D0539949

Harry smiled. All those years he had lived in Rory Gallagher's shadow, all those years he'd felt he had been second-best, had second choice, taken what Rory Gallagher didn't require. Now he had what Rory wanted, he could see it written all over his face, and the years fell away; they simply disappeared. The smile stayed fixed on his face. 'Kate and I have been together for some time now, and I think I'm right in saying . . .' He glanced at Kate and raised an eyebrow, but she fixed her eyes on the ground. 'I think I'm right in saying that she looks to me to protect her and take care of her. In fact,' he glanced at Kate again, 'I have been thinking of asking her to be my wife.'

'Your wife?' Kate jerked up and stared at Harry open-mouthed. But before she could say anything else, Rory grabbed her arm and spun her round to face him.

'His wife?' His expression was one of total disbelief. 'Kate, he's not serious? Surely he's not!'

Also by Maria Barrett:

ELLE
DANGEROUS OBSESSION
DECEIVED
DISHONOURED
INTIMATE LIES

BREACH OF PROMISE

Maria Barrett

WARNER BOOKS

A *Warner* Book

First published in Great Britain in 1998
by Little, Brown and Company
This edition published by Warner Books in 1998

Copyright © Maria Barrett 1998

The moral right of the author has been asserted.

*All characters in this publication are fictitious
and any resemblance to real persons, living or dead,
is purely coincidental.*

All rights reserved.
No part of this publication may be reproduced,
stored in a retrieval system, or transmitted, in any
form or by any means, without the prior
permission in writing of the publisher, nor be
otherwise circulated in any form of binding or
cover other than that in which it is published and
without a similar condition including this
condition being imposed on the subsequent purchaser.

A CIP catalogue record for this book
is available from the British Library.

ISBN 0 7515 2094 2

Typeset by Palimpsest Book Production Limited,
Polmont, Stirlingshire
Printed and bound in Great Britain by
Clays Ltd, St Ives plc

Warner Books
A Division of
Little, Brown and Company (UK)
Brettenham House
Lancaster Place
London WC2E 7EN

For E.P.J.B.
Practice makes perfect.

Acknowledgements

Another book, another baby, a great deal of hard work, a good few cases of wine and several scary, hairy moments when the novel that is almost never was. I am indebted to my team, William, Lily and Edward, for their long-suffering patience and love, to my team captain Emma Aylward for her tolerance, efficiency and hard work and to our team manager, Jules, for doing what he does best: directing from the sidelines!

I would like to thank David Rees and Ian Hamilton from Grenalls for their help with my research into the gin industry, along with Eleanor Bannister and Jane Merrimen of the IDV Gin Group. Any mistakes are mine. Thanks must also go to Sarah and Jerry Hicks of the Folly Wine bar in Petersfield (an excellent bistro and hostelry!), and all their staff for letting me into their trade secrets; to Kirstin Cliffton and Zoe Quick who answered all my legal questions and to my bank, Lloyds, who talked me through the loan business. Again, any mistakes are mine. I would like to thank my editor Barbara Boote, and all the backup at Little, Brown, Helen Anderson and Mic Cheetham. Finally, thank you Emma for everything you do in a day's work and thank you Jules, for not only the work, but everything that goes with it to make a happy life.

Chapter One

Alice rolled over in bed and felt the cool, empty space which a few moments earlier had been occupied by a warm, breathing body. Immediately she sat up. The light was on in the bathroom but the door was closed and, stuffing the pillows into a support for her back, she watched it, waiting for the outline of a figure to appear through the glass panel. She was upset – no, more than that, she was raging. It had been a crappy week, she had been made redundant, her period was worryingly late and if he thought he could just turn up here any old time for a quick one, then he had better think again. She glanced at her watch. It was eight o'clock on a Saturday night, for God's sake! He couldn't just run out after he'd had his fun and leave her in alone to watch *Casualty*! She braced herself as the door opened.

'Hi, babe.' She felt a flash of anger, but bit her lip. He crossed the room and dropped his wet towel on the floor next to the bed. 'You got any plans for tonight?' he asked casually, taking his shirt off the chair. He pulled it over his lean, tanned body and began to fasten it.

'I thought I had,' Alice said.

He glanced across. 'Oh yeah? What happened?'

'You,' Alice stated flatly. He bent to pull on his under-wear and grinned at her, obviously thinking she was joking. Alice's mouth twitched. 'And where are you off to?' she managed to ask, amazed that her voice sounded so normal.

'Rory's stag do,' he answered. 'Should be a riot. Harry's hired the downstairs at the Wine Gallery for him, he's got a stripper, a tit-o-gram, the whole—'

'Christ! You men are so goddamn immature!' Alice yelled, jumping out of bed and storming across the room to the bathroom. She banged the door so hard that the glass panel rattled dangerously. 'And what the hell is a tit-o-gram, as if I didn't know!' she shouted, yanking it open again and pulling on her towelling robe. 'It's so damned derogatory – so, so arrogant! You're all the same, all you want is—'

'Whoa! Hang on a minute, Al.' He held up his hands. 'Who rattled your cage?' He stared at her with an amused expression on his face, clearly expecting her to break into laughter or at least a grin, but Alice did neither. Instead, she slumped down on the red velvet chaise at the end of her bed and dropped her head into her hands. The tears welled up in her eyes and spilt over, falling heavily to leave tiny splash marks on the plush crimson pile.

'Al?' He was embarrassed; this wasn't part of the deal. Alice was a good-time girl, they all knew that! She was fun, a good laugh, game for anything, a terrific lay. A vision of her draped erotically over that very same chaise a couple of hours earlier flashed into his head and he turned away, hurriedly taking up his jacket. 'Alice? You all right?' Uncomfortable, he rattled his car keys in his pocket.

She jerked up. 'Of course I'm all right! Why the hell

shouldn't I be? I've got a nice bottle of wine in the fridge, I can send out for a takeaway and there's bound to be a good movie on later. Christ!' she finished. 'You're a bloody shit, you really are!'

He stood there, not knowing quite what to do. The truth was that he wasn't a shit, not like most who passed through Alice's bedroom and Alice's life. He was just the latest and probably the last in a long list of failed attempts at love and happiness.

Alice wiped her face on the sleeve of her dressing-gown. 'Go on, go if you have to. Piss off!'

'Look, Alice, if I'd known you didn't have any plans, if you'd said, then I could have—'

'Could have what?' she snapped. 'Stayed an hour or so longer? Had one more quick fuck before you disappeared?' She shook her head. 'Oh, please, spare me.'

But he really did feel bad. He had known Alice only a couple of weeks, and it'd been one hell of a blast. It wasn't that he wanted to get involved, but he didn't want to dump her either. 'Look, Alice,' he said, 'why don't you come along, a bit later on, I mean, to the party? We're bound to go on to a club or something, and you could join us; you know most of the guys . . .'

'Yeah, I know them,' Alice muttered, in the biblical sense, she almost added.

'Well, come on then, it'll be a laugh – do you good, cheer you up a bit.' He had put on his jacket, ready to leave. He wasn't in a huge hurry, but he did want to get out of there. 'Come on, Alice, what d'you say?'

Alice shrugged; she really couldn't be bothered to say anything.

'It's the Wine Gallery,' he said. 'Off the Fulham Road,

yeah?' Finally she nodded and saw him visibly relax. 'Right, well, I'll see you later, then?' Again she nodded. She glanced down at her hands and became absorbed in the fate of a torn cuticle until she heard the front door slam and was sure he had gone. Then she looked up again and listened for a moment for any sound of his return. There was none. All she could hear was the deathly silence of loneliness.

Alice's black mood lasted roughly an hour, but an hour of self-pity was about as much as she could take, so she showered, did her hair and make-up and dressed to kill. At ten she left her flat, and by half-past she was at the Wine Gallery. Her cab pulled up outside just as Harry, best man to the groom, appeared on the pavement, waving his arms to flag down the approaching car.

'Alice! Blimey, what a coincidence.'

Harry, a brief one-time lover of hers, helped Alice out on to the pavement. 'This is luck itself, Al,' he exclaimed, unaware that she had turned up to join the party. 'You couldn't help me out of a jam, could you?' He glanced behind him at the groom, Rory Gallagher, who was slumped over the railings of a rather smart house several doors down from the Wine Gallery. 'Five lagers, three vodkas and he's absolutely smashed. Wasted! Can't get any sense out of him at all, and it's barely halfway through the evening. He's bloody useless!' Harry smiled. 'Lightweight!'

Alice nodded. She had a grim premonition of what was coming next.

'Alice, I've got to get him home, he's chucked up twice and I can't just leave him in a corner. You couldn't—' He was interrupted by a loud straining noise behind him and turned to see Rory throw up a third time into the wooden planter of a bay tree on the front steps of the house. 'Jesus!

See what I mean?' He dashed over and lifted the slumped body of the groom-to-be, heaving him up and dragging him along the pavement towards the cab.

'Oi, mate?' The driver hung his head out of the window. 'I'm not having that geezer honk all over my cab, ta very much.' He put out his indicator, ready to move off. 'You can find another cab.'

'No, wait!' Harry dashed forward, glancing imploringly at Alice. 'This young lady here will take him home and make sure he doesn't throw up in the back of the cab – won't you, Alice?' Alice's heart sank. 'And there's an extra tenner in it for you.' Harry pulled a wad of cash out of his pocket, but the cabbie shook his head. 'Twenty, then?'

'No, mate, it's thirty and nothing less,' he said.

'OK, thirty,' Harry agreed and, having secured the ride, turned to Alice. 'Please do this for me, will you? I know it's a lot to ask, but just get him home for me. I can't leave the party; I'm in charge, I'm supposed to be settling all the bills, organising everything. *Please*, Al?'

Alice looked at Rory, probably the only one of the crowd she hadn't slept with. She liked him, he was decent, honest, head over heels in love and sure about it too, committed – not like most of the good-time johnnies who passed through her life. 'What's the alternative?' she asked.

'I'll have to ring a mini-cab and leave him to the fate of the driver,' Harry answered. 'Chances are he'll be dumped at the front door of his flat, there'll be a frost tonight – not unheard of in May and he'll die of hypothermia at three or four this morning.' He smiled. 'There isn't any alternative, really. Alice, please, just see him home for me, would you?'

Alice sighed heavily. She was too bloody soft, that was

her problem, couldn't say no. 'OK,' she said. Harry grinned and heaved the dead weight of Rory forward, propping him against the side of the cab while he opened the door for Alice to climb in again.

'Thirty-four Park Road, Clapham,' he said. 'Then wherever the young lady wants to go. Here.' Harry handed over the cash and, with great effort, bundled Rory inside the taxi, where he collapsed on to Alice's black suede, spike-heeled shoes.

'If he pukes on my shoes I'll expect a new pair,' she said.

Harry laughed and slammed the door shut. 'Thanks so much, Alice,' he shouted. 'You're wonderful, I love you!'

Alice nodded as Rory groaned. If only, she thought, and settled back for the ride to Clapham.

'Can you wait?' she asked the driver, jumping out of the cab. They had driven across London with the windows down, and a blast of cool air on Rory's face had revived him sufficiently to stagger – with Alice's help – out of the taxi towards his flat. 'I won't be long,' she called over her shoulder. They struggled to the front door of a large Victorian house and Alice propped Rory up against the wall while she searched his pockets for keys. There was no sign of them.

'Rory?' She shook him gently; he had begun to snore. 'Where are your keys?' He moaned quietly, shrugging her aside, and turned into the wall. 'Rory?' Alice was beginning to lose patience. She pulled him round to face her and shook him a great deal harder. '*Rory?*' she snapped. 'Keys!' But he was too far gone to be any use. She swore vehemently under her breath. What now? She was damned if she was going to waste any more time on this; there was only one thing for it – she would have to leave him in the porch and hope that a neighbour found him and took him inside. He'd be fine; it was a mild night, there was no danger of hypothermia. 'Rory, I'm going now,' she said loudly. He made no response. Dragging him over a few inches, she let him slide sideways down the wall into the porch and slump in a heap on the floor. His head dropped forward on to his chin. 'Sorry,' she said quietly, 'I've done what I can.'

Alice turned and headed back towards the taxi. But just as she was about to climb in, she looked back and stared at the heap on the ground. A germ of an idea started in her head and, during the few moments while she stood and stared, it grew and spread until suddenly it rampaged through her like a virus. Alice always had been and always would be an opportunist. She knew what was wrong with her – the dull, low ache in her stomach, the bouts of weeping, the faint, sick and sinking feeling each morning – and she knew, just looking at the pitiful mess called Rory by the front door of No.34 Park Road, Clapham, that here was a God-given chance that could not be missed. Without dwelling on it – Alice was not one to contemplate – she turned to the cabbie and asked, 'Can you hang on a bit longer?'

He shrugged indifferently and, her mind made up, she hurried back to the house. 'Come on, Rory,' she said, heaving him to his feet. He was just conscious enough to make it possible. 'You'll have to come back with me,' she told him, half dragging and half carrying him back to the taxi. She pulled him inside with help from the driver and let him flop on to the seat.

'Battersea,' she called, giving her own address. The taxi swung round and headed off.

'You all right, love?' the driver asked over his shoulder.

Alice smiled grimly. 'Perfectly,' she answered, 'or I soon will be, anyway.'

Back at the flat, Alice gave the cab driver another £10 for helping her get Rory up the stairs and into the bedroom and left him there while she made a note of it in her diary. She would get the money back from Harry, it was the least he could bloody do. Putting the kettle on, she went through to the bedroom to attempt to undress Rory. His clothes were damp and smelled of sick, and she didn't want him sleeping on or in her bed in that state. She didn't really want him sleeping on or in her bed at all, but she had formulated a plan and a few dirty sheets were a small price to pay for what she was after.

Pulling off the jacket and unknotting the tie first, she then unbuttoned his shirt and eased it off his body. He was an athlete, Rory Gallagher; that's why he couldn't drink, he carried no weight. Alice gently trailed her fingers across his chest, tracing the hard shape of his muscles from his shoulders down to his abdomen. He murmured and reached out, catching her hand. She froze, suddenly embarrassed, but he didn't open his eyes, he simply pulled the hand down to his mouth and held it there, against his lips. 'Kate,' he murmured and for the first time in her life Alice was so consumed by envy that it physically hurt. She removed her hand, stared down at him for a while, then muttered, 'Get a grip, Alice, you don't want love, you want security.' But she didn't smile as she said it and the words left a rather bitter taste in her mouth. She sighed heavily and went on with the task of undressing Rory.

Rory woke with a terrible feeling of dread. Even before he opened his eyes he felt it, a sort of heavy sinking in the pit of his stomach, but that was before the hangover hit him. Once that happened, all he could do was stagger out of bed, slam several doors in a failed attempt to find the bathroom and finally throw up in the kitchen sink. Thankfully there was nothing but bile; he had well and truly emptied his stomach the night before.

'Jesus! Where the hell . . . ?' He laid his head against the cool stainless steel of the sink and closed his eyes. He had absolutely no idea where he was.

'Rory?'

He spun round. 'Alice! My God! I mean . . .'

Alice never wore anything in bed and last night was no exception. As she came into the kitchen, her nakedness was clearly visible under the thin silk wrap she wore.

'Oh, Christ!' said Rory.

'Thank you,' she replied archly.

'I didn't mean that, I meant . . . oh, God . . .' He looked at her again. 'We didn't . . . er, I didn't . . .' He stopped, unable to read her face, and swallowed hard. There was a silence, then weakly he asked, 'What happened last night?'

Alice hesitated. She too had thrown up that morning and it was this that had finally decided her. Instead of putting Rory straight and telling him the absolute truth, something she would usually have done without fail, she shrugged and turned away.

'Alice?' Rory's voice faltered. He crossed the room and

took her by the shoulders, turning her back to face him. 'Tell me, please.'

'You were drunk last night,' she said. 'I turned up at the party and Harry asked me to take you home, you could hardly stand up. When we got back to your place I couldn't find the keys in your pockets, so I brought you back here.'

Rory's misery hung on his face. 'And?' He held his breath, swallowing back the urge to throw up again.

Alice stared at him. It was such an intense misery, tinged with horror, that for a moment she almost laughed. But it was only a moment, then the laughter quickly turned to anger. Was she really so awful that the thought of a night with her was bordering on the horrific? She shrugged a second time.

'Alice?' Rory's voice was desperate, which incensed her further.

'Oh, for God's sake, Rory! Work it out for yourself,' she snapped, pulling away from him and crossing to the kettle. 'You were drunk; let's just forget it, shall we?'

'Forget it? Forget it?' He dropped his head in his hands and a cold sweat broke out on the back of his neck. He couldn't remember a thing, not leaving the party nor meeting Alice. How the hell had he ended up in bed with her? He was in love with Kate, he was going to marry her in July – or at least he had been going to, up until last night. Dropping his hands away, Rory straightened, took a deep breath and went back to the bedroom. He had to get out of there and think it through, get some sort of hold on reality.

Looking round, he found his clothes left in a neat pile on the chair, and sat on the edge of the bed to dress. But as he glanced at his shirt, properly folded; his trousers, the crease in each leg pressed together; his socks in a pair, turned over at the top; his tie rolled, he wondered how on earth he had managed that in the throes of drunken passion. He stared down at them and tried to think. Of course he hadn't managed it, someone had undressed him, which meant that he had been too incapable to do it himself, let alone get it up and make love to a woman whose reputation preceded her. He looked round the room again, this time for Alice's clothes, and saw her dress on a hanger, her underwear and stockings neat on the dressing-table. There was no sign of passion there, no disarray in the room, no hint of abandonment at all. He *couldn't* have done it, he was sure he couldn't have. His clothes smelled of sick; he must have been puking his guts out. How could he have had sex if he couldn't keep the contents of his stomach down? Rory sat still for a few moments working it all out, then he hurriedly dressed, holding his breath against the whiff of sick, and grabbed his jacket from the back of the bedroom chair.

'Alice?' he called. 'Alice?'

She was in the kitchen drinking coffee.

'I'm off,' he said from the doorway. 'Thanks for putting me up.'

Alice looked across at him and saw the open, honest expression, the kindness in his face. He smiled at her and she smiled back, but still she didn't put him right about last night. 'It was a pleasure,' she told him.

Rory nodded uneasily. 'Do I owe you any money, for cabs, dry cleaning? Did I break anything?'

'Only my heart,' she quipped. He ran his hands nervously through his hair, still not quite sure what to make of the situation.

'Just kidding,' Alice said.

He relaxed slightly. 'Well, I'll see you sometime then,' he remarked.

'Yes.'

'Bye, Alice.'

Alice looked down at her coffee cup. 'Bye, Rory,' she answered. She heard his footsteps going along the passage to the front door. It opened, then there was a pause. A few moments later he walked back to the kitchen.

'Alice, sorry, I forgot my keys. Where are they?'

She swirled the grey-brown coffee round her mug, realising that she really didn't fancy it at all, then stood to take her cup across to the sink. 'I don't know,' she said over her shoulder. 'That's why you were here in the first place.'

'Oh, shit!' He rubbed his hands wearily over his face. 'This is all I bloody well need!' he muttered.

Alice looked round. 'I could ring Harry for you if you want, ask him if anyone picked them up last—'

'No!' Rory snapped. That was the last thing on earth he wanted, to let everyone know that he'd spent the night here. He glanced at Alice, saw her face and said more gently, 'I mean, thanks for the offer, but I think I'll go across to the wine bar and ask them myself.' He dug in his pockets. Alice stared at him.

'Alice, look, I'm really sorry but I . . . . couldn't borrow a few quid, could I? I ran out of cash last night, and I er . . .'

Alice shrugged. 'Sure,' she said. 'My purse is in my handbag, it's in the bedroom.' She went to move, but Rory pre-empted her. 'I'll get it,' he said. 'It's the least I can do.'

'It's on the bedside table,' she called after him as he hurried along to the bedroom. He disappeared and Alice waited. In a few moments he reappeared, his face ashen. He handed her the bag, she found her purse and held out a tenner. 'Is ten enough?'

'Yes, great. Thanks.' Rory clutched the note and seemed frozen between staying or going. He opened his mouth to speak, but no words came out.

'You all right, Rory?' Alice asked.

He swallowed hard, then said, 'I'd better go.'

Alice turned to face him. 'Are you sure . . . ?' She broke off, a puzzled frown on her face, and watched him hurry back along the passage to the open front door before she could finish her question. He turned, offered a half salute and then disappeared, slamming the door behind him. Wondering what on earth could have upset him so much, Alice walked along to the bedroom, sat down on the edge of the bed and reached for a tissue. As she did so, she saw it: the small three-pack of condoms she had bought yesterday and the discarded wrappers of the two she had used earlier on in the evening. She picked up the box and looked at it.

'Oh, well,' she murmured, knowing now exactly what had upset Rory. Sometimes, she thought, things have a peculiar way of moving outside our control. Sometimes, we just have to let them be. 'That's it, then,' she said aloud. And glancing down, she laid a hand on the still flat plane of her stomach and smiled.

Chapter Two

Alice lay in bed for some time before she could summon up the energy to rise. She stared blankly at the bright blue silk suit she had chosen for the wedding, which was hanging in front of the wardrobe, the small mother-of-pearl buttons winking at her as they caught the morning sun through the window. She rolled over, felt sick and rolled on to her back again. The nausea receded. Reaching across, she opened the drawer of her bedside table and took out the chemist's bag she had placed there last night; it felt like a dead weight in her hand. Opening it, she removed the packet, peeled off the Cellophane and pulled out an instruction leaflet. *First step*, it read, *the simple-to-use home pregnancy test*. She scanned the directions, a knot of tension tightening in her chest. It seemed easy enough, she thought – a quick pee in the right place and there's the rest of your life sorted. Of course it was pretty much sorted already; even without the test, Alice was certain she was pregnant.

Sitting up, Alice took the tester stick, climbed out of bed and made her way along to the bathroom. Her nerves faded for a moment with the effort of concentrating on what she was doing: removing the cap from the stick, sitting in position, holding the indicator steady with one finger over the window to stop splash-back, then trying to pee, aiming it at the special chemical end, mid-flow, and covering her entire hand in the process.

'Yeuch!' she muttered. 'Not exactly glamorous.' She replaced the cap and finished off; then, leaving the plastic stick on the side of the wash-basin while she rinsed her hands, she watched it with grim fascination as the small window changed colour and a thin blue line appeared. That meant she had tested properly; nothing to blame there, she thought, as she picked it up and sat down on the edge of the bath. Her heart was hammering so hard it was making her almost breathless. There was knowing in one's heart and then there was knowing for sure, the indisputable evidence in hand. She watched the big window fill; sweat prickled her skin and she held her breath. Within seconds another thin blue line appeared; it deepened, then widened slightly. There was no mistaking it; according to the test and without a single doubt, she was pregnant. Alice dropped the indicator and stood up. 'Oh, God,' she murmured. 'Oh, my God.'

Alice began to pace the floor. Of course she was pregnant, she'd known for ages – well, not for certain, but she'd had a pretty good idea and she was prepared, in many respects; she had thought it all through. That's why she had done it today; it was her last chance, her deadline. Despite not being absolutely certain until now, Alice did know that she wanted this baby, she had worked that one out long ago. At thirty-eight, single and going nowhere fast, she wanted it and she wanted the life that went with it – marriage, security, love. She had always thought that if she did get pregnant, on her own, with no means of support, she would be able to deal with it rationally, unemotionally. But she couldn't. Perhaps she hadn't realised the strength of the maternal instinct until it hit her; perhaps it was the hormones or perhaps just the idea that she, Alice, despite a lifetime of disasters, had finally managed to create something wonderful, which was growing inside her own body. The only rational thing she could say about it was that her biological clock must have been ticking away silently for years and had now finally gone off. The only unemotional thing about it was the depth of her plan. Marriage and security were uppermost, the love was an optional extra. She wanted the baby more than she could remember wanting anything else in her life before . . . and she was in no doubt that she was going to get it.

Picking up the testing kit, Alice carried it through to the bedroom and placed it on her bedside table. It lay there, the irrefutable proof; her insurance policy. She stood there for a moment, glancing up at her wedding outfit. A brief pang of something like guilt struck her, but she was too insulated to really feel it, too wrapped up in herself. People would get hurt, she knew that, but people got hurt every day and survived, didn't they? She'd never liked Kate anyway; she was too sleek, too well cared for, too lucky by far. It was about time life dealt her a blow. Besides, Alice thought, crossing to the dressing-table to lay out her make-up for the day, often these things made a person, built character. Look at her – she'd had a hell of a lot of shit and she hadn't crumbled. She sat down, ran a brush through her hair and then leaned forward to the mirror to really stare at her face. She had to look after herself now, herself and her child – surely that was more important than anything else? A child's happiness came first, no matter what it cost. Alice noticed the faint blue shadows under her eyes and added a concealer stick to the array of make-up. Then she glanced at her watch. It was just after eight and the wedding was at two, so she had plenty of time. Straightening, she continued to stare at her reflection in the mirror. She wondered if she should feel any pain, a flicker of doubt even, but she felt nothing. She had a mess to sort out and the sooner she did it the better. No matter what it cost, she reminded herself, and Alice knew that the price for this baby was going to be very steep indeed.

Rory sang loudly and badly out of tune in the shower as he soaped and scrubbed his body with some rather exotic smelly stuff that Harry had given him. He didn't usually go in for expensive pongs, but Kate liked them and it was his wedding day after all. Besides, he'd probably sweat so much by the time it was all over that he was going to need all the camouflage he could get.

Turning off the hot tap and giving himself a quick blast of icy water, he hollered with the shock of it and then stepped out of the shower. Reaching for a towel, he dried himself vigorously and wrapped his faded old towelling robe round his body. Funny how parents never threw things away! As he walked along the passage to his old bedroom, his mother called up the stairs.

'Rory? Rory, there's someone to see you.'

He stopped, went back to the stairs and peered down from the galleried landing to the hallway. 'Who is it, Mum?'

His father appeared from the sitting-room and Rory said, 'Shouldn't you be in church, rehearsing the choir or testing the organ or something?' He smiled, but his father didn't smile back and Rory had an odd sense of unease. 'You OK, Dad?' he asked, but the Reverend Michael Gallagher didn't reply. He moved aside and glanced behind him as a figure came out of the sitting-room. 'There's a young lady here, Rory . . .'

Rory leaned forward to see who it was. 'Alice? Good Lord! Alice? What on earth . . . ?' The sight of her brought back the grim memory of his stag night and Rory flushed. He had thought about it a great deal in the few days that followed and had convinced himself that, despite the sight of the open box of condoms, he couldn't have made love to Alice that night. He'd had neither the desire nor the physical capability.

He stared at her for a few moments, then remembered his manners and said, 'Sorry. It's nice to see you, Alice; you'd better come up, I'm just getting ready.' He moved back, letting go of the banister, and saw that his palms had left a smear of sweat on the polished wood. He wiped them on the towelling robe and told himself not to be alarmed; this was a coincidence, nothing untoward. 'Would you like some coffee?'

Alice seemed tense. 'No thanks, Rory, it rather turns my stomach at the moment.' He glanced down at her; she did look a bit peaky. Behind her, Rory's father stood watching the scene with an icy air of disapproval. The Reverend Gallagher had a strong sense of propriety and a young lady turning up unannounced on the morn of his son's wedding was not, in his book, accepted behaviour. He scowled at Rory but the look went unnoticed. Rory was too busy worrying what the hell Alice was doing there to notice his father's reaction.

Alice bit her lip. Now that she was here at the vicarage, now that she had met the Reverend Gallagher and Mrs Gallagher, spied the church festooned with garlands of flowers and seen Rory – seen how terribly happy he looked, despite her appearance, how fresh and honest and thoroughly nice he was – her nerve almost failed her. But only almost.

At the top of the stairs she listened to his small talk about the wedding as she followed him silently along the passage and into a boy's bedroom, still decorated with sports trophies and shots of friends stuck on the walls. Rory closed the door, glanced round and said, 'Mum keeps threatening to take them all down and redecorate, but I won't let her; it's my past.' He reached up and peeled off a photo of two adolescent boys, bare-chested, standing in bright sunshine and holding a huge tuna fish aloft for the camera. 'That's Harry and me thirteen years ago, deep-sea fishing in the Med,' he said, looking at the picture closely for a moment before holding it out for Alice to see. 'Kate's mother invited us out to the South of France with Kate. She wanted company for her while she swanned off with her new boyfriend, but of course Kate didn't want to have anything to do with us – stupid pubescent boys, she called us, and she was a good two years younger than we were.' He smiled. 'The boyfriend ended up taking us out all the time, fishing and sailing, and Kate's mother was furious.' Alice glanced at him and noticed how his eyes creased when he laughed. 'It was a blast, fantastic! We had a brilliant time.'

Alice didn't want to ask, but she had to; curiosity was a peculiarly masochistic thing. 'How did you meet Kate? Were you at school together?'

'No, not at all. I was at school with Harry, but Kate and

I met when she came to Tonsbry for her summer holidays. Leo, who owns it, is her uncle. He introduced us and her mother encouraged it, knowing I was the local vicar's son. Of course we didn't get it together for years; we lost touch when I went away to university and only met up again a couple of years ago.' He took back the photo and stuck it up again. 'But that year, the South of France holiday, was the year I fell in love with her,' he said, more to himself than to Alice. 'I was fifteen – it was the silver bikini that did it. A ghastly bit of kit that left a trail of sparkly bits wherever she went. We called her "Tinkerbell", it really got on her nerves. I carried a torch for her all those years; I never quite got over her, or the bikini!' Laughing, he looked up. Then the laughter died. 'You all right, Alice? You've gone very pale.'

She shook her head, then crossed to the window and stood silently looking out at the view.

'Alice?' Rory had an uneasy sense of disaster. He felt sudden panic in the air and realised it was his. 'Alice, is there something wrong?' His voice wavered slightly. This is ridiculous, he told himself; I'm just tense, there can't be anything wrong, this is my wedding day, there simply can't be. But at that moment Alice turned and Rory saw her face. His whole body jolted with fear.

'I'm pregnant,' she said. Rory closed his eyes. For a moment everything went blank, just blank. There was no noise, no image, no smell, nothing. Then seconds later the shock hit him so hard that it knocked him backwards, literally. He staggered back against the wall and pressed his nails into his palms; he tried to swallow, but his mouth had dried up.

'You're sure?'

She nodded. His mind was racing, images spinning, crashing into each other. That night, that fateful night, had he slept with Alice? Had he somehow managed to make love to a woman he hardly knew and certainly didn't love? He felt sick, the floor swam up towards him and he slumped down the wall with his hands on his thighs and his head between his knees. He stayed like that until the sickness receded, then he looked up at her.

'Alice, what are you saying?'

'That night . . .' she began, than she stopped and moved away. If she was going to do this, if she was going to lie so cruelly to save herself, then she couldn't look at him – she couldn't watch his face as she did it. She turned to the window again, her body only half towards him as she continued. 'I didn't say anything because you were engaged, I didn't want to spoil things. I mean, let's face it, Rory, we hardly know each other. I'm a friend of Kate's . . . I –' She broke off, suddenly embarrassed by that admission. After a pause she went on, 'It was a stupid fling, a drunken mistake, it should never have happened . . .'

Rory snorted loudly and Alice flinched. All the time she spoke she was aware of the destruction her words would create. It wasn't a nice feeling, but it was a case of survival and she was hanging on in there by the skin of her teeth. She faced him. 'Rory, we didn't use a condom – or rather we tried to, but you were too drunk so we gave up after two failed attempts. I thought I'd be safe, I had no idea I'd get . . .' Her voice trailed off. A few moments later, she said, 'I really didn't think I'd fall pregnant. I'm sorry . . .'

'You're sorry?' Rory stood upright. 'Christ, Alice! You're sorry? You turn up here on the day of my wedding to tell me that from one stupid fucking drunken mistake I made you pregnant – and you're *sorry*!' Suddenly he swung round and slammed his fist into the wall. There was a hard crack as his knuckles hit the plaster and again Alice flinched. 'Jesus Christ! I can't believe this!' he cried. 'I just can't . . .' He swung back to face her. 'Couldn't you have taken some kind of morning-after pill? Couldn't you? Hmmm? This is the late twentieth century, you know, Alice, you can get things like that.' He was shouting and Alice braced herself for what was coming next. He would want her to get rid of the baby, it was inevitable, and she had her arguments ready. She waited, but he didn't say it. Rory dropped his head in his hands and then, seeming to calm slightly, he said, 'You're absolutely *sure* you're pregnant?' She bit her lip and nodded, still waiting for the ultimate question – how much would it cost?

'And it's mine?'

Again she nodded.

'How many weeks are you?'

'Only about, five, I think, my period's only just late.' Rory glanced up at her and Alice held her breath. She was fudging dates, she was at least eight weeks gone, but he didn't have to know that; if she was clever, he never would. 'I'm sorry.'

'I see.'

There was a long, painful silence which seemed to last for ever and Alice stared so hard at the ground that her eyes lost focus. Then she heard Rory move across the room towards her. He stood in front of her and placed his hands on her shoulders. 'Alice,' he said. Here it comes, she thought, I wonder how much he'll offer me.

'I'm sorry, too.' His voice cracked and he had to swallow

hard. Alice heard that swallow, she felt the enormous physical effort it took him to keep control. There was another long, painful silence, then: 'Don't worry, Alice,' he said, after what seemed like an eternity. 'I'll look after you, both of you.' And releasing her, he crossed the room and left, quietly closing the door behind him.

Alice slumped down on to the bed. For a long time she just lay there, staring up at the sloping ceiling, at the photographs of Rory's life, of Kate Dowie and Harry Drummond, of Tonsbry House, of university and cricket and squash – of every moment, it seemed, caught on camera. She was nowhere to be seen, not even in a group photo. Like a burning comet she had spun out of infinity, crashing into the orb of Rory Gallagher's life and destroying it. She was so ashamed of what she had done that it paralysed her. For a fleeting moment she thought of jumping up and racing after him, telling him it was all an elaborate lie, confiding in him and asking for his help, but she couldn't even raise her head off the pillow; she just lay there inert and the moment passed. She had started a chain of events that would run into each other, link up and grow. There was no turning back. She heard raised voices downstairs, shouting, the slam of a door, and she rolled on to her side, curling herself up into the foetal position.

Not once, she thought, not once had he asked her to get rid of the baby, nor even mentioned it. He had assumed its right to be born and his responsibility for its life as a matter of course. Alice was thoroughly ashamed, frightened of the consequences of her actions, but she was also achingly relieved. Rory was everything she had thought he would be. He had acted with honour, he had saved her, but it was an action that would cost him his happiness. The plan had worked.

There was no going back.

Harry Drummond was eating a hearty full English breakfast in the restaurant of the Dog and Duck in Tonsbry village when Rory strode in. It was a quarter to twelve; he had been out for a run, showered, changed into cords and a weekend shirt – pale pink cotton twill with button-down collar – and smelled strongly of aftershave. He glanced up as Rory came in, mumbled something through a mouthful of toast, then stopped chewing and stared at his friend.

'What's up, Argie?' 'Argie' was an old school name derived from Rory's initials. 'You look terrible. What the hell's up?' He stood, dumped his napkin on the table and moved towards Rory.

'Listen, Harry, can we go somewhere private? I need to talk to you.'

Harry glanced behind him at the garden. 'Out there?' Rory nodded and he led the way outside.

'OK, what is it?' Harry dug his hands in his pockets and turned towards his friend. He was relaxed, obviously thought this was some kind of minor upset. 'Don't tell me, you're worried I've lost the rings?' He smiled. 'No? You want to rehearse your speech again?'

Rory stood motionless, feeling as if his feet had rooted themselves to the ground. His whole body ached, ached so much that he wanted to fold his arms around himself and curl into a tight, defensive ball. He hesitated, knowing he held the outcome of the rest of his life right there in what he said next, but the hesitation was transitory. Rory believed in realising what was right; he always had done and he always would do. The need for honesty and integrity was as basic to him as the need to eat and breathe. It was woven into the very fabric of his nature.

Harry cuffed him on the arm. 'Come on, Rory? What the hell's up?' He was still smiling, but his eyes had become vaguely wary. 'Last-minute nerves?' he tried.

Rory shook his head. 'Something awful has happened, Harry,' he began. 'I mean, I've done something awful, terrible, I . . .'

Harry's smile faded, though not completely – it sagged at the corners, but left an echo of itself on his face. 'Come on, Rory,' he said, still not taking the situation particularly seriously. 'For God's sake spit it out. What the hell can be so bad?'

'Alice, Alice White,' Rory managed to say.

'Alice White?' Harry frowned. 'What the bloody hell has Alice White got to do with it?' He was losing patience, but he hung on in there. He had a fleeting premonition that things were about to go badly wrong.

'My stag night,' Rory said. 'I . . . we . . .' He broke off. He had always liked to think of himself as strong, courageous almost, but this was the hardest thing he had ever had to say and he wasn't sure he could do it.

Harry stared at him. The smile had completely vanished. 'Go on.'

'I was pissed,' Rory said. 'Apparently . . .' He hesitated again, then blurted, 'Apparently we had sex. I don't remember it, but we did and—'

Harry held up his hands to interrupt. 'Whoa! Hold it right there, Rory.' He took a pace back and looked away for a moment. Then, having thought about it, he asked, 'Who says you did?'

'Alice.'

'Ah, Alice.' Harry digested this piece of information, then said, 'Rory, you were so pissed that night you couldn't even stand up, let alone get it up. Come on, you don't believe her, do you?'

'Yes! I do. Of course I do. Why would she say it if it wasn't true?'

'I don't know – but look, even if you did end up in bed with Alice White, you wouldn't be the first bloke to make a dreadful, drunken mistake and you won't be the last. It happens, you know! You weren't married at the time and from the look on your face you feel like shit about it, so . . .' Harry shrugged, but inside he was seething. Rory Gallagher had had everything, place at Cambridge, top job with a big firm of accountants, loads of money and, to top it all, Kate Dowie. Yet here he was whingeing and moaning because he'd made some sort of minor cock-up – pardon the phrase – and couldn't act like any normal bloke and forget about it. It really pissed Harry off. 'Look, Rory,' he began coldly, 'I don't approve, but I'll forget you ever told me this and you forget it ever happened, all right? Don't let it ruin the rest of your life. Stop whining and get on with it! It was a mistake, the sooner forgotten the better. OK?'

Rory rubbed his hands wearily over his face, then looked straight at Harry. 'No, it's not OK,' he said. 'I wish it were. There's more.'

'More? What more? What the hell else could there be?'

'Alice is pregnant,' Rory said quietly, 'and it's mine.'

At this, Harry exploded. 'Yours!' he cried. 'Are you kidding? Oh, get real, Rory!' He began to pace, his face flushed with anger. 'Christ! Bloody Alice! She told you that, did she? Alice, who's serviced most of the men I know and all their friends. Christ, I don't believe this! She said you were the father of her child, from one quick, drunken bonk?' He stopped and faced Rory. 'You surely don't believe her?'

'Yes, yes I do.'

Harry shook his head and almost laughed. 'Come on, Rory! What evidence has she got? Has she had a paternity test? She's making it up, man. She's having you on.'

'But why? Why would she make it up?'

'Because she saw you coming, that's why. Let's face it, who else would take a claim like that seriously? Alice, the tart with a heart! You're too bloody nice, Rory, any fool can see that; she thinks she's on to a good one.'

Rory shook his head. 'I don't think so,' he said firmly. 'Honestly, Harry, I really don't . . .'

Suddenly Harry stared at him. It was as if realisation of what Rory was saying had just dawned. 'You genuinely believe all this claptrap, don't you?'

Rory didn't answer, he just hung his head.

'You believe it!' Harry shook his head. 'You do! You believe it.' There was a silence and Harry turned away. He thought of Kate, then he thought of all the times he'd wanted her, coveted her almost, of all the times he'd known he could make her far happier than Rory ever would, given half the chance. Harry's mind flashed back to his boyhood. Even at fifteen he'd known it, despite the fact that she was drawn to the tall, athletic and clever Rory Gallagher. Christ, it had even been Harry she'd met up with again first in London! If only he hadn't introduced her to Rory, if only he had kept them apart. How many times had Harry thought that over the last two years? How many times had he lamented that one big mistake?

He turned back to Rory and asked, 'So, what now?' And as soon as he said it, he recognised the opportunity of the situation. He saw what was in it for him. For the first time in years he wasn't dominated by the sheer strength of Rory's charm, or overpowered by his physical presence. Harry was the Army officer, yet Rory had always been the leader and now, for the first time in years, Harry actually felt equal. Rory had fucked up and he'd done it royally! He stared at his friend, knowing he should say otherwise, knowing it was his duty to advise the best he could, persuade him to take time to think it all through carefully, to maybe postpone the wedding, to talk to Kate. But Harry ignored all of this. Instead, he asked, 'Are you going to cancel the wedding?'

Rory looked down at the ground. A tense, expectant silence created a gulf between them and it took him all his courage to look up again. 'I don't know, I really don't,' he said finally. 'What else can I do, Harry? What else *can* I do?'

Harry took a risk in saying what he said next, but it was a calculated risk. He knew Rory's honesty was integral to his character. 'You could forget all about it,' he said, carefully choosing his next words. 'Lie. Do nothing, go ahead with the wedding, pretend the whole thing with Alice didn't happen and deny everything.'

'For God's sake, Harry. How can I lie? If I say nothing – forget it, as you suggest, go ahead with the wedding today – and it turns out that I am the father of this child, then Kate would never forgive me. Alice could bring a paternity suit, and where would that leave me? I would have married

Kate under false pretences and deceived her in the worst possible way. Surely you see that, don't you?'

Grudgingly, Harry did see it. He saw Rory's integrity which he knew he should defend, but he couldn't help thinking of himself. This was a complete and utter mess, yet right through the centre of it was a clear, straight path for Harry. He would have to be there for Kate, take charge of the situation today, save her from the embarrassment, ease her pain. He would have to look after her for quite some time to come, help her get over this and comfort her. And at the end, when she was finally through the other side and had forgotten it, then who knows who she might think she loved? His loyalty was divided, but he really didn't have to think twice about who to defend. He glanced up as Rory appealed to him.

'You do understand, Harry? You do see that I've got no choice? That I have to do the right thing? Tell me you understand! Please, Harry!' Harry wasn't sure if this was an appeal to agree or disagree; he felt the turning point lay in his hands. He kept quiet for a few moments.

'Harry?'

Finally he answered. 'Yes,' he said, 'I understand. You must do the right thing.'

'Oh, God!' Rory put his hands up to his face. 'What a fucking mess!' Harry put out a hand to pat him on the shoulder, but thought better of it. They had been friends, close friends for a very long time, but all that would have to change now. If he wanted Kate, and he did, then he would have to take sides.

'It's one hell of a mess,' he said, 'and it's going to need some very careful handling. I'm afraid that you'll have to make yourself pretty bloody scarce.'

'What d'you mean, scarce?'

'For God's sake, Rory! You should get the hell out of it and leave things to me! No one will want to see your face after I break the news.'

'After *you* break the news?'

'Yes. Who else did you think was going to tell Kate? Alice?'

'No. Me, of course.'

'You? Christ! Get a grip, will you!' Harry's temper finally snapped. 'The best thing you can do, Rory, is bugger off. I think you've already done enough damage, don't you?'

'But I can't just leave! What about Kate? I owe it to her at least to tell her myself.'

'Why? What good will that do? Do you really want to see her pain? Don't you think that might just be considered rubbing her nose in it?' It was crucial that Harry told Kate, that he should be her comforter, the one she turned to and leaned on.

'No, I . . .' Rory broke off and dropped his head in his hands. The thought of not seeing Kate, of not being able at least to explain, was so terrible that it made him feel sick with helplessness and despair. Loss overwhelmed him. 'Do you really think that's how she'll feel, Harry, that I'm making it worse by trying to talk to her?'

'Yes! I don't see how she can feel anything else. You've made up your mind, she isn't going to change it, so let her be. Let me handle it.' He *had* to handle it. What if somehow, in some way things were resolved, or Rory changed his mind? Harry couldn't risk it. This was his moment, his opportunity.

'But that's running away, it's cowardly, it's—'

'It's the only decent thing you can do. This isn't just you

and her, it's arrangements and money that's been spent, people to phone, cancellations to make, the whole fucking thing, Rory. You are going to call off a wedding, and you can't stand around making an emotional mess out of it. Kate has to be told, comforted, and then things have to be done.' There was a silence, Harry was sure Rory was almost swayed. But a few moments later he found he was wrong.

'No, no, I can't do it. I cannot run away, I—'

'You have to!' Harry suddenly snapped. That was a mistake.

'No!' Rory said. 'No, Harry, I don't have to. In fact, quite the opposite. I know what is right, and leaving you to tell Kate is definitely not. I will tell her myself.' He stopped and swallowed hard. He could just walk away, take Harry's advice, simply go and let him get on with it. But Rory wasn't a coward, he was facing up to Alice, to what he had done, and he owed it to Kate to face up to her as well.

'Oh, Christ . . .' he murmured. 'What a mess!'

'This really isn't the right thing to do,' Harry cut in. 'I really don't think . . .' But Rory had started towards the pub.

'Look, Rory?' Harry called after him, and he turned. 'If you have to tell Kate yourself, then promise me one thing,' he said. 'Promise me that after today, after you've destroyed her hopes and dreams, her happiness, that you'll have the grace to leave her alone and let her get on with her life.'

'What do you mean?'

'If you love her, then whatever happens you have to leave her alone, let her start again.'

Rory stared at the ground. He didn't know if he could do what Harry was asking, how could he never see Kate again? But Harry was insistent; he had to protect Kate – and, of course, himself.

'Rory! Say it, goddammit! Make the promise.'

'OK!' Rory stood straight and faced Harry. 'Yes, whatever you want,' he answered. And with that, he walked away back to the pub and out of Harry's life for ever.

The grounds of Tonsbry House were a short walk from the village across the fields, down by the stream and over Priory Lane. Another time Rory might have enjoyed it, now he walked slowly and with grim determination towards the task he had undertaken.

Jumping the gate of the farthest field, he made his way up to the house, his shoes wet from the heavy dew that often accompanies the beginning of a brilliant early summer's day. He arrived at the back façade of Tonsbry, its lichen-covered golden stone glowing in the morning sunshine, and stood for a while looking up at it. Then he picked up a stone. It was a long-standing arrangement, almost a ritual. He aimed the stone at her bedroom window and let it fly. It hit one of the tiny leaded-glass panes and bounced off with a loud ping. He waited. Moments later, a sleek dark head appeared at the window, then Kate's face, pale and even more beautiful than he had ever seen her before; her hair was piled high on her head, caught up with just a pin, and a white bath sheet wrapped tightly round her torso showed the long curve of her neck and the slope of tawny-skinned bare shoulders.

She opened the window and leaned out.

'Oh! Oh, gosh, Rory! You shouldn't. It's bad luck to see the bride . . .' She broke off and pulled back slightly, glancing down to check that the towel was still in place. She flushed, suddenly embarrassed by her appearance, then saw something in Rory's face and her own became guarded.

'Rory? What's wrong? What are you—?'

'Kate, I'm sorry,' Rory interrupted, 'but we have to talk, privately. Can you come down right away?'

She put a hand up to her hair, a nervous habit she had, and pulled at a loose strand. 'What's wrong? Can't you tell me now?'

Rory braced himself. He shook his head and said, 'I'd rather you came down, Kate.'

Kate looked briefly over her shoulder, then called out, 'OK, wait there, I'll be down in a few minutes.' And just as she closed the window, Rory caught the look of terrible dread and panic that crossed her face and wished to God he hadn't.

'Hi!'

Rory spun round. He had been looking out over the grounds of Tonsbry House and hadn't heard Kate cross the lawn towards him. She looked wonderful, fresh and lovely; radiant. It took his breath away. When she moved forward to kiss his cheek he flinched, and it shocked her. 'Rory? What on earth?'

'Kate, I have to tell you something,' he said quickly. 'Something awful, something . . .' He broke off, short of breath, dizzy with fear. 'Kate, something's gone wrong, we can't . . . I mean, I can't . . . I can't marry you today, Kate, I can't . . .'

Kate took a pace back. She stared at him for a moment, then shook her head. 'No, no, this isn't happening,' she said, a peculiar smile on her face. 'Rory, stop it! This is ridiculous. What's going on?'

He moved forward, took her hands in his, then dropped them again suddenly and clenched his fists by his sides. Kate froze, staring at him. 'Kate, I've made a mistake,' he mumbled. 'I've done something awful, terrible, I—'

'For God's sake, Rory!' she cried. 'Tell me what's happened. Just *tell* me!'

Rory stopped. For a split second he felt as if he wasn't really there, that he had somehow been lifted out of himself and was watching this happening from above. He took a breath, he saw Kate as he would always see her from that moment on, in pain and very scared. He said, 'I got drunk, I slept with Alice White and she's having my baby.' That was it, he had said it. Another moment of suspension, a silence, then he looked up at Kate.

'I don't believe it,' she said, shaking her head. 'I'm sorry, but I just don't believe it!'

Rory closed his eyes. 'Oh God, Kate,' he said, 'it's true, it's fucking true, believe me. I did it, I fucked up our lives, I don't know how or why, I can't even remember it but I did it . . . Oh God!' He wrung his hands. 'Kate, I'm so sorry, I don't know how it happened, I—'

'Stop it!' she suddenly shouted. 'Stop it, stop it, stop it!' She put her hands up to her ears. 'I don't want to hear it! I don't want to know what you did!' Her voice was strangled by the sobs that rose in her throat, but she would not cry. There was another silence which closed in on them and separated them completely. Kate held herself up with every nerve and sinew strained at the effort. She took a breath.

'Have you told Harry?' she asked.

He nodded.

'Leo?'

'No, I didn't think . . .'

The silence again.

'Christ, Kate! Say something, rant at me, shout at me. Say something, anything, please!' This wasn't fair, silence made it worse. He reached for her hand, but she backed away. 'Please, Kate, please don't shut me out, don't just—' Suddenly the smack came out of nowhere. It hit him hard on the side of the face, a full, sharp slap, and it knocked him back a pace. He clutched his face and stared at her. 'You, you . . .'

'I think,' she said, clenching her hands together so tightly to stop them shaking that her knuckles were white. 'I think that you should leave.' Her voice was choked with anger and grief as she turned away from him.

'But, Kate?'

Somehow she managed to lift her head and propel her body forward, her legs so weak with the shock that she wanted to drop to the ground and crawl the few yards to safety. She didn't turn back.

'Kate, I . . .' Rory stopped. What could he say? Words were futile. He stood and watched her walk back to the house, he watched her move slowly across the terrace, knowing it was the last time he would ever see her and powerless to do anything about that fact. As she turned towards the yew hedge, he saw a figure step out of the shadows and move towards her. She walked one last pace into an embrace and her whole body slumped, as if the life had just drained out of her. She stood for what seemed to Rory like eternity; then the figure moved her forward, back towards the house. Rory could see who it was and his stomach lurched. 'Harry Drummond,' he murmured and, unable to move, he watched his friend take Kate out of his life for ever.

*   *   *

Later, much later, when the caterers had left and the guests arriving at church had been turned away, when the jazz band had been cancelled, the wine left unopened in its cases in the cellar and the glasses packed back in their boxes, Kate Dowie stood at the long, stained-glass window on the staircase of Tonsbry House and looked out at the front lawns. The marquee was still there, the huge cream canvas old-fashioned type, with guy ropes and striped lining. The flowers were still arranged and the tables and chairs in place for the guests who never came.

'The ghost wedding,' she muttered bitterly under her breath and felt a hand on her shoulder.

'Kate?'

It was Leo, her uncle and the only one she might have confided in, but she didn't answer. She didn't want sympathy, it just made her want to weep and she had no intention of doing that, she was damned if she was going to do that!

'Kate? How do you feel?' She kept still, frozen beneath his touch. Why did everyone keep asking her how she felt? How did they *think* she felt? She stared out at the marquee and said nothing.

'Kate, darling, come away, come and have a cup of tea or a drink or something . . .' His voice trailed off and Kate could hear the desperation in it. She stiffened, feeling the threat of tears, and pressed herself closer to the glass, further away from her uncle. 'Kate?' She shook her head.

'Go away,' she whispered. 'Please, go away.' She wanted to be left to her misery. Hadn't she been humiliated enough without having to break down in front of them all? She felt the pressure of his fingers as he squeezed her shoulder, then he was gone. His footsteps receded down the small flight of stairs, along the passage, and Kate closed her eyes. Nothing changed. Even doing that couldn't blank out the image of the failed day, the cancelled wedding and the terrible pain of Rory's words.

Along the passage, Leo Alder opened the door of the morning-room and stepped inside. He closed it softly behind him.

'Well?' Kate's mother Adriana was smoking, her filter-tipped cigarette – long and thin and menthol – ringed with a thin gold line. She flicked the ash into a small Limoges plate which she held in one hand, and said again, 'Well? Come on, Leo? What did she say?'

'She said, as I thought she would, to leave her alone.'

Adriana glared at her brother, a man she neither liked nor understood, and drew hard on her cigarette. She uncrossed her legs, encased in natural extra-sheer, high-gloss stockings from La Perla, and stood up. 'I'll speak to her,' she announced. Leo shifted slightly to a defensive position in front of the door. 'I don't think so,' he said.

'Oh, for God's sake, Leo, stop being so pathetic!' she snapped. 'If I want to speak to my daughter, then I will!' She stubbed out her cigarette in the porcelain dish, regardless of her brother's pained and shocked expression, and moved towards the door. She had taken off her hat, a navy and white large-brimmed affair trimmed with feathers and silk, and her still dark auburn hair had escaped its French pleat in places, softening her face. Leo thought for a moment how much of her beauty she had given to Kate, then she said, 'Get out of my way, Leo!' in that clipped sharp way she had and he thought, very thankfully, how little of her personality she had passed on. 'Kate needs me,' she went on, 'she must want to speak to someone, it's not good for her to bottle it up like this. I must go to her, Leo, really I must; it's not healthy, she needs a stiff brandy and a good weep.'

'Really, Adriana,' Kate's father – Adriana's first husband, John Dowie – started, 'if Kate says she wants to be left alone, then—' But he didn't finish. She turned on him with the same withering look she had given Leo.

'Shut up, John! If you were any good at anything at all except books and tutorials, then I might seek your opinion. As it is, you're not, so keep it to yourself!' There was a discreet cough from a figure by the window and Adriana glanced across. 'Yes?' she demanded.

Adriana's latest husband – number four, and the only one who had ever managed to stand up to her, Pierre Glibert, Comte de Grand Blès – turned and looked at her. With a smile that stopped her in her tracks, he said, 'If your daughter desires solitude, Adriana my darling, then that is exactly what she will get.'

Adriana opened her mouth to speak, but closed it again as the Comte held up his hand to silence her. She swallowed down a mouthful of air and stared at her very costly navy Bruno Magli shoes. 'I only want to help her,' she said quietly.

The Comte crossed to her and took her arm, gently leading her back to her seat. 'Of course you do,' he said. 'She's your daughter, you love her.'

The room fell silent. Everyone loved Kate. Fearless, funny, beautiful Kate who had no pretensions and not one unkind bone in her entire body. Mrs Able, Leo's housekeeper at Tonsbry, sniffed loudly and Harry stared down at his hands.

At that moment the door to the morning-room flew open.

'Ah, everyone's in here, I see.'

Kate stood in the doorway, her hair still held up on top of her head by an old clip, wearing the pair of scruffy cut-off denims and small white T-shirt that she had thrown on in her haste to meet Rory. She smiled, a bright, false smile that was supposed to make her look strong, but instead made her look so vulnerable and fragile that Leo thought for a moment that if she were pushed, just a fraction, she would crack and shatter into a thousand tiny irreparable pieces. She didn't come in, she said, 'I was looking for some scissors – Leo, Mrs Able? You wouldn't know where I can find any, would you?'

'Scissors?' Adriana couldn't keep the shock out of her voice. She had seen Kate fail before, she had seen her daughter upset and distraught over minor things that could be soothed away with reasoning or a kiss or the purchase of something new, but she had never seen this person here before – this brittle, hollow girl who looked as if someone had just killed her spirit and literally sucked the life out of her. She drew in her breath and felt Pierre's hand tighten over her own.

'Yes, scissors,' Kate answered, turning to her mother. 'I am going to cut up my wedding dress!' She stared around the room, not really seeing any of them. 'You see, Harry's been talking about this ball at the Officers' Mess, haven't you, Harry? And I thought, why waste such a pretty frock, why not cut it short, dye it black and wear it to Harry's ball?' She smiled again, but the sinews on her neck stood out as if it cost her enormous physical strain to do so. 'I even thought I might cut out the sleeves and add a plunge neckline. I've got spectacular boobs, I thought I might show them off a bit. Now that I'm no longer engaged, of course!'

The room was frozen with shock.

'Well? Are there any scissors around, Mrs Able?'

Leo said, 'There are some right here, Kate dear, in the sewing box.' He stood up, went to the Victorian mahogany sewing table and opened it. Taking out the dressmaking scissors, he crossed and handed them to Kate. 'Are you sure you want to do this now?' he asked quietly.

Kate took the scissors. 'Of course!' she replied loudly, for all to hear. 'Why not? I've no other use for the dress, so I might as well get on with it.' She turned. 'Thanks, Uncle Leo,' she said. 'I'll show it off when I've finished.' And closing the door behind her, she left the drawing-room choked with a stunned and saddened silence.

Up in the bedroom she had always called her own, Kate walked across to her wedding dress, still hanging on its padded silk hanger from the top of the wardrobe, still with the fine tissue paper over the shoulders, and took the scissors to its hem. She opened them, held a thick fold of wild Thai silk between the blades and prepared to cut. Her hand began to shake. Steadying it by holding the wrist with the other one, she closed the scissors over the dress and heard the resonant crunch of the silk as it cut. Quietly, and alone, Kate at last began to sob.

Chapter Three

Four Years Later

Leo Alder's nurse at Tonsbry House was married with three school-age children, and children were expensive nowadays with their CD players and Nike trainers, their computer games and football strips. She had taken a part-time job with a private nursing company to help pay for all these things, but she found that the more she earned, the more they spent as a family and there was never enough to put away in the bank. She was well qualified, honest and pleasant, she worked hard and nursed Leo through his last few months of cancer with care and kindness, but when the offer of a small lump sum came in, just for a few phone calls about Mr Alder's condition, she thought it through and took it without any qualms. It wasn't ethical, breaching patient confidentiality, but it wasn't illegal and the money was more than welcome.

So she rang the number she was given, once a week at first, then every few days as his condition worsened, and the day he died she made her phone call before she even telephoned the doctor. She used her mobile, as she always had, was put straight through to the gentleman she always spoke to and said: 'Mr Alder died this morning at ten minutes past nine. Will there be anything else you require from me?'

The voice on the other end told her that there wasn't, and that the lump sum promised would be delivered to her home address in cash by the end of the day. So she thanked the man, disconnected the line and went out of Leo Alder's bedroom and downstairs to inform the housekeeper and to phone the doctor from the study to come and certify his death.

In the warm, balmy air of the small island of Mustique, just as dawn was breaking, a telephone rang in the cool, darkened sitting-room of a large, spacious villa whose gardens ran down to the white, sandy beach and whose long sweeping windows overlooked the dazzling, clear azure-blue sea.

A pair of heels clicked over the marble floor, along the corridor towards the ringing phone. The call was answered.

'Hello?'

'It's me. Just to let you know that Leo Alder died this morning, an hour ago, at nine-ten.'

There was a long silence, and the caller became impatient. 'Hello? Are you still there?'

'Yes, I'm here,' the answer came. 'Start proceedings today.' Then there was a click and the line went dead.

Kate Dowie cycled up towards Pimlico from Victoria, expertly manoeuvring her bicycle through the traffic towards the filter lane and turning left into Egerton Square.

She swung up on to the pavement, slowed, then stopped, climbing off and taking a padlock out of the huge basket on the front that advertised: *KATE DOWIE – HIGH-QUALITY CATERING SERVICES*. Attaching the bike to the iron railings, she lifted a pile of small red-and-white striped paper bags with handles out of the basket, along with a couple of large plastic containers and, with her arms full, made her way across the road towards her building. She noticed that she was back before the van this morning and made a mental note to call Rebecca on the mobile to check that there hadn't been any problems. Kate had been doing the sandwich run that morning, delivering freshly made exotic and hugely expensive sandwiches around the City on her bicycle, while Rebecca, one of her best chefs, was out in the van delivering the orders for ready-made luncheon food. Usually she was back long after the van and Becca had already made a start on the dinner-party menus, so this morning she was slightly worried as she unlocked the front door and kicked it open with her foot. There was a great deal to do today, three dinner parties and preparations for a large cocktail party in the City tomorrow night. Stopping at the hall table, Kate glanced at the post, grabbed the bundle for her, which was tied with a rubber band, and flicked through it as she made for the stairs. Mostly white envelopes, she noted, with a surge of delight. After four hard years, *KATE DOWIE – HIGH-QUALITY CATERING SERVICES* was doing as much business as it could handle and could now safely be called a success.

But it hadn't always been like that. When Kate took it over against everyone's advice, the autumn after Rory left her, she had found that instead of being the going concern she had been sold, it was an ailing business with no more than two clients who entertained once a month. She had hocked everything to buy it too, refusing her mother's offer of a loan and digging in her heels for independence and a chance to prove herself. To prove *what* about herself she hadn't known in the beginning. But as she worked, touting for business, throwing her whole self into every dinner party she produced, getting up at four every weekday morning to make exotic sandwiches and flogging them on foot in the offices around the City; and as she learned to grow her own herbs and blend her own coffee, expertly choose a menu and complementary wines and finish every meal with home-made whisky truffles – a touch she was now quite famous for – she realised that it was to prove she was worth something. To rebuild her confidence in herself and to make sure that although she had failed once – and she had considered Rory jilting her a failure, for a very long time she had blamed herself – she would never, *ever* do so again.

All those years ago, Alice had thought Kate too lucky by far; maybe she had been for a while, but Kate had learned to make her own luck now. She was less sleek, still beautiful, but it was a beauty that was unselfconscious – a beauty that had a peculiar habit of going unnoticed; then she would turn or smile or say something funny, catching people unawares, and it was so startling that it took one's breath away. Kate had changed, much as Alice had thought she would. In many ways she was a completely different person; she seemed multi-layered, complex, ungiving even, but underneath – to the people she worked with and cared for – she was still the same funny, kind and clever Kate.

Reaching the top of the first flight of stairs, Kate dropped the plastic containers down on the floor, along with the paper bags and the post, then fished her keys out of her pocket where she'd just dropped them and went to unlock her front door. Just as she did so, it opened and Stefan stood in front of her, as immaculate as ever, tanned, muscular and barefoot in grey jogging shorts and a white T-shirt.

'Hello!' Kate bent to pick up her things. 'Were there any calls?'

'A couple,' he said, taking the containers she handed him and leading the way inside and along to the kitchen. Stefan and Kate had been friends for three years now, close friends. He lived upstairs and had his own key to her flat, letting himself in every morning after she'd left for the City to answer the telephone for a couple of hours and take messages. Kate had a thing about answerphones and only used one when it was really necessary. She felt that the sound of a real voice could often make the difference between a booking given to her and one to another caterer. Besides which, Stefan had shed-loads of charm and, seeing that so many of her clients were women, she knew that his answering the phone was a great asset to her.

'Did Mrs Varrall call about Friday night?' she asked, going immediately to the fridge to take out an asparagus and prawn mousse to check it was set. 'I left the menu plans on the desk for her, did you see them?'

'Kate?'

'Hmmm?' She inserted the fine blade of a knife, lifted it out and was happy that the mousse was set. 'I must call Becca before I do anything else,' she went on, putting it back in the fridge and taking out the ingredients for what she was about to prepare. 'She's late today, and I'm just hoping that she hasn't run into any trouble. Unlikely, I know, but I can't help worrying, we've got so much on today, I—'

'Kate?'

Kate stopped in mid-sentence and glanced over her shoulder at Stefan. 'Sorry, Stefan, I'm gabbling. Did you want to say something?'

Stefan hesitated. The phone call hadn't come out of the blue, he'd been waiting for it and was sure Kate must have been too, despite the fact that she seemed to go on hoping blindly, regardless of what the doctors said. Still, now he was faced with it, he didn't know where to start. He felt suddenly cold with apprehension.

'Oh, Lord, you're not going to tell me you can't work on Friday afternoon, are you? I really was hoping to get away early to go down to Tonsbry to see Leo. When I spoke to the nurse a few days ago, she said things had worsened . . .' She stopped. 'Sorry, if you can't do it, then so be it. I shouldn't be burdening you with all this stuff—' She turned and saw something in his face. 'Stefan?'

'Kate, look, forget Friday. I'm afraid that you had a call this morning and there won't be any need to go down, I mean . . .' He broke off for a moment and stared down at his hands. 'Look, I'm really sorry, Kate, but—'

'Leo's dead,' she said. 'He's dead, isn't he?'

Stefan nodded. He wasn't sure what to expect, quite how Kate would react. She had a defiant streak in the face of disaster or pain that got her through most things, but this was different. This was death and this was Leo. Stefan had never probed or delved into Kate's life, just taken what she had chosen to give him in the way of information, but he didn't have to be a genius to see that her uncle had always been there for her, stable and secure at Tonsbry House in the midst of her mother's absence and many marriages and her father's abandonment of things real for things intellectual.

He reached out to touch her arm, but Kate turned away.

'I'm OK, Stefan,' she managed to say. 'Really, I'm OK.' She moved across the kitchen to the window and stood with her arms wrapped tightly round her body. Stefan watched her and could see that she gripped her arms so fiercely that the blood drained from her fingertips. He moved to the kettle, switched it on and reached up to the cupboard to take out the cognac that Kate used for cooking. Pouring a slug into a cup, he added a tea-bag and made her some weak tea. Adding two hefty spoons of sugar, he walked across to her and silently handed it over. Kate took it and downed a large gulp, but said nothing. Her hands shook and he realised that she was shivering.

'Kate, drink the brandy and tea, come on.' He wondered if he should call someone, Harry perhaps, but his instinctive dislike of the man prevented him from doing so. He looked across at Kate. She seemed to be sinking, retreating into herself and losing awareness. 'Kate?'

She started, then he saw her raise the mug and drink. Slowly she finished the tea and shuddered, the brandy hitting the pit of her stomach. A bit of colour had returned to her face. Stefan stood silently, not sure what to do. Would she want him to stay, or was he intruding? There was more, more to tell, but he didn't think she had the strength to face it.

'Stefan?'

He glanced up. Some of the hollowness of shock had gone and her eyes were bright with unshed tears. It reassured him, it seemed more normal somehow, easier to deal with. Then she said, 'Who rang? Was it my father or Mrs Able?' and he floundered for a few moments, knowing that the truth had to come out and dreading it.

'No,' he said, watching her face intently, 'Rory Gallagher rang.'

The change in her expression was so swift and so violent that it took him aback. Her eyes narrowed and hardened and a rush of colour flooded her face as the blood rushed to the surface of the skin. 'Rory Gallagher!' she fired at him. 'What the hell has he got to do with Leo?'

Stefan swallowed hard. 'He rang from Tonsbry, he worked for your uncle on the estate. He wanted to ring, he—'

'Worked for him?' Kate cried, throwing up her hands in horror. 'Worked for him? What the hell do you mean, worked for him? How? Why?' She had begun to agitate, her movements coiled tight with anger. 'The last I heard, he was married and living in Notting Hill. What the hell do you mean, Stefan?' She was becoming hysterical. 'I don't understand! How can Rory have had anything to do with Leo? How can he know Leo's dead? How can he? Why did he ring? Why? I can't see—'

'Calm down, Kate! Just calm down.' Stefan took her by the shoulders and, with some effort, held her still. 'Kate, Rory worked for Leo, managing the estate, that's all I know. He rang because he wanted to make sure that you would be all right. That's all, OK?' But it wasn't all. Stefan didn't mention that Rory had rung before, many times, or that he liked the man, from what he knew of him – liked the fact that he so obviously cared for Kate.

Kate hung her head. She was silent for a few minutes

and Stefan could see that she struggled with her tears. She hated to cry in front of anyone, he knew that. 'I'm sorry, Kate, really, about Leo,' he said. She nodded and he moved away to the other side of the kitchen to give her the space she needed. 'Shall I ask Becca to cover for you today? I can give her a hand and you could maybe take some time off?'

Kate glanced up. 'No,' she said quickly. 'No, thanks, it's kind, but I – I just think I should work, I mean I'd like to.' She wrung her hands, then wiped her face on her apron. 'Sorry.' She took some kitchen roll and blew her nose loudly and inelegantly. 'It's better if I work, it always is.'

There she goes again, he thought, burying herself in work, cutting herself off, but all he said was, 'Yes, sure.'

'It's not even as if it's a shock or anything. I mean I expected it, I knew in my heart it was coming and, well, I should be prepared in a way, I . . .' She blew her nose again as her eyes filled with tears. 'Oh God, sorry . . .'

Stefan stepped forward, put his arm around her shoulder and gently propelled her into the sitting room. He eased her into the sofa and went back to the kitchen for some more tea. When he returned, Kate said, 'Stefan, you've cleared up! You shouldn't have done, it's too kind, it's . . .' She stopped to blow her nose a third time and said through her handkerchief, 'God, this is so pathetic. I'm sorry, blubbing all over the place. You shouldn't have done all this, really, it was so kind, it—'

Stefan handed her the cup. 'It was nothing,' he said quickly, when in actual fact it had been a great deal. When he heard about Leo's death he had been desperate to do something for Kate, to show her how much he cared, so he'd spent a good few hours frantically tidying, clearing the paraphernalia of Kate's successful business from every surface, polishing and vacuuming, opening windows and generally restoring a very beautiful but much neglected flat. It was all he could think of to do.

'Besides,' he said, rubbing at a smear on the mirror above the fireplace with the hem of his T-shirt, 'think of all that you've done for me.'

'I gave you a job washing-up,' Kate said. 'It wasn't much.'

'Maybe not to you,' he answered, 'but it was a whole lot to me, at the time anyway.' Stefan took a pace back and stared at Kate while she sipped her tea. It had meant everything to him back then; she had rescued him – that was how he liked to think of it – met him in a café by Waterloo station on a freezing-cold night when he was down to his last tenner with nowhere to sleep, and saved him from poverty. She had bought him a coffee, chatted to him for five minutes and then, on the spur of the moment and stuck for help, offered him a night's work washing-up at a buffet party for thirty. That was the beginning.

Clean-shaven and in a fresh white shirt and black jeans, provided by her courtesy of a friend, he had slicked back his black hair and was discovered to be hauntingly good-looking. In the company of an élite media party, waiting tables as well as washing-up, in the space of three hours he had totally reinvented himself. He left behind Stephen Briggs – formerly of Acacia Avenue, Maidstone in Kent – glad to be rid of him, and became Stefan Vladimar, public-school educated with an obscure but fascinating Eastern European background. He became an actor resting between roles, and by the end of the evening had secured his first piece of business. It wasn't a part, but it paid damn well and he was a young man with a verve for life, along with a keen and healthy appetite for sex. He had never known how much he loved women until he tried, and then he loved them as much and as long as they required. In fact, he had an extraordinary talent for it. On the surface it was escorting them to dinners, drinks parties, receptions and opening nights; underneath it was making them feel exactly how they wanted to feel, and that really was a talent.

Now he had a regular clientele and a flat above Kate's – half the size but smart, smart enough to entertain in. He worked out, kept his body tanned, muscular and waxed as smooth as his close-shaven, chiselled face. He wore Armani for media women, a hand-made suit from Simpsons of Piccadilly for City executives and lawyers, Paul Smith for the doyennes of advertising and Calvin Klein fine cotton underwear for all of them. He was select and élite, and he was making a small fortune.

'Stef?'

He looked up. He had been so lost in thought that she startled him. Immediately he felt guilty for thinking of himself and not Kate, and he flushed.

'Stef, what exactly did Rory say?'

Stefan bent and took Kate's cup from her, carrying it through to the kitchen. There he washed it up and wondered what the hell to say in reply. He knew the Kate and Rory history, or parts of it, but it was before his time and although he had talked to Rory on the phone, he had never met him. What Rory Gallagher had actually said was: 'Leo died at ten past nine this morning. Could you tell Kate for me? I didn't want just anyone ringing her up, I wanted to make sure she was with someone who cared about her when she heard. How is she, I mean is she well, and happy? You will look after her, won't you? Let me know if there's anything I can do, but don't tell her about Tonsbry, not unless you really have to.'

'Stefan?'

'He said that Leo had died and that he wanted to make sure that you heard it from me, not just anyone.'

'Did he ask about me?'

Stefan nodded.

'What?' She moved a little closer, and Stefan could smell the brandy on her breath; she had obviously had an empty stomach. Despite the fact that Kate cooked for a living, she had no real interest in eating. 'What did he ask?' There was a peculiar edge to her voice.

'Nothing – well, not really. He said . . . erm . . .' Stefan broke off, not knowing how to proceed. In all the time he'd known Kate she had never mentioned Rory Gallagher; it was as if she had wiped him from her life entirely. Did she really want to know, or was it some kind of reaction to Leo's death? He felt himself sweat. What if he opened up all the old wounds? She was vulnerable enough already, wasn't she? Regardless of her tough defences, Stefan made his decision. Gallagher might come across as a nice guy on the phone, but if he'd hurt Kate so badly once, he could do it again and Stefan wanted no part in causing that. 'He just asked me to tell you, that was all,' he lied.

'Oh.' It was as if someone had punctured Kate and let all the air out of her body. 'I see.' She seemed to slump with disappointment, and Stefan hoped to God he'd done the right thing. 'So that was all,' she said to herself. She turned away, her whole stance suddenly angry, defiant almost.

Then she said, 'I must ring Harry. He's on exercise, but I might be able to get a message through to him.' And Stefan thought, oh no, not Harry, and really did wonder if he had done the right thing.

'Flora! Don't do that, please!'

Rory Gallagher didn't look up. In the kitchen of a small labourer's cottage on the Tonsbry Estate, he sat at the scrubbed pine table with his daughter and tapped another figure into his calculator, totalled, then wrote down the sum in his analysis book. The sharp chink of metal on china continued.

'Flora, I'm warning you . . .' He began another depressing calculation, his pencil working down the column of figures, his mood sinking second by second. Suddenly there was a crack. He glanced up, reached swiftly across the table and grabbed the butter knife. 'Stop! Now!' He placed it at his side and stared at his daughter. 'When I say don't do something, I mean it.'

Flora pursed her lips. 'Why?'

'Why what?'

She began to trail her finger in the small dollop of jam on the side of her plate, making patterns with it on the table top.

'Flora, for goodness' sake! Have you finished?'

'Yes.'

'Yes what?'

She bent and licked the mess of jam off her plate. 'YesthankyoupleasemayIgetdown.'

Rory smiled. 'Three going on twenty-three. Yes, you may.' He watched her small, compact figure slip off the chair and go across to the sink to wipe her hands. Where she got such pristine habits he had no idea; he was hardly domestic and she had no motherly example to follow. 'Do your face while you're there,' he said. 'Your mouth is covered in jam.'

'Daddy . . . ?'

'Yes?'

'What're you doing?'

'My accounts, I'll just be two more minutes.'

'Daddy . . . ?'

'Yes?'

'When will you be finished?'

Rory sighed, dropped the pencil and looked up. Flora, across the small kitchen, stared at him with a fierce look of concentration. 'Now,' he said. 'Right now. Go get your boots on.'

'Hooray!'

'Bugger the accounts,' he muttered, well out of Flora's earshot. It was a deeply depressing task anyway, and he desperately needed some fresh air.

'You're off out then, are you?' Mrs Able came down the stairs of the cottage carrying a basket of dirty towels. She had been housekeeper at Tonsbry for thirty years and had known Rory most of his life. 'You look shattered, boy.' She came across to the table and dropped the basket down on the floor. 'It's a sad day for all of us – and just when you'd got settled, too.' She patted him on the shoulder, then fumbled in her housecoat for her handkerchief. Having blown her nose, she said, 'Let me take Flora, for this morning anyway, give you a chance to get a bit of rest.'

Rory smiled, but shook his head.

'You've done so much, Rory lad, there's nothing more you can do now.'

'No, perhaps not.' But had he really done enough? He'd brought his business skills to a badly mismanaged estate and tried so hard to sort things out, but had he achieved anything except the very smallest of triumphs? He didn't think so – and in that respect he'd failed Leo, failed to make his last few months less painful, failed to help him die peacefully. Rory hung his head. The last three years had been so swamped in failure, personal and professional, that he wondered if he would ever get it right again.

'Ready!'

They both looked at Flora, who suddenly appeared from the porch, boots on the wrong feet, hat on but ears sticking out at right-angles, her coat only on one arm. Despite himself, Rory smiled. Flora always had that effect on him.

'What a clever girl! Come here, though, and let me put them on the right feet.' Rory sat Flora on a kitchen chair and knelt, pulling off the wellies and quickly reorganising them.

'Daddy . . . ?'

'Yes?'

'Are you better now?'

He glanced up at a small, concerned and sincere face. 'Better, sweetheart? What do you mean?'

'You were set up this morning—'

'Set up?'

'Yes. I heard you, and I thought that you must have hurt yourself.'

'Oh, upset, you mean.'

'Yes!'

Rory looked away and held his breath for a few moments; it was the closest he had come to tears. He had liked Leo, Leo had given him the chance of a life again and he would be eternally grateful for that. 'I was, sweetheart, you're right, and I had hurt myself.'

Flora leaned forward and kissed her father's face, a round wet kiss. 'Kiss it better,' she said and, boots righted, jumped off the chair and ran to the front door. Rory stood and walked across to the porch after her.

'Bring her over to John and me for lunch, then,' Mrs Able said. 'We need a bit of life today.' She sniffed and dabbed at her eyes with her rose-printed handkerchief.

Rory pulled his own coat on and stuffed his feet into his boots, then turned and said, 'Thanks, I will.' He planted a very uncustomary kiss on the housekeeper's cheek and pulled open the door. The last thing he heard before he stepped outside was a loud, resonant disapproving cluck from Mrs Able, but as he glanced over his shoulder at her she was smiling.

'Come on, Flora,' he shouted. She was hovering by the paddock fence with a handful of grass, trying to lure one of the ponies across to her. 'Those sheep'll be waiting!' Flora turned and ran over to him, taking his hand.

'Good girl. We have to get a move on, or there'll be mutinous sheep all over the Tonsbry estate.'

'What's mutniss?'

'Rebellion,' Rory said. Suddenly he bent, scooped up a squealing Flora and ran across the small courtyard with her, tickling her as he ran. 'Pirates and Captain Hook and Daddy coming to gobble you all up!' he cried. Flora screamed even louder and for a few minutes Rory Gallagher forgot his grief and the very bleak future of Tonsbry House and estate. He had Flora, and it wasn't the first time he had marvelled in his luck at that fact.

*   *   *

Adriana was packing when Pierre came into the bedroom. She had neatly lined up dozens of outfits on to the bed and was carefully laying them in her case with precision and order. Her face was pale, but her eyes burned with a curious and almost erotic excitement.

'And where are you going, my darling?' he asked, peeling off his shirt and letting it drop on to the floor.

Adriana glanced up. The sight of her lean, bronzed husband would usually have had the right effect, but this morning it did nothing but irritate her. 'I've booked myself on the Air France flight to Paris this evening. I've got a car coming for me at three.'

Pierre sat down on the bed. 'Why Paris?'

Adriana laid a fine, gauzy, silk chiffon suit in her case, then changed her mind and placed it on a pile of discarded clothes on the ottoman. 'I want to be near Kate, and you know how much I dislike London, so I've rung Manni and asked him to open up the apartment.' She glanced at her watch. 'He's picking me up at Charles De Gaulle tomorrow morning. God, there's so much to do and I can't get hold of Lorna – she's disappeared, bloody typical, just when I need—'

'It is her day off, Adriana, you can't expect her to wait around to see if you might decide to hop on the next flight to Paris and need her to pack for you.' Pierre spoke with his usual slightly mocking tone, but Adriana ignored him.

'May I ask why you've decided to abandon me for gay Paris?' He was flicking through a copy of the novel she was reading on the bedside table. It was one she had been recommended by a friend, but neither liked nor understood, and he noticed that she'd made a shopping list at the top of page 30 in ink, in her small, neat hand. It made him smile.

Adriana looked up. 'Leo died this morning,' she said.

Pierre's smile vanished. He looked at his wife and noticed how her gaze trailed across his body and down to his crotch. As he watched, he saw a certain look cross her face, a look he knew intimately, and felt himself harden.

Adriana untied the sash on her silk robe and slipped it off her shoulders. She was magnificently tanned, her body had been sculpted in California over the last few years and she had the shape and physique of a woman in her prime. Stepping forward in just her high-heeled backless slippers, she straddled him, keeping her body half an inch from his. Leaning forward, she traced his lips with a hot, wet tongue.

'Tell me,' Pierre whispered, 'why does that fact seem to turn you on so—' But she silenced him by gently biting his lips and he sighed, closing his eyes. After many years of dominating people with his wealth and power, Pierre had met his match. His wife knew exactly how to manipulate and it horrified him, yet fascinated him and filled him with insatiable desire.

Chapter Four

Jan Ingram ran across the lobby towards the open lift, her wet heels slipping on the cream marble floor, her tired, hungover body weighted under the strain of lap-top, take-away breakfast, handbag and a Tesco's carrier stuffed with the extra papers she couldn't fit into the computer case. She lost her balance just as she got there and fell into the compartment against the wet raincoat of an accountant from some company on the second floor.

'Bugger! I mean, shit, sorry!' She righted herself, with his help, and glanced down at the small coffee-stain on his mac. 'Oh God, I'm so sorry, these bloody cups.' She dabbed ineffectually at it with a crumpled, lipstick-stained tissue from her own coat pocket until the man said sharply, 'It's quite all right. Really!' and inched distastefully back from her.

'Oh, right, er . . .' She swallowed hard, the tears that continually threatened just below the surface welling up. 'Sorry,' she mumbled. She stared down at the floor, shuffled to one side as the lift stopped to let the accountant out, then counted the remaining three floors up to her own office in her head, unable to face any of the other passengers. She hurried out, holding the leaking coffee cup away from her overcoat, and, using the side of her body, pushed open with a hefty shove the plate-glass door to Ingram Lawd Financial Services.

'Jesus!' The carrier-bag fell on the other side of the door and damp papers scattered everywhere as she struggled to keep hold of the coffee. 'Shit! Cindy!' she yelled, 'If you don't mind?'

A tall, slim girl with immaculate hair sauntered out from behind reception and bent with huge effort to gather up the papers. Jan just made it to the desk, dumping her bag, lap-top and leaking coffee down on the blotter. She held on to the edge of reception for support and glanced down at her mud-splattered tights. 'What a sodding morning,' she muttered. She was soaked and dishevelled but she couldn't be bothered to worry about it, not any more.

'Can you bring that lot down to my office when you've gathered them up, please?' She glanced down at Cindy, waiting for an answer before picking up the brown paper bag; none came. 'If it's not too much trouble, that is?' she added sarcastically. Jan had the sudden urge to kick her hard. Bloody rude, useless trollop, she thought, another of Duncan's glamorous and totally stupid recruits. But she decided to let it go, it wasn't worth the aggravation.

Silently, she turned and walked along to her office, holding her coffee and Danish, and leaving a small trail of water dripping off her coat as she went.

A few minutes later Jan sat at her desk, still in her wet coat, and put her head in her hands. The door to her office was closed, so she was perfectly safe. She closed her eyes for several moments and her head swam. Bloody Duncan, bloody, sodding, stupid egotistical pig! She felt the tears well up and let them slide out from under her lids. Her make-up was ruined anyway, what difference did it make? Who the hell cared what she looked like? She sniffed and wiped her nose on the back of her hand. Christ, she was pathetic! She looked up, dropping her hands away. Sad, that's what she was, old and sad. She leaned back, pulled open the drawer and rummaged in it for a hanky, finding instead a rather dog-eared pack of travel tissues. She used one to blow her nose, wiped her face while she was at it and felt marginally better. 'Get a grip, Jan,' she murmured. 'You've got the whole sodding day to get through yet.' Slipping off her coat, she turned to the two newspapers that had been delivered on her desk, the *Independent* and the *Financial Times*, and took up the *Independent* first, glancing over the features. There was a time when it had been the *FT* first and foremost; as soon as she sat down she'd have been scanning the pages, making notes, buzzing down the corridor to Duncan when something good came up. Not any more, now the sight of the FTSE 100 Index filled her with a kind of despair, a feeling of waste and futility. She sighed, blew her nose again, flipped the plastic lid off her coffee and turned to the paper. Clipped to the top was a small memo, typed, brief and impersonal. It said: Jan, please find attached review of business for the Tonsbry Estate. Leo Alder died yesterday. Please go over file and we'll talk this morning. Duncan.

'Bloody man!' she burst out. 'Who the hell does he think he is?' She closed her eyes again for a moment, too upset to do anything. Then, recovering, she unclipped the papers and glanced over them. For the first time in weeks she left her own tragedy behind for a few minutes and thought of Leo Alder. 'Poor Leo,' she murmured. She had liked him, had never approved of Duncan's policy regarding Tonsbry

House. Taking her Danish out of the bag, Jan wondered briefly if she should try to find the file before she did anything else, but another glimpse of Duncan's memo decided her against it. Twenty years they had been married, she and Duncan, and in the past three months twenty years had been reduced to a one-line memo. Savagely, she bit into the pastry and a dollop of apricot jam squished out and plopped on to the front of her shirt.

There was a peace and quiet in the Officers' Mess of the Blues and Royals that was cherished by the men and staff alike. Breakfast was a hallowed time for reading and eating in male, bonded silence. It was a time when even married men escaped the quarters and sneaked across for full English breakfast or fresh kippers without the whine of children or forced conversation with the wife.

And Harry Drummond loved it. In fact, the good-looking, thirty-two-year-old Captain loved everything about life as a soldier. At six foot two, blond and well built, a sportsman – rugby, squash and cricket – Harry was ideally suited to his chosen career. He wasn't uniquely selfish, it tended to be part of the criteria for the Army, but he was immensely self-obsessed. He was very pleased with life, and very pleased with himself.

This morning, his head buried in the *Sun* – purely for the sports coverage and to keep abreast of conversation amongst the men – he chomped enthusiastically on a slice of wholemeal with Cooper's marmalade, his own jar, and relished the silence. He had just finished a two-week exercise and gone straight off for three days R and R in Scotland with Tully's sister. Kate knew nothing about it, of course; there was no reason why she should do. It was a relationship that had been rumbling on in the background for years, well before Kate, and one that he felt entirely justified in having. Harry was a dynamic man, he had a strong and healthy sexual appetite and it was hardly his fault if Kate had no particular interest in that direction. Besides which, it had taken years – three, to be precise – to talk her round to his way of thinking, and no one in their right mind would have expected him to be celibate for all that time.

Harry smiled. The memory of the last three days filled him with satisfaction. Good scoff, good fishing and a damn good lay!

'Morning, Captain Drummond!' One of the young subalterns sat down opposite Harry, spread his napkin on to his lap and waited for one of the Mess staff to take his breakfast order. 'Did you get your message?'

Harry glanced up.

'No, what message was that? I've just come in for breakfast, there wasn't anything urgent in my pigeon-hole.' Harry began to butter another piece of toast.

'The Colonel didn't get hold of you, then?'

He stopped buttering. 'Get hold of me? No, why the hell should the Colonel want me?'

'I don't know. Something about some girl ringing you urgently? It might have been your girlfriend, I'm not—' But the young lieutenant didn't finish his sentence. Before he had the chance, Harry jumped up and disappeared in search of the Mess Sergeant to find out what was going on.

Five minutes later, having discovered that it was Kate who had been trying to get hold of him, Harry was at the pay phone. He dialled the number of Kate's flat, went straight through to her answerphone and found himself in the unenviable position of having to weigh up what she might or might not know and bluff his way through the rest. 'Ah, Kate,' he said, 'you're obviously not there. I . . . er, I heard that you were trying to get hold of me and I've been up in Scotland for a few days' rest – last-minute thing, invited by one of the chaps. Gosh, Kate, I hope you're OK. They said it was urgent and I'm er . . .' He faltered at this point, knowing he had to say something loving and reassuring but not knowing how. 'I'm worried, awfully worried. I wonder if you can call me back, or I'll call you a bit later on, see if you're in then.' Loving, he thought, racking his brains. 'I'm . . . Oh, yes, I'm thinking of you, Kate dear.' It came out in a rush as he suddenly realised how much tape he'd used. 'A lot. Hope you're OK. Bye for now. Bye.'

He hung up and breathed a sigh of relief. It wasn't that he was unaffectionate or prudish in any way, it was just that he didn't really have that sort of relationship with Kate. It was close – Lord, he'd worked hard enough to make it so – but it wasn't intimate in the way that most love affairs were. In all honesty Harry wasn't even sure if it was a love affair, more a long-standing friendship which he had somehow managed to mould and stretch into something else. He sighed heavily again, but this time more with frustration and confusion than relief, then he made his way back to the dining-room and tried, without appetite, to finish his breakfast.

Jan had finished the *Independent* and was about to glance at the *FT* when the door of her office was flung open. She started, dropped the last of the Danish on to her lap and bent to retrieve it. When she looked up, her soon-to-be-ex-husband was standing at her desk, glaring at her.

'Jan! What the bloody hell . . . ?'

She popped the last bite into her mouth.

'There's a board meeting in five minutes. Don't tell me you've forgotten.'

'No. Of course not, I . . .' She stopped as she registered the look of distaste on his face and pulled lamely at a frizzed strand of hair. 'I'll be there.'

'Well, you'd better get a move on then. Christ! Look at the state of you!' He turned, glanced back at her once more with a half-derogatory, half-pitying look, then clicked the door shut hard behind him.

Jan chewed numbly for a few moments, then her anger exploded. 'Bloody Duncan!' she burst out. 'That man has a bloody nerve!' Wasn't it enough that he had humiliated her, betrayed her, dumped her like old baggage for a woman twenty years her junior? Wasn't it enough that she still came into work in this sodding company, still provided the financial skill that they'd built on for fifteen years together, sacrificed everything else for? She felt the tears well up yet again and snapped open her handbag to pull out her compact. 'Christ! Look at the state of me? What did he expect? I'm forty-three, not twenty-three!' She smeared some powder over her face, dabbing mercilessly at the blotches on her skin, but her tears ran down and made a mess of it so she gave up and yanked a hairbrush through the frizz that should have been a perm.

She dropped the brush, glanced at her watch and picked up the phone. Clearing her throat, she dialled, then said, 'Cindy? Have you got those papers off the floor yet? Good. If you could let Mr Lawd have them, he needs them for the meeting. Yes, the meeting now. Thank you.'

She replaced the receiver and went over to the filing cabinet where she rifled through to look for the Tonsbry Estate file, guessing it might be on the agenda of the meeting that morning. She found it, pulled it out and looked at it. To be honest, she wasn't sure she could face it. It was complicated and sensitive, and she had liked the man as well; she'd liked him very much. She didn't have the heart to talk about foreclosing less than twenty-four hours after his death. I must be getting soft in my old age, she thought, ignoring the impulse to re-do her make-up once more.

But it wasn't soft she'd become, she knew that – it was stale. She'd had a rotten taste in her mouth for some time now, and Leo Alder's piece of business seemed to sum it all up.

They had made money, heaps of it; they'd been successful, Ingram Lawd, so successful that they had an offer on the table from a major High Street bank. The sort of offer every company dreams of; the kind of success every business wants. But for what? At what cost? Offering loans to people in stricken circumstances, in the pit of the recession, sometimes in order to enable them to simply survive, and then charging them extortionate interest, crippling them all over again. Repossessing properties, reselling them, making more profit.

Jan smoothed her skirt and buttoned her jacket over her blouse to cover the jam stain. And what did she have now? Apart from money and a sore conscience? She had sacrificed children, friends, interests, everything for Duncan and Ingram Lawd; everything. She walked across the office and pulled open the door just as Duncan stepped into the corridor. He was laughing at something a colleague had said, and Jan felt a pain so sharp that it made her wince. 'Nothing,' she said quietly. 'I've got nothing.' But she pasted a smile on her face and followed him into the meeting.

Kate poured the last of the organic double cream into the ice-cream maker, threw the empty carton away in the bin and, satisfied that she had the formula right, switched on the machine and waited a few minutes until it whirred into life. Then she cleared the work surface, opened her book and wrote down exactly what she had done, using the scribbled notes she had made along the way. It was now ten-thirty and Kate had been creating ice-cream recipes for nearly five hours. Unable to do the sandwich run, due to Stefan's insistence that she needed a break, and unable to face sleep, she had got up at four a.m., driven to New Covent Garden Market to buy a box of fresh fruit and set about doing what she always did when troubled or confused: she threw herself into her work.

Three batches of ice-cream and four hours, forty minutes later, Kate made the last entry in her book, put the cap on her pen and laid her head down on her arms on the work surface. Her eyes were sore, dry and gritty from crying and lack of sleep, so she closed them for a moment to relieve them and felt the sharp ache in the pit of her stomach, the shocked, painful realisation that she was never going to see Leo again. She snapped them open and took a deep breath; then she stood up, surveyed the mess and set about clearing it up. If she carried on, didn't stop at all, just worked herself into exhaustion like she had when Rory left, then there wasn't any time to think, to hurt or grieve, there wasn't time for anything except just existing.

Kate filled the sink with very hot water, squirted in some washing-up liquid and went first to the kitchen door to open it, then to the window. It was stuffy in the kitchen and she wanted to let a blast of cold air blow right through. As she did so, the phone rang. She hurried towards the sitting-room to answer it, heard the answerphone click on and realised that she obviously hadn't heard it at all that morning, with the door to the kitchen closed and the ice-cream maker going. Reaching the phone, she saw that she was right and that she had three messages stacked up. Stefan must have put it on for her last night so that she wouldn't be disturbed. As the machine ran on, Kate heard the sound of her own voice on the message and waited to see who it was ringing. It was a peculiar feeling, listening in, intrusive in a funny way, even though the message was for her. Her own voice finished, there was a beep and she heard: 'Kate, darling, it's Mummy!' Without thinking twice, and with great relief, Kate picked up the phone.

'Mummy, I am here; sorry, I just got to the phone.'

'Oh, Kate, thank goodness! How are you, darling? I just heard and . . . well, I know how much Leo meant to you . . .' Adriana's voice trailed off lamely. Leo was her brother, but she had never made any pretence about the relationship. She had neither liked nor respected him, had seen him just once in thirty years, and that time only because Kate insisted on them coming together for her fiasco of a wedding. 'I'm sorry, Kate,' she said, 'for you.' That much was true; she couldn't bear the thought of Kate being upset.

Sympathy; Kate's throat filled with tears and she had to swallow them down. 'Thanks, I—'

Adriana cut in. 'I'm in Paris, Kate, I flew in this morning just in case.'

'In case of what?'

'In case you need me, darling – I'm here for you.'

Kate faltered again. It was incredibly kind – it made her very tearful – but it was also very out of character. Kate knew her mother loved her, she had always known that, but Adriana loved her in a more distracted, more selfish way than most mothers loved their offspring. Kate didn't resent that fact, she had never known anything else; it was simply the way Adriana was.

'Thank you. I'm sorry I didn't call you, I . . .' I didn't think of it was the truth, because her mother had no part in Leo's life; but 'I've been too upset' was what Kate said. 'How did you find out?' Leo had left all his arrangements to his solicitor – he had told Kate that several weeks ago – but she didn't think her mother would have been on the list of people to notify.

There was a silence on the other end of the phone, then Adriana said, 'I rang the house.'

'Did you?' Kate was surprised, but in her grief she didn't think to question why.

'Yes – look, Kate?' Adriana's tone had changed, her voice had hardened, but Kate didn't pick it up; her grief insulated her. 'Kate, will you promise me something?'

'Well, yes, I suppose so. What is it?'

'That you won't do anything without talking to me.'

'What d'you mean – do anything? What sort of thing?'

Adriana sighed. 'Nothing specific, I mean . . .' She hesitated, then said, 'Just remember that I'm here in Paris if you need me, OK?'

Fresh tears, and Kate had to blow her nose. 'Thank you.'

She heard her mother tut at her tears on the other end of the phone and was immediately embarrassed.

'Darling, I've got to fly,' Adriana said. 'I've several appointments this morning. I'll call you later on in the week. Do you need anything from Paris?'

Kate was reassured; this was far more the Adriana she knew. 'No, no thanks.' Her mother would have bought her virtually anything she wanted had she asked, yet she never thought to enquire after Kate's business or ask about Harry.

'OK then, darling, we'll speak soon.' Adriana blew a kiss down the line. 'Bye-bye now, take care, sweetheart.' And she hung up before Kate even had time to reply.

Kate held the empty phone for a few moments, not entirely sure of her reaction to the call, then she dropped it back in its cradle and pressed the replay button on her answerphone. The first message was from Harry, and his loud, self-assured voice filled the room. Kate leaned back against the wall and closed her eyes. Why, she thought miserably, after all this time and all he's done for me, does Harry still fail to move me? Cutting him off, and deciding the other messages could wait, she walked back through to the kitchen to get on with the clearing-up.

Chapter Five

The following day, Kate woke before it was light. She glanced at her watch, a luminous Mickey Mouse face with a red plastic strap, and saw it was five minutes past six. Wide awake, she sat up, pushed her hair off her face and climbed out of bed. Pulling on some scruffy jeans and a grey cashmere sweater, she reached for socks and then something to put on her feet; a well-worn and highly polished pair of riding boots. She went into the bathroom, washed her face, cleaned her teeth and ran a comb through her hair. She was ready. Without make-up, in an outfit hastily thrown on, and oblivious to the fact, Kate looked incredible.

Walking through the flat, she turned on lights, opened the shutters and then the windows to air the place, tidied a few cushions on the sofa and some papers on the table and went into the kitchen for some coffee. Kate was an expert coffee blender, it was one of her talents – different beans, special essences to tailor-make a coffee to suit a client or a particular meal – but at home she drank instant, any old brand, with powdered milk and a sweetener. Made, it was usually a rather murky, indifferent-tasting liquid, but she didn't mind; at least she didn't have to think about it. What is it they say, she thought, sipping but numb to the taste: 'A cobbler's children are always the worst shod?' Kate hated to cook at home, she had a freezer full of ready meals from M & S and ate those or piles of toast with Marmite – if she had to eat at all, that was. And if she ever entertained, which was rare as she worked most nights, she would order take-away pizza and offer it to her guests straight from the box.

Kate took a last sip of her drink and threw the remainder down the sink. She grabbed a grissini from a jar on the side and nibbled it as she went into the bedroom for her bag. Dumping it in the hall, she closed the windows in the flat, switched off the lights and made her way to the front door. She checked that the envelopes for Stefan and Becca were on the hall table, with instructions for the business, all typed, plus menu plans, invoices and last-minute ideas for stand-in recipes. It was now Wednesday and she had plans to be away only until Friday, as they had a busy weekend ahead, but had doubts about doing even that. If the call hadn't come from Leo's solicitor then she would have simply gone down to Tonsbry for the funeral, stayed just for the day and come straight back. She didn't want to be there without Leo; she was dreading it, and she didn't want to leave her business either. The work kept her going; without it she was frightened that she might just crack up.

About to open the front door, Kate remembered the present for Mrs Able and dashed back for it. She found it in the fridge and placed it carefully in her bag; it was a box of home-made truffles. Finally ready, she left the flat and locked up before going downstairs and out to the car she had hired for the week. She felt sick, a knot of tension was churning her stomach, but there was no way out. Shivering, she looked up at the slowly lightening sky and then climbed into the car. Taking a deep breath, she started the engine and drove off.

Rory rolled over in bed, flung out an arm in the direction of the alarm clock, hit it, knocked it off the bedside table and lay there in the darkness listening to it bleeping under the bed. Finally he dragged himself out of bed, fumbled around on the floor for it and switched it off. Shivering in the unheated air of his bedroom, he grabbed his sweater and hurried towards the bathroom for a quick wash. On the way across the landing, he saw the light on in Flora's bedroom.

Poking his head round the door, Rory found his daughter sitting up in bed with her Lion King annual, talking herself through the story. He smiled, then sighed, knowing that he would now have to get her up as well and drag her out with him to make a start on the ploughing. Had she been asleep, as she was most mornings, he would have left her and been back well before she woke up, but awake was a different story. Flora awake needed careful and watchful management.

'Morning, sweetheart. You're awake early this morning.'

'Hello, Daddy. I'm reading.'

'Yes, I can see that. We'll have to get up in a few minutes. I want you to come and help me on the tractor this morning.'

'Why?'

'Why?' Rory hesitated, not knowing if he had the energy this morning to go through the whole explanation, but also knowing that Flora couldn't be fobbed off. 'Well, I have to make a start on ploughing the field up at the top, because – you know Mick? Well, he's ill and he can't do it.'

'Why?'

Rory sighed. 'Why what?' he asked, coming into the room and picking up yesterday's clothes. He checked them for stains in the hope that she could wear them again today.

'Why's he ill?'

'He's got a cold.' It wasn't the right answer, but trying to explain a vasectomy was beyond him.

'Oh, OK.' Flora rolled her eyes, then closed her book and dropped her legs over the side of the bed.

Rory smiled. 'Good. Right, clothes on, then into the bathroom for a quick wash and teeth-brushing session.'

Flora looked at what he was holding and said, 'Oh, Daddy! I can't wear those, yeuch! I wore them yesterday, that's dirty.' She clambered off the bed, took the clothes out of his hands and dropped them back on the floor.

'Hey!'

Glancing up, she picked them up again and jauntily walked across to the laundry basket, dropping them in and dusting off her hands afterwards. She then found herself something else from the pile of neatly ironed clothes on the window-seat. 'If I wear a red top, then I've got to have red tights as well,' she muttered, searching for a pair of red woolly tights. She found them, along with a red cardigan and red dungarees. 'Here, this is nice,' she announced. Duly chastened, Rory took the clothes, folded them over his arm and hurried her through to the bathroom with him to dress.

Kate arrived at Tonsbry just as it was getting light; it

was mid-November and the days were short and cold. She pulled into the long tree-lined drive and stopped the car, climbing out and sniffing the air. It was sharp and damp, with a hint of wood smoke, and it was so evocative, so reminiscent of childhood, of bonfire nights and long walks, winter afternoon tea in front of the fire, of watching Leo ride, staying out in the grounds until the very tip of nightfall and coming in for a hot supper in the kitchen with Mrs Able. It was so reminiscent of everything secure and happy that, for the first time since Leo's death, Kate really gave in to the feeling of loss as she rested her head against the ice-cold metal of the car and closed her eyes. She willed him back with all her heart and mind, she willed Leo back in her life – kind, caring, safe Leo. But when she opened her eyes again there was nothing but the empty, dull ache in her stomach and she knew it was pointless. She climbed back into the car and drove on up to the house.

Flora sat at the edge of the field and watched her father in a miniature tractor on the horizon, right up in the corner of the field almost hidden behind the clump of trees, as he rounded the machine and turned it, starting back to plough another far from perfect furrow. She should have been up on the tractor with him, but she didn't like the noise and vibration and had complained so much that he'd deposited her at the edge of the field and told her that under no circumstances was she to move. Every now and then he would put his arm out of the cabin and wave and she would stand on the wall, as she'd been instructed to do, and wave back so that he could see her. But now, bored and cold, she sat on the wall and kicked her legs, swinging them back and forth, trying to knock the dry-stone wall to see if it would move. All she longed to do was go up to the house to see Mrs Able and gobble a nice warm fairy-cake straight from the oven. She needed a diversion and, looking all around for one, spotted a figure coming her way. She stood up and waved, the figure waved back and headed closer. Flora jumped down.

'Hello!' she called. The figure was a lady who smiled and called 'hello' back, then made her way over the stile and across the field to the low stone wall.

'What are you doing?' Flora asked. 'What's your name?'

'Kate, and I'm taking a walk. What's your name, and what on earth are you doing here on your own?'

'My name's Flora. You've been crying.'

Kate flushed. 'Yes, I have. You didn't answer my question.' She squatted to Flora's height. 'Shouldn't you be with someone?' There were two families on the estate; Flora must belong to one of them, she concluded.

'I am. Daddy's over there. He lets me play here when he's working. D'you want to see my secret place?'

Kate stood and put her hand up to her eyes, trying to spot the tractor. She could see that the field was half ploughed and she would have liked to wave at whoever it was in the tractor to let them know she was here. But she couldn't see anyone, not that it worried her particularly; Flora was quite safe, just as she had been roaming freely around the estate as a child. Just to make sure though, she said, 'Where did you say Daddy was?'

Flora rolled her eyes. 'Not again!'

Kate smiled; the child was very comical. 'Yes, again. Is he over in that field?'

'Yes, he's over there, on the tractor. Come on, d'you want to see my secret place?' Flora had taken hold of Kate's sleeve and hung on to it.

Kate couldn't resist. 'I'd love to, but shouldn't we go and tell your daddy where we're going first?' She disengaged the little fingers from her sweater and tucked them into her hand. They were cold and much smaller than she had expected.

'Oh, no, he'll know where I am. He always does.'

'I see.' Flora was so matter of fact, so sensible that Kate smiled again. 'You're sure about that?'

'Uh-huh.'

Kate loved children but had no real experience of them. It didn't occur to her that Flora wouldn't have any idea whether her father knew where she was or not; she was only three, after all.

'All right then, Flora,' Kate said, 'where's this secret place? I hope it's not too far away.'

'Oh no, it's just over the fence and behind the trees.' Flora started off, tugging at Kate's hand. 'Come on.'

Kate let herself be led, but she had a pretty good idea where the secret place might be and wanted to see it almost as much as Flora did. If she had guessed right, it was the tree house that Leo had built for her. Holding hands, Flora and Kate made their way across the fields, over the small stream and into the copse.

'There!' Flora announced. 'Up there.'

Kate looked up and smiled. She had been right. 'It's brilliant,' she said. 'Is it all yours?'

'Uh-huh.'

'Wow!'

Flora turned and stared at Kate for a moment, as if she

couldn't quite believe her, then she beamed. 'Would you like to go in it?'

'Oh, yes please, do you mind?'

'No, as long as you're very careful.'

Kate almost burst out laughing. 'Oh, I will be,' she said solemnly, 'I promise.' And once again, Flora turned to stare.

'OK,' she said. 'I'll go first and you can stand behind me in case I fall.'

'Very sensible,' said Kate, and did just that.

Rory jumped down from the tractor, kicked its huge wheel hard with his steel-toe-capped boots and swore loudly. The bloody engine had gone and he had only half finished the field. Christ, he hated anything mechanical, had only just managed to pick up the rudiments of ploughing because Mick was going off for his op – how the hell he was supposed to fix a buggered diesel engine he had no idea. He swore again and reckoned that this was going to put him back several hours. He'd have to get a mechanic in, which meant funds they didn't have; then there was Flora, she needed to be fed and taken to nursery school before he had any hope of getting back to it. 'Shit!' he muttered. 'Perhaps Mrs Able . . .'

He turned and stared at the far distance. He could take her up to the house now and perhaps leave her there. He couldn't see much from where he was standing, half behind the clump of trees, so he walked out to the middle of the field and looked for Flora again. Searching the wall, he waved his arms in the air and shouted across the open field.

'Flora!' His voice carried on the wind, but he couldn't see

any sign of her. 'Daft child. What on earth . . .' He waved and shouted again, whistling after that, a loud piercing noise that swept over the fields. 'Flora?' Still no sign of her. He was cross. 'Trust her to be playing and not sitting where I told her to,' he murmured. He climbed up on to the tractor and took the keys out, then jumped down and strode off. With the days this short, there was no time to waste.

At the dry-stone wall, Rory stopped. He glanced up along the edge of the field, then jumped up on the wall and scanned the stretch of land in front of it. He felt a sudden rush of panic.

'Flora! Flora, where are you?' He cupped his hands to his mouth and called her name again. There was no answer, no sign of her.

'Oh, Jesus!' He jumped down again and headed across the next field, the tractor no longer a priority. He shouldn't have left her alone, it was stupid, he should have kept her with him. Still shouting her name, he began to jog. She must have gone home, though how she'd have got there on her own he had no idea. 'Please be at home, Flora,' he muttered, suddenly breaking into a run. 'Please be at home!'

Kate looked at her watch; it was nearly eight o'clock and they had been playing for over half an hour. That was long enough to be gone, she thought, just in case anyone was wondering where the child had got to. 'I'm afraid, Flora, that we have to go now and try to find your mummy and daddy.'

'Why?'

'Because you have to go home. I should think you want your breakfast, don't you?'

Flora shook her head. 'Just one more minute,' she said, holding up three fingers. Kate smiled, she had fallen for that old chestnut twice already.

'No, no more minutes, I'm sorry.' She bent and kissed the top of Flora's head. 'We can play again another day, if you like.' Kate stood, crouching down under the low roof, and made for the step-ladder. 'I'll go down first, you follow me, then you can jump the last few steps and I'll catch you.'

'Hooray!' Flora shouted.

Kate climbed down, waited with arms outstretched and only just caught the small, lithe body which came hurtling through the air. 'Whoa! The last few steps I said, not the whole thing.' Flora shrieked with laughter and Kate continued to hold her. 'Come on, you,' she said. 'Tell me where you live, and I'll give you a ride all the way home.'

'Gully Cottage,' said Flora as Kate lifted her up on to her shoulders. Kate thought nothing of it, why should she? 'Gully Cottage it is, then,' she said and they made their way, slowly meandering, back to where Flora lived.

Rory ran back to the cottage via the road, the quickest and most direct route, certain he would find Flora at home. He didn't; it was deserted. He switched on all the lights, darted into every room calling out her name – then, leaving the door open and the small house ablaze, he ran out and up towards Tonsbry House. He would need John Able and perhaps a few others from the farm to set up a search party. There was a lot of land; he couldn't do it on his own. She must have simply wandered off, he told himself over and over; she was bound to be around somewhere, maybe even playing on her own. But he was filled with dread. The image of his child alone and frightened played itself out in his mind until he was almost sick with fear. Reaching Tonsbry, he ran up the steps and into the open house.

Kate gently lifted Flora down on to the ground in the cobbled yard in front of Gully Cottage and called out. The door was open and the lights were blazing. Taking Flora's hand and calling out again, she led the way inside and was amazed to find the downstairs empty.

'Hello?' She went to the staircase and shouted up. 'Hello? Is anyone at home?' She turned to Flora. 'D'you know where Mummy is?' Flora shook her head, her face curiously blank.

'Perhaps we should go and find Daddy again, then,' Kate suggested.

Again Flora shook her head. 'I'm hungry,' she said. 'I haven't had my breakfast yet.'

'Oh, oh dear.' Kate was beginning to feel nervous; she wasn't at all sure what to do next. 'D'you think Daddy will know you're at home?' she asked.

Flora shrugged.

'I see.' She glanced around for an indication of who might live there, a handbag or some photos, but found nothing. Apart from a child's clutter, nursery paintings, outdoor clothes on the hooks by the door, the place was decidedly unhomely; it looked as if the family had just moved in. 'Look, Flora,' Kate squatted down. 'Does Daddy have a mobile phone so that we can ring him and let him know we're at home?'

'What?'

'Does Daddy ever carry one of those little phones in his pocket and ring people up on it?'

'Nope.' Flora shrugged again. 'I'm thirsty,' she said. 'Can I have a drink, please?'

Kate stood up. 'Right, fine.' She worried for a moment longer, then looked down at Flora's earnest little face and smiled. 'Seeing you asked so nicely for it, yes, you may. What would you like?'

'Milk, please, in a cup.' Kate crossed to the draining-board and found a mug. 'No,' Flora interrupted, 'not that one, that's Daddy's . . .' She dragged a chair across the kitchen floor, clambered up on to it and reached for a small cup in the plate rack above the sink. She just got it, wobbled precariously for a few seconds, then handed it to Kate and climbed down. Kate went to the fridge, found the milk, poured it and gave it to Flora.

'Why don't you sit down and drink it,' she said, 'while I just ring Mrs Able at the house and let her know I'm here with you?'

'OK,' said Flora, and she sat down to drink her milk.

Mrs Able hurried across the stone floor of the hall at Tonsbry House, towards Leo's study where the phone was ringing. She was trying not to run, her arthritis was playing up and her joints ached, but she couldn't stop herself. She was worried sick, the child was barely three and a half and they had no sense at that age; she could have gone off anywhere, with anyone. Flinging open the door, she reached the desk before the phone cut off.

'Tonsbry House, hello?'

Kate was instantly relieved to hear the housekeeper's voice. 'Mrs Able? Hi, it's Kate.'

'Hello, Kate. Look, dear, I can't talk on the phone; you see it's needed, something's happened, Flora Gall—' Mrs

Able stopped suddenly, realising that so far as she knew Kate had no idea that Rory lived on the estate. They had all tried hard to keep it from her, to spare her feelings, as Leo had insisted they should.

'Flora? Did you say Flora?'

'Yes, dear, she's—'

'That's why I'm ringing,' Kate interrupted quickly. 'I'm at Gully Cottage with a little girl called Flora. I found her on the estate and I just wondered who her parents were. We've been—'

'Flora? Flora's there with you?' Mrs Able put one hand up to her chest. 'Oh, thank God for that! Thank God! Hold on a minute, Kate.' She dropped the phone and darted, as much as her stiff joints would allow, across to the window. Opening it, she shouted out at her husband who was just heading off the front lawns towards the drive. 'John? John! Flora's safe, she's at home. Yes, yes, she is, at Gully Cottage. She's with . . . John! John, come back for a minute. John!' She sighed, exasperated, as her husband dashed off. There was a scene brewing, she was certain of it.

Mrs Able went back to the phone. 'Kate? You still there? Listen, Kate dear, there's something you ought to know, it's about—'

'Flora! Get down!' Kate put her hand over the phone as Flora climbed up on to the chair by the sink again and reached for the small bowl that matched her cup. 'Hang on a minute, Mrs Able,' she said. 'Flora? Please get down before you—' Suddenly Kate dropped the phone and sprang three feet across the kitchen, just in time to grab Flora as she toppled backwards. 'Whoa!' she cried, stumbling back and hitting the wall. 'Caught ya!' Flora's face, ashen with fright, changed instantly to relief at Kate's smile. 'Phew!' Kate said lightly. 'That was a close one.'

Flora smiled back. 'We nearly fell, didn't we?' she said.

'Yes, yes, we did,' Kate answered, sounding far braver than she felt. She had crunched her shoulder and the pain was excruciating. 'Come here with me a minute, you, and let me just say goodbye to Mrs Able.' Kate picked up the phone again and put it to her ear. 'Sorry about that. What were you say . . .' She stopped and looked at the receiver. In her flight, she had cut herself off. 'Blast!' she muttered, replacing it and wondering whether to call back. She glanced at the pad by the side of the phone and saw the number of her flat in London written down. Curious, she flicked through the pages, knowing she shouldn't really but unable to resist. She saw a message in Mrs Able's old-fashioned, neat handwriting and took the pad across to the table. Staring at the message, it took her several minutes to decipher it and, as she did so, an awful sinking realisation dawned on her. She glanced up at the running footsteps out in the courtyard, the door of the cottage was flung open and, as she turned, a look of horror and dread crossed her face.

'Kate!'

'Rory!'

'Flora?'

'Daddy!'

Rory was across the room in seconds and had scooped his daughter up into his arms. 'Where on earth have you been?' he cried, trying to keep a tight control on himself. The urge to shout at her, scold her, shake her even – to make her understand how dangerous, how absolutely terrifying it was to go off on her own like that – almost overwhelmed him. Hugging her tightly, he reined in his anger and let relief wash over him. She was safe, that was all that mattered, she was safe and home. He stayed like that for some time, not wanting to let her go, but she wriggled free and finally he placed her carefully down on her feet. 'Where were you, you monkey? Daddy's been looking everywhere for you!'

Kate sat silent and inert and braced herself.

'I went off to play with Kate,' Flora said. 'She's my new friend. We went to the tree house.'

A deep, hot blush spread over Kate's face and neck as Rory slowly turned his attention from his daughter to her. She looked at him for a moment, at the expression of sheer disbelief on his face, then dropped her gaze and stared blankly at the table. 'I'm sorry,' she murmured, 'I didn't—'

'You're sorry!' Rory said. 'You take my daughter off without telling anyone where you were going, a child you've never met before, and meanwhile I'm worried sick, I've got the whole estate out looking for her and the police alerted, I—' He stopped and threw up his hands. 'Good God, Kate! What on earth were you thinking of?'

'Daddy?'

'I asked you a question, Kate!'

'Daddy, Daddy!'

'Not now, Flora. Kate? Answer me. Was this some kind of perverse revenge?'

'Revenge?' Kate repeated, the word not making any sense to her, then suddenly the meaning hit home. 'Revenge?' she cried, jumping up. 'Who the hell do you think I am, Rory? I had no idea she was your daughter, why should I have? I had no bloody idea you lived here. When did that all happen, eh? How very cosy for you and Alice. How did you talk Leo into that one, huh? Always fancied Tonsbry, did you? Wormed your way in here, seeing that you're not married to me.'

'For God's sake, Kate, it's nothing like that.'

'Daddy!'

'Not now I said, Flora.'

'But, Daddy . . .'

'Flora, stop! I'm in the middle of . . .'

Flora looked imploringly from her father across to Kate, and Kate caught the panic on her face. 'Flora,' she said, 'what's the matter?'

'There's nothing the matter with her!' Rory snapped. 'Nothing that a short, sharp slap for running off with a stranger won't cure.'

'Rory, that's unfair, I—'

'Oh, you're the world's leading expert in child care now, are you?'

'No, I just think that there's something the—'

'Daddy!' Flora cried. 'I need to do a . . .' But she didn't finish. She looked down as a slow puddle of urine formed on the floor by her feet and then burst into tears.

'Oh, Christ! Just what I need,' Rory snarled.

'Rory, don't be so bloody mean!' Kate implored.

'I'll be what I damn well like!' he shouted. He'd just about had enough. The fright of losing Flora, the shock of seeing Kate, his grief, the ruddy great mess on the estate – all of it just suddenly exploded inside him. 'Just get out of here, Kate! Stop telling me what to do and get out.'

'God, Rory, you're a tyrant, you really are!' Kate shouted back.

'Well, it's damn lucky that you didn't marry me, then, isn't it?'

Suddenly Kate froze. Her face took on a stricken look,

then a flicker of pain crossed it, pain so intense that it made Rory wince. 'Oh God, Kate, I didn't mean that, I really didn't. I'm sorry, I . . .' But Kate dashed past him and, before he could say anything else, ran out of the door. Rory ran after her. 'Kate? Kate, come back, please!' he shouted. 'Kate!' But he was wasting his breath; she had gone. 'Oh God, Kate, what a bloody mess.'

He turned back inside and saw Flora, small, wet and sobbing her heart out. 'Oh, sweetheart,' he said, hurrying across to her and kneeling down to hug her. 'I didn't mean to shout at you, but you must never go off with people you don't know, Flora, it's very dangerous. Daddy was very worried.' She hiccuped loudly and he patted her back, holding her close until she calmed down. He felt terrible; he had handled the last five minutes deplorably. He hardly ever shouted at Flora, yet just now he had very nearly lost his self-control. 'Listen,' he said gently, releasing her and wiping her face with his hanky. 'Let's get you clean and dry, shall we?' She nodded forlornly. 'And then we can have some breakfast and I'll take you to nursery. How does that sound?' Flora nodded again and even managed a smile. 'Good,' said Rory, planting a kiss on her forehead. 'Come on, then.' He took her hand and led her up the stairs. 'All better now?' he asked halfway up.

'Yesss,' Flora said quietly and Rory sighed. If only the rest of life's problems were quite as easy to solve, he thought, and he bent and picked up his daughter to give her another hug.

Chapter Six

It was eight-thirty a.m. and, after a sleepless night and with a pounding headache, Kate sat in her hire car at a traffic-light junction in the middle of rush-hour traffic in Chartwell, the nearest market town to Tonsbry, struggling to find first gear. She had driven the car so badly that morning that she shouldn't really have been behind the wheel at all, and now, with cars stacking up behind her and horns blaring, she felt very near to despair. She yanked the gear-stick this way and that, crunching through the gears, but she just couldn't find it. Finally, managing to engage one of the gears, she moved forward and promptly stalled; the engine died.

'Oh God . . .' She was stuck, close to tears and with the bonnet of her car directly in the line of the oncoming traffic. Several cars behind her sat on their horns and, unable to think of anything else to do, Kate flung open the car door, jumped out and shouted, 'OK, OK! I'm doing my best. Just be bloody patient, will you?'

She climbed in again, took several deep breaths and pushed her hair back off her face. The despair and tears had hardened into a white fury as she disengaged the gears, pumped the clutch a couple of times and switched on the engine again. She shifted the gear-stick, the lights changed and she found first gear. There was a knock on the passenger side of her window.

'Oh Christ! What?' she snapped, briefly turning to see who it was. As she did so, she let her foot off the clutch, shot forward two feet and stalled a second time. Letting out a roar of frustration, she swore, pressed down the window and snarled, 'What the hell do you want?'

Rory glanced over his shoulder at the line of ever-increasing traffic and shouted above the blaze of car horns, 'I thought you might need a hand?'

Kate threw up her hands and cried, 'Go away! Just . . . oh God!' She was near to tears. 'Just go away, Rory. GO AWAY!' As she restarted the engine, slammed it into gear and screeched off with her foot right down on the accelerator, the lights were just switching from amber to red and her car narrowly missed the oncoming traffic.

Ten minutes later, Kate parked her car, locked it and glanced at her watch. She was almost half an hour late for her appointment with David Lowther, Leo's solicitor, and was in a black, thunderous mood. She hurried up Chartwell High Street towards one of the town's oldest buildings, found the dark green door of Lowther & Crest and went inside.

'Hello, Kate Dowie to see Mr Lowther. I'm terribly late, I'm afraid, I—'

The receptionist interrupted her. 'Don't worry, Miss Dowie, Mr Lowther has allowed time. Can I take your coat?' She stood up, a neat, tidy woman in sensible tweeds and brown lace-up shoes.

Kate glanced down at her own long black velvet coat

with its wide fur collar and cuffs and immediately felt self-conscious. 'No, thanks, I'll hold on to it.'

'Right, well, I'll show you the way, then.' The receptionist led the way along the corridor and Kate snatched off her velvet hat with its sunflower trim as she fell into step behind. At the door to Lowther's office, the receptionist knocked lightly, was ordered to 'Enter' and held the door open for Kate. Lowther stood up as Kate fixed a smile on to her face and walked into the room. But as she did so, another figure got up as well. Kate let out a small, stifled cry and the smile on her face froze.

'Ah, Kate!' David Lowther greeted her. A short, round and balding man about her mother's age, he stepped forward and held out his plump, nicotine-stained hand. 'How nice to see you again, Kate, my dear. You know Rory Gallagher, I presume?' Lowther smiled, but Kate could do nothing, not return his smile nor answer him. For a few moments she stood, completely numb, and stared blankly at him. Surely he knew? Surely he had some idea of her history? She was too shocked to speak. Then Lowther coughed and said, 'Shall we sit?'

Kate nodded, Rory sat down again and she took up her place on the chair next to him in front of the desk. She gripped her hat in her hands and rolled the velvet tightly between her fingers.

'I'm sorry, Mr Lowther,' she began tensely, 'but could you tell me what this is all about?' She swallowed hard. 'I thought I was seeing you about a matter concerning my uncle. I don't understand what connection Rory Gallagher has, and I—'

David Lowther held up his hands to silence her. He was fond of dramatic gestures; they added to his feeling of self-importance. 'Kate, my dear.' He was also fond of using terms of endearment, since they helped him to patronise people. 'I will explain everything in due course. First, may I offer you both tea or coffee?'

Kate shook her head and Rory said, 'No, no, thank you. I'm a bit short of time actually.' Kate thought: The arrogance of it! It incensed her.

It obviously irked Lowther too, because he said, 'Well, I'll try not to take up too much of your time then, Mr Gallagher,' with a distinctly cynical edge to his voice.

Rory smiled. He had taken an instant dislike to this trumped-up little solicitor and, ignoring any hint of sarcasm, remarked, 'Thank you, that would be very kind.'

Lowther coughed. 'Right, we'll get on then.' He shuffled the papers in front of him on his desk. 'I've asked you both here for the reading of Leo Alder's last will and testament and I have done it today, before the funeral on Friday, because Mr Alder had some express wishes about the funeral that he would like both of you to carry out.'

'Both of us?' Kate couldn't keep the shock out of her voice. It didn't make sense. How could Leo have involved her with Rory when he of all people knew how she felt? How could he have done that?

Lowther watched her for a few moments, then asked, 'Is there a problem with that?'

'Yes! Of course there's a problem,' she burst out. 'Mr Gallagher and I are hardly friends, Leo knew that, in fact we—'

'Kate!' Rory glared at her. 'Kate, why don't we let Mr Lowther finish telling us what Leo wanted before you go—'

'Before I what?' she demanded.

'Nothing,' Rory said quietly. 'Let it go, Kate, please?'

'Let it go? What did you mean? Tell me? I have a right to know. You can't just—'

'*Kate!*'

Suddenly she stopped and looked at Rory. She had forgotten for a moment where she was or what she was doing there, and the situation came back to her now with painful clarity. Embarrassed, she dropped her gaze and said, 'Sorry, please go on.'

Lowther was unflinching. He nodded solemnly and continued with the reading. 'This is the last will and testament of Leo Campbell Alder, of Tonsbry House, dated the third day of October, nineteen ninety-four. He states that he is of sound mind and body and asks that Kate Dowie and Mr Rory Gallagher both be present at the reading of this will and at his funeral, the arrangements for which he has left to me. He would like you, Kate, to host any mourners who might want to come back to the house after the service.'

Kate hung her head.

'And he would like Mr Gallagher to support you in that role.'

She jerked up. '*Support* me? What the—?'

Rory stared hard at her and she stopped in mid-sentence. She stared down again and bit at her nail, refusing to look at either Rory or Lowther.

'Now the will.' The solicitor looked directly at Kate. 'Would you mind if we dispensed with the formalities? I think it might be a bit easier if we do.'

She shrugged. She wasn't bothered either way, she just wanted to get out of there and away from Rory. His very presence in the same room angered her.

'Good.' Lowther paused. 'Now, Kate, I don't know if this is going to come as something of a shock to you, my dear, but Mr Alder has left his entire estate to you.'

'To me?' Kate sat up. She shook her head. 'No, no, that's not possible,' she protested quickly. 'He was going to leave it to my mother, I'm sure he was, he couldn't do anything else, he—' She broke off abruptly and stared at Lowther, who sat blank-faced opposite her. 'There must be some mistake,' she said. 'It should go to my mother, it—'

'There's no mistake, my dear,' he interrupted. 'Leo Alder wanted you to have the house and estate. It was in his former will as well, it has been his wish for many years.'

'His former will? Years?' Kate repeated numbly. She was almost too stunned to take it in. 'I don't understand,' she murmured. 'Why? Why did he leave it to me? What was he thinking? Why?'

There was an uncomfortable silence, then Lowther said, 'It was entirely his decision; who are we to question it?'

'No, of course, but . . .'

'Kate, dear, there is more to go through, and if Mr Gallagher wants to get away quickly then we had best move on.' The solicitor's sharp, vaguely patronising tone went right over Kate's head.

'Yes, of course,' she agreed quietly.

'There are several conditions of the will, regarding the couple who kept house for Mr Alder, the tenants and of course Mr Gallagher.'

'Mr Gallagher?' Again the shock and anger.

Rory glanced sidelong at Kate. Her anger was like an open wound.

'Yes, Mr Alder has requested in his will that Mr Gallagher

be kept on as estate manager for at least an interim period of one year.'

'A year?'

'Yes, one year, provided that is agreeable to Mr Gallagher.'

Rory nodded, but said nothing. He had known that Leo was fond of him, but this stipulation did seem a bit bizarre. Leo had loved Kate, he would never have done anything to willingly upset or distress her.

'He has also asked that Mr Gallagher be consulted on every decision regarding the house and estate, and that he be a joint signature on all relevant bank accounts.'

'A joint signature? That can't be right!' Kate shook her head. 'I'm sure it can't. This is all highly unusual.'

Lowther shrugged. 'I'm afraid that this is a highly unusual situation. Mr Gallagher was in the process of trying to bring some sort of business order to the estate – isn't that right, Mr Gallagher?'

Rory looked up. 'Yes, I was beginning to make some headway.'

'I believe that Mr Alder thought you were on the right track and wished you to continue what you were doing.'

'What do you mean, some sort of business order?' Kate asked, butting in. She felt as if she was one pace behind Lowther and Rory, that she was missing something. 'Why was Rory on the right track?'

Lowther sighed. 'I'm afraid that this will also probably come as a shock, Kate. In simple terms, Tonsbry House and Estate are heavily in debt.'

'In debt?' Yes, it was a shock, Kate was momentarily stunned. She was silent for a minute or so, then she asked, 'What sort of debt?'

The solicitor coughed, as if the next sentence was

something unpleasant in his throat. 'Over the past few years, Kate – in an attempt to try to rescue the estate from a fall in value, low profit margins on the livestock and farming land, and virtually no rentals from the farm buildings – Mr Alder took out a large loan with a company called Ingram Lawd.' Lowther pulled out a piece of paper from the pile in front of him. 'He took out an agreement to re-mortgage the house and estate with this company four years ago. It was at the height of the property slump, with interest rates likely to rise, and his loan was on a variable rate. You understand what that means, do you?'

No, Kate wanted to snap, of course not, that's why I run a successful business! But she didn't, she said, 'That it's affected by interest rates?'

Lowther missed her sarcasm. 'Yes, exactly. If interest rates go up, or down, then so do your repayments. Unfortunately for Mr Alder, interest rates rose six per cent in the space of one year and it nearly ruined him. He fell into arrears with his mortgage payments, ended up taking out a bank loan in order to try to meet those repayments and got himself into a vicious circle of debt. Now,' Lowther stopped and rifled through his papers, 'the situation today is slightly better. Interest rates have fallen, Mr Gallagher has managed to get things on to an even keel and the debt has been reduced, but not to any great extent. The estate manages to keep up repayments, but only just and there's still the sum of three hundred and fifty thousand pounds outstanding—'

'Three hundred and fifty thousand pounds?' Kate interjected. 'My God, that's impossible, I—'

'I'm afraid there's more.'

She turned to Rory. 'You know about this?'

He nodded.

'So what have you done about it?' she demanded.

Rory ignored the suggestion that he was somehow responsible and said patiently, 'I've been trying to salvage what I can, get the estate into some sort of order, rent out the farm buildings and sell some of the livestock. Leo just wasn't well enough, he . . .' His voice trailed off. Neither of them needed reminding of what Leo had suffered. 'He did what he could,' Rory finished.

'If I may, Mr Gallagher?' Lowther passed them both a set of accounts. 'This is the current situation; Mr Alder asked me to have these produced so that you had something to work from. As you'll see, I've had the property valued and that's the figure there in the right-hand column.'

'But that's nothing! Are you sure?'

Lowther nodded, but Kate glanced at Rory for further confirmation. He agreed.

'There's no market for this type of property at the moment,' the solicitor said. 'It's too run-down for what I'd call the "millionaire market" and not cheap enough for the developers. Plus there's no call for development in this area, we're too rural.'

Kate looked at him. 'So what you're saying is that I've got a debt on Tonsbry worth more than the property?'

'Yes, for the moment.'

'And that I can't sell to realise the debt; all I can do is try to make some savings, increase profit in whatever way I can and just keep it ticking over, paying off both loans with every penny that comes in.'

Lowther nodded. 'Yes, that's about it. Obviously there are some finer points to be discussed but—'

'But I've got it in one, right?'

He raised an eyebrow at her sharpness. 'If you wish to put it like that, yes.'

'I fail to see that there's any other way to put it!' Kate was not only upset, she was almost insanely angry. For Leo, her beloved Leo – the only one who ever put Kate first – to do this to her, saddle her with debt, with a crumbling old house, and thrust her into a relationship with a man she hated, was so terrible that she could hardly believe it. She stared down at her hands and clasped them tightly together to try to stop them from shaking. It was all a farce, all those years she had meant nothing to him. In the end he was as selfish as her mother – no, worse even, because her mother had never pretended to be anything she wasn't. She wanted to scream, it rose in her throat and threatened to choke her.

'Kate? Kate, are you all right?' Rory reached out and touched her arm, but she jerked away.

'Don't touch me!' she cried, holding her arm into her body as if his fingers had burned her. She turned away from him and was silent for some time, while Lowther looked down at his papers and let her compose herself.

Finally Kate looked up. 'So what if I give up and declare myself bankrupt to get rid of the place?'

Lowther hesitated, then said, 'You can do that, it's always an option. But I have to tell you that if you do so, then you're likely to lose your catering business as well. Everything in your name will be sold in order to pay off the debt.'

'My flat?'

'Yes, I'm afraid so.'

Suddenly Kate dropped her head in her hands. Rory wasn't sure if she was crying and was at a loss to know what to do. He couldn't even comfort her; she wouldn't let him.

But Kate wasn't crying, she was too angry and too shocked for tears. She felt as if she had just been cut off from the real world. She heard Lowther cough, she heard the rustle of papers and the sound of the phone ringing in another office, but the noises had no meaning. She was suspended in a muffled, painful silence. She stayed like that for some time until Lowther said, 'Kate, my dear, I am afraid that I have another appointment. We must get on.'

'Get on?' What else was there to discuss? There couldn't be any more. 'I'm sorry,' Kate said, lifting her head, 'but I really could do with some air. Can we leave the rest until after the funeral?'

The solicitor tried hard to hide his relief, but Rory picked it up. He caught something else too, in the man's expression, only he wasn't able to identify it.

'The rest is formality, I can put it in writing for you, if you like,' Lowther offered.

Kate got to her feet. Her legs felt unsteady and she had to hold on to the back of the chair. 'Thank you,' she murmured. Lowther rose as well and stepped forward to help her. 'I'm quite all right,' she insisted, avoiding his hand. Picking up her coat, she turned towards the door. 'Really, quite all right,' she repeated blankly. 'Thank you.' And without another word she walked out of the office, leaving the door open behind her.

Rory watched Lowther for a moment, then rose himself. 'There's nothing else you need me for, is there?'

The solicitor shook his head. 'I can contact you at Tonsbry House, can I? I trust you're not going anywhere?'

'I wouldn't think so, not just yet anyway.' Rory turned

towards the door. He was worried about Kate; if he hurried he could probably catch her – although what he intended to say to her if he did, he had no idea. 'Thanks, Mr Lowther,' he said, then stopped at the door with an afterthought. 'You'll let us know the exact arrangements for the funeral, will you? How many and that sort of thing?'

Lowther shrugged. 'I can give you the list of those I was asked to contact, but who else might just decide to turn up on the day I'm afraid I don't know.'

'I see.' Lowther really was a pompous little man, and decidedly unhelpful for a family solicitor. 'Whatever you have will help, thank you,' Rory remarked and, not wanting to waste any more time, he quickly said goodbye and left the office. Hurrying along the corridor, he smiled at the receptionist and made his way out on to Chartwell High Street. 'Damn!' he muttered, looking both right and left. There was no sign of Kate. 'Damn!' he said again and, pulling on his overcoat, he walked forlornly back to where he had parked the Land-Rover.

As soon as Rory Gallagher had left his office, David Lowther quietly closed the door and went to the telephone. He took out his diary and looked up the number he needed, then sat down, picked up the phone and dialled. His call was answered and he said, 'Hello, it's David Lowther here,' modulating the tone of his voice an octave lower to extract the most from it. He smiled. 'Yes, very well in fact.' The smile faded. 'Of course I didn't "enjoy it"! It was all very distressing. Yes, it was a shock, I don't think she was expecting anything of the sort. Yes, I did, I made it quite clear that the debt extended to everything she owns – yes, and the catering business. Shocked again, I'd say, and quite distressed. No, no, I don't think she'd oppose anything that got it off her hands, particularly not knowing that Gallagher is part of the whole inheritance.'

Lowther lit a cigarette while the person on the other end spoke. He relaxed back in his chair, dragging deeply on the nicotine. 'No, it wasn't easy to convince him to do it; Leo was opposed to it for quite a while. He kept on about the fact that Gallagher and Kate would never be reconciled and that—' He was interrupted. 'I don't know, I think it was the fact that he felt he was leaving too much of a burden for Kate to handle on her own.' He smiled again. 'Thank you, yes, and to my skill in persuading him. In the end, of course, he asked my advice and I gave it to him. No, I'm certain there won't be a reconciliation; Leo was right, she was furious, and upset too. There's no love lost between those two. No, no, of course I wouldn't expect there to be – no, I didn't mean that I . . .'

He broke off and sat forward. Why didn't these conversations ever go his way? Grinding out his cigarette, he said, 'I'm sure it'll be worth it; I can't see her wanting to do anything else. Yes, I'll keep in touch and ring as soon as I can get some idea of how the land lies.' He doodled with a pen on the pad in front of him, feeling thoroughly bad-tempered. Square after tiny square he drew, filling in each one with thick black ink. 'The funeral's Friday; yes, I did, I don't think it'll work at all, they can't even talk civilly.' The call was winding up and Lowther was disappointed; it was never long enough. 'Right, I will, of course, thank you. Yes, I—' But he didn't finish what he was going to say, for the line went dead. 'Shit!' he said to the silent phone, feeling thoroughly annoyed and frustrated.

He buzzed his secretary and immediately asked her to

come in for dictation. 'Yes, now!' he snapped over the intercom. 'This minute, if it's not too much trouble.' Then he sighed, letting out a small amount of built-up tension, and felt marginally better. Nothing improved his mood like the prospect of bullying the nice young girl who had the misfortune to work for him.

Duncan Lawd was on the phone to Carol-Anne. It was mid-morning, she was still in bed and had been describing to him exactly what she was going to do to him when he got in from work that evening. He was excited, his face was flushed and he had pushed aside the pile of papers he should have been working on so as to be able to concentrate fully on what Carol-Anne was saying. She was building up to a crescendo and Duncan was sorely tempted to just slip his hand down under the desk when his eye was caught by the small red flashing light on his phone that told him he had another call waiting. He closed his eyes and tried to ignore it, but his secretary had been told to hold everything unless urgent.

'Carol-Anne,' he said gently, 'I've . . .' She let out a tiny, breathy moan and Duncan sighed. She was into her stride. 'Carol-Anne,' he began again, 'I'm sorry, darling, but I . . .' The moan deepened. He wondered briefly if it was worth it to interrupt her and decided it wasn't. Without hesitating, he cut her off.

'Hello, Duncan Lawd.' He sat forward, all thoughts of Carol-Anne forgotten. 'Yes, yes, I did. I set the wheels in motion a couple of days ago. No, not yet, these things take time, I gather there's a funeral on Friday and we usually like to give it a few days after that, I—' He was cut short. 'Of course we can, I wouldn't advise it, but if that's what you want . . .' The red light on his phone was flashing again; it had to be Carol-Anne. 'I might be able to send someone down at the weekend if you really think—' Again he was cut short. The red light continued to flash. Suddenly he smiled. 'But that's far more than we discussed! No, no, of course it's acceptable, but . . . yes I will, on Saturday then. I quite understand, as soon as we can, yes. I'll let you know. OK, right and—' He heard a click and the line was disconnected. 'Thank you,' he said, smiling, then went back on the line to Carol-Anne.

'Darling, what happened? We were cut off and I've been trying to get through to you ever since.' There was a simper on the other end, then a short giggle and Duncan glanced at the door. 'Wait a minute, sweetie,' he said, 'I'll just be a few seconds.' Standing, he quickly crossed to the door, flicked the lock and returned to the desk. He unzipped his fly, sat down and relaxed back in the chair. 'Now where were we? You naughty girl.' There was another giggle, then a low murmur and Duncan eased his hand down under the desk. 'Ah yes,' he whispered, 'that is so good . . .'

Nothing turned him on like the smell of money.

Chapter Seven

It was late Friday afternoon, the funeral was over and the wake was drawing to a close. Rory stood across the room from Kate, by the door, so that he could see people out once they had said goodbye to her and offered their condolences. He didn't want to be there in the midst of such animosity and anger, but Leo had requested it and Rory was still a man of honour. He was there, no matter what it cost him personally. And it did cost him. Ever since the first moment when he had seen Kate at Gully Cottage, that terrible fiasco which had resulted in him saying things he should never have said, he had known that their relationship was doomed for disaster. Emotions were raw, the pain hadn't died or even lessened and the memories were still too vivid, too close. There was no hope of friendship, no hope of even a kind word between them, and he realised that it was stupid of him ever to have considered it. But he had, and that was what really cost him. Over the past few years, through all the failure and regret, Rory had somehow held on to the small hope that, despite everything, at the end of it might be Kate – Kate forgiving and, if not loving, then at least liking him again, a friend.

As he looked across at her now, he knew how misguided that hope had been. And in knowing that, every moment in the same room with her, every glance at her and every word she said just reminded him of his loss.

And as for Kate, she could hardly bear the sight of him. The fact that Leo had asked it of her hurt her almost more than Rory's presence. Every time she looked at him she felt sick. The disappointment of years ago flooded back and threatened to overwhelm her. It tainted her grief, tarnished her memories of Leo and Tonsbry and fuelled an almost insane anger which burned away inside her. Kate was hanging on to her dignity by a thread. She didn't understood Leo's request, she didn't understand what Rory was doing at Tonsbry in the first place and she was consumed by the injustice of it all.

There were only a few mourners left now and Mrs Able circulated, collecting up plates and dirty glasses while Kate stood patiently talking to an elderly relative. She wasn't concentrating on the conversation, she had hardly heard a word that had been said all day. Her eyes kept darting anxiously towards Rory as if she were keeping track of the enemy. He watched her as closely as he could and saw that, over the past four years, Kate had grown in confidence and poise. She had changed, she held herself straighter, her smile was less quick, less given to please, and she dressed differently too; she had always been stylish, but her clothes now seemed to be chosen for herself. There was no sign that she had worried about what to wear today. At the funeral she had worn her long black velvet coat and hat, sombre and respectful, but back at the house she removed that and underneath wore a long, straight, printed silk skirt with red poppies against a deep blue-black background, a soft black sweater and a bright crimson chiffon scarf. She looked extraordinary amongst the black and navy tweed, the dull grey stockings and brown felt hats, like a rare and exotic bird.

'Rory, it's nearly five,' Mrs Able said, passing him on the way through to the kitchen. When he started and tore his gaze away from Kate, the housekeeper gave him a look that said: stop mooching, lad, and get on with it. It made him feel about fifteen again. 'You'd better ring the vicarage,' she went on, 'and tell your mother that you'll be late. Tell her from me that if she needs a hand giving Flora her tea and putting her to bed to let me know. All right?' Self-conscious, Rory nodded.

Out in the hall, she stopped and glanced over her shoulder. 'There's no point in crying over spilt milk, lad,' she said sharply. 'What's done is done, you just have to get on with it.' He feigned puzzlement, but Mrs Able just clucked. 'Tell Kate the truth; she deserves it and it has to come from you – that's what Mr Leo always said.' Her voice wavered at the mention of her former employer, but she covered it with a cough and Rory thought that whatever he and Kate had to put up with in all this, it was nothing compared with the Ables who had been with the family for most of their working lives. Rory glanced at her and stepped forward to take the tray.

'Here, Mrs Able, let me.' It occurred to him as he took the glasses from her that he had never known or used her Christian name and nor, as far as he could remember, had Kate. Her husband managed the household and was always John, while she kept the household and was always Mrs Able. 'Kitchen, Mrs Able?'

'Ay,' she said. 'Then you call your mother.' And she

led the way, holding the door open for him as they went.

Rory returned to the drawing-room as the last of the mourners were taking their leave. Kate was embraced and kissed and John Able had coats ready to be collected in the hall. Rory waited until they made their way over to the door, then escorted them out into the courtyard to their cars. It was dark, barely five o'clock and the night had come down, cold and damp, closing in. He shivered but not oppressively. He liked the long nights and always had, the constant turning of the seasons reassured him. Life moves on, he thought; it was the one thing that had kept him going throughout the trauma with Alice, it put his problems into perspective. Remembering that time, a time really only barely past, he dug his hands in his pockets and looked up at the sky, which was already patterned with stars. He wondered where the hell Alice was now. Australia, last count, but she hadn't planned to stay. Maybe she had, maybe she hadn't and, to be honest, he didn't really care much so long as she left him and Flora alone.

Standing to wave as the last car drove off down the drive, Rory then made his way back to the house. He knew Kate wouldn't want him hanging around, but he wanted to call his mother at the vicarage to let her know he was on his way home and he couldn't believe that Kate, even as angry as she was, would begrudge him a phone call.

Walking into the hall, Rory immediately thought of Leo and all of a sudden the loss hit him – a feeling so acute that it took him by surprise. He had been waiting for Leo's death, in many ways had prepared himself for it during the last few months, had thought he knew what to expect. But just the sight of an unlit, empty grate in the hall rendered all that useless. Leo had been Rory's friend, unexpected and generous, and he missed him.

Without thinking further, Rory crossed to the stone fireplace and knelt to see if the grate had been swept; it had. So he got up, went through to the passage that led to the kitchen and made his way along to the store-room. He found the basket of kindling and everything else he needed, and dumped it all on top of a small pile of logs. Back in the hall, he knelt and began to lay a fire – paper, a few fire-lighters, some kindling, coal and a couple of the smaller logs – all the time remembering how Leo had always had a fire in the hall; always – it was part of the house. He dug in his pocket for his lighter, and set the flame to the edge of the paper. Still kneeling on the cold stone floor, he watched as the paper took, igniting the fire-lighters and setting up enough flame to burn the coal. Within a few minutes, the fire was under way and Rory was satisfied. As he sat back on his heels, warm for the first time that day, behind him Kate said coldly, 'What on earth do you think you're doing?'

He jerked round, twisting his knee. 'Oh, Kate, I'm sorry, I was . . .' he faltered, feeling ridiculous. 'I was making a fire,' he stated obviously.

'So I see.'

'I thought . . .' He stopped. What had he thought? That in lighting a fire he could in some way bring Leo to life again? It sounded so foolish. 'I thought it was cold in here,' he finished lamely.

'How considerate,' Kate replied archly. 'So, if you've finished . . . ?' She nodded towards the door.

'Yes, sorry. Of course.' Rory got to his feet. 'Listen, I . . . I couldn't just use the phone, could I?'

Kate gritted her teeth. 'No, you bloody couldn't,' was what she wanted to snap, but she held it back and said nothing.

'It's just that I want to ring my mother to let her know that I'm on my way and to wait to put Flora in the bath.'

Kate shrugged. The mention of Flora softened her, although she had no idea why; she should have resented the child, disliked her on principle. 'You can use the phone in Leo's study,' she said coldly. 'I'm going in there now.'

She turned and Rory followed her across to the three-windowed room at the front of the house that Leo had adopted as his study and private sitting-room. Kate opened the door and Rory walked in after her. He could smell polish and hothouse freesias and saw a tall square vase filled with them – the dark red flowers, long-stemmed, with a touch of burning orange in the centre.

'Leo loved them,' Kate said, noticing Rory's look. But as soon as she said it, she was angry with herself for feeling the need to explain anything at all to him.

'Of course.'

She went and stood by the window with her back to him while he crossed to the desk to make his call. She was being polite, but it was a bad choice in such circumstances; she should have focused in on the room, not out of it. Staring at the front lawns of the house, she felt again their power to conjure up an image of that terrible day and cut her off from reality, to plummet her once more into deepest, darkest despair. Turning away abruptly and back into the room, she listened to Rory's conversation for a few moments . . . his cosy, familial conversation . . . and suddenly the most enormous resentment welled up inside her. A resentment so violent that she wanted to lunge across the room and snatch the phone from his hands.

'Oh, did she?' Rory continued, oblivious to Kate's anger. 'I see. No, no problem. Yes, I agree, it's better to leave her there then. Yes, I will, first thing, about eight, eight-thirty. Give her a big kiss for me. Thanks, Mum, bye.' He put down the phone and turned. 'She fell asleep,' he said. 'My mother put her to bed, Flora's got her own little room there . . .' His words seemed to ricochet off the walls of the room and fall empty on to the floor. There was such a force of malevolence all around him that it quite shocked him. He said tentatively, 'Kate? Are you all right?' But it was a mistake; he should have simply ignored what he felt and walked out. He should have gone home.

'Me? Oh, I'm fine, Rory, just fine!' she said coldly, her voice oddly detached. 'Please, go ahead, make your calls, and one to Alice while you're at it, to let her know that you'll be late home for dinner and that no, today wasn't too bad and she could probably have shown her face if she'd had any guts.'

Rory stared down at the floor. 'Kate, please,' he said quietly.

'Please what? Please don't mention Alice? Why is that, Rory?'

'Kate, it isn't fair, you—'

He was about to say, you don't know the whole story, but Kate snorted derisively and said, 'Fair? *Fair!*' Her voice rose sharply, emotion cutting through it. 'What the hell has fairness to do with any of this, Rory? Were you *fair* when you dumped me four years ago? Were you *fair* when you came back here? Was Leo, in giving you the cottage? Knowing that I would have to see you and Alice day in and day out if I ever came back!' She threw her hands up in the air, close to tears. 'Fair? What's fair, eh? Tell me!'

'I don't know,' Rory said. 'Please, Kate, I don't know anything, I—'

'"I don't know,"' she mimicked. 'Please, Kate, don't ask me to explain, I can't, I'm far too pathetic to have to face up to it and give you an explanation. I'll just bugger off with Alice and live happily ever after, but don't ask me to apologise for ruining your life, for costing Leo thousands of pounds, for humiliating me in front of hundreds of people, for . . . for fucking Alice and giving her a—'

'Stop it, Kate!' Rory suddenly shouted. 'That's enough!'

'Enough?' Kate moved closer to him, like an animal moving in for the kill. 'You've had enough, have you?' She spat, inches from his face. He could smell her breath, hot and acidic. 'Very brave. Very in character – do your bit then scarper, leave before the shouting starts, let Harry—'

'Let Harry what? I never *let* Harry do anything, I—'

'You what? Had a pressing engagement? Do me a favour, Rory! You were too much of a coward to face Leo and everyone else for that matter, just like you're a coward now – not bringing Alice, the pair of you not able to face me, not—'

'I don't *live* with Alice!' Rory suddenly cried. 'She's not here! She . . . we . . .' He broke off at the sight of Kate's face. She staggered back several paces and felt behind her for the wing chair to hold on to. Rory hung his head. When he lifted it again a minute or so later, Kate had somehow managed to regain her composure. It was as if the shock had deflated her anger. She stared blankly at him, waiting.

'Alice and I were only together for a short time, she . . .'

He swallowed hard. For some ridiculous reason he had always imagined this differently, telling Kate, putting the past to rest. He had imagined some sort of sympathy, forgiveness even, a reconciliation, but this was nothing like that. Just a cold explanation and Kate staring at him, unseeing, unfeeling. 'We were never meant to be,' he said. 'Alice left me eighteen months ago, that's why I came here. I was in a mess, struggling to hold down a job and child care, my parents going backwards and forwards from here to London to help out with Flora, and . . .' he shrugged, 'and to help me too. So we came and lived with them for about a year, then Leo offered me the cottage. I wanted to start afresh, so he asked me to help him with the estate and the cottage came as part of the deal. It was . . .' Again Rory broke off. How could he possibly explain what coming here had meant to him? 'It was incredibly generous of him, he knew how much it would hurt you and yet . . .' He struggled with the words. 'He helped me out of a terrible situation and it made a huge difference, it . . . well . . .' he shrugged again. 'It changed my life, and Flora's.' Shaking his head, he said, 'I'm not a coward, Kate. Facing you that day, telling you about Alice, it was the hardest thing I've ever had to do and then, then I—'

'Stop it, Rory!' Kate cut in. 'I don't want to know, not about that day, not now, not ever.'

Rory said nothing. There was a tense silence for a few minutes, then Kate asked, 'So what happened? To you and Alice?'

Rory glanced up. 'You really want to know?'

She looked at him. 'Don't read too much into it,' she answered. 'It's curiosity more than anything.'

'Alice was ill,' Rory said. 'She had post-natal depression,

badly, and things were never right. As soon as Flora was born she just sort of . . . well, fell apart, I suppose.'

'Poor Alice!' Kate said sarcastically and immediately wished she hadn't. 'I'm sorry, I didn't mean that.'

'No.'

But of course a part of her did mean it, a part of her wanted Alice and Rory to have suffered and struggled and hurt – it was just, it was punishment. 'I'm sorry,' she said again; it wasn't a lie, her better nature had won through. 'What happened? Are you divorced?'

'No, we were never married. My father suggested we wait until the baby was born. I think . . .' Rory shook his head, 'I think my parents saw things happening that I didn't. I think I was in shock for most of that year, and grieving; I'd lost the only thing that really mattered to me—'

'Don't, Rory!' Kate suddenly snapped. 'Just don't, all right?' She wasn't going to shoulder his guilt or take the burden from him. He'd done what he'd wanted to do at the time, so let him live with that. She had, hadn't she?

He dropped his head. 'I'm sorry,' he mumbled, but he wasn't. He'd had to say it, just to get it out of the way.

When he glanced up a few moments later, Kate was no longer looking at him but had sat down on the window-seat and was reaching across to the lamp on the table. She lit it and light flooded into the room, dispelling the shadows and making everything much clearer.

'So you never married?'

'No, we never got round to it. When Flora was born Alice got ill, she couldn't cope and it was never an issue, there wasn't the time or the energy.'

'What happened to her? To Alice, I mean?' Kate wasn't sure why she kept asking, whether it was the need to get things straight or an almost macabre satisfaction in Alice's demise. 'I'm sorry,' she added quickly. 'I mean, if you don't want to say, I quite understand.'

'No, no, it's OK. Alice had this big thing about motherhood, she wanted it so badly, wanted Flora so badly that when it happened and it wasn't what she expected – you know, a crying baby, exhaustion, constant work – she felt inadequate, as if she'd done something wrong. It kind of went downhill from there. It was the depression, some sort of chemical imbalance we found out later, but at the time it was just Alice going under. I had to take weeks off work to look after Flora. Alice coped, sort of, but she would leave Flora to cry, forget to change her, bath her, sometimes even feed her. I couldn't leave her alone with the baby for long periods of time, so my mother came up, but that just made it worse, emphasised the inadequacy. She had something eating at her, something she couldn't get over, it . . .' He stopped. He was about to say that it was guilt, but he knew he couldn't tell Kate that – not today, maybe not ever. He remembered how he had felt when Alice told him. Quite simply, he had wanted to kill her. 'I don't know why you fuss and love that baby so much,' she had said almost casually one morning. 'She's not even yours.' It had ripped through Rory with such force that it was the closest he had ever come to physical violence.

He closed his eyes for a moment now, seeing the terrible image of himself and Alice, shouting, screaming, locked in misery, and knowing that for one awful, frightening moment he was inches away from knocking her senseless. He looked up and saw Kate staring at him. She knew she shouldn't ask, Rory's face was sufficient answer, but she had to. 'What happened to Alice? In the end?'

'She left us. She packed a bag one morning and walked out. She called me a week later and told me that she didn't want Flora and that I could have legal custody if I wanted it.'

'Did you?'

Rory almost smiled. 'It never crossed my mind to do otherwise.' It was ironic really, he thought, that Alice had lied and schemed so viciously to keep her baby and then deserted her. Ironic that it was Rory, the duped father, who had ended up loving Flora. And he did love her, she wasn't his by blood but she was as much a part of him as any child he could have created. 'There's something irresistible about that little girl,' he said, and this time he did smile.

On impulse, Kate smiled back. 'I know,' she answered, 'much to my detriment,' and there was a moment, so fleeting that Rory almost missed it, a moment of pleasure, of shared intimacy which led him to ask, 'So?' But the moment he said it, he regretted it. Kate froze.

Harry Drummond screeched to a halt in his bright orange MG, peered at the sign on the gatepost at the end of the drive, then spurted forward and slammed the car into reverse. He swung back into the drive and turned the car around, swearing loudly as he did so and reaching across to the passenger seat for the map once more. Why the hell could he never find bloody Tonsbry House? Good Lord, he'd been there often enough as a boy and a few times with Kate over the past couple of years, but he hadn't a clue where it was now. It was along this road somewhere – well, according to his map and as far as he remembered it was, but he was buggered if he could see it. Crunching through the gears, he found first and sped off back the way he had come. A mile or so along, he slowed at a pair of rusting wrought-iron gates, an entrance he had ignored first time round, and stopped. Leaning across to the glove compartment, he found his torch, switched it on and shone it out of the window at the stone pillars supporting the gates. 'About bloody time!' he snapped, finding the words 'Tonsbry House' etched into the stone. 'The first damn thing I'm going to do is put up a proper bloody sign!' And revving the engine, he swung into the drive and accelerated towards the house.

Rory and Kate walked across the stone floor of the hall together, if such separateness could be called together, their footsteps echoing in the silence that enveloped them. At the fireplace Kate stopped. The fire was a good idea, she could see that now, it gave off a warmth that had been lacking all day. She stood close to it with her hands outstretched towards the flames and Rory watched her face soften. He saw an opportunity to talk and took it; he said, 'I should never have behaved like I did the other day, when Flora was missing.'

Kate didn't look up. 'No, you shouldn't have.'

'I'm sorry. It was rude, unforgivable.'

She focused in on the fire, the flames were almost hypnotic. Unforgivable, she thought, what an odd word to use. She wasn't aware that forgiveness came into it at all; he had apologised, and that was the end of it. She didn't care enough to want to forgive.

'Kate?'

She glanced up.

'Kate I—' But Rory didn't finish what he was going to say. He was interrupted by the crunch of tyres on the sweep of drive outside, the slam of a car door and footsteps – strong, heavy shoes with metal blakeys on the heel – up the stone steps towards the half-open front door. There was a knock and a voice shouted, 'Hello? Kate? Hello?'

Rory jerked back as if he'd been hit. The voice called out again and he drew in his breath. His shocked gaze went from the door to Kate, then back to the door again. He knew who it was, but could hardly believe it. 'Harry?' His questioning glance went to Kate once more, the door swung open and instantly he faced a man he hadn't seen for four years. 'I don't believe it! Harry Drummond!' he burst out.

'Rory Gallagher?' Harry stared, shocked into silence for a few moments; then he turned to Kate, her face aghast, and dashed towards her. It was as if Rory wasn't even there. 'Kate! Kate, darling.' He was across the hall, sweeping her into a hug before she had a chance to even utter his name. He released her, still stunned into silence, then took her hand in his and held it tightly, murmuring, 'Kate, dear, darling Kate.' He pressed the hand to his lips and, ignoring Rory as best he could, said, 'Why didn't you tell me the funeral was today? I've been worried, Kate darling. I called the flat and Stefan told me you were here, then he mentioned the funeral and . . .' Harry broke off to press her hand to his lips a second time, acutely aware of Rory behind him, then slowly turned to follow Kate's gaze. 'Ah,' he said, 'I see!'

'Do you?' Rory asked, as calmly as he could manage and all the time thinking: what the hell is going on here? 'Perhaps you could tell me then?'

Harry ignored that and turned to Kate. 'Has he been upsetting you?' She shook her head. She couldn't bear to look at either of them. Harry was being ridiculous, over-protective and macho, and Rory was acting all hurt and shocked as if he hadn't ever expected Kate to get a life without him.

'No,' she said. 'No, he hasn't.' But she didn't mean no, she meant yes, of course he has, only it wasn't the way Harry meant it, it was just that she couldn't be in the same room as Rory without feeling upset. 'I mean . . . oh, I don't know, I mean of course not, not at all. I, he—'

'He what?' Harry was spoiling for a fight. 'He shouldn't even be here, if you ask me.' He turned to Rory. 'I think it's about time that you left.'

'Oh, really? And who says so?'

'I do.'

Rory stared at the man he had once considered his closest friend and felt the anger rise in his chest. Of course he knew why Harry had dropped him, had even understood for a while – the fact that Harry didn't want to hurt Kate, that he wanted to be there for her, the victim, the injured party. Of course he had understood, he'd wanted his best friend to help the woman he loved and trusted him to look after her. But then, later, when Rory in turn had needed a friend, when he had become a victim himself, Harry had been unmoved, too busy, too involved with Kate to be able to spare the time, the energy or the friendship.

'And who are you to tell me what I can and can't do?' Rory demanded.

Harry let the comment hang in the air for a few moments. He squared himself up, lifting his head a little higher, and glanced at Kate. Then he smiled. All those years he had lived in Rory Gallagher's shadow, all those years he'd felt he had been second-best, had second choice, taken what Rory

Gallagher didn't require. Now he had what Rory wanted, he could see it written all over his face, and the years fell away; they simply disappeared. The smile stayed fixed on his face. 'Kate and I have been together for some time now, and I think I'm right in saying . . .' He glanced at Kate and raised an eyebrow, but she fixed her eyes on the ground. 'I think I'm right in saying that she looks to me to protect her and take care of her. In fact,' he glanced at Kate again, 'I have been thinking of asking her to be my wife.'

'Your wife?' Kate jerked up and stared at Harry open-mouthed. But before she could say anything else, Rory grabbed her arm and spun her round to face him.

'His wife?' His expression was one of total disbelief. 'Kate, he's not serious? Surely he's not!'

Kate yanked her arm free. 'Why not? Is it really so hard to imagine that I might have a life of my own, that someone else might want to marry me?' The resentment and anger lying so close to the surface suddenly exploded. 'Christ, Rory! You think that because you didn't want me no one else will. You arrogant, self-important—'

Rory grasped her shoulders and held them. 'No! No, that's not what I meant at all.'

'Then what?' She shrugged off his hands and moved away from him towards Harry. 'Marrying Harry doesn't seem such a ludicrous idea to me, in fact quite the contrary.' She felt for Harry's hand and clung on to it. 'It's what I need. Harry's always been there for me, I trust him, he's . . .' She faltered, searching for the right word, the right meaning. He was Harry, as plain and simple as that; she'd never thought of him as anything else. The fact that she had never been drawn to him, that she had just drifted anchorless towards him, escaped her now. The fact that she had never felt a burning passion, an all-consuming desire, seemed irrelevant. Harry loved her, he had just proposed to her in front of a man who filled her with such fervent rage that it left her almost senseless, and she could never ignore that. She could never let Harry down in the way she had been let down herself. Never.

'He's the man I admire and respect,' she said, swallowing down the sudden threat of tears.

Rory stood still, knowing that the ground had suddenly shifted underneath him. 'Is he? Is he really?' He stared hard at Kate, willing her to look at him, to return his gaze so that he could see, just for a moment, if she really meant what she said. It didn't matter that Kate was angry, that she hated him even, he could stand that; but if she loved someone else, if she loved Harry, then it changed everything. Kate hung her head. She stared down at the ground and clamped her jaw shut, squeezing Harry's hand so tightly that her fingertips left imprints on his flesh. How dare he question her? Why should she lie? She felt the urge to shout at him, to rail against him; but Harry took a step forward, releasing her hand, and said, 'That's enough, Rory. I think you'd better go.'

'Kate?'

She didn't look up.

'Jesus, Kate! Why didn't you tell me? Why didn't you at least let me know—'

'Why the hell should I?' she suddenly cried. 'You're not part of my life, I haven't even seen you for years. I don't owe you anything, nothing – Christ, I don't even like you, I . . .' But she didn't finish, for Rory turned and strode across the hall and through the half-open front door, slamming it hard behind him and running down the steps.

There was an ear splitting silence except for the hiss and crackle of the fire, then Harry said, 'Well, that's that, then!' And beside him Kate burst into tears.

Chapter Eight

Harry lay in bed, Kate's bed, a four-poster which she had revamped several years ago, hanging fine white muslin instead of the faded, heavy, dark Victorian brocade which belonged to it and covering the high mattress with white bed-linen and a mountain of pillows encased in sharp, crisp white cotton. Leo had been shocked at first, but he had sold the brocade for what he considered to be a ridiculous sum to a dealer in the Portobello Road and from then on had been quite chuffed with the whole idea of redecoration.

Harry leaned back against a stack of deep pillows and popped a hand-embroidered cushion Kate had brought back from France behind his head. He forgot about his hair-cream, the one that smelled divine but left a faint trace of oil on anything it touched; he forgot about everything except the moment. He was content, happy in fact, despite Kate's peculiar mood. Rarely had he slept so well, seldom had he felt this good and never had sex with Kate been so satisfying. Never had sex with Kate come anywhere near, in fact. Most of their love affair had been spent with him cajoling and gently bullying and Kate complying, dutifully almost. She had always been remote, detached, it was part of the way she was. Only not last night; last night Kate had loved Harry with a force he'd not experienced in her before, with a passion he didn't know she possessed. She had been different, not the Kate he knew, and for a while – for a few intense moments – he thought he knew exactly what Rory had seen in her.

So now, lying in a bed he had not been privileged to lie in before, looking across the room at a woman who had agreed, virtually if not completely, to marry him, a beautiful woman with a property and land behind her, Harry felt pretty damn good – about life, about Kate, and most of all about himself. It was true that he hadn't been planning to marry yet, but Kate was a hell of a catch – looks, charm, money – and Harry was ready to settle down; it would do his career good, put a bit of substance behind him. Of course it would all have to end with Tully's sister; Harry didn't want to start off on the wrong foot, but the thought of that dampened his spirits so he decided not for the present – perhaps better to see how things went first, see how long it all took to come together. Besides, Sasha Tully was quite a girl and he wasn't about to give her up on a whim.

Moving the pillows slightly, Harry wondered about a cup of coffee and glanced at Kate who was sitting wrapped in a blanket on the window-seat. One long, pale slim leg was uncovered, but Harry was unmoved at the sight. It was cold out of bed and he really didn't want to be lumbered with the task of making the drinks.

'Kate?'

'Hmmmm?' She didn't turn from the window, but tucked the uncovered leg back inside the blanket and returned to her view.

'I don't suppose you fancy some coffee, do you?'

She shrugged.

'No? Oh.' He pulled the duvet higher up under his chin, irritated by her lack of interest in him and wanting to penetrate her mood. 'What are you thinking, Kate?'

She turned. 'I was thinking about the house,' she answered. 'There's something . . .'

'Were you? I suppose you were thinking what changes would need to be made once we're married.'

'Well, er . . .'

'There's probably a master bedroom, isn't there? We could move into that, have it redecorated of course. Has it got an en-suite bathroom? You know this is a wonderful house, it could be really spectacular if we spent a bit of money on it. I was thinking last night that it might be worth thinking about me giving up the Army – you know, living here full-time, eventually that is, helping to run the place. Of course we'd want to have a family one day, and this is just the sort of home that's ideal for kids—'

'Harry!'

'What?' He grinned. 'It *is* wonderful for kids! Isn't it? They'd have loads of freedom, space to run around and we could entertain a lot, fill the place with friends, always have something going on . . .'

'Harry!'

'Sorry, am I running away with you?' Harry laughed and climbed out of bed. Naked, he crossed to the window-seat and pulled Kate to her feet. 'I'm sorry, I don't mean to rush things, Kate darling.' He turned her face up towards his and kissed her mouth. 'You don't really mind me going on, do you?'

'No, I . . .' Kate looked away and her heart sank. She hadn't told him about the debts yet, or about Rory living a stone's throw away; she hadn't had much chance, and when she did she hadn't had the nerve. Turning back to him, she said, 'Look, Harry, there's something I need to tell you about the house.'

Harry nodded absent-mindedly. He was staring over her shoulder out of the window at the view Kate had been so absorbed in since she had woken. 'It's a spectacular view,' he said. 'Stunning!' His mouth brushed Kate's hair and he stepped round her to have a closer look. 'What's that small building across the valley, with the smoking chimney?'

'One of the cottages, Gully Cottage, I think.' She didn't think, she knew. She knew because she had been watching it all morning.

'Really? I didn't know there were cottages on the estate. Is it leased, or could we perhaps think about letting it for summer holidays, shoots, that sort of thing?'

'It's leased,' Kate said quickly.

'Ah, I see.' He turned away. 'It's worth thinking about though, Kate, I mean long-term. Perhaps I'll pop down there later on this morning and have a look at the place.' He saw her face and added, 'From the outside, of course.'

'Of course,' she murmured. This is your chance, she thought, tell him about Rory and then about the house. But Harry placed his hands on her shoulders and leaned down to kiss her mouth. She felt the warm wetness of his lips and gently pulled away.

'What?' Harry nuzzled her neck. 'Where's the heat of last night?' he whispered. 'Where's that unstoppable—'

'Harry, don't!' Kate moved out of his embrace, pulling the blanket tighter around her body, than she crossed to the bed and bent to pick her clothes up off the floor. Had it been real desire, she wondered, folding her skirt, or had it been a fierce, passionate attempt to banish the past? To forget the sadness? What she'd felt last night had been so intense it took her breath away, yet was it Harry who had made her feel like that, or was it something far less safe, less tangible? Kate pulled on yesterday's knickers and bra and threw the blanket back on the bed.

'You're getting up, are you?' Harry asked, sneaking back under the duvet.

'I'm going to find some clean clothes and then have a bath.' Kate tried to temper the note of irritation that crept into her voice. 'Why?'

Harry reached over to the bedside table and took up his pack of cigarettes. 'I wondered about a cup of coffee?' he wheedled. Noticing Kate's glare, he dropped the pack back. 'Milk, two sugars?'

Kate sighed, 'Fine.' She took clean underwear, her jeans and a long-sleeved T-shirt out of her bag, still unpacked, and picked a towel off the old-fashioned cast-iron radiator. It was damp; the radiator didn't work.

She glanced back at Harry before she crossed to the door. He had reshuffled the pillows and slunk down ready for a snooze.

'Harry?' she began, but now wasn't the right time; she knew that.

'Hmmm?' came the lazy, disinterested reply.

'Nothing,' Kate murmured; and taking her wash-bag from the chest of drawers, she silently left the room.

Stefan ran towards platform twelve with an old duffle-bag over his shoulder, his battered leather flying-jacket gripped tightly in his hand. He was late, he heard the guard blow the whistle and saw the barrier close. Reaching it seconds later, he leaped athletically over the bar and sprinted up the platform. Halfway along, he narrowly missed collision with a woman struggling to run in a tight skirt and high heels, carrying a briefcase, heavy lap-top and a bulging handbag. He swerved to the right, stopped short and, as the guard began to slam shut any open doors on the train, he doubled back, grabbed the woman's bags, took hold of her arm and literally dragged her along to the last open door. As the train started to move off, Stefan jumped up, threw the baggage down in a heap and then leaned out and bodily lifted the woman aboard. He dumped her on her feet, the door slammed, the guard called out an obscenity at him and they were off. Stefan started to laugh.

'My God! That was incredible!' Jan Ingram was still panting from the effort of having nearly missed the train and the thrill of being lifted high into the air by a six-foot-two Adonis. She wondered for a moment if she had died and gone to heaven, then she too started to laugh. 'Do you make a habit of rescuing helpless women?'

Stefan's laughter faded to a grin and he bent to hand the lady her possessions. 'Always,' he answered. 'I'm very good at it, but only on old rolling-stock. Automatic doors have played havoc with my chivalry!'

Jan knew she was being flirted with quite shamelessly, but she didn't mind. Make the most of it, Jan, she thought, it's a hell of a long time since that happened. She smiled back, took her things and thanked the young man. 'I don't suppose I can buy you a drink when the buffet opens?' she said, not in the least expecting him to agree. 'By way of a thank you?'

Stefan nodded. 'That would be very nice, thanks.' He

never refused a drink from a lady; you never knew when business could crop up. 'Where are you sitting?'

'Oh, right, yes, um . . .' Surprised, Jan wafted towards the front of the train. 'Up there, near the front.' She felt suddenly embarrassed; had she really just propositioned a young man?

'In first class?' Stefan said. Jan nodded. 'OK, I'll find myself a seat, dump this and come on up.' He smiled again and bent to pick up his bag, showing the neat muscular curve of his bottom in tight, faded Levi's, then he turned and headed through the doors to find a seat.

'My God,' Jan murmured, 'I don't believe I just did that!' She fiddled with a strand of hair which had already lost its perm and fell lifelessly over her forehead. That was the first time she had felt even remotely attractive for years! She flicked back the strand of hair and smiled to herself. Then she remembered why she was here and depression set in again. Picking up her bags, she sighed miserably and made her way along to her seat.

And why am I here? Jan thought ten minutes later, leafing aimlessly through a magazine between bursts of staring morosely out of the window. I must be bloody mad! But she wasn't mad, she was just desperate and she knew exactly why she was there, pathetic as it was. She was there because Duncan had asked her to be, because – no matter how hard she tried to hate him, how angry she was, how humiliated and hurt – when he said dance, she danced. When he said, 'Jan, we need this Tonsbry deal and it means a hell of a lot to me,' she found herself sitting on a train to Chartwell, near Winchester on a Saturday morning because Duncan had suggested that she would catch whoever was to inherit Tonsbry there at the weekend, the day after the funeral. She hated her weakness, she despised the fact that she even listened to him but there it was, twenty years was a hell of a long time to just wipe out with one affair. Jan closed the magazine, sighed miserably again and, just as she did so, Stefan materialised by the side of her seat and said, 'Shall we go for that drink?'

Surprised, Jan blinked twice, nodded, smiled and then blushed, avoiding the eye of the man opposite her. She rose, made a hash of getting out of her seat and finally managed to stand straight. 'Buffet's this way,' she said. 'It should be open now.' She led the way, wondering what the hell she was doing and why she had asked him for a drink in the first place. As they got to the buffet and she turned to ask him what he'd like, he smiled at her and she immediately remembered what and why. She felt a shiver run down the entire length of her spine and blushed again, this time a deeper, darker red.

'What'll you have?'

'A beer?'

'A beer; yes, right, good. Um . . . I'll have a gin and tonic . . .' Jan faltered momentarily over her decision but then thought, what the heck, I've a grim task ahead and a stiff gin won't do me any harm. She went to the bar, ordered the drinks, paid for them and asked for a receipt. As she turned, clutching a miniature bottle of gin, a can of tonic and a can of lager, and two plastic cups, she saw Stefan had been watching her. 'Business,' she said, embarrassed. 'I need the receipt for business.'

'Of course.' He flipped the ring on the can and drank his beer, ignoring the plastic glass. A professional woman was a better prospect. 'Cheers,' he said, wiping his mouth on the back of his hand. 'Shall we move?' He nodded towards the corner. The bar was standing room only but corners, in Stefan's experience, were often more intimate than a table for two. He gently eased Jan backwards so that she was standing against the carriage wall and he was in front of her. It was a position he liked.

'So,' Jan said, 'I'd better introduce myself. Jan Ingram.' Stefan took her hand and held it a touch longer than was necessary. 'Stefan Vladimar. Pleased to meet you, Jan, and thanks for the drink.'

'My pleasure.' Jan took her hand back and struggled to think of something to say, but her mind went blank.

'So, Jan, where are you headed?' Stefan could sense her unease; it radiated off her in waves. 'It doesn't seem very fair to be working on a Saturday!'

'No, it isn't!' Jan took a big slug of her gin for Dutch courage and swallowed it in one gulp. But as it went down a large burst of carbon dioxide came up and she had to turn away to belch behind her hand. 'Oh, sorry, excuse me.' Her cheeks flamed as her excitement slowly sank towards misery. 'I don't usually,' she stammered, 'I mean work on a Saturday, but I . . . it's an extraordinary piece of business and my husband – I mean my ex-husband, well almost, we're separated – he asked me to do it and I well . . .' She broke off as Stefan touched her arm. It was a simple gesture, unprovocative and comforting and as she stared down at his hand, long, slim fingers with clean well-cared-for nails, she forgot her insecurity, her unhappiness, the fact that she was very probably making a complete fool of herself standing in the British Rail buffet car flirting with a man about fifteen years her junior, and she smiled.

There was a moment of relief as they both relaxed, then she said, 'I'm sorry, I was gabbling, wasn't I?'

Stefan shrugged, then smiled. 'A bit, perhaps, but only enough to be charming, not boring.'

Jan's smile turned to a short, throaty chuckle. 'Are you to be believed?'

He held out his arm and flexed his bicep muscle. 'Have a feel, it's all real and it's all paid for!'

Jan declined and took another sip of gin.

'So where are you off to then, Jan?' Stefan smiled. 'Under the strict orders of the soon-to-be-ex-husband?'

'Oh, yes, well, I'm seeing a client this morning and on a Saturday in order to catch them at home. It's a bit of a . . .' Jan stopped. She had been about to say that it was a bit of a grisly task, that she had to serve notice to foreclose on a loan, but realised that it didn't sound particularly impressive or even nice and was better kept to herself. 'A bit of a bore, working on a Saturday,' she finished. 'And you? Where are you off to?'

'I'm going to visit a friend, a surprise visit. Her uncle just died, and I think she could do with cheering up.'

'That's nice.' Very nice, Jan thought, it must be a girlfriend. Her face fell and Stefan said, 'She's been a good friend for years, I live in the flat above her. She's got this rather pompous, stuffed shirt of a boyfriend, and I can't imagine he'd be much good at offering comfort and support. He's the stiff-upper-lip type.'

'And you're not?'

'Good Lord, no! Do I look that sort?' Stefan glanced down at his casual, slightly scruffy attire and smiled. 'I cry at *Little House on the Prairie*!'

Jan laughed. 'Actually,' she said, 'you know, so do I!'

And touching drinks in a mock toast, they both drank to that fact.

An hour later the train arrived at Chartwell station bang on time, much to Jan's disappointment. She had rather hoped for a long delay, some sort of spectacular hold-up on the line, but for the first time in her long experience of British Rail there was not a single hitch. She said goodbye to Stefan without either of them discussing their ongoing travel, left him her business card and tried very hard to forget him on the way back to her seat. He would never ring – why should he? – he must have dozens of women after him. Collecting up her things, feeling woozy after drinking so early in the day, she felt foolish for even considering it and embarrassed about leaving her number. As she stepped off the train and made her way along the platform, she tried hard not to look over her shoulder but succumbed to the temptation before going through the barrier. She turned, wondered if she should suggest giving him a lift in her taxi and searched the oncoming crowd for sight of him. There was none; to all intents and purposes, he had disappeared. Jan blinked several times, stood on tiptoes to see above the mass, then wondered briefly if she had imagined him. She was jostled as people tried to get through the ticket barrier and a few moments later gave up. She walked out of the station to the taxi rank, found a cab and told the driver where she wanted to go. Disappointed, she climbed in, popped a mint into her mouth to take away the taste of gin and tonic and settled down into her seat. Despite the morning ahead, despite feelings of embarrassment and despite Duncan, Jan felt a burst of self-confidence for having even attracted a man like Stefan in the first place.

'Grey old day, love,' the driver called over his shoulder.

'Oh, I don't know,' Jan answered. 'It's a lot brighter than I expected!'

Chapter Nine

It was nearing lunch-time and Mrs Able stood at the long oak table in the kitchen of Tonsbry House, kneading a mound of bread dough. She had her sleeves rolled up, her apron on and her arms covered up to the elbows in flour. Across the table from her sat Harry Drummond and, as he talked, his dialogue was occasionally interrupted by a hefty, almost angry thump of the bread dough on the table top.

'So you're saying that there's no other staff for this place then, Mrs Able?'

'Aye.' Staff, she fumed, no one's ever called me staff before, cheeky blighter. She banged the dough hard on to the table and plunged her hands into it.

'What about house parties, that sort of thing? D'you get people in?'

'No, never had much call for it.' House parties? What was the boy on about? This wasn't a Nancy Mitford novel! She threw some more flour on the surface and slammed down the dough, sending a scattering of white dust towards Harry. He coughed and vaguely thought of another conversation opener, but quickly dismissed it. She might have been Mrs Able, but she certainly wasn't ready and willing!

He smiled at his sudden wit but, not knowing the joke, the housekeeper wondered if he was one short of a load. She bristled and said, 'No doubt you'll want to read the papers in the drawing-room 'til Kate gets back from her walk. There's a fire made up.'

'Ah, right.' Harry stood. At last some sense out of the woman. He would have to talk to Kate about her; if he stayed, then she would have to go. 'Will you be bringing coffee through later?'

There was another thump of dough on wood as Mrs Able's hands seemed to wring the life out of it.

'Right, well, you know where I am,' he said, unnerved by the sight of the helpless dough. 'I'll be off then.'

She didn't look up. Listening to his footsteps recede, she wiped her hands on her apron and sank down into a chair. Where in God's name did Kate find that one? she wondered. Either she had missed something, or Kate wanted her brains tested! She picked up the lump of very well-kneaded dough and plonked it into the basin ready for proving. But just as she was going to place it next to the Aga, the front door-bell sounded. So, leaving it where it was, she untied her apron and hurried along the passage to the hall.

'Hello, Rory. You shouldn't have bothered with ring-ing.'

Rory stood uneasily outside on the stone steps. 'Sorry, but I didn't want to just walk in . . .'

'Why not? It's never bothered you before, lad.' She smiled but Rory flushed, embarrassed.

'Kate might not approve . . .' he began.

'No, well, Kate's out walking, so come on in and don't

worry about it.' She turned towards the kitchen and glanced back at him. 'You coming?'

'Well, I thought I might wait for her actually, see if she's all right. I'll wait in the drawing-room if that's OK?'

'Oh Lord!' Mrs Able suddenly remembered Harry Drummond. 'No, no, that's not OK!' she exclaimed. Did Rory know about Harry? What if he didn't know and Kate was keeping it a secret? The thought of him finding Harry in the drawing-room threw her into a complete flap. 'It's not clean,' she went on hurriedly. 'I haven't opened the shutters or drawn the curtains. Wait in Mr Leo's study, it's warmer and brighter at this time of the year with the three windows. Go on . . .' She ushered Rory in that direction. 'I'll bring you a cup of tea, I should think you're gasping . . .'

'Mrs Able?' Rory found himself at the door to Leo's study before he had a chance to look round. 'Mrs Able, are you all right?'

'Me? Oh yes, dear, fine. Why shouldn't I be? Hmmm? Absolutely fine!' She flung open the door and propelled Rory forward, closing it quickly behind him. 'Just fine,' she muttered, wiping a small line of perspiration off her top lip. 'Dandy.' She hovered outside the door for a moment wondering what to do, then she swung round at the sound of tyres on the drive outside.

Jan climbed out of the taxi, took the driver's card and arranged for him to wait for her in Tonsbry village. She didn't know how long she would be, but she really didn't care; she was past worrying about expenses, in fact it almost gave her pleasure to think of running up a huge taxi bill. She paid the cabby, tucked the receipt in her purse and reached for her things. It was only the second time she had ever been to Tonsbry, but as she straightened and looked up at the house she understood how someone could mortgage their life to keep it. It was beautiful, old and faded and mellow, and it was etched with the pattern of countless lives. She could almost feel the presence of the people who had loved and shaped Tonsbry.

God, I must be getting old and sentimental, she thought. Or maybe I've always been that way, perhaps it's latent, this feeling of wanting to belong. She gripped her lap-top and briefcase, walked up the stone steps towards the open front door and knocked.

'Hello?' Mrs Able was at the door before Jan's hand had left the wood; it made her jump.

'Oh, gosh!' She put her hand up to her chest, slightly unnerved by the flushed, elderly woman in grey tweed and stout lace-up shoes. 'Good morning. Sorry, I wasn't expecting someone so quickly.'

'No, I don't suppose you were,' said Mrs Able. She had spotted the briefcase and she never trusted people with briefcases. 'What can I do for you?'

'Jan Ingram,' Jan said. 'I wonder if I might have a word with . . . er . . .' She faltered, not knowing who to ask for. 'I'm from the loan company Ingram Lawd,' she announced with more confidence than she felt. She lifted her head a little higher. 'I would like to speak to whoever is now in ownership of this property.'

'Ah, I see.' Mrs Able kept her grip firmly on the door, and the door firmly only half-open. 'May I see your identification?' Mr Leo had told her to always ask for confirmation, and one couldn't be too sure these days.

'Oh!' Jan was taken aback. 'Oh yes, of course, I should have a card here somewhere.' She rummaged in her bag, but discovered she had given Stefan her last business card and asked, 'Will my travel card do? Or my driving licence?'

'If it has to.'

She took them out and handed them across to Mrs Able. She felt absurd, still a touch light-headed from drinking on the train, standing out in the cold and being inspected by an ageing housekeeper.

After peering at the blurred mug-shot on the travel pass and matching it up to Jan, Mrs Able was sufficiently satisfied that she was who she said she was to open the door and usher her inside. 'You'll have to wait,' she said. 'Miss Dowle's not back from her walk yet.' Then Harry and Rory sprang to mind and she experienced a jolt of panic. Wait where? She couldn't put this woman in with Kate's fellow – that was impolite – and she daren't put her in with Rory in case Kate got upset – anything to do with Rory seemed to upset her – but she didn't want her in the kitchen and she couldn't leave her here in a draughty old hall. The housekeeper tried to think fast, but it wasn't her strong point. 'Oh dear,' she muttered, 'you'll have to wait in the . . . er . . . morning-room – no, I mean the dining-room, that's it! It's the only room free . . . I mean clean.'

'That's fine, I'll—'

'This way,' said Mrs Able, taking Jan's arm and leading her across the hall towards the dining-room. 'Come on, it's just here.' She opened the door, Jan walked in and turned to say how lovely it was; but before she could open her mouth the door was shut firmly behind her and Mrs Able's footsteps could be heard hurrying away along the passage.

How odd, she thought, suddenly alone in the silence.

But then she remembered who she was and what she was doing here and realised that, if anyone was odd, it had to be her.

Out on the estate, Kate swung her legs up over the last gate that separated the farming land from the grounds of the house, sat on top of it for a few moments looking back towards the stream, then jumped down and headed on into the grounds. Her shoes were wet – one of the few decent pairs she possessed, black suede loafers – and she realised she should have worn boots. Her feet were soaked through, but she didn't feel the cold; she was numb to it. She took in the view, the sights, smells and sounds of Tonsbry, but it didn't come to life for her, it felt like a dead weight around her neck. She trudged miserably on, hoping for something to happen, some sort of revelation even, but nothing did. At the drive she stopped, took one final look back and then glanced up towards the house. Halfway up the drive, duffle-bag slung over his shoulder, she spotted the unmistakable figure of Stefan. When Kate called out to him, he turned and threw both arms above his head in a jubilant wave. She smiled for the first time in days and broke into a run.

'Kate!'

'Stefan!' The two fell into an embrace, Stefan sweeping Kate off the ground and hugging her tightly. 'Why didn't you tell me you were coming?'

He released her and took a pace back to look at her. 'Spur-of-the-moment decision,' he answered.

'Then why didn't you at least ring from the station? I could have picked you up!'

'Ah.' He shrugged and grinned. 'I travelled gratis, courtesy of British Rail, and jumped over the barrier at Chartwell to avoid the ticket collector.'

'Stefan, I'm shocked!'

'It's the thrill of it, Kate. Of course I'd have paid if I'd been asked to, but once we arrived at Chartwell and no one had rumbled me it seemed rather silly to give myself up at the barrier.'

'And from the station to here?'

'Some young man in a Land-Rover gave me a lift from the side of the road.'

Kate smiled. 'Oh well, by whatever means, you're here now!' She hugged him again. 'It's so good to see you!'

'And it's so good to see you too, Kate,' said Stefan, kissing her face. 'You're too thin, you need some of my special love and attention!'

Kate smiled. 'Don't be silly, I couldn't possibly afford your prices!' She slipped her arm through his and they started for the house.

'So? What's new? How's the business going?'

'Kate, you've only been away since Wednesday! But it's going fine, Rebecca is very capable and I am simply brilliant myself . . .'

'Any bookings?'

'Two. I brought the diary for you to look at. I thought you might want to give me instructions in case you have to stay on a bit.' Stefan patted his duffle-bag. 'It's here.'

'Thanks, I'll look at it later, but I won't be staying; I want to get back to work and, well . . .' she shrugged, 'I don't feel very comfortable here, I . . .'

'You've seen Rory Gallagher, then?'

'Yes.'

'Your mother rang by the way, she asked me if you'd seen him.'

Kate stopped walking. 'My mother asked you if I'd seen Rory Gallagher?'

'Yes. She wants you to ring her. I asked her if she wanted the number for the house and she seemed a bit – sort of upset.'

'She would never ring me here; she's only rung the house once since the day she left it in 1963. She and Leo didn't get on. I think she always felt that the house should have been hers by right; she was the oldest, but Leo was the male.'

'And he left it to you, not your mother.'

'Yes.' Kate lapsed into silence for a few moments.

'How did she take it?'

Suddenly Kate clapped her hand over her mouth. 'She doesn't know! My God! I haven't spoken to her since I found out, I . . .' She broke off, was silent again for a few moments more, then said, 'She can't know about Rory either. How can she know that Rory Gallagher works here?'

'Maybe she spoke to your uncle?'

'I very much doubt it.' Kate really couldn't think, but then so much had happened in the past few days that was hardly surprising.

'Perhaps it just filtered through to her – things do, you know. She knew Leo was ill, didn't she?'

'Yes, but . . .' Kate shrugged. She couldn't deal with this now, she didn't have the energy. 'Come on,' she said, starting off again, 'you haven't seen Tonsbry before, have you?'

'No.'

'Well, I'll show you round then. It's a beautiful place.'

And as she said it to Stefan, she suddenly realised that, for the first time since the will was read, she meant it.

Twenty minutes later, after a brief tour of the outside of the house and the gardens, Kate and Stefan climbed the stone steps to the entrance of Tonsbry and Kate dug in her pockets for the brass key to unlock the door.

'it never used to be locked, you know,' she said, 'but today it's just silly to leave it open all the time. It's an invitation to any old body.' She reached forward, inserted the key and was about to turn it when suddenly the door burst open to reveal Mrs Able, attempting to look as if she hadn't been standing there all that time waiting, which of course she had.

'Mrs Able! Are you—'

'Kate!' the housekeeper cried. 'Thank goodness!'

And at the sound of her voice and Kate's name, the doors to the study, the drawing-room and finally the dining-room flew open one after the other.

'Kate!' exclaimed Rory.

'Rory!'

'Stefan?' Jan queried.

'Jan?' Stefan asked, turning to Kate.

'Kate?' Harry demanded.

'Harry . . .' Kate murmured. She glanced at Stefan, then they disengaged themselves and stood apart.

'Oh dear,' twittered Mrs Able. 'Oh dear, dear me.'

'Who on earth . . . ?' Rory began.

'Stefan, this is Rory Gallagher and Mrs Able,' said Kate. 'You know Harry. Rory, Mrs Able, this is Stefan, a very good friend of mine from London.'

'Jan?' Stefan said, moving across the hall. 'This isn't the

business you . . . ?' He broke off as her face drained of all colour. How the hell am I going to deal with this, she thought, and felt weakly for the wall behind her.

'Oh dear,' Stefan muttered. Reaching for a chair, he said, 'Here, sit down, Jan; you've gone very pale. Are you all right?' Jan covered her face with her hand and nodded. But she was far from all right, she was ridiculous; she should have been able to cope with this, this was business and she was a professional! But the very thought of revealing to Stefan exactly what she was here for, the very idea of intruding into the grief of these people to tell them that they were about to lose their home was almost unbearable. She felt sick. What on earth had possessed her to agree to Duncan's request? Why the hell hadn't she been stronger, or even seen this coming?

'Stefan? Is this a friend of yours?' Kate asked.

'Yes.'

'No!' Jan said. 'I mean, we met on the train.' She wondered if she could just stand up and walk out without doing anything at all, without saying anything at all. It crossed her mind for a split second that she might just grab her bag and run for it, but it was only a split second. She was here, she had a job to do and she had to get on with it. Besides, she was letting her feelings get in the way and look where that always got her! Taking a very deep breath, she stood and said, 'Look, I'm sorry, but I'm not here with very good news, I'm afraid. I need to speak to the present owner of this property.'

'That's me, I think,' Kate said. 'Kate Dowie, I'm Leo's niece.'

Jan tried to ignore the gaze of five pairs of eyes from all directions and went on. 'I'm from Ingram Lawd, my name is Jan Ingram and my company had a loan arrangement—'

'Yes, I know,' Kate interrupted. So the vultures were out already! 'I'm fully aware of the loan that your company had on the property.'

'Loan?' Harry piped up. Kate ignored him, her face set in a grim look of determination.

Jan braced herself; this was going to be even more awful than she had anticipated. 'Miss Dowie,' she ventured, 'is there somewhere we can go to talk more privately?'

Kate hesitated; private meant bad news. 'Leo's study,' she said, 'this way.'

Jan followed her and at the door Rory asked, 'Do you want me to stay?'

'No,' Kate answered. 'I don't *want* you to, but I suppose you should. You know as much about the situation here as anyone.'

'Situation, Kate?' Harry called. 'What situation? Shouldn't I come in with you?'

Kate turned. 'Oh, thanks, Harry, but no. Could you make Stefan a coffee?'

'Make Stefan a coffee?' Harry said, but his indignation was lost on her. She had already gone into the study with Rory and Jan Ingram and shut the door behind them. Harry glared across the hall.

'It's OK,' Stefan said, 'I think I can manage that myself.' He turned towards Mrs Able. 'If you'll show me where the kettle is, Mrs Able, I'll make us both one, shall I?'

'That'd be lovely, Stefan,' she answered, throwing him one of her rare smiles. 'This way.' And Harry huffed, loudly and rudely, before turning on his heel and stomping back into the drawing-room.

*　　　*　　　*

Jan placed her computer on the desk in the study and leaned forward to smell the freesias, glancing around the room as she did so. It was a wonderful room: untidy, masculine, full of light and books and CDs. It smelled of polish and flowers, the wood panelling glowed and a feeling of permanence suffused everything. Standing straight, Jan saw Kate staring at her and flushed. 'It's a lovely room,' she said and instantly regretted it. She was forgetting herself, she was here to foreclose on a loan and she couldn't afford sentimentality.

'Miss Dowie,' she began, 'firstly, I'd like to say how sorry I am about the death of your uncle.' It was a standard opening, an attempt to smooth the way. Kate nodded. 'Unfortunately, his death has had repercussions in terms of the loan facility on the house and estate, and I'm afraid that we have had to re-evaluate our position on the loan.' The words came out, but they sounded so worthless that Jan was almost embarrassed to say them. It was a well-used company procedure, she'd said them time and time again in all sorts of situations – only then she'd been safe, smug and secure. 'If people can't manage their affairs, then their affairs get taken away from them,' Duncan had often said, 'it's as simple as that.' But it wasn't simple. Jan had managed Duncan, managed her life, given it everything she'd got and then one day she'd woken up and it was all gone. It was nothing she'd done, it was beyond her control.

'We . . .' She lost track of what she was saying for a moment. Picking it up again, she said, 'The current position is, I'm afraid, that because we have no guarantee of repayments – Mr Alder fell into arrears with his mortgage payments on several occasions in the past – we are not prepared to transfer the loan to any other party.' She paused for a second to let this piece of information sink in. 'Therefore the only thing left to us – and we are quite within our legal rights – is to foreclose on it.' Jan stopped and glanced down at the floor before continuing, 'Are you aware of what this means?'

Kate shook her head; she didn't trust herself to speak. Her heart was thumping in her chest and her palms were damp with sweat.

'Well, it means that we would require repayment of the loan in full within three months.'

'In full?' Kate looked frantically at Jan. 'You can't be serious! How on earth would we be able to do that? Surely you've done your homework and know the current value of the property?'

'Yes, we do. That's one of the factors that we've had to take into account.'

'Then how am I expected to pay back the loan if I can't sell the property to cover it?' She turned to Rory. 'Rory? Is this right? Can they do this?'

'I'm not sure. I think that they have to give you an option, but I'm not certain of that.'

'*Is* there an option?' Kate asked Jan.

Jan hesitated, then she pulled out a chair and said, 'Do you mind if I sit?' She did so and, really not at all sure why she was doing this, went on, 'Yes, there is an option, but we do not *have* to give it to you. Once a borrower falls into arrears with their payments, then I'm afraid that the protection given in the mortgage contract is no longer valid, and we are well within our rights to demand repayment of the loan in full at any given time. But you can appeal with the help of a solicitor, and we would very probably have to hear the appeal.' This information wasn't normally offered voluntarily.

'How do we appeal?' Rory asked.

'Through your solicitor, as I said.'

'What sort of appeal do we make?'

Again Jan hesitated, then said, 'Look . . .' She rubbed her hands over her face, the effects of the alcohol were catching up with her. 'This isn't really my business, but you would need to ask to continue repayments and if you were able to prove that you could meet them – perhaps start some sort of business venture that was going to increase income on the property – then we would have to reconsider.'

Kate looked at Rory. 'A business venture?'

He shrugged. 'Something like opening the house to the public, yes?'

'I don't know, it's a possibility,' Jan answered.

'No,' Kate said, 'it isn't. Leo looked into that years ago. The house didn't meet the criteria for the National Trust and without some sort of backing it's impossible to do; there're too many regulations for public safety, that kind of thing.'

'Well,' Jan commented, getting to her feet, 'as I said, that's not my field. I've told you more than we usually divulge, I'm afraid I can't say any more.'

Kate stared at her. She looked suddenly rather tired and sad and, despite her own situation, Kate felt sorry for her. 'So,' she asked, 'how do we leave it?'

'The situation today is that I have served you notice on foreclosing the loan. There's a clause in our contract that means you have twenty-one days in which to appeal. I've got some papers here that I have to leave with you.' Jan unclipped her briefcase and took out a brown card folder which she handed across to Kate. 'I have to inform you that if you do not meet the demand for repayment of the loan in full, then we will serve notice to repossess the house.'

'Repossess the house!' Kate was stunned.

'Yes, that's normal procedure. We would then sell the property to cover your debt and would pursue you for the outstanding sum.'

'Very nice too,' Rory said. 'Is that legal?'

'Perfectly, Mr . . . ?'

'Gallagher. What happens if you more than cover the debt? If you make a profit?'

'That's business, Mr Gallagher.'

'Yes, but not very honourable business, is it?'

Jan didn't answer. He was right, of course; it was how they had made so much money, but Jan wasn't proud of it and she wasn't going to admit it. She stood straight and smoothed her skirt. She needed the loo and to use the telephone, but it wasn't the situation to ask. So she picked up her bags and said, 'I'm sorry, I . . .' She broke off. She had been about to say that she understood how this must feel, but in truth she didn't and it would have sounded trite. 'I'll be in touch,' she finished lamely.

'Yes, thank you,' Kate said.

'I'll see you out,' Rory added. He moved towards the door and held it open; Jan took her cue, said a brief goodbye and headed out of the study. Rory saw her across the hall, she thanked him and left the house without a backward glance. She wondered where Stefan was, but immediately dismissed the thought. You've made quite enough of a fool of yourself for one day, Jan told herself. And struggling in her high heels on the gravel, she trudged on up the drive.

* * *

Kate joined Rory in the hall. 'You could do with a drink and something to eat,' he said, 'you look exhausted.' She shrugged. He was right, the sudden shock had worn her down, but she didn't think she could face food. 'A cup of coffee would be nice,' she told him.

'Come on, then.' He went to take her hand, but she avoided the gesture and walked on ahead of him to the kitchen.

Stefan was in there alone, Mrs Able having gone into the village for supplies. He looked up from his *Hello!* magazine as Kate and Rory came in, searching their faces for clues.

'Was it bad news?'

Kate pulled out a chair and slumped down into it. Behind her Rory quietly went about making the coffee. 'It was *very* bad news. The loan company want to foreclose on the loan. The loan is for more than the house is worth, and I end up with bugger all.'

'You're kidding!'

'No. Negative equity, I think it's called, but that's the down side. The up side is that the company will in all probability repossess the house unless we appeal, and then send the bailiffs in, I presume, when they're ready.'

'Repossession?'

'Yes.'

'Can they do that?'

'Yes.'

Kate put her head in her hands. 'You know, I didn't think I wanted this place. For the last few days I saw it as a real millstone around my neck, but by God, when someone wants to take it away for nothing it makes me want to fight to the death for it!'

'Do you mean that?'

Kate glanced round at Rory, shrugging. 'No, probably not. Perhaps . . .' She stopped.

'Perhaps what?'

'Nothing.'

'Perhaps if I hadn't been involved, you might have done, right? Perhaps if you hadn't had to face me here, you might have felt like fighting for it?' Rory couldn't keep the anger out of his voice. 'Is that it, Kate?'

'Drop it, Rory,' Kate said. She laid her head back on her hands.

'Is there anything I can do to help?' asked Stefan.

She smiled at him. 'It's very nice of you, Stef, but I really don't see it. Ingram Lawd have decided to foreclose on the loan that Leo took out several years ago, and even if I sell Tonsbry I won't be able to pay it off. I currently have a debt of roughly three hundred and fifty thousand pounds and a property worth just over two hundred thousand. It's as simple as that.'

'Good God, Kate! How long have you known this?' came Harry's voice.

Kate turned towards the door. 'Oh, Harry,' she said, without feeling, as he stood in the doorway of the kitchen; how long he had been there none of them knew. 'Come on in, you might as well join the party.' She glanced at Rory. 'Another coffee, please, waiter.'

'Kate, don't be funny,' Rory said.

'Believe me,' she replied coldly, 'I don't feel in the slightest bit funny.'

Harry had come into the room and slunk into a chair opposite her. 'Are you saying that the estate is in debt, Kate?'

'Give that man a round of applause,' Kate said. 'In debt, broke, bankrupt! Loved and cherished, yes – but absolutely penniless, I'm afraid.' She had an almost hysterical urge to laugh at the look of horror on his face. 'So am I, come to think of it.'

'Oh, God!'

'So might you be too, Harry, when we get married,' Kate said, her voice rising manically. 'I'll have to check that, but I think you'd be liable for all my debts as well.' She smiled and shrugged. 'Isn't life fun, eh?' Then she slapped her thigh. 'It's a whole barrel of laughs sometimes, a whole . . .'

'Kate,' Rory said quietly. 'Don't, please.'

Suddenly Kate stopped, dropped her head and swallowed hard. 'I'm sorry, Harry,' she said. 'That's about it, I'm afraid, my inheritance – a great white elephant of a house.' She stood and crossed to the window.

'But, Kate, this is awful!' said Harry.

'Isn't it?' she murmured.

Stefan stood up. 'Kate, look, I really don't think I should stay.'

She turned. 'You're very welcome to, Stef, if you can stand my mood.'

'No, it's not that, it's that, well . . .' He stared down at his hands. He thought he might go after Jan. It was a rash, spur-of-the-moment idea, but he couldn't think of anything else to do and he couldn't just sit here feeling maudlin, doing nothing. 'I just think I'm in the way. You've got things to sort out—'

'Too right we have!' Harry snapped.

'Do you want me to stay?'

Kate looked at him. 'No, no, you're right, I've got a lot of thinking to do and I guess I need some space.'

He took his duffle-bag off the back of the chair. 'Shall I see you out?'

'No.' Stefan crossed to the window, put his arms around her and kissed the top of her head. 'Perhaps I can get Jan to stall calling in the loan if I catch up with her. I'll ring you,' he said. 'It can't be as bad as it looks now, it never is.'

'No, maybe not.' But Kate wasn't at all convinced. The prospect of bankruptcy, or of letting Tonsbry go for nothing was devastating. She had loved Leo and Leo had loved Tonsbry. As Stefan left, she turned and called after him, 'Thanks!'

He shrugged, offered her a half-smile and hurried on his way. Kate turned back to the window.

'Kate?' Harry demanded.

'What?' She kept her gaze firmly on the scene outside.

'Kate, why the hell didn't you tell me?' Harry glanced sidelong at Rory. 'Did Rory know?'

She didn't answer. Rory inched towards the door and slipped out of the room. Harry noted his disappearance and thought: bloody coward, deserting a sinking ship! 'I just can't believe it,' he went on. 'This is just awful, really awful. Thank God we weren't already married, I could stand to lose everything – my commission, my career, my flat . . .'

Kate stared at him. 'Harry?' she said coldly.

'You led me to believe last night and this morning that you had inherited a large house and grounds and a substantial amount of money . . .'

'No, I didn't!'

'And I bet that's the last we'll see of *him*, slinking out of the door like a snake. Good God, Kate, bankruptcy! You'll have to let it go; there's no question about it, none at all.'

'Will I?'

'Of course. This changes everything, Kate, I mean, we certainly can't go rushing into any sort of arrangements with this hanging over our heads; it would be foolish, dangerous even.'

'Of course.'

'Of course! Yes, you see my point.' Harry began to pace the floor. 'To be honest, Kate, this isn't at all what I'd bargained for, it's serious stuff. I don't know if I can afford to get involved.'

'No.'

'No, exactly. And there'll be all sorts of legal things that you'll have to do, sort out. It's a nightmare, all of it! We can't make any announcements yet, Kate; we couldn't possibly announce an engagement with this going on in the background.'

There was a long, uncomfortable silence; then, curiously unmoved, Kate said, 'No, I don't suppose we could.'

Harry looked at her for a moment, unsure of her attitude.

'I need some time to think, Kate. We both need time to think, you especially.'

'Of course.'

'I know it must be hard to understand, but I don't know if I can commit myself in this sort of situation.'

'No.'

'You mustn't take it personally, Kate, it's nothing to do with you; it's circumstances. Look,' he walked over to her and took her limp, cold hands in his, 'Kate, I think it might be best if I went back to the regiment now, cut the weekend short and gave you time on your own to get your head straight.'

'Yes.'

'I could pack and be out of your hair in the next half an hour.'

'Yes.'

'You do understand, don't you, Kate?' Harry looked at her imploringly, but there was no need.

'Of course,' she said. She understood; it was perfectly clear, and the odd thing was that she didn't mind nearly as much as she had thought she would. 'You must do what you think is best, Harry,' she told him.

'Yes. Yes, I must.'

He dropped her hands, suddenly embarrassed by the idea of physical contact and, relieved, Kate said, 'Shall I see you out?'

'Oh!' He wasn't sure how to handle this; Kate's mild acceptance had come as a bit of a disappointment. 'Oh no, don't bother,' he answered, 'I can collect my things and find my own way. I'm sure you've got plenty to be getting on with.'

'No, not really.' She didn't see any point in lying just to be polite. 'But do as you wish.' Kate switched on the kettle. She hadn't had that cup of coffee she'd been promised and suddenly she wanted it.

Harry turned towards the door. 'Are you all right, Kate?' he asked, more out of duty than consideration.

'Fine,' she replied, spooning Nescafé into a mug. 'Just fine.' And as she reached for the sugar, she heard him head off along the stone passage towards the hall, then moments later he had gone. 'I'm really fine,' Kate said aloud to the empty kitchen, 'why shouldn't I be?' And, sitting down with her coffee, she put her head in her hands and burst into tears.

*   *   *

At the end of the drive to Tonsbry House, Jan took a good look up the road in both directions and tried to decide which way the village was. She had no idea. It had started to drizzle, her shoes had rubbed a blister on her heel, she was cold and tired. So, taking out her mobile phone, she dialled the number on the card she'd been given, asked the cab company to contact the driver who had brought her to Tonsbry House and request him to pick her up here. Told that there would be a thirty-minute wait, she replied, 'No, there bloody well won't! It takes ten minutes from Tonsbry village to here, and I'm paying a waiting charge. I'll expect him by quarter to!' She switched off the phone.

Desperate for a pee and looking around for a discreet bush, Jan – not a lover of the great outdoors – decided that a cold, damp pee was better than none at all and, spotting a possible site in the field over the road, made her way across. She dropped all her things on the wet grass and struggled over the gate, landing badly on the other side and twisting her ankle. She tramped painfully along the edge of the muddy field to a clump of trees near the hedge, scanned the ground for any creepy-crawlies, then peeled down her layers and squatted somewhat unsteadily. Anxious and uneasy, she went about her business, with one eye on what she was doing and one on the horizon for intruders.

Stefan jogged up the drive with a careful, regular stride, covering the ground quickly and easily, his athletic body hardly noticing the pace. At the entrance he slowed to a walk, scanned the distance for any sign of Jan, then spotted her things on the opposite side of the road. He crossed, called out, heard a sharp gasp of breath and, concerned for her, vaulted over the gate. Greeted by a sight which took him completely by surprise, he knew intuitively the distress his appearance would cause. So, without a word, he vaulted back, crossed the road and waited. It was not in his nature to compromise a lady.

Jan hurriedly finished what she was doing, stood up and rearranged her clothing. Peering through a gap in the hedge, she saw Stefan across the road. Thank God she hadn't answered his call; of course he would know what she'd been doing, but at least she hadn't been caught in the act. She made her way back to the gate and was considering the most dignified way to get over it when Stefan materialised just as she'd put her foot on the first rung.

'May I help?'

She nodded, climbed up halfway and he lifted her the rest, right up into the air and over the gate. Jan felt feather-light and girlish; in fact she weighed almost ten stone and was hardly a spring chicken, but there was something about Stefan that made her feel that way despite the obvious age gap. 'Thank you,' she said, picking up her things and straightening her clothes. They crossed the road and she saw Stefan's duffle-bag on the ground. 'You're not staying?'

Stefan shrugged. 'I was in the way,' he said. 'I think Kate needs some time on her own; I should have thought about that before I came dashing across the country.' He looked at Jan. 'Not a very nice business to be in?'

She flushed and looked down at her hands. 'No.' She felt suddenly tearful. 'I shouldn't have come, I . . .'

'You came because your husband – soon-to-be-ex –

asked you to and, no matter how much you think you hate him for deserting you, you can't say no to him.'

Jan jerked up. 'What the hell . . . ?'

'It's all right.' Stefan placed a hand on her arm. 'I just know how you feel, that's all.'

She swallowed down the urge to cry in one large painful gulp and, unzipping her bag, fumbled in it for a tissue. The one she found was crumpled and smudged with lipstick, but she managed to blow her nose on it. It was the sympathy which undid her. 'I shouldn't have come,' she said tearfully. 'I realised that as soon as I walked in. Kate Dowie – that's your friend, is it?' Stefan nodded. 'She seems nice, too nice for all this to be dumped on her.' Again he nodded. 'I'm not even sure that it's the right thing to do, foreclose on this particular loan. Sometimes – well, over the past few months that is – I've had to question Duncan's ethics, not openly of course but to myself privately . . .' She stopped as her voice faltered. Stefan took a clean white linen handkerchief out of his pocket and handed it to her. She dabbed at her eyes and said, 'Why am I telling you all this? I don't even know you.'

'Because you like me?'

She shook her head.

'Then it's because you think that I really do understand. And,' as she glanced up at him, 'you need someone to talk to.'

'Perhaps.'

Jan blew her nose on the hanky, then remembered it was Stefan's and flushed. 'Sorry, I'll take it home and wash it.'

He smiled. 'Don't be daft! You're welcome to it.'

'Thanks.' She wiped her eyes again and took a deep

breath. 'So how come you're so understanding? Are you a counsellor?'

Stefan shrugged. 'Something like that.' It wasn't that far from the truth. Part of his charm for the women he escorted was that he possessed a tacit understanding of their problems and that he listened – listened in a way that their husbands, lovers and male colleagues never did. 'Look,' he said, 'seeing as we're both here, shall we share a lift to the station and travel back to London together?'

Jan looked at his face for a few moments to check whether he was sincere. All she saw there was the same well-cut, chiselled features and easy, clear blue eyes she had seen earlier. If he was deceiving her, then he was a past master at it and it certainly didn't show.

'OK,' she replied, 'if you like.' Probably he wanted to help his friend, possibly he even liked her; whatever the reason, she decided to go with it. What did she have to lose, that she hadn't lost already? 'I rang for a taxi about ten minutes ago, it should be here any minute.'

'Great,' said Stefan. Then he smiled at Jan and bent to pick up her bags and his own.

Chapter Ten

'Daddy, come on, Granny said supper's ready.'

Rory turned from the window of Gully Cottage, the one that faced up towards the house, and looked at Flora. She had her napkin tucked into the top of her jumper and a faint smear of ketchup across her mouth.

'Have you been eating tomato sauce on its own?'

'No.' She shook her head resolutely.

'Flora? Are you sure?'

'Yup.'

Rory followed her through to the kitchen and saw a dollop of ketchup on the tablecloth. 'She's been at it again,' he told his mother.

Faye Gallagher glanced over her shoulder. 'At what?'

'The ketchup.'

'Oh, Rory, it doesn't matter. All children like ketchup.' She smiled indulgently at Flora. 'So do I, come to think of it, especially with fish fingers.'

Rory laughed. 'There's no need to encourage her.'

'I'm not,' said Faye Gallagher, 'I'm perfectly serious! Anyway,' she finished serving and turned, with two plates of food in her hand, 'what's so interesting about Tonsbry tonight? You haven't taken your eyes off that window since you came in.'

'Kate,' Rory answered.

Faye put down the plates and went back for her own. 'Flora, did you wash your hands?'

'Yup.'

'What about Kate?' she asked Rory.

'I don't know, there've been no lights on up there all day and she had some bad news this morning. I . . .'

'Have some food as well, Flora, not just ketchup,' said Faye. 'You what, Rory?'

'I just hope she's not sitting there alone in the dark, feeling miserable.'

'How bad was bad?' Faye asked.

'Pretty bad.'

'Perhaps she's gone back to London?'

'Yes, maybe.'

'Where's London?'

'It's a big city, Flora,' Rory said, wondering if he would ever manage a serious conversation uninterrupted at home again. 'Like the one in the story about the little polar bear, remember?'

'Yup. Can I have some more ketchup, please?'

'Eat your potatoes first, then you can have some more.'

'Why don't you go up and see if she's all right?' Faye stopped eating and leaned across to Flora. She took the spoon out of the little girl's hand and scooped some peas and mashed potato on to it. 'Here, eat,' she said. 'I don't think there's any point in you sitting here fretting,' she went on to her son.

'I'm not fretting, Mum.'

'What's fretting?'

'Worrying. Here, put some chicken on your spoon.'

Rory watched his mother and Flora for a few minutes, then put his knife and fork down on his plate. 'Actually, you're right . . .'

'As always.'

'Yes, as always.' He smiled. 'I *am* fretting, and I think I will just pop up and check she's OK.'

'Good idea.'

'What's a good idea?'

Faye rolled her eyes at Rory and he laughed, leaning across to kiss the top of Flora's head. 'What's a good idea, Daddy?'

'Never you mind,' he said. 'Come on, eat your supper.'

'Where're you going?'

'I'm just popping out for a little while. I'll be back to put you in the bath.'

'Can I come?'

'No, eat your supper.' Rory stood up and took his coat down off the hook.

'Why can't I come?'

He pulled it on and said, 'Because if you did, then you wouldn't be able to have any of the apple cake and ice-cream that Granny's got for pudding.'

'Apple cake?' Flora turned to her granny. 'Is there apple cake, Granny?'

'Bye,' Rory called as he left the cottage, but there was no answer. The last thing he heard was his mother saying, 'No, only after you've eaten some of this lovely mash and chicken, come on . . .' And smiling, he switched on his torch and made his way up to the house.

The house was dark and deserted when he arrived, and it unnerved him. He wasn't sure what he would do if he found Kate had gone back to London; with Tonsbry so unresolved, it was something he just couldn't bear thinking about. But he discovered the back door unlocked and knew she was still here. So he let himself in, switched on the lights as he went and made his way along to the kitchen. It was Kate's favourite place, and if she wasn't in bed then she would very probably be there. He opened the door, shone his torch swiftly round the room and saw her, head on the table, her coat pulled around her shoulders and fast asleep. Rory went through to the hall to fetch a travel rug from the chest and then returned to the kitchen. As gently as he could, he opened out the rug and tucked it round her, then he switched on a light – so that if she woke she wouldn't be in darkness – and turned to leave. Just as he was closing the door after him, Kate called out.

'Rory? Is that you?'

He came back into the room. 'I'm sorry,' he said, 'I didn't mean to wake you.'

Kate sat up and rubbed her face. 'It's OK, I've been asleep for ages,' she said. For the first time in days she didn't feel any anger at the sight of him. 'Thanks,' she pulled the blanket round her, 'for this; I'm frozen.'

Rory stood by the door, wanting to keep his distance. Kate had just woken and she looked exactly as he remembered, fuddled and awry and so sexy that it made his heart stop. It quite shocked him, the intensity of the feeling, and he had a strong desire to get the hell out of there. But Kate asked, 'Are you coming in?' and he found himself shrugging and answering, 'I'll make some tea, shall I?'

'I think I could do with a bloody stiff drink,' she said. 'I'll look in the pantry, there's bound to be something there.' She stood and stretched and then, still holding the rug round her shoulders, disappeared through the door into the pantry.

'Cooking sherry?' she called out. 'Some rather wicked-looking home-brewed beer, or there's this . . .' She put her head round the door. 'Tonsbry Original,' she said, holding a bottle aloft. 'I think it's gin – will it do?'

Rory nodded and she came out. He wasn't at all sure how to handle this sudden change in Kate. One minute she couldn't bear the sight of him, the next she was offering him drinks. He stood uneasily across the kitchen and watched her.

'I don't know what we can put with it,' she said. 'I don't think I can be bothered to find anything. Will neat do?'

'Kate?'

She was searching for glasses by the sink and didn't bother to look round. 'Hmmm?'

'Kate, why the change?'

She stopped what she was doing and hesitated, then still without looking at him said, 'Purely selfish, I'm afraid. I don't want to be on my own, not tonight.' She turned with two glasses in her hand and avoided his eye as he came further into the room.

'I don't think there's any ice,' she said, placing the bottle on the table and sitting down. 'Never mind.' She peeled the seal off the cork, twisted it and opened the bottle. 'Let's just drink.' And pouring without ceremony, she thrust a glass towards Rory, who sat down as she took a hefty slug from her glass. 'Hmmmm.' She reached for the bottle and looked at it. 'Not bad. It's rather palatable, actually. Sort of herbal taste, a bit like a liqueur. You know, I think it's better on its own. Nice label, too. I wonder where it came from, it must be—'

'Kate?'

She looked up at him, then put the bottle down. There was a brief silence, then she said, 'You want to know what I'm going to do, don't you?'

'I think we need to talk about it at least.' He took a sip of gin. 'You've got other people to consider, Kate, and I think you need to make a decision fairly quickly; it's only fair.'

'I know.' She drained her glass and refilled it, taking another gulp before she went on. 'You'll have to bear with me,' she said. 'I did find out about all this only today, and I'm still trying to take it in. But . . .' She wetted her finger and ran it around the rim of the glass, making a high-pitched ringing sound.

Rory reached out and stopped her, placing his hand over hers. 'Kate? Talk to me.'

She took back her hand and tucked it down on her lap. 'But I have given it some thought,' she went on, 'and I think it's all rather ironic really – my life, I mean.'

Rory stared at her.

'You see, it's ironic that you went off with Alice because she was having your baby and because she desperately wanted that child, despite the fact that it ruined our happiness – and then she walked out on both of you, leaving the baby she wanted so much. Then there's Tonsbry, my inheritance, an inheritance I wasn't sure I wanted, to be honest; that I'd practically decided to sell – to someone nice, of course, who would look after the place – and then I find that it's about to be taken away from me and I can't bear the thought of that happening.' She swallowed down another mouthful of gin and plonked her glass on the table.

'Does that mean you want to keep Tonsbry?'

'I don't know!' She shook her head. 'How could I let someone like that Ingram woman waltz in here and take what Leo tried so hard to save, what he loved? They'd get it for nothing, then probably carve it up into executive apartments or something equally as ghastly and I'd still be left with a huge bank loan. God, Rory!' She reached for the bottle and poured them both another glass of gin. 'But how? *How* do I keep it? It's impossible! Some sort of business venture? Increase profit? You've pulled out virtually every trick in the book to do that already. So how do I do it?'

'I don't know, Kate. I haven't got any answers at the moment, but if that's what you want to do, then give it a go.'

'It's a hell of a risk on my own.'

He was silent for a moment, then he asked, 'What about Harry? He'll support you, won't he?'

Kate shrugged. She bit her lip, drank another slug of gin and avoided Rory's gaze.

'Kate?'

'Harry's gone,' she said flatly. 'He doesn't want to get involved.'

'Oh, I see.' Rory watched her for a while. 'Are you all right?'

She didn't answer. 'Classic,' she said finally. 'Comfort from the first man who jilted me over the second.' She shrugged. 'But I'm fine actually. You forget, I'm an old hand at broken engagements, I've been through it all before!'

'Oh, for God's sake, Kate!' Rory suddenly exploded. He'd been lulled into a false sense of security, thinking that Kate could actually be reasonable – yet two minutes into the conversation she was back carping at him, going on and on about the past. 'Are you ever going to let it go and just get on with life?' he asked.

'What do you think I've been doing for the past four years?' she snapped back. 'Certainly not crying into my soufflé.'

They glared at each other, then he noticed that she was shivering, despite the coat and the blanket. 'You're cold,' he said, his anger forgotten, 'you're shivering.'

Kate's anger was deflected too and she said, 'I think it's my feet. They got wet on the walk across the estate, and now they're like blocks of ice.'

'Here.' Rory bent and lifted one of her feet up on to his knee. She was about to pull it back but the warmth of his hands stopped her. 'God, you're not kidding, your shoes and socks are soaked.' He slipped off her shoe, rubbing her foot. 'You should take your socks off; your feet will never warm up with these on.' She shrugged, and Rory pulled up the bottom of her jeans and peeled off her wet sock, his entire body on alert, acutely conscious of the intimacy of the act. Gently he rubbed her toes in his hands, warming them. It was something he had done for her since she was a girl; it felt totally natural and at the same time so intensely erotic that he found himself holding his breath. 'The other foot, please,' he said. Kate changed legs and he repeated the action. 'Better?'

'A bit,' she answered.

Rory placed her foot on the floor and went to stand. 'I'll get you some socks from the boot-room; they'll warm your feet up instantly.'

'No,' Kate said, 'don't go anywhere.'

He looked at her, then sat down again. Bending, he

unlaced his boots, removed them and took off his socks. 'Here, then, have mine.'

She smiled. 'Old habits die hard.' She had a drawer full of Rory's borrowed socks at the flat; she'd never been able to throw them out. Taking the socks, she pulled them on and said, 'Thanks, you're right, I feel instantly warmer.' She tipped her head back and closed her eyes, suddenly quite a bit drunk.

Rory slipped his bare feet back into his boots. 'I think we need something to dilute this gin,' he said, looking at her. 'We'll be plastered otherwise.'

Kate opened her eyes and sat up. 'I'll get it.'

'No, don't worry, I can find—' They both stood up at the same time – Kate a bit wobbly on her feet from the gin, Rory with his boots undone. Inevitably they collided, Rory lost balance slightly and, as he stepped forward, he staggered out of his boots, lurching forward and grabbing whatever came to hand to stop himself from falling flat on his face. That was Kate. As they stumbled back in a kind of clumsy tango and fell against the wall, Kate found herself with Rory pressed hard against her body and closed her eyes for a moment. Then he kissed her. The kiss didn't take her by surprise, she had almost expected it, but the effect did. For a second she was so shocked by the response of her body, by the sheer physical pleasure she felt that she opened her eyes again and stared fleetingly at Rory's face.

Moments later, reality hit. Yanking her face away, she cried, 'What the hell are you doing?' And she shoved him back with such force that he crashed back against the table with an almighty thump.

'What d'you mean, what the hell am I doing?' he shouted, the blow against the corner of the table sending an intense pain up one side of his body. 'I was kissing you, and I didn't feel much resistance either!'

'Resistance? What was that then?' Kate stumbled away from him across the kitchen. 'Get out of here!' she snarled. 'Go on, get out of here!'

'Get out of here? What have I done? You invited the kiss, you made me think—'

'I did nothing of the sort! That's typical of you, isn't it? Typical! Changing things to suit you, taking advantage. God, you make me sick.' Confused and upset, Kate backed towards the wall and pressed herself into it. How could he have possibly imagined that she wanted to be kissed by him? After all that he'd done to her? 'I want you out of here, off the estate!' she shouted.

'Off the estate?'

'Yes! As soon as possible. I don't care what Leo wanted, I just want you away from me, away from here. Go on. Go!'

Rory stared at her, suddenly speechless. 'You don't mean that, Kate!'

'Of course I do! Why the hell shouldn't I?' She was so angry that she couldn't think straight. The blood pounded in her head, hammering against her skull.

Rory stood where he was, still staring at her, unable to take it in.

'Go on!' she cried. 'Get out!'

The force of her voice brought him to his senses and he bent to secure his boots, then went to get his jacket. He didn't rush, his movements showed none of the distress he felt as he took the coat off the back of the chair, pulled it on and walked across to the door which was still open; the passage outside was in darkness. He wanted to look back at Kate, just to see her face, to really convince himself that she meant it, but he didn't – his pride got in the way and he wouldn't let himself.

Without another word or the longed-for backward glance, Rory walked out of the kitchen, along the passage to the back door and was gone before Kate let out her breath.

The house was silent, eerily so, its shadows sinister and unnerving. She sank down to her feet and curled herself up. Then out of the darkness a piercing bleep cut through the chill, damp air and Kate lifted her head. She pulled herself up and lumbered along the passage, across the hall and into the study. She didn't switch on any lights, she couldn't bear to. Picking up the phone, if only to put an end to the noise, she held it to her ear and murmured, 'Yes, hello?'

'Kate? Kate darling, it's Mummy!'

There was silence and Adriana said, 'Kate, are you all right, darling?'

'No!' Kate burst out. 'No, I'm not! Everything here is awful, just awful, and I really don't know what to do.' Her anger translated to tears which streamed down her face.

'Just calm down, Kate darling, calm down.' Adriana lit a cigarette on the other end of the line and reached for her glass of wine. Having broken the habit of a lifetime by ringing Tonsbry, she was now glad that she had. 'Take a deep breath, darling,' she coaxed. 'Sit down and tell me all about it. I've known that house a long, long time and I'm absolutely sure that I'll know exactly what to do.'

An hour later, in her apartment on the Rue Raynouard in the district of Passey in Paris, Adriana began the tiresome task of packing. She hated packing for London; the English were so understated in comparison with the French, and she didn't possess that kind of clothes any longer. She would have to stock up at N. Peal as soon as she arrived and make a mercy dash to Simpsons and Harvey Nicks. It was all very bothersome, but her irritation was minor and her desire to be close to Kate, to make sure she did the right thing, overshadowed any other emotions.

Taking things out of drawers and laying them on the bed, Adriana ticked them off her list as she went along. She was a meticulous person; every last detail had to be attended to and when she did something, anything at all, she did it properly, regardless of what that might entail. When she packed she made lists: suitcase, overspill bag, hand luggage, vanity case and handbag, each piece of baggage had its own list of contents, each item on each list was collected and laid in a neat pile before being double-checked and then put in the case. Of course, usually she would have a member of staff to lay things out for her and actually pack while she managed the whole thing. But tonight she had decided to leave on the spur of the moment, again, and there was no one available for the task. As she laid out her suit to travel in, along with new stockings, shoes and underwear, she heard the front door close and hurried across the bedroom to call out to Pierre.

'Darling! I'm in the bedroom.' She listened for a few moments, heard him exchange a few words with the maid, then busied herself as she waited for him to come in. She glanced up as the door opened and said, 'Ah, Pierre darling. There you are! I tried to call you several times to let you know—'

'And where are you off to this time, Adriana?'

Adriana had the grace to blush. She stopped what she was doing and sat down on the edge of the bed. 'I had a telephone call from Kate this evening,' she said, only slightly altering the truth. 'She's in a terrible state and I think she needs me. Whilst I will not under any circumstances go to that ramshackle old house, I cannot stay in Paris. I have to go to London to be at least within driving distance. You do understand, don't you?'

Pierre took off his jacket and left it on the ottoman; someone would hang it up for him later. 'This is a rare display of motherly concern, Adriana,' he said. 'I'm very impressed.'

'There's no need to be sarcastic, Pierre! I may not be the most conscientious of parents, but I always go when I'm needed.'

Moving his jacket aside, he sat down. 'Adriana, I've only just arrived in Paris, having abandoned my holiday to follow you here. Are you expecting me to come to London as well?'

She shrugged.

'And what sort of state is Kate in? She always appeared to me to be a very competent young woman.'

'It's this bloody house!' Adriana burst out. 'Leo's left her Tonsbry, and it's turned out to be riddled with debt and Rory Gallagher.' She stood up and pressed her hands together. 'Bloody Leo! That man should never have inherited the house in the first place, he hadn't got a bloody clue! Flower gardens and loans for all sorts of stupid get-rich-quick schemes, all of which failed – spectacularly, I might add. And to cap it all he's written into the will a tenancy on the estate for Rory Gallagher of all people!

As if Kate didn't have enough to cope with, fighting loan companies and bankruptcy, she's got to face that little bastard every day as well.' Turning to her dressing-table, Adriana picked up her hairbrush. 'I told her to get rid of him,' she said, pointing the Mason Pearson at Pierre. 'And to sell the bloody place! I said I'd bail her out of all debts if she just got rid of it and him and got on with her life!'

Pierre calmly stood and took the brush from his wife before she did any damage, then sat down again as she went on.

'But she's talking about some sort of business venture, keeping the place going, and that's when I thought – I have to go, I can't let her get herself all involved and tied up in something she'll regret for the rest of her life. I said to her, I said, "Kate, I will not loan you money to make as big a fool of yourself as Leo made of himself. Get out of it while you still have the chance!" I said—'

'Adriana?'

She took a breath and looked at him.

'Adriana, you didn't tell me that Leo had left the house to Kate and not to you.'

She shrugged and turned away so that he couldn't see her face. 'It didn't seem important.' She waved her hand in the air dismissively.

But Pierre knew his wife better than she thought he did; he knew the whole history – had made it his business to find out – and he made a mental note there and then to keep a more watchful eye on her. 'Of course,' he said. 'Why should it be?'

'Exactly!' She turned back to him, her face composed, but he thought he could detect a faint trace of anger in her eyes.

'So when are you leaving?'

Adriana smiled. 'I knew you would understand.' She came across to him and bent to kiss his cheek.

'Don't I always?' he asked.

She laid her beautiful, soft and remarkably youthful hand on the side of his face. 'Yes,' she said quite truthfully, 'you do.' Then she straightened. 'So? Will you be joining me?'

But Pierre shook his head. 'Not at the moment, darling.' Adriana was easier to watch from afar. 'Perhaps in a week or so.'

'Whatever you want,' she answered and, leaving a trace of her perfume where she had touched his skin, she went back to her lists and neat piles and continued with her packing.

Chapter Eleven

Jan Ingram entered the building where Ingram Lawd had their offices, ambled across the marble lobby to the lift and called it. She was late, the lift took an age and there was a time when she might have run up the five flights of stairs to get in that few minutes earlier. But not now. Now, she carefully placed her two Harvey Nichols carrier-bags on the floor beside her, pulled out a copy of *Vogue* from one of them and finished the article she had started in the taxi on the way across town. She didn't even bother to glance at her watch. She was more than late, she had missed half the morning, but then she could afford to; it was her business.

By the time the lift arrived at the fifth floor, Jan had closed the magazine, ruffled her hair to reshape it after the chill wind outside and lightly touched up her lipstick. She walked out and into Ingram Lawd, smiled at the receptionist – another new, immaculate twenty-something – and determined that the first call she made would be to the recruitment agency. Surely they must have more mature women on their books?

She sauntered down the corridor to her office, not unaware of the fact that the place was deserted because the morning meeting was in progress, but blissfully regardless of it. She opened the door and went in, dropped her bags on the floor in front of her desk, flicked through her mail and buzzed her secretary.

'Morning, Molly. Could I have some coffee, please? No, I know I've missed it but I'm sure Duncan will let me know the salient points, thank you.' She sat down, aimlessly opened a couple of letters, glanced at the Tonsbry House file on her desk and then the phone rang. She picked it up.

'Yes, Molly? Oh, really? Yes, please, put him through.'

Smiling, Jan waited for her secretary to connect her, then said, 'Stefan! Hello, how are you?' She fiddled with the telephone wire, winding it round and round her finger. 'Yes, fine, thanks. No, I haven't, I've literally just got in but it's on my desk, I was planning to go through it a bit later.' She disentangled her finger and opened the file, giving the first page a cursory glance. 'No, no decisions yet.' She laughed. 'Of course I'm doing it to keep you hanging on. What other reason would there be?' She closed the file. 'Yes, I'll let you know, of course I will. Can I get you on the mobile number you gave me? Good.' Again she laughed. 'Well, I'm not sure I'll need the twenty-four-hour option but thanks anyway.' She reached down to her bag. 'OK, right, thanks for calling. Yes, I will, and you. Bye!'

Replacing the receiver, she reached for her bag and took out first her cigarettes, then her compact. She checked her reflection, touched the corner of her mouth with her finger-tip where her lipstick had smudged and took a cigarette from the packet. Lighting it, Jan sat back in her chair and inhaled deeply. For the first time in a long while she felt in control. Yes, she was going to look at the Tonsbry file; yes, she very probably would do something about it, but she would do it because she wanted to, because Kate Dowie had made an impression on her and because she felt that in some small way she was making up for her sense of disillusionment with the business she had created. Of course helping Stefan came into it, and spiting Duncan was an added bonus, but they weren't the reasons. One short hour on a train from London to Chartwell and the small fact that she had attracted a young man and kept him interested and entertained had gone a long way to restoring Jan's self-confidence. Life is so often made up of small gestures which have far-reaching effects, and this was one of them. As Jan heard the familiar voice and Duncan's unmistakable temper in her small outer office she actually looked up, then smiled, and that was something she would not have done a week ago.

Moments later, the door burst open and Duncan Lawd strode in.

'What the hell happened to you?' he demanded.

Jan arched a newly plucked and reshaped eyebrow. 'None of your business,' she retorted. 'But out of courtesy I will tell you. I—'

'You had your hair done!'

'How nice of you to notice.' Jan touched her glossy, coloured hair, cut for the first time in her life by an extraordinarily expensive stylist in a top London salon, and smiled. It was worth every overpriced penny for the look on his face.

'It's very short.'

'Yes.' She had had the awful, erroneous home perm cut out and a totally new, up-to-the-minute shape cut in. It suited her, in fact it took years off her and she knew it.

Armed with the haircut, she had then spent a fortune at the Bobby Brown make-up counter and far too much money on clothes: a few well-cut, designer items and six sets of outrageously sexy bras and knickers. She was wearing a set now, in sheer black, edged with lace, and even on her untoned, fuller and rather wrinkled figure she had to admit they looked fantastic. They *felt* fantastic too. What was it the woman in Rigby & Peller had said? Wearing knickers that would turn on the Pope gave you enormous confidence. Jan's smile widened. By God, she was right!

'Is something funny?' Duncan came over to the desk and perched on the edge. Jan noticed he had a slight limp.

'Nothing at all,' she answered. 'What's wrong with your leg?'

He coloured. 'Strained a muscle,' he mumbled, flicking through the pile of post she hadn't opened.

'Strained a muscle? How on earth did you do that, Duncan? The only sport you're any good at is table football.' She watched him as his colour deepened. Yesterday it might have depressed her; today it intrigued her. 'Come on, spit it out.'

He fiddled with the letters. 'Aerobics,' he murmured, not looking up.

'Aerobics!' Suddenly Jan burst out laughing.

Duncan stood up and slammed the post down on the desk. 'Go on, laugh! Just because I don't want to end up on the slag-heap like the rest of my contemporaries, just because I want to take care of myself, look good, feel good.'

'But, Duncan,' Jan cried. 'Aerobics! A shiny leotard and leopard-skin tights!' She hiccoughed and managed to bring her giggling under control. 'I mean, really, is it honestly you?'

Duncan shuffled uncomfortably from foot to foot, but his strained muscle ached so much that he had to sit down again. Jan did have a point; in fact he had hated it. He'd been twenty years older than the instructor at the front, a strapping Australian youth with bulging muscles and a black all-in-one leotard, and only a quarter as fit as the rest of the class. It wouldn't have been so bad if he hadn't done his leg in halfway through and had to limp out of the studio, puce and sweating, while the rest of them throbbed and bobbed to the beat. The instructor, the Adonis hung like King Kong, had called out, 'Cheerio, try the beginners' class next time, mate!' and Duncan had felt utterly ridiculous. Given his own way, he would happily never have repeated the whole experience. But he didn't tell Jan all this, he said, 'I was rather good at it actually,' and then picked up *Vogue* before she could question him further.

'What's this?' he asked. 'A new image for you too?'

Jan shrugged. 'Just sick of the *FT*,' she said. 'Which reminds me, what happened in the morning meeting?'

Duncan's mood changed; it was like a switch flicking on. 'The Tonsbry Estate,' he answered. 'How did you get on on Saturday? It was on the agenda this morning.'

Jan avoided his gaze. 'Fine,' she said. 'I'll have a report for you by the end of the week.'

'A report by the end of the week? Come on, Jan, you can tell me now, for God's sake!' Duncan was smiling, but it was a cold smile; she knew it well.

'There's some work to be done, some figures, that sort of thing, I—'

'You're stalling, Jan. I know all the figures, there's nothing to sort out. I want that loan foreclosed, I—'

'*You* want the loan foreclosed?'

'You know what I mean, Jan; we need that piece of business in, it won't look good if it's left outstanding . . .' Duncan glanced up as Jan's secretary came into the office without knocking.

'Coffee, Jan?' Molly edged past Duncan and placed the cup and saucer on the desk. She had been with Jan for five years and was fiercely loyal; she thought Duncan had behaved appallingly, and was in the unique position of being able to let him know that. 'Mr Vladimir something called again, Jan,' she said. 'I told him you were in a meeting and would be free in a few minutes.' She glared at Duncan as she said this, but it went over his head.

'It's Vladimar,' Jan corrected. The Polish name rolled fluently off her tongue and Duncan stared at her. She had been saying it all night, even in her sleep, so it was little wonder it sounded so good now. 'Stefan Vladimar – and if he calls again, could you put him straight through?' Molly nodded and, with a smug grin, left the room.

'I'll not keep you then,' Duncan stood, 'since you're expecting a call.' His temper was up and it showed. Jan felt a prickle of intense satisfaction. 'Jan, I want that Tonsbry business sorted quickly,' he said. 'I don't want it hanging round our necks like the proverbial albatross!'

'What's the hurry?' she asked. It was a genuine question, not just uttered to rile him. Sure, it was a big loan, but the business was well in profit; there was no panic. 'I said I'd do it by the end of the week; there isn't any reason to rush it, is there?'

'If I say we need it sorted, then we need it sorted!' Duncan suddenly snapped.

'Hold on, wait a minute!' Jan rose too, even though she

wasn't usually one to retaliate. 'Who the hell do you think you're talking to? I'm not . . .' But the phone rang and she stopped in mid-sentence. They both looked at it for a moment, then she picked it up.

'Stefan!' she exclaimed. 'Yes, yes, I did get the message. What can I do for you, we only spoke a few minutes ago.' She smiled. 'Lunch? Today?' Glancing down at her diary, she flicked to the day's page and said, 'Perfect! Where, and what time?' Duncan stood where he was for a few moments, not sure how to take this sudden change in his wife; then, not wanting to listen further to her social arrangements, he walked towards the door. He watched Jan for a short while, saw her face animated, looking younger than he'd seen it for years, then finally turned to leave. And, as he returned to his office, cross and irritated by her sudden confidence, he noticed that his strained muscle felt decidedly worse.

Rory swung the battered old Land-Rover into the back courtyard of Tonsbry House and switched off the engine.

'Flora,' he said, opening his door, 'you stay here while I just pop inside for a few minutes. I won't be—'

'No, Daddy, I want to come in and see Mrs Able.'

'I'll be two minutes, Flora.' He jumped out of the car. 'Just stay there.'

'Daddy! Pleeeease!'

Rory sighed, tutted irritably, then slammed his door shut and walked round to the back passenger door. He opened it, unclipped Flora's car seat and helped her out. 'Why am I so nice to you, young lady?'

But Flora ignored him as she jumped down and ran towards the house, shrieking, 'Mrs Able? Mrs Able!' She had disappeared inside before he even had time to blink.

'Flora!' Kate turned from washing-up in the sink as Flora scrambled into the room and darted across to Mrs Able. She had a stinking hangover, the beginnings of a chill, and felt thoroughly upset, confused and wretched.

'Hello, Flora dear,' said Mrs Able, relieved to have the morose atmosphere in the kitchen lightened for a few moments. 'How pretty you look in that dress!'

'It's a pinafore skirt, not a dress.'

'Oh, pardon me.' Mrs Able smiled. 'Well, it's very nice, whatever it is. Shouldn't you be at nursery?'

'No. Daddy and I are packing.'

'Packing?' The housekeeper looked across at Kate, who shrugged.

'Yes,' Flora went on, oblivious to Mrs Able's distress. 'I've had to put all my toys in a big plastic bag, and Daddy says that I can choose three books and keep pink teddy out to go in my case but everything else, all my clothes as well, they all have to go in the bags.' Flora spread her arms. 'We've got tons of them . . .' She looked at Mrs Able with her arms outstretched. 'This many. Are there any cakes?'

'Of course, dearie, I'll get the tin.' She crossed to the cupboard near Kate and said again, 'Packing? What's going on, Kate?'

Kate flushed. She was about to offer some sort of pallid excuse when there was the sour scrape of a chair across the stone floor up to the sink. 'Can I help you?' a small voice asked.

'Oh . . . yes, why not?'

Flora climbed up on the chair next to Kate at the sink and started to roll up her sleeves.

'Shall I help?' Kate asked.

'Yes, please.'

She pushed the sleeves up above Flora's elbows.

'Thank you,' said Flora. She plunged her hands into the warm soapy water and reached for a mop.

'Where's your father?' Mrs Able asked Flora. She was worried and kept glaring across at Kate for some answers.

'Dunno.' Flora looked at Kate and pulled a face. 'He's been ever so grumpy today and he's still wearing the same clothes he had on yesterday. Yeuch! His feet smell, pooheee!' Despite her mood, Kate smiled. 'He says this is an adventure; I like adventures, do you?'

Flora turned her full gaze on Kate, a small pointed face with clear questioning eyes, and Kate had the sudden memory of herself at that age, always on an adventure with her father, moving house, staying with friends, looked after by countless foreign girls with no interest in her and no language skills. She nodded and said, 'I had lots of adventures when I was a little girl,' but she said it with a heavy heart, weighed down by the memory of it.

'Hello, Rory love,' said Mrs Able and Kate spun round. 'D'you want some tea?'

'No, thanks. I just called in to see Kate.'

Again Kate flushed. Flora had been right, Rory still had on yesterday's clothes and by the look of him he had slept in them – if he'd slept at all, that was.

'Kate, I'd like to talk to you,' he said, 'in private. Could you mind Flora for me, Mrs Able?'

'Of course.'

'Kate?'

Kate glanced down at Flora, nodded, dried her hands on a tea-towel and turned from the sink.

'Where're you going?' Flora called out.

'To Leo's study. I won't be long,' Rory answered.

Flora shrugged. 'OK then.'

He opened the door, waited for Kate and went out after her. As he closed it behind them, he heard Flora say, 'I've had enough washing-up now, Mrs Able. Can I have a cake, please?' And he found that he had a terrible ache in his chest at the thought of her.

In Leo's study, Kate stood by the desk and waited for Rory. None of the anger she had felt last night had survived. Confusion, yes, and misery, but the blind fury had burned itself out and in its place was left a sadness which draped her like a cloak. She turned, looked at his face as he came in and thought immediately of Flora.

'Kate, I wanted you to know that I packed up last night and I've made arrangements to leave today.'

'Oh, I—'

'I've got all the house accounts, ledgers, legal files and so on in the boot of the Land-Rover,' he went on, not giving her a chance to speak. 'I'll bring those in for you and if I can use the Land-Rover to move our stuff out, then I'll return the keys along with the cottage keys a bit later on this afternoon. Is that all right?'

Kate nodded numbly and he took a breath. 'However, before I go, I want to say something. I'd like you to hear me out and think about what I've said; that's all I ask. Is that OK?'

Again she nodded. She had begun to feel very cold and wrapped her arms around her body.

'Kate, last night I had an idea. It's to do with Tonsbry and starting a small business on the estate. Now look,' he dug his hands in his pockets and avoided her gaze, 'I know you don't want me in your life – you've made that very clear and I understand, I accept it – but this idea, if it's feasible, then I would really like to have a go at it.'

Kate opened her mouth to speak but Rory held up his hands to silence her. 'I know what you're going to say, but I've thought it all through. You wouldn't have to see me at all, you could go back to London and leave me to get on with it. I wouldn't live here; I could find rooms for me and Flora in the village, or maybe go home to the vicarage for a while, and you wouldn't have to get involved at all once you've given the go-ahead.' He moved a pace forward and instinctively Kate took a step back. 'I wouldn't be doing this to muscle in on your life, Kate, honestly I wouldn't; I'd be doing it for Leo, because Leo loved this house and because . . . well, because Leo was very kind to me when I needed it and . . .' He broke off. There was a silence. 'And well, because I think it's a bloody good idea and it could work.' He glanced at her briefly, then looked away.

Kate felt behind her for the chair and sat down. 'Can you tell me what this idea is?'

'I can, but I think I need to go away and talk to some people first. If it's feasible, and I should know by this afternoon, we could discuss it then.'

She stared down at her hands and through the silence she heard a little voice saying 'Daddy says this is an adventure' over and over again.

'Will you give it a chance, Kate?'

Kate looked up. 'Yes,' she said, 'of course.'

Rory nodded. Inside his pockets, he relaxed his hands. He turned to go.

'You know, I've been trying to work out why Leo left this house to me and not my mother,' Kate said, and he turned back. 'For the past few days it's gone on and on in my head, and just now I realised the reason.' She dropped her gaze back to her hands. 'When I was a child, after my mother left, my father and I were always on the move, especially in the school holidays, to friends, relatives or guest-houses. You see, my father's rooms in college were no place for a little girl for long periods of time and he was always trying to farm me out. "Adventures" he called them. We didn't have a home, not really, not like most people. And then Leo found us. I was six, and from the first weekend here I always had my own room; this was my house. Leo never went anywhere, he was always here, and I think he knew what a difference that made to my life as a child.' Kate smiled, just for a moment. 'Of course as I got older and I saw more of my mother, Tonsbry featured less, but I suppose Leo always saw it as my home.' She faced Rory again. 'How could I not fight for that? My home. And Flora's home, too.' Rory recognised the apology. 'Look, even if this idea doesn't work,' Kate went on, 'don't move Flora, keep her where she is until we know what to do with the house.' She stood up, all trace of emotion gone, and said, 'OK?'

'Yes, OK,' Rory answered. 'Thank you.' He didn't add anything else, he saw no necessity. 'I'll come back after lunch, shall I?'

'Yes.'

And without another word, he turned and left Kate alone in the study.

For lunch, Stefan had picked a restaurant he had never been to before; it was important to him, to start all this on new ground. He arrived early, took his seat by the window and waited for Jan. He had been in the escort business for two and a half years now, he'd seen more than most and nothing much fazed him, but he had to admit to a certain nervousness today. This was the second date with Jan in less than forty-eight hours; it was something he rarely did and he was looking forward to it with an almost boyish excitement. Hence the nerves. Also, he hadn't told her what he did for a living – he hadn't found the right moment, and he wasn't sure that he would. Jan was beginning to look a little more than a business proposition and, if he was honest with himself, helping Kate was now just an excuse.

Glancing round for a waiter, he decided to order a bottle of wine, something else he rarely did at lunch-time, and spotted Jan as she walked into the restaurant. He stood to wave, saw her smile and felt an immediate sense of relief that she was here. She came across, he pulled out a chair for her and she sat down.

'You look fantastic!' were the first words he uttered.

'I feel it,' she replied. 'It's amazing what spending tons of money will do for morale!' They both laughed as the waiter materialised to take their order.

'Would you like some wine?'

'I'd love some.'

'White? A Chardonnay?'

'Perfect.'

Stefan glanced briefly at the wine-list and made his choice. He had become adept at wine-lists, it was part of the job; women liked him to order for them.

'So?'

Jan slipped off her coat. 'So,' she said.

'You got home all right on Saturday, then?'

'Yes.'

'Good.' They both smiled and Stefan went on, 'I really enjoyed Saturday, regardless of all that happened with

Kate.' And he had, it wasn't just part of the professional patter. The train journey back had led to dinner, and the few hours they'd spent together were some of the best Stefan could remember.

'So did I.' They fell into silence but it was a comfortable one, without any necessity to speak. Jan took out her cigarettes, lit one and blew the smoke out of the side of her mouth. It was an ordinary gesture which Stefan found incredibly erotic.

'So,' he said again.

Jan smiled. 'So what?' The waiter appeared with the wine and interrupted them. Having poured it, he left the bottle in a cooler and placed menus in front of them. Jan ignored hers, took a sip of her wine and said, 'The loan, on Tonsbry House and Estate?'

Stefan was genuinely surprised. It wasn't that he had forgotten, it was just that it hadn't seemed right to mention it yet.

'What about it?' he asked.

'Well, there's something awry there,' Jan said. 'I think Duncan is plotting. He wants the business settled instantly and got in a real flap about it when I stalled him, which indicates to me that he's got something up his sleeve.'

'Like what?'

'Oh, I don't know, a potential buyer, development plans, it could be anything, Stefan. He's a very shrewd operator.'

Stefan touched her hand. 'Not that shrewd.'

'Thanks. Anyway, I've decided to postpone things, until I find out what's going on.'

'You have? How?'

'I thought I'd misplace the file, temporarily.' She ground

out her cigarette and opened the menu. 'Well, for a few weeks anyway – give Kate Dowie a chance to sort herself out. That is what you wanted, isn't it?'

'What?'

'For me to hold things up a bit?'

Stefan at least had the grace to look embarrassed. 'Well, yes, but—'

'I thought so.' And despite the fact that Jan had been preparing herself for this moment, despite the fact that she had not been under any illusions as to the purpose of all this, she couldn't help feeling disappointed. She stared down at the menu to avoid looking at Stefan.

'Jan?'

She was expecting hearty thanks, so didn't bother to look up.

'Jan, there was a but,' he said. She was concentrating on the starters, thinking she might as well get a decent lunch out of it. 'I was going to say: but it isn't the reason we're having lunch, or the reason I had such a good time on Saturday night.'

She continued to stare at the words on the menu.

'Jan, look at me, will you?'

Finally she raised her head. 'Look.' Stefan hesitated for a moment. 'Jan, are you really hungry or can we just skip lunch and go home to bed?'

For a second the excitement was such a jolt that Jan thought her whole body had seized up. Then immediately reality struck. So this was one favour for another, she thought – and it made her feel old, pathetic and insulted. 'Thanks for the offer, Stefan,' she said, snatching up her cigarettes and stuffing them into her bag, 'but lunch would have been enough.' She stood, pulled on her coat and –

before he could say a word, or even reach out to stop her from leaving – she turned tail and fled.

'Jan!' he called after her. 'Jan!' But there was no point, she had left the restaurant. 'Shit!' Stefan said aloud. He sat there stunned for several minutes, then he got up, left a £20 note on the table for the wine and walked out of the restaurant. Outside he looked up and down the road to see if he could spot Jan, but there was no sign of her; she had gone. Tucking his hands in his pockets, he made his way up towards the tube, then saw a free taxi-cab and flagged it down. 'Pimlico, please,' he said, climbing in. But for once, the thought of going home alone thoroughly depressed him.

Kate was in the study when Rory arrived back at the house that afternoon. She had been trying to read, without success, and trying not to think about what might or might not be about to happen. She was confused, still upset and had a constant nagging in the pit of her stomach which, if she hadn't known better, she might have called excitement. She heard Rory come in, talk to Mrs Able for a few minutes and then cross the hall towards her. She tried to gauge his mood from the tone of his voice but was unable to; he spoke quietly, as he always did, and she could pick up nothing.

'Kate?' He was there in the doorway as she looked up, and she caught her breath at the familiarity of him.

'I'm sorry I'm a bit late, I got held up, but it wasn't wasted time.' He crossed to the desk and plonked two carrier-bags on top of it before taking off his coat and hanging it over the back of the chair. He started to lift bottles out of the bags and line them up on the desk. 'Are you OK? You look tired.'

'I'm fine!' Kate snapped. Rory looked up. She felt a flash of irritation but didn't know if it was directed at him or herself.

'Good.' He turned all the labels on the bottles to face them and stood back for a moment. 'I found a still on the estate,' he said.

'A still?'

'Yes, it was used for making gin about forty years ago.'

'Where?'

'Where what?'

'Where did you find it?'

'In one of the outbuildings, next to an old store-room. It's not that far from the house actually, which would make perfect sense of course.'

'What would?'

'I'll tell you in a minute.'

Kate was beginning to get agitated as Rory crossed the room to the sideboard and picked up two whisky tumblers. 'I had a hunch it'd be there – more than a hunch really, I was pretty certain, once I'd looked into it.'

'Rory?'

'Hmmm?' He had brought over the glasses and was unscrewing bottle tops. 'Right. Come over here, Kate.'

She stood where she was. 'Rory, what's this all about?'

'I'll tell you in a minute. Come on, come over here.'

Sourly Kate crossed and stood beside him.

'OK,' he began, taking the top off the first bottle. 'Oh, wait – we need a spittoon, or we'll be plastered.'

He went to the sideboard, took out a tankard and said, 'This will do.' Back at the desk, he poured the first measure. 'A standard brand-name gin,' he said. 'Sip it.'

Kate took it, sniffed it, then said, 'Rory, for goodness'

sake! Tell me what's going on! Is this some kind of a joke?'

'No, no joke and all in good time. First we taste the gins, then we go from there. OK?'

'No, it's not OK, but . . .' Kate sipped, rolled the flavours round her mouth, then spat it out. 'Gin,' she said. 'So what?'

'You'll see in a minute,' Rory answered, pouring her a measure from the next bottle. 'Here.'

She took it, sipped it, let the taste develop and then spat it out. 'That one is nicer; what is it?'

'It's Bombay Sapphire. A nice, exclusive and expensive gin. Here.' He poured a third measure. 'Supermarket gin.'

Kate tasted, then almost immediately spat it out. 'Tastes like it!' she said.

Finally Rory poured the last measure. 'Tonsbry Original,' he said. Kate sipped, held it in her mouth, rolled it round and then swallowed. 'Nice.' She held out her glass. 'Can I have another tot?'

Rory poured her one, then a second for himself and they both sipped. 'It *is* nice,' Kate said. 'It's very nice, smooth and almost herbal.'

Rory swallowed his drink and picked up the bottle. 'Kate,' he said, 'I think we may have something here.' He ran his fingers over the blue etched glass down to the label. 'I really think . . .' Then he stopped and put the bottle back on the desk. 'Right, the facts,' he said, reaching into one of the carrier-bags. He took out a brown envelope, pulled out a fold of papers and smoothed them flat on the desk. 'The gin we're drinking, Tonsbry Original, was made and bottled right here on the estate up until 1959. Early on this century it was apparently quite common for country estates to distil and bottle their own gin, and Tonsbry was no exception. There was a small industry going here and, according to some records my father found, in 1947 over five thousand bottles a year were produced.'

'Is that all?'

'Is that all! Kate, that was incredible! Don't forget we're talking about 1947, post-war, and a small local distillery. Anyway, I was talking to my father and he says he can remember it quite well as a boy; it was a very popular drink, it sold for miles around and some bottles even sold up in London. Your grandfather apparently hired a master distiller from one of the big gin companies when he took over the distillery and, according to village myth, that chap discovered some sort of secret ingredient that made the gin really special. He—'

'Rory,' Kate interrupted, 'this is all very interesting, but where is it leading us?'

'It's leading us—' Rory stopped, took both of Kate's hands in his, then said, 'Kate, I know this is going to sound bizarre, but just hear me out, OK?'

She frowned, uncertain and uncomfortable with his touch.

'OK?' he insisted.

'OK,' she agreed, gently pulling her hands away.

'Right, well this morning I found a still, right?'

'Yes, but—'

'No buts, just listen. According to my father, the still I found is very probably, even today, in good working order. Apparently they were solidly built, and he says there's not much you can do to a still to destroy it apart from dismantle it. So . . .' Rory paused for breath, but not for long; he was really fired up about this. 'What we have here on the estate is the basic tools and a hell of a lot of potential for restarting the Tonsbry distillery.' He picked up the bottle of Tonsbry Original again. 'Kate, this stuff is amazing! It's easy to drink, looks sophisticated and trendy and we've got the licence to make it!'

'To make it?' Kate burst out. 'Rory, are you suggesting that you go into gin production?'

'Yes! What else did you think . . .'

'I thought, when you said restart the Tonsbry distillery that you meant a museum, not a bloody gin factory!' Kate walked away, then turned and came back. 'Rory, you cannot be serious! You were right, this is bizarre.' She shook her head. 'In fact it's the most bizarre thing I've ever heard. What in God's name do you know about distilling gin?'

'But that's just it!'

'What's just it?'

'I don't need years of experience or knowledge, I've got my father!'

'Your father?' This wasn't just bizarre, it was bordering on the realms of surreal. 'What does the Reverend Gallagher have to do with making gin?'

'Not gin necessarily, but home-brewing and pretty much everything actually. That's why I'm so late. He can talk for hours on the subject – he's been doing it for years.'

'Oh, Rory, this is ridiculous!' Kate cried, stomping across to the window. She stood with her back to him, looking out and trying to calm down.

'No, Kate,' he said, 'it isn't ridiculous, it isn't ridiculous at all. D'you think I'd have mentioned it to you if I hadn't thought it through? Christ, Kate, this is exactly the sort of thing Leo and I had been searching for months back and never found! And if we hadn't discovered that old bottle of gin last night and drunk it, then we might still be searching.'

Kate stared at him, not even half convinced.

'Don't you see,' he went on, 'it's almost fate, the way we found the gin last night; it's as if it were meant to happen and everything's there for us, it's—'

'It's crazy, Rory!' Kate said. 'That's what it is. Crazy!' She walked back to the desk and picked up the sheaf of papers, glancing through them. 'OK,' she said, 'let's just say that I did think it was a good idea, what then? Hmmm? No—' She held up her hand to stop him speaking. 'I'll tell you, shall I? Firstly, if the still you found was still operational, and by some fluke you managed to find a manufacturer who made glass bottles like this, and your father had sufficient knowledge to be able to make gin, what about the recipe? What went into Tonsbry gin that made it taste so special? Second, what if you even found the recipe and managed to produce this stuff, where would you sell it and how? Where's the money for marketing, advertising? What do you know about the drinks market? Third and most important, how long would all this take? Months, years? Doesn't gin have to be matured, like whisky, in barrels for several years? I haven't got years, Rory, I haven't even got months. I need a project that could be up and running in a matter of weeks. I need—'

'You need this, Kate!' Rory said. 'Look.' He took the papers from her and put them back on the desk. 'Gin is ready to drink once it's made, there's no maturing period. If the still works, then I clean it and get in a store-load of fuel. My father thinks it's probably coal-run. Then I get in the basic ingredients . . .'

'Which are?'

Rory reached for the papers and rifled through them, then said, 'Which are: grain spirit at roughly ninety pence per litre plus the botanicals, and these are juniper, coriander, angelica root, orange peel, lemon peel or cinnamon and of course whatever else it is that makes Tonsbry so special. Add to that a cost for heating, bottling and packaging, all of which I'd have to work to keep right down, but . . .' He pulled out another sheet of paper with some figures on it. 'I reckon I could produce Tonsbry gin at somewhere between a pound and one-fifty per litre, then add on packaging and marketing, but I also reckon I could sell it for between twenty and thirty pounds for a seventy centilitre bottle.'

'Thirty pounds for a bottle of hooch! Rory, that's ludicrous.'

'Maybe, but that's what some of these really trendy brands sell for. It's all image, Kate, and if I get that right, then who knows?'

'You have done your homework, haven't you?'

Rory glanced up, not sure if she was being sarcastic, but Kate smiled and he smiled back. 'Actually,' he said, 'I was up all night thinking about it.'

'I see.' Now it was Kate's turn to pick up the bottle. She ran her fingers over the name 'Tonsbry Original' etched into the glass. 'Where would we sell it?' she asked.

Rory felt a surge of triumph: 'We.' Kate was interested. 'What about starting with the people you sell sandwiches to in the City?' he replied. 'Give a few bottles away free and put the word out that we can sell direct from here and deliver. We could also target some of the more trendy bars, but I'm absolutely positive that, if we got that far, the selling wouldn't be a problem.'

'If we got that far . . .' Kate murmured. She continued to gaze at the bottle, then suddenly she said, 'What about the loan? And what about a licence?'

'The estate has a licence already; it's expired, but my father rang someone in Customs and Excise at lunch-time and they don't think it'll be too difficult to renew it. The loan . . .' Rory shrugged. 'That's what we've really got to sort out before we do anything else. That, and finding the recipe.'

Kate put down the bottle. 'I don't know, Rory, it all just sounds so complicated.'

'What did you expect? Nothing is easy, Kate, this isn't a get-rich-quick scheme, it's a proper business venture.'

'Would it cost much to get going? I mean, would we have to buy in a lot of raw materials?'

'No, not to start with, we could buy in small quantities and see how we get on. Look . . .' Rory held up his hands. 'Why don't we make a start on researching this recipe, and if we find it then we'll go from there?'

Kate hesitated. Everything in her head said: don't get involved, take your mother's advice, get out now before you get hurt. Her mother had even offered to get Pierre to pay up the remainder of the debt if she let Tonsbry go. And yet everything in her heart willed her to go with it, willed her to fight and at least give it a chance. There was a silence. Rory said nothing, too frightened that any word from him now would sway her in the opposite direction. Then finally, Kate nodded. 'OK,' she said, 'I'll give it a try.'

'Right, come on, then,' he said, careful to cover any emotion. 'Let's get looking.' He walked across to the bookshelves and pulled the library steps along to where he wanted to start. 'You ring your friend and find out if he managed any results from the Ingram woman, and I'll go through the book collection.' He glanced back at her and smiled, a friendly, nothing-hidden sort of smile. 'It's bound to be here,' he said, 'I'm sure of it.' And climbing up the steps, he began looking on the top shelf, with an old copy of the Tonsbry household accounts.

Chapter Twelve

Jan arrived back at Ingram Lawd mid-afternoon, having taken a long walk through Hyde Park and stopped for a coffee in a smart patisserie off Knightsbridge. She had been gone for nearly three hours and she felt calmer but still upset; walking into her office, the first thing she did was buzz Molly and ask her to hold all calls. The next thing she did was to get out the Tonsbry House file. She sat with it in front of her for some time before opening it, thinking about lunch, about Stefan and about herself. 'So much for the new confident me!' she muttered under her breath. 'One proposition and I scarper like a frightened deer.' She smiled. Hardly a deer, dear, more like a sad old doe.

Jan opened the file but her mind was far from it. Had she overreacted? she wondered. She had to admit that bed with Stefan had crossed her mind more than once or twice in the past forty-eight hours, so why had it come as such a shock? Had he really meant to trade favours? Or was it a simple case of I like you, you like me, let's do it? Jan flushed at this thought and hastily glanced down at the file. The words swam, she continued to dwell on her thoughts.

Maybe she was kidding herself that she was getting

involved in this business because she wanted to; maybe it was the same old situation, falling for the same old line. Was she really prepared to chuck in her business sense, upset Duncan, upset the way they did things – had always done things – in order to take a moral high ground that she had never been interested in before? Or was it just for the sake of an affair? Jan really didn't know, and the hour in Hyde Park had done nothing to enlighten her.

Closing the file, she slipped it into her drawer. She had told Stefan she would lose it for a couple of weeks, and that's exactly what she intended to do. She had promised herself that she would look into it thoroughly to see what, if anything, Duncan might be up to, and any more than that she couldn't think about right now. Right now she was going to finish off some work, smoke a cigarette and then go home.

Kate sat on the floor of the study with the telephone by her legs, her head in her hands. It was virtually dark outside, but she and Rory hadn't lit the lamps. They worked by the light of the fire, as if turning on the lights would signal the length of time they had been looking already, with no results. She picked up the receiver one more time and dialled Stefan's number. There was no reply. Dropping it back in its cradle, she said, 'No news from Stefan on the loan, and no recipe. We've been at it for a couple of hours now, Rory. I'm beginning to think it's all a bit hopeless.'

Rory closed the huge old-fashioned ledger he was reading and looked across at her. 'Kate, the fact is that there was gin produced at Tonsbry, I've got all the figures and dates and stuff right here.' He held up the ledger. 'And that means that there has to be a record somewhere of *how* it was made.' He smiled reassuringly. 'There *has* to be, Kate, I'm sure of it.'

Kate shrugged. She wanted to believe him, had begun to feel almost desperate to do so, but still she couldn't get her head round it. 'Well . . .' She stood up and walked across to the fire to stretch her legs. 'Of course, recipe or not, there won't be any sort of business if we aren't able to get a bit of help from that Ingram woman.'

'I'm sure your friend is doing his best.'

'Hmmm. What time did I leave that message? I wonder if he's got it yet? Perhaps I shouldn't keep hanging up, maybe I should leave another message, say we're waiting to . . .' Kate stopped as the phone rang. 'That'll be him!' She moved quickly back to the desk and grabbed the receiver. 'Hello?' Rory watched her as her face fell and a voice on the other end said, 'Kate, darling? How are you?'

'Oh, Mummy, hi, I'm fine.'

'You don't sound fine, darling, you sound positively suicidal! Look, I rang to tell you that I'm in London, arrived this morning, and I've got a suite here at the Langham Hilton. Why don't you leave that rat-infested place and come up to town tomorrow? You can stay with me here, there's no need to go back to your poky little flat – let me pamper you for a few days? We could shop, have some treatments –'

'Thanks, Mummy, but I can't.' Kate's face set in defiance. 'I can't leave at the moment, and Tonsbry isn't rat-infested nor is my flat poky.'

Adriana laughed lightly. 'No offence, darling I only meant that there's tons of space here – and of course you can leave, you can desert the place any time you like, and no one would think any the worse of you.' She paused and Kate heard her take a sip of wine. 'What on earth is there to stay for anyway?' There was a faint, steely edge to her voice.

'Gin,' said Kate.

'Gin?' Adriana laughed again. 'Dear girl, what on earth do you mean?'

'Do you remember ever hearing of a gin being made on the estate, Mummy?'

There was a short silence on the other end, then Adriana said, 'Possibly. Why?' The 'why' was sharp and demanding; Kate tensed.

'Well . . .' She hesitated, unsure of Adriana's reaction. 'The thing is, we've found a still on the estate, in good working order, and we're thinking of trying to set it up again to manufacture a specialist gin.'

'To manufacture gin?' Adriana cried. 'Are you completely stupid?' Kate winced; she had been right to be hesitant.

Adriana's temper exploded. 'What in God's name are you thinking of, Kate? Manufacture *gin*! You don't know the first thing about brewing, you can't possibly enter into something like that, it's ridiculous! I won't let you, Kate, it's a recipe for disaster. You'll set it all up, incur more and more debt and it'll fail, spectacularly, just like every other pathetic little venture of Leo's. And who's "we" by the way? Who on earth put you up to this hare-brained scheme in the first place?'

'Er . . .'

'Is it that crackpot boyfriend of yours, the one from the Army who hasn't got two brains to rub together?'

'No, no, it's no one you know, it's . . .'

'It's Rory Gallagher, isn't it?' Adriana snarled. 'It is, isn't it? Go on, admit it!'

'Yes! All right, it's Rory but—'

'But what? There are no buts, Kate, he saw you coming! How you can consider even being in the same room with that toad, let alone going into business, I don't know. It's beyond me, Kate, it really is! I've a good mind to come down there and drag you by your hair out of that horrible house and away from any more stupid mistakes.'

'But I don't think this is a mistake,' Kate said, finding a slither of nerve to cling to. 'I think it's worth a try, I really do.'

'Oh, do you? Well, you mark my words, young lady, you'll fail – you'll lose money hand over fist and you'll end up in big trouble! And I will not bail you out. Not this time . . .'

'You've never bailed me out!' Kate suddenly cried. 'I've never asked for your help and I have no intention of failing.'

'Give it up, Kate,' Adriana hissed through clenched teeth. 'Just stop this nonsense now and sell the bloody place! Get rid of it.'

Kate was silent.

'Did you hear me, Kate?' Adriana's voice rose and even Rory heard her. Still Kate said nothing. 'If you don't answer me, Kate, I shall hang up now!' Adriana threatened. There was a brief silence, then a click and, moments later, the line went dead.

Kate replaced the receiver, then slumped down on a chair. 'She's right, you know,' she said. 'This is a stupid idea. We'll never do it, never.' She stared down at her hands and Rory closed the book he was looking at. That's it then, he thought, it's over before it even started; a fitting epitaph for us, Kate and me. He stood, crossed to the window and looked out as the silence in the room deepened.

'But,' Kate said suddenly, getting to her feet and taking up the ledger Rory had left on the floor, 'we can have a bloody good try, can't we?' And turning from the window, Rory saw her grim, defiant smile.

Duncan stood outside Jan's office and knocked lightly on the door. She called out and he went in. It irked him to do so, but she had told him earlier that she would no longer talk to him unless he respected her privacy. They were separated, she'd said coldly, and that meant at the office as well as at home.

'Is it all right to talk?' he asked archly.

'Not particularly. Do I have any choice?'

'No.' But despite his bravado Duncan stood just inside the door, unwilling to come right into the room. For the first time in years, he was not quite sure of his position.

'I haven't made up my mind about the Tonsbry Estate yet, if that's what you want to know,' Jan told him. 'I think it needs some careful thought. I'm not happy about just foreclosing on the loan for the sake of it, Duncan; I don't know that it's in the best interests of the company.'

'In the best interests of the company?' Duncan exclaimed. 'Since when did you decide what is and isn't in the best interests of the company? I think you're rather overstepping the mark here, Jan.'

'Am I?'

'Perhaps you've forgotten who owns fifty-one per cent of this company!'

'And perhaps *you're* forgetting that I still own forty-nine per cent!' Jan snapped. 'That makes me pretty important, especially when it comes to potential buyers.'

'Whoa!' Duncan held up his hands. He swallowed hard, glanced away for a few moments and by the time he looked back at Jan he had composed a smile on his face. It was a smile that made her shiver. 'Jan,' he said, 'don't you think you are being a little over-zealous about all this?' He came into the room and stood over the desk so that she had to look up at him. 'I realise that you've been flattered by this so-called admirer, and I also realise that it's a very long time since anyone took any interest in you, but . . .' He shrugged. 'I shouldn't let it go to your head if I were you.' He smiled again and Jan saw the venom in his eyes. 'It's all rather sad, really, thinking that you're more important than you are. You surely don't think that a man so much younger than you—'

'How do you know he's younger?'

'A shrewd guess, my darling. The hair, the make-up, all this effort.' He laughed and shook his head. 'Come on, Jan, what would a young, virile man find attractive about a woman your age?'

'I'll tell you, shall I?'

Duncan jerked round.

'Stefan!' Jan cried. 'What on earth—' She broke off, knowing this wasn't the time to reveal any more than she absolutely had to.

Stefan was leaning against the door-frame. He wore a dark blue Paul Smith suit with a pale indigo shirt unbuttoned at the neck and brown suede crêpe-soled loafers. He looked immaculate; he took her breath away. 'She's clever, funny and far more exciting than a woman half her age.' He stood upright and came across to the desk.

'Oh, and then there's the sex.' He smiled at Jan. 'Stefan Vladimar,' he said, holding out his hand to Duncan.

Duncan took it, his smile fixed on his face, and said, 'Well, there's no accounting for taste, is there?' He dropped Stefan's hand within seconds and turned towards the door.

'Jan, I don't expect any further delay on that matter we discussed,' he remarked. 'You'll let me have the file in the morning, I take it?'

Jan made no reply. She sat where she was and looked the other way.

'Good. Right, well, Mr . . . ?'

'Vladimar,' Stefan repeated.

'Yes, that's it, Mr Vladimar. Goodbye, nice to make your acquaintance.' And without saying anything further, he walked out of the room.

Stefan turned to Jan. 'Was that the—'

'Husband, soon-to-be-ex-husband, yes,' she said. 'It was. Nice, isn't he?'

'Very, but rather misguided,' Stefan answered. 'You all right?'

Jan nodded, then she dropped her head in her hands and covered her face for a few moments. There was something about Duncan's ridicule that really got to her; perhaps it was the disappointment that after so many years he could behave in that way, perhaps it was the fact that he was always so close to the mark. Clearing her throat of tears, she looked up again and said, 'Your timing was perfect, Stefan, thank you.'

He shrugged.

'What are you doing here, by the way?'

'I couldn't get through on the phone and I couldn't leave it the way we did after lunch.'

'No.'

He dug his hands in his pockets. 'Look, I also wanted to say that I shouldn't have behaved like that at lunch-time, it was rude and I offended you. I'm sorry.'

Jan didn't answer.

'About this loan business . . .'

She braced herself.

'When I left Tonsbry just after you, I had an idea that I could help Kate in some way, I don't know how – maybe by getting you involved, asking you to help, but . . .' He moved closer to the desk. 'Can I sit down?'

Jan nodded and he perched on the edge. 'But I'm not in this for what I can get out of it. I like you, as mad as it may sound after only forty-eight hours, but there you are. I'd like to see you again and if I can persuade you to help Kate then all well and good, but if I can't . . . well, so be it.' He sighed, then said, 'Phew, I think that's the longest speech I've ever made!'

She smiled. 'Well, I'm sorry too. I acted like an idiot, running off like that. Anyway, what I said on the loan business still stands; it's as much as I can do at the moment, and it's as much in my interest as anyone else's. OK?'

Stefan nodded. He was about to reach out and touch her face, but Jan anticipated the move and bent to get her cigarettes out of her bag. When she had straightened and lit up, Stefan said, 'A month. Give it a month.'

She smoked in silence. He did have a point. A month would give Kate Dowie a chance to put together a business proposal and decide if she wanted to appeal, and it would give Jan a chance to take her time looking into the whole business. It would also give her time with Stefan, to make up her mind whether or not she wanted to get involved. She flicked her ash. Hardly the most professional of decisions, she thought, but then had Duncan been professional when he'd rogered his secretary?

'OK,' she answered. 'A month.' And before she could back away, Stefan leaned forward and kissed her.

It was nearing midnight, the fire was dying and the study was growing cold when the phone rang. Rory took the call. Kate looked up from a huge file of old papers, half listened to the conversation, then went back to what she was doing.

'That was your friend Stefan,' Rory said. He crossed to her, then squatted down where she was sitting. 'He's got us a month to sort things out.'

Kate kept her head down and chewed her fingernail.

'It's better than nothing, Kate. It'll give us a chance to get things up and running, in the initial stages at least, and we can put together a pretty decent business proposal in that time.'

She nodded but still didn't answer him. He stood and stretched, wondering if they ought to jack it in for the night, then suddenly she called out and he spun round.

'It's here!' she cried. 'I've got it! Cornflower gin, in brackets "Tonsbry Original Dry London Gin". This is it! There's a list of ingredients and measures and loads of figures and stuff. Look!' She jumped up and held it out for Rory. 'I don't believe it! I've actually found it!'

Rory took the file and looked down at the hand-written notes, pages of them, then up at Kate. He grinned. 'Well done, Katie,' he said. 'Bloody well done!' And, unable to stop himself, he put out his arms and scooped her into a hug. But it was a mistake; he shouldn't have done it. The past reared its monstrous head again and, struggling against him, Kate suddenly pushed him violently away.

'Don't, Rory!' she snapped. 'Don't do that, please.'

She moved across the room, putting as much distance as she could between them and he said, 'I'm sorry, it was automatic, I just . . .'

'You have no right to touch me!' she said angrily. 'If we are going to work together, then I am prepared to bury my feelings for the present, but that doesn't mean I've forgotten them. Is that clear, Rory?'

He gritted his teeth; she was speaking to him like a child.

'I really can't do it if you don't understand that one simple point,' she emphasised.

'OK,' he agreed, suddenly very weary. 'I understand.' He picked his coat off the back of the chair and headed for the door. 'Look, we're both tired, I'll go now and we'll sort things out in the morning. OK?'

'Yes.'

'I'll see you tomorrow, then?'

'Yes,' she said again.

'Right.' Rory stepped out into the cold hall and glanced back at her. 'Bye.'

She nodded. And not knowing what else to say, he waved, attempted a pathetic half-smile and left her alone. Then he made his way home, steeling himself against the cold and the awful feeling of sinking disappointment that swamped him.

Chapter Thirteen

Harry heard footsteps across the carpet of the sitting-room in the Officers' Mess and slunk down a little further into his armchair. He raised the paper and kept quiet. With any luck, whoever it was would see he wanted a little privacy and bugger off. No chance.

'Drummond! Is that you?' He recognised Nick Tully's voice and considered remaining silent to see if he'd go away, but Tully crossed the room and gave *The Times* a sharp whack with the back of his hand. Harry lowered it.

'What on earth are you doing here sulking on a Saturday afternoon? You're not on duty, are you?'

Harry sighed heavily. 'No,' he answered, 'I just fancied a bit of peace and quiet, that's all.'

'Yeah, yeah. Got nothing better to do, more like.' Tully grinned. 'Well, you soon will have!'

'What the hell's that supposed to mean?' Harry snapped.

'Whoa!' Tully sprang back. 'No need to be so tetchy, Harry, old mate.' He dug in his pocket and pulled out a single cigarette. It was one of his habits, carrying his fags in singles, and he did it so that he didn't have to offer them around. It annoyed Harry; not that he smoked himself, it just annoyed him. 'God, you've been so bloody morose the past week, Harry, no one would think your girlfriend has just inherited a substantial house and estate and that if you play your cards right you could become "Lord of the—"'

'Shut it, Tully!' Harry snarled. 'Just shut it, OK?'

Tully raised his eyebrows. 'What did I say? All I said was that before long you could be married and thinking about giving up the regiment.'

'Giving up the regiment?' Tully swung round at the voice and Harry saw the Colonel crossing towards them. If he'd been within range he would have given Tully a bloody sharp kick.

'You're not thinking of giving up the regiment, are you, Tully?' the Colonel asked.

'No, sir.'

'We'd miss him, eh, Drummond? Not that he's much good as a soldier, mind you, but he does play a damn good game of cricket.'

Tully laughed loudly and Harry cringed. It was coming, he could feel it coming. 'Not me, sir,' Tully said, bringing his laughter under control. 'Drummond! His girlfriend's come into a great deal of money and I was advising him to capitalise on that and ask her to marry him.'

'Oh, were you now, Tully? That's very unusual for you, showing a bit of good sense.' Smiling, the Colonel turned to Harry, his habitually blank face showing a rare spark of interest. 'This true, Drummond? All thoughts turning to spring, the rising of sap, love and all that?'

Harry flushed, badly. 'Not quite, sir.'

'Not quite? Oh, shame!' The spark was extinguished. 'I was just saying to Janey the other day, actually, that none of our young lads are married yet. Great shame, it's good for the regiment to have a few of you under the thumb.

Hwa-hwa!' The Colonel always found himself immensely amusing. Tully joined in heartily with the laughter and Harry managed a hasty guffaw.

'You know, sir, I don't think Drummond's being entirely honest with us,' Tully said, grinning. 'I bet he's got something up his sleeve! He's been pretty shady the past week.'

Harry attempted to kick Tully hard on the shin, but he missed and clunked the sofa table instead.

'Have you, Drummond?' The Colonel's face lit up again in a way Harry found most unnerving. 'I say, come on, spill the beans!'

'Not at all, sir,' Harry insisted. 'There's nothing to tell, really. I, we . . .' He stopped. Harry had never enjoyed much attention in the regiment; he was a good soldier, competent, reasonable at sport but rarely asked to play, liked but not popular. He fitted in without ever standing out, did well without any show of brilliance. He simply got on with it. But now, as he glanced up at the Colonel's face – amused, curious, focused on him – he caught a brief glimpse of what it might be like to be a star. Suddenly, and without thinking twice, he said, 'We haven't set a date or anything, or even made a formal announcement.'

'Announcement, announcement?' the Colonel trumpeted. 'So there *is* something to announce, is there?'

Harry was taken aback; he hadn't expected such alacrity.

'Not exactly . . . well, sort of, I suppose.'

'Good Lord! Congratulations, Drummond! I say, what splendid news. Hush-hush of course, mum's the word.' He thrust out a hand to Harry.

'Why, Harry. You sly old dog!' Tully burst out. 'You could have told me at least.'

Harry shrugged, smiling uneasily. His whole arm was throbbing from the Colonel's ultra-firm handshake.

'We must have you for drinks!' the Colonel declared. 'A drinks party is definitely in order, I think; I shall go over to quarters and tell Janey immediately. A celebration in your honour, yours and Kate's.'

Harry flushed to the roots of his hair. 'Oh, I don't think—'

'Nonsense! Has to be done.'

'Well, er, smashing . . .' Harry murmured. 'Thank you, sir.'

'Not at all, Drummond. Splendid news! Splendid! Eh, Tully? You next, eh what?' He nudged Tully hard in the ribs, chortled merrily and turned to leave. Glancing back, he said, 'Leave it all to us.'

'What, sir?'

'The drinks. Sometime this month.' And he smiled again before crossing the room and calling out to the Mess Sergeant for a large gin and tonic.

After the Colonel had gone, Harry sat glumly staring at the fire. Tully watched the Colonel settle himself down on the opposite side of the Mess, well out of earshot, and then cuffed Harry on the arm.

'Buck up, Harry!' he hissed. 'It's not every day you get a royal invitation to drinks.' He grinned. 'Rather you than me, I've heard that the gin's watered down and there's no getting away from Major Scunner's wife.' He rolled his eyes. Mrs Scunner was infamous in the regiment, she was in charge of teaching first aid and liked to recruit virile young officers to practise mouth-to-mouth resuscitation on. 'You never know,' he said, laughing, 'you might be picked to help with her St John first-aid course!'

Harry abruptly stood up. 'All right, Tully,' he said, 'it's not that funny!' He folded his paper and dropped it down on to the armchair. 'I'm going to my room. Call me if anyone rings.'

'But, Harry—'

'Just shut it, Tully,' he snapped. 'You've said quite enough for one day!' He headed out of the Mess towards the stairs.

'But, Harry, listen, there's something—'

Harry turned at the door just as the Colonel looked across to see what the commotion was about. Tully shut up; he smiled rather sheepishly and Harry continued on his way. Oh dear, thought Tully; in the light of recent events and Drummond's odious mood, this could be a very bad move indeed. Famous for his practical jokes, Tully often found that not everyone shared his wild and somewhat warped sense of humour.

Harry made his way along to his room and, at the door, dug in his pocket for his keys. He was in a foul mood, irritable, depressed and thoroughly ashamed of himself. What an idiot! Whatever had possessed him to tell a lie like that? And how the hell was he going to get out of it? Engaged? About to attach himself to a young woman worth a fortune? 'Oh, God,' he muttered, resting his head against the door. 'What have I done?' When he went to turn his key in the lock, he found to his dismay that the door was already open. Oh great, he thought, to cap it all I even forgot to lock my room! All I need now is for my stereo and wallet to have been nicked and it'll have been another perfect day. He turned the handle, heard a slight scuffle inside and immediately tensed. Bracing himself for an intruder, he swung the door open and stepped into the room.

'Good God! Sasha!' The sight that greeted him should have made him laugh. Tully's sister was wearing nothing but a pair of black stockings, a black lace suspender belt and the cap and tunic of his No. 2s dress uniform. 'Sasha, what the hell are you doing here?' He came into the room and hurriedly shut the door behind him. 'Christ! Come away from the window, for God's sake.' Darting across the room, he yanked the curtains shut and propelled Tully's sister over to the bed. 'I'm engaged, for pity's sake.'

'Engaged?' Sasha Tully blinked rapidly several times, her face draining of all colour. 'Engaged!'

'Oh, God, no! I mean, not really but I just told the Colonel . . .' Harry slumped down in the armchair and dropped his head in his hands. 'Never mind,' he said miserably, 'it's far too complicated to go into.'

Sasha stared across at him, six foot of one hundred per cent male, who at this moment looked just like a little boy. Her heart melted and her shock softened. 'Harry?' Sasha murmured. 'Don't you want to see my medal? It might take your mind off things.' Harry swallowed hard. Whatever else she was, Sasha Tully was one hell of a girl. Large-breasted, small and perfectly formed, she had the creamy, luscious flesh of a Rubens painting; the curves on her hips and bottom swelled indulgently, and she adorned them frequently with black silk and lace.

'No, I don't!' Harry growled. An inventive girl, God only knew where she'd hidden it. 'Put something on, Sasha,' he implored, looking away from her. 'Please!'

'But I've got something on,' she answered. 'Come on, Harry.' She lay back on the bed and the tunic fell open to reveal the full round breasts with hard dark brown nipples. 'This isn't like you.' Harry glanced back and, uncomfortably hard, shifted in his chair.

'Oh, Harry,' she wheedled. 'Come on, what's the matter?'

Harry leaned his forehead against the tight ball of his fists and closed his eyes. 'What's the matter?' he murmured. 'I'll tell you what's the matter. My life's a mess, my relationship with Kate is on the rocks, nothing is what I thought it would be and now I've gone and got myself invited to a celebration drinks party with the Colonel.' He groaned. 'If this is your idea of a joke, Sasha, then I'm afraid I don't find it at all funny!'

Suddenly Harry felt hands pull his fists away and gently ease him to his feet. His eyes shut tight, he let himself be led, unable to resist. 'No joke,' Sasha whispered in his ear. 'Nick thought you needed cheering up.' She unzipped his fly and her long, deft fingers snaked inside his pants and found his erection. He groaned again. A few moments later, she said, 'Would you like to see my medal now?'

Despite himself, Harry nodded and silently she turned him round to face her, loosening his jeans and pants down over his hips. 'Look,' she whispered. She slipped the tunic off her shoulders and ran her fingers down over her breasts to the top of her suspender belt. There she had pinned a piece of striped ribbon and a gold-covered chocolate coin. Harry smiled, then bent his head to her breast and took her nipple in his mouth. 'It's edible,' she said, 'the medal. Taste it and see.' And gently easing his head down her torso, she pressed herself back against the wall and opened her legs. Harry gripped her thighs, brought his mouth to the smooth white skin and, still wearing his cap, she wrapped her fingers in his hair and let out a low, hoarse cry of pleasure.

The still-room, as it had now become known, and the adjacent store-room were about five minutes' walk from the house. Kate ran all the way. She was tense, excited. The past week had gone in a flash, in a mountain of arrangements, discoveries and sheer hard work. She had the final confirmation in her hand – a fax from a glass manufacturer in Bagshot undertaking to make the bottles they needed, for the price they wanted – and she couldn't wait to tell Rory. Everything else was in place, now all they had to do was make the gin. And that, they all seemed to think, was practically done.

'Kate! Hooray! Kate!' Flora, who had been sitting with Mrs Able, jumped up and darted across to Kate as she came in. Kate bent and hugged her, lifting Flora up on to her hip before she did anything else. Together they walked across to Rory and his father.

'I've got confirmation for the bottles,' she called out.

Rory was shovelling coal on to the fire and didn't stop what he was doing, he just lifted a hand in salute and carried on. Kate went back to Mrs Able and they stood together looking at the still, a huge copper boiler-like construction with a condenser attached and a brick, coal-fuelled fire underneath. Rory's father, the Reverend Michael Gallagher, joined them; he was pink and sweating from the heat.

'How far have you got?' Kate asked him.

'We've been going about two hours and the steam is definitely coming off cleaner. I would hazard a guess at another three to four hours to get the inside of the still completely clean.'

'But how will you know when it's completely clean?' Mrs Able queried.

'The steam will come off odourless. All we've done is filled it with water and we're boiling the water to clean it. Quite simple really.'

'Aye.' Mrs Able didn't look at all convinced.

He turned to Kate. 'You got the bottles sorted out, then?' She handed the fax across. 'Great, well done! Is it within your budget?'

'Yes, well within.' Rory had set out a budget for the initial process and so far they had come in under it.

'Have you seen what Flora and Mrs Able have been doing, Kate?' He pointed to a trestle table in the corner of the outhouse. 'They've been working that old Purdy's labelling machine. It goes pretty well now, doesn't it, Mrs Able?'

'Aye, Reverend.' Despite protestations that everyone should call him Michael, Kate and Mrs Able still found 'Reverend' easier to say. 'We're up to one bottle a minute, aren't we, Flora love?'

Kate took a good look at the machine. She was amazed that they had even got it working at all, let alone so well. That was something she hadn't bargained for in all this – the amount of equipment that was still here, put away carefully and lovingly and that, with a bit of cleaning and repair, was turning out to be as good as new. It gave her a feeling that she was reviving a tradition, something that belonged to the house and her family. It gave her a sense of Leo, which had helped so often in the past week of grieving. None of it was quick or easy, not by modern standards, but it all worked, and that was what mattered.

'I've got the hang of that capping machine too, Kate

dear.' Mrs Able reached across the table and lugged a heavy-levered contraption towards her. She picked up a bottle and a cork cap, fitted them both into the machine and, with a flick of her wrist and a twist of her hand, she yanked the lever and the bottle was capped.

'Brilliant!' Kate cried, genuinely impressed. She hadn't been able to fathom that machine out at all. Mrs Able beamed. She was hot and sticky from the heat in the still-room, her hair had come free of its grips and hung irritatingly round her face, her blouse was grubby and the arthritis in her fingers ached from fiddling with the machines, but she was delighted. She and John had felt more useful this last week than they had done for years. At last at Tonsbry there was something to look forward to, work to be done, a fight to be had. The house was alive again, people coming and going, deliveries, phone calls – everywhere she looked, there was activity. It reminded her a bit of the war – not the fear, of course, or the terrible loss, but the sense of pulling together, of working for something they all believed in.

''Scuse me, love?'

They all turned towards the open doors.

'I got a delivery here from Spice and Nice, is it for you?'

'Oh, yes!' Kate said. 'Wait, I'll come and get it.' She hurried across the still-room and out to the van parked in the yard.

The driver unlocked the back, took out a cardboard box and said, 'Can you check it's all here, tick them off and sign here, then print your name . . . here.' He handed her the box, took a pen out of his back pocket and waited while Kate checked the botanicals they'd ordered, then signed his form.

'Thanks. See you again, I hope.' He climbed back into his van and started the engine as Rory came out, hot and exhausted from shovelling coal. He glanced at the box. 'What's that?'

Kate dropped it on the ground, bent and opened the plastic bag of juniper berries inside it. She took out a handful of them and stood crushing them gently in her fingers to release their aroma. 'This,' she said, holding them out for Rory to smell, 'is . . .'

'Gin!' he completed.

Kate grinned. 'Yes, gin!' she agreed, and they both started to laugh.

Adriana flicked the switch on her remote control and the television screen in her bedroom went blank. She glanced at the tea-tray by her side, picked up a wafer-thin cucumber sandwich and abandoned it after one bite. She was bored, irritated and sick of waiting. Dropping her legs over the side of the bed, she padded barefoot to the bathroom and stood in front of the large, well-lit mirror, for want of something better to do, and stared at her reflection. She looked immaculate, of course she did, she had been in and out of beauty salons all week. She had lost weight, a couple of pounds, and her bust was definitely firmer. Her skin glowed, her nails were perfect, yet Adriana was unhappy; deeply unhappy. She had been waiting for a call from her daughter for nearly five days now and still the silence went on.

Wretched girl, she thought, viciously plucking a grey hair from her head. I'll be damned if I am going to ring *her*! But the thought of Kate alone in that terrible house, making a fool of herself with that horrible man, almost brought tears to Adriana's eyes. Almost . . . There was nothing else for it, she decided; she would have to resort to plan B.

Taking a last glimpse of herself, Adriana left the bathroom and went back to the bedroom. She sat down at the dressing-table, picked up the phone and dialled the number she had written down several days ago on the hotel notepad. When her call was answered, she said, 'Hello? May I speak to Captain Drummond? Yes, of course I'll hold. Yes, tell him it's the Comtesse de Grand Blès. Thank you.' And she settled down to wait for Harry.

Harry sat up in bed feeling even more miserable than he had done two hours earlier. Sex with Tully's sister was draining, it had taken his mind off things in the short term but in the long term he was now stressed and knackered. He reached for a toffee from his bedside drawer, unwrapped it and popped it into his mouth. Some people smoked after sex, some went to sleep, Harry chewed toffees. As he chewed, his mouth loosened with saliva, he made discreet little slurping sounds and had to pick the odd bit of sticky sweet off his tooth with his fingernail.

'God, Harry!' Sasha moaned. 'Do you have to do that?'

'Yes!' he snapped. 'I do.'

She rolled over and stared up at him. 'Oh dear,' she said, 'you really are in a bad mood, aren't you?'

Harry ignored her so she sat up. 'Look, Harry, I may not be brain of Britain but I am quite good at listening to people's problems.' He still ignored her. 'I might even be able to help.'

'Help?' He swallowed down his sweet and reached for another one, offering Sasha the bag first.

'Thanks.' She took a toffee and pulled the duvet up over her chest. 'Yes, help,' she said. 'Right, your relationship's on the rocks. Why's that?'

'Oh, God,' Harry moaned, 'it's too long to begin to explain.'

'Try.'

He turned to look at Sasha. 'You really want to know?'

She nodded. Actually she didn't want to know at all, but she did want Harry, badly; she adored him, and she had a theory that if she was around often enough – pleased him, listened to him, laughed at his jokes and understood his problems – then she might just get him.

'Harry, I'm a friend,' she said. 'Come on, let's talk it through.'

He took her hand. 'I walked out on Kate last week,' he said. 'I'm not proud of it, but I really don't know if I can afford to get involved. She's in trouble, you see, in debt to be precise; she's inherited this ruddy great house and estate and it turns out that it's a dead donkey, hocked right down to the toilet rolls.' He stared at Sasha's hand – very feminine, manicured nails with pale pink polish – and remembered Kate's, always smelling of onions or garlic or some sort of food, always dry, with carrot under her fingernail. He kissed one of Sasha's fingers and smelled a mixture of her perfume and her sex. 'The thing is that this debt might extend to me. I mean, she could be declared bankrupt and if we were together – well, it wouldn't reflect at all well on me, would it? Army officer, pillar of the community, that sort of thing.'

Sasha nodded sympathetically.

'I told her, I said, "Kate, I just can't afford to be mixed

up in all this, it could ruin my reputation."' He looked at Sasha. 'I was right, wasn't I?'

'Oh, yes,' she said, entirely in her own interest. 'Absolutely.'

'But there's something else. You see, somehow or other – I'm not quite sure how really – but I seem to have told the Colonel that Kate and I are engaged and well . . . he got all sort of fired-up about it and wants to throw a drinks party for us and . . . oh, God . . .'

As Harry hung his head, Sasha stroked the back of it gently, reassuringly and thought – *fast*. She wasn't known for her quick mental responses – she preferred the dizzy blonde guise – but this was important. She didn't want Harry engaged, not in any way at all; reality or fantasy. 'Well, the first thing you must do, Harry,' she said, removing her hand and sitting up straight, 'is tell the Colonel that Kate's estate has complications in probate.'

'In probate?'

'Yes, it's just a legal term for—'

'I know what it is, Sasha!' Harry snapped. She took heed of the warning and reverted to type. 'Sorry, of course you do. Well, tell him that – and that Kate isn't going anywhere because there's too much to do, sorting the house out, etc. You could leave a note in his pigeon-hole saying you had a call this afternoon, and then make yourself scarce for the rest of the weekend.'

'Scarce?'

'Yes! You could come up to London with me if you like?'

'Hmmm. Then?'

'Well, once you've got out of the drinks party for the time being, you can subtly take Mrs Colonel aside one day and tell her that things aren't going at all well – you

221

know, do the wounded fiancé bit, get her on your side and then, finally, break the news that Kate's dumped you a few weeks later.'

'Kate's dumped me?' Harry was a bit taken aback by the potential dent to his pride.

'It's the only way,' Sasha said, 'if you want to stay squeaky clean.'

'Hmmm. You really think so?'

'Yes, I do.'

Sasha reached up and stroked Harry's hair again. 'God, Sasha,' he moaned, suddenly aroused, 'you understand me like no one else. You know that, don't you?'

Sasha made soothing, murmuring sounds.

'I don't know what I'd do without you. I mean, if only, if only it wasn't for . . .' He broke off at the sound of knocking on the door.

'Wasn't for what, Harry?' Sasha prompted.

The knocking came again.

'Harry?'

'Ssssh!'

'Captain Drummond, sir! There's a call for you. The lady is waiting on the line, a Comtesse de something-or-other – French, I think.'

'Shit!' Harry dropped Sasha's hand, threw back the covers and jumped out of bed. 'That's Kate's mother!' He strode towards the door, realised he was naked and grabbed his underpants off the floor.

'Captain Drummond?'

'Yes. Hang on a minute, Corporal!' Harry crossed to the door. 'Sasha!' he hissed. 'Get under the covers!'

'But, Harry—!'

'Just do it!'

She pulled the duvet up over her head and lay still as Harry opened the door.

'Shall I tell the lady you're on your way, or will you call back?'

'I'll be right there, thanks, Corporal.'

He closed the door, standing deep in thought for a few moments until Sasha came out of hiding and said, 'I'll wait here for you, shall I?'

Startled out of his brief reverie, Harry hurriedly began to dress, glancing across at Sasha as he pulled on his shirt and trousers. 'Oh God, Sasha, I don't know . . . er . . . no, probably best not to, I'd have thought!' The idea of Kate's glamorous and wealthy mother waiting to speak to him had thrown him into a minor flap.

'Why not?'

'Oh, well . . . I might be ages, she might have rung off and I'll have to wait for her to call back or something, you just never know. Besides,' he finished buttoning his shirt, 'you must have loads of better things to do than hang around here waiting for me. Hmmm?'

She hadn't, this was the best thing she could think of, but she nodded and murmured, 'Of course.'

'Great!' Harry wasn't an out-and-out snob, but he was hugely impressed by the rich and titled and couldn't wait to get out of the door. 'I'll see you soon then, Sasha?' He had turned the door-handle and glanced fleetingly back at her, still warm in his bed.

She nodded again. 'Do I get a kiss?'

'Oh God, yes! Sorry!' He darted back, kissed her chastely on the cheek and was at the door again before she had a chance to slip her arm round his neck. 'Thanks, Sasha,' he said.

'Yes. Harry, I . . .' But she didn't finish; Harry had left the room.

Stefan stood on the corner of the Fulham Road and watched both ways for Jan. They had arranged to meet at seven, but it was now seven forty-five and there was no sign of her. The film started at eight; he had the tickets, a big box of Maltesers and a table booked for ten at his local Italian restaurant. He was beginning to feel let down – no, more than that, he was beginning to feel a bit of a prat. Taking his phone out of his pocket, he rang the switchboard of Ingram Lawd for the third time – no reply – then tried Jan's mobile again: switched off. He wondered what to do. Should he give it another half an hour and feel thoroughly ridiculous in the process, or should he just jack it in and go for a drink? He glanced up the road to left and right one last time and decided to jack it in. She wasn't going to show; for whatever reasons she had, she was going to stand him up. And no matter how hard he tried to shrug it off, the thought of that left him feeling utterly depressed.

Turning towards the Goat and Boot, Stefan dropped the chocolates in the bin along with the cinema tickets and made his way up to the pub. He was about to go in when he heard his name called and spun round expectantly.

'Stefan? Stefan, darling! Over here!'

He saw one of his long-standing clients parked across the road and waving at him from the driver's seat of a Mercedes 80 SL. Disappointed, but keen not to show it, he crossed and bent to the window of the car. 'Hello, Loïs. What are you doing here? Not kerb-crawling, I hope?'

Loïs Makinny laughed loudly and waved a well-decked hand in the air. 'I was waiting for a friend, but he hasn't shown up. I don't suppose you're free by any chance, are you, Stef? I've got a table booked at La Caprice, fancy a bite?'

Stefan didn't really fancy a bite, but Loïs was very loyal and she really only cared for his company in public. She liked to humiliate her ex-husband by high-profile dining and party-going with Stefan and a few other select young men. He glanced quickly up the Fulham Road, not really knowing what he expected to see, then nodded and smiled. 'Loïs, I'm starving,' he said. 'I'd love a bite!'

She laughed again. She had a deep throaty chuckle which drew attention to her; it was all part of the act. She reached over, opened the passenger door for Stefan and he climbed in beside her. 'You look very chic, Stef, my love. You been stood up as well?'

Stefan shrugged. Seeing Loïs take a long, thin cigarette out of a box on the dashboard, he reached for the lighter, flicked it and lit her cigarette. 'I presume you'll still charge her full price,' she said, smiling and blowing smoke out of the side of her mouth.

'It wasn't business, Loïs,' he answered.

'Oh, dear.' She patted his thigh, then started the engine. 'Oh, well,' she said, 'take consolation from the fact that this woman is obviously stupid!' She put her foot down and accelerated away.

'Stupid?' Stefan reached for one of Loïs's cigarettes. He didn't usually smoke, but she liked him to keep her company.

'Yes, Stefan darling. To turn down for free what we all have to pay for seems to me to be just plain daft!' And she laughed again heartily, flicked her ash on the floor and Stefan winced.

*   *   *

It was ten-fifteen. Sasha sat in her car, parked on a meter outside the Langham Hilton in Portland Place, and waited for Harry. He had said he didn't need picking up, that he could get a cab after dinner, but Sasha had offered, suggesting that he might save himself the fare – and Harry, being Harry, was unable to resist the temptation of a free lift.

But as she sat, Sasha worried. She worried about Harry, about herself and most of all about Kate Dowie. For the first time that afternoon she really thought she might have got somewhere, that there might be a small gap in the wall of Harry's adulation for Kate, that it might just possibly be over. But one phone call from the Comtesse de bloody Camembert and he was back on the case, rushing to dress for dinner in London and to discuss Kate 'openly and seriously' – his words – with her mother.

Of course Sasha had offered to drive him up to town and let him stay the night at her flat, both of which he took up without a qualm. So she had rushed to the Nine Elms Sainsbury's, as soon as she had dropped him off at the Langham, to buy croissants and fresh coffee, three different types of cereal, eggs, bacon, sausages, mushrooms and tomatoes for grilling. But was any of that really likely to make a difference? What did Kate's mother want? And whatever it was, would Harry give it to her? Sasha sighed miserably and glanced at her watch. Her thirty minutes on the meter were up, so she took another pound coin out of her purse and, climbing out of the car, inserted it in order to continue her lonely vigil.

Inside the hotel, in the Memories restaurant, at a discreet

table for two, Adriana sat with Harry and covered a small, bored yawn with the back of her hand. She dropped the hand back on to her lap and reached for her glass. As she took a sip, Harry realised he was a few seconds behind her and hastily picked up his own drink. He was sadly under the misconception that it was polite to drink whenever your host drank, but had failed to register that Adriana was drinking water while he drank wine. The result was that he had lost track of the conversation and the clarity of his vision was beginning to suffer. As he replaced his glass, it was immediately topped up by a silent, hovering waiter who upturned the now empty bottle in the ice bucket and asked 'Madam' if she would like another.

'Thank you, yes,' Adriana replied, wondering why on earth Kate had kept in touch with this rather well-meaning but dull and pompous young man. She coughed politely to refocus Harry and said, 'We were discussing the idea of a little financial help for you and Kate, in order to get you both on your feet in London, perhaps to buy a restaurant?'

'A restaurant?'

Adriana waved her hand dismissively in the air. 'Whatever,' she said impatiently. They had been through all this before. 'But particularly to get her away from Tonsbry and this ridiculous gin business.'

'What gin business?'

'The one Kate told me about!'

'Oh, yes.' Harry wasn't at all sure what she meant – he seemed to have missed that part of the conversation – but he did detect Adriana's irritation and decided, through a haze of exceptionally good claret, that it was best to agree with Adriana no matter what.

'Naturally there would be no need to mention the gift to Kate; it could be transferred into your name and you could say it was your own capital. Of course Kate would have the voting share of the business, but I wouldn't see any problem in giving you a little bonus for yourself once you and she were settled.'

'What sort of settled?' Harry asked, trying not to slur his words.

'That's really up to you, Harry,' Adriana told him, smiling sweetly, although behind the smile she thought: if Kate wants to marry him, then I shall have to deal with that when I come to it. Her main priority was to get Kate away from making the biggest mistake of her life.

'And you want me to take some leave and go down to Tonsbry to convince her that it's all back on?'

'And that trying to save that monstrosity of a house will ruin her life.'

'But why?'

'Why what?' Adriana almost snapped.

'Why will it ruin her life? And why don't you just give her this lump sum to pay off the debts on the house?'

'It will ruin her life, Harry,' Adriana said, as if speaking to an imbecile, 'because she will become obsessed. I've seen it happen. She will think she can save Tonsbry, make a go of it, and she will spend the rest of her life in debt struggling to do it.' Adriana lit a cigarette, despite the fact that Harry was still eating. She saw him grimace, but decided it was his own fault if it took him more than an hour to eat a main course. 'And I will not bail her out of debt precisely for that reason,' she went on. 'If I wipe the slate clean now, then in a few years' time she'll be back to square one. Tonsbry eats money, I saw what it did to Leo – no life, no family, only that ruddy house – and I will not let that happen to Kate!' Adriana ground out her cigarette and clicked her fingers, calling for the bill. Talking about Tonsbry always put her in a vitriolic mood.

'Harry,' she said, 'I hope you'll forgive me, but I've got a wretched headache.' She dropped her napkin on to her plate and stood up. 'Could you put the bill on to room one-four-eight?' she said to the waiter. 'Harry? Will you excuse me?'

As Harry struggled to his feet, the full effects of the wine took their toll and he held on to the edge of the table for support. 'Of course! I'm sorry, I hope you feel—'

'Yes, thank you.' Picking her small Chanel Kelly bag off the table, Adriana managed a tight smile and said, 'I shall be in touch. You'll make a journey down to Tonsbry?'

'Yes, of course. I'll go in the next day or so. Please leave it to me.'

Adriana concealed her horror at such a prospect and nodded. 'Good night, Harry,' she said.

'Oh yes, right . . .' Harry made a lunge sideways to kiss her as she passed, but was not quick enough and caught the table-cloth, pulling it with him and knocking over three glasses and the small vase of flowers as he did so. 'Good night!' he called, as she disappeared out of the restaurant. Then he slumped back into his chair.

'Would sir like some more wine?' the waiter asked, having just produced a new bottle.

'Yes, please,' Harry replied. 'Put a cork in it, would you, and I'll take it home with me.' He folded his napkin and laid it on the table. 'Thanks, thanks very much.' And standing, he took the bottle that was handed to him and strode out of the restaurant.

*   *   *

It was nearing midnight when Jan finally finished her paper work. She had calculated all the interest payments on the Tonsbry Estate, gone back three years to see the rise in rates, the extent of the leverage and the profit on the loan. She was satisfied that there was no reason why they had to foreclose; it was good business, provided Kate Dowie was prepared to meet repayments. However, there was a clause in the contract which stated that Ingram Lawd had a right to foreclose on a loan if they felt it appropriate and this, she was certain, was the clause Duncan intended to use.

Jan closed the file and stood up. She had worked with Duncan for many years now and was pretty sure she knew every trick in his book, but this . . . this urgency on the Tonsbry business . . . just didn't make sense. They didn't have a potential buyer, she had checked; and there were no redevelopment plans – again she had checked the files. So what the devil was he up to? If he wanted that loan foreclosed, then it had to be in order to buy the property at a reduced rate. Why else put an end to a piece of business that was bringing in a good rate of profit? And if he wanted that property, then what did it have that Jan, or Kate Dowie for that matter, didn't know about? Jan left the file on her desk and took the office keys from her drawer. She left her own office and walked along the corridor to Duncan's, switching on lights as she went. When she reached his room the door was locked. She rifled the bunch for the right key, unlocked the office and went in.

The first thing Jan did was try the filing cabinets. Three were open, but the fourth was locked. What was in it that Duncan didn't want anyone to see? Second, she looked through the desk; there was nothing there. She didn't really know what she was looking for or what she expected to find, but she did know that there had to be something. Turning to his diary, she flicked through the pages. Meetings, lunches, aerobics . . . she allowed herself a smile at that one. Duncan was fastidious about his diary; the pages revealed a detailed account of his life. Each social or business arrangement had not only the time – in the twenty-four-hour clock – the venue, address and telephone number and an allocated time slot, but also the taxi booking and various personal notes, such as: 'Prince of Wales check suit/pale blue stripe shirt (Pinks)/blue Hermès tie' alongside 'dinner at the RAC Club'. It fascinated Jan, it always had. She was one to scribble down a time and place and leave the rest in her head, so this exceptional habit made for interesting reading. As she flicked through and read the personal notes, she almost missed a meeting slotted in for Monday at eleven-thirty, a simple note in pencil with nothing else written by it. She skimmed over it, ignored it, then a page or so on thought for a moment and turned back. It was very odd sandwiched between two meetings, both of which were detailed; the second even had a list of sandwiches that Duncan's secretary was to order for the working lunch. She stared at it for a few moments, then sat down in his chair and turned back to the beginning of the year. She scanned each page and, sure enough, she found five other instances of this pencilled note for a one-hour meeting. No venue, no name, no other specifics. It was most peculiar, suspicious even and, although she had no idea what it could mean, she did feel an overwhelming urge to find out.

Closing the diary, Jan left it exactly as she had found it – Duncan would notice otherwise – and stood, making a mental note of what she had seen. Don't be ridiculous, Jan, she told herself, it's just an aberration, a mistake, but it niggled at her and as she re-locked his office and made her way back to her own, she couldn't get it out of her mind.

At her own desk, Jan checked her diary for next week's appointments and wondered if she ought to follow up this meeting of Duncan's. But she dismissed the idea as plain silly – chasing her estranged husband around London, taking an almost perverse interest in his private life. She sat down, lit a cigarette and thought about it.

The thing was, she was certainly free on Monday; it was strange, very strange, for Duncan not to write down any details at all. Perhaps she should take a look and see who he was meeting? Just a quick look, stand outside and try to catch a glimpse. She flipped back to the current week, glanced down at the pages and it was then that she saw her arrangement for Friday, that night. She clapped her hand to her forehead and let out a groan. How the hell could she have forgotten? And why hadn't he rung to remind her? Jan rummaged in her handbag for her mobile and saw it was switched off. She swore out loud and reached for the phone on her desk. Dialling Stefan's number, she heard it ring, the answerphone clicked on and she swore again. Waiting for the bleep, she finally said, 'Stefan? I'm so sorry about tonight, really I am. You're not going to believe me, I'm sure, but I simply forgot. You see, I was working on this Tonsbry Estate file and I lost track of time. I've been doing it all day and I just sort of carried on and . . .' She stopped, aware that she was babbling. 'Well, whatever. I'm sorry anyway, I hope it didn't ruin your evening. Look, call me soon? Please?' And not knowing if he was listening, or out, or so angry that he wouldn't ever return her call, she hung up. 'Bugger!' she said. Then she dropped her cigarettes, keys and mobile into her bag, grabbed her coat and left for home.

Stefan reached for Loïs Makinny's velvet overcoat and draped it around her naked shoulders. She had to be nearing sixty, but her body was well cared for and still looked good. She held on to the coat and sat up. Reaching for a cigarette, she said, 'Stefan, that was . . .'

He silenced her with a brief kiss and stood up. This wasn't really Loïs's kind of thing, but every now and then she needed a little physical comfort and he had never refused her. Tonight was one such occasion. They had met her ex-husband in La Caprice, there with his new wife, and it had upset her far more than she would admit. 'Would you like some coffee?' Stefan asked.

Loïs shook her head. 'It keeps me awake, Stefan darling, and I should like to go home to bed now.'

Stefan pulled on his trousers and a sweater. 'I'll drive you,' he said. 'I'll get a cab back.'

'Thank you, dear.' She too dressed, not bothering with her underwear but stuffing it into her handbag, and when she was ready she went out into the hall to wait. 'The little red light on your answerphone is winking at me, Stefan,' she called. He kept the phone on a table in the hallway. 'I hope it's the woman who stood you up, calling to apologise.'

Stefan joined her. 'I'll listen to it later,' he said. He didn't want to think about Jan, not now. 'Car keys?' Loïs handed him the small gold keyring with her car and house keys. 'Ready?'

Loïs nodded and Stefan put his arm around her. She looked tired and a little sad. 'Did anyone tell you that you really are lovely, Loïs Makinny?'

She smiled. 'Isn't that what I pay you for, Stefan?'

He stopped. 'No, Loïs, it isn't. You pay me to escort you out to dinner and be good company. You don't pay me to think that you're lovely.'

Loïs kissed his cheek affectionately. 'Thank you, darling boy.' She opened the door and waited for him to take her arm. 'You are wasted in this job, Stefan,' she said. Then she turned, suddenly serious. 'Get out before it spoils you!'

Stefan shrugged. 'Maybe,' he replied. But as he said it an image of Jan popped into his head, and he knew that the 'maybe' wasn't as bland as it might have been.

Chapter Fourteen

It was Monday morning and Jan was tired. She shouldn't have been, she had done nothing all weekend, but she was tired and depressed. It was the depression that wore her out, following the stress and anxiety of waiting for Stefan to ring or return her call – or at least let her know that he had got her message. There had been an ominous silence all weekend and, even though she tried to tell herself that he was busy, had things to do, might not even have got the message in the first place, she couldn't bring herself to ring him again on Saturday or Sunday or even now on Monday; and she couldn't help thinking that he had taken offence and decided not to call her again. That depressed her because, combined with the niggling idea that Duncan was up to something underhand – an idea she simply couldn't dispel – she was beginning to wonder just exactly who she could trust.

Possibly no one, she thought, glancing at her watch, or perhaps everyone and I'm paranoid. Certainly during the past twenty years that she had been married to Duncan, he had always operated within the law, as far as she knew, and had never done anything underhand or dishonest. But then carrying on an affair with his secretary for eighteen months was about as underhand and dishonest as it could get. So, where did that leave her? Jan bent, took a large M&S carrier-bag and a small vanity case from the drawer in her desk and went to get her coat. Where it left her was very suspicious, of everything and everyone. She buzzed Molly and said, 'Molly, I'm going out for a couple of hours, I've got a doctor's appointment. If Duncan wants to know where I am, tell him Harley Street and that I'll be back at lunch-time.'

Then she pulled on her coat, picked up her handbag and the carrier and left the office. She thought briefly that she must be slightly mad to do what she was about to do, then she smiled to herself. She *was* mad, completely, and so bloody what? Better mad than stupid and this time, whatever Duncan was up to, he sure as hell wasn't going to get away with it.

Down in the street below, Jan made her way along to the pub on the corner and went straight through the bar to the ladies', where she locked herself in a cubicle. Taking out the contents of the carrier-bag – things she had bought that morning on the way in to work – she stripped off her coat and pulled on a new beige raincoat, a scarf and knee-length black boots. Then she scraped back her hair, secured it with clips and took an old shoulder-length blond wig from the vanity case, along with a hand mirror and a new hat. She put on the wig, checked it in the mirror, brushed it, then added the hat. Almost ready, she stuffed her overcoat, shoes and handbag into the empty carrier and let herself out of the cubicle. Jan checked her reflection, added a red lipstick and tied the scarf stylishly around her neck. Then she left the pub and immediately outside found the black cab she had ordered waiting for her.

'Hello? Cab for Ingram?'

'Yes, love. Where to?'

'It's a bit tricky, actually,' she said, opening the door and climbing into the back. She leaned forward. 'What I'd like to do is ask you to follow another cab. Would that be possible?'

The driver shrugged. 'You're paying, love,' he said. 'The meter's running already.'

'Fine. I'll let you know which one it is then,' Jan told him and sat back, turning to watch the entrance to the Ingram Lawd building. Minutes later, earlier than she had expected, she watched Duncan leave the building. She held her breath, saw him glance at his watch and hoped that her assumption had been right. Duncan always travelled in London by black cab, and she was sure one he had ordered earlier would turn up any minute now.

Duncan waited . . . and Jan waited unseen in her taxi on the corner. As he shuffled impatiently from foot to foot and glanced at his watch a second time, Jan fidgeted on the back seat. 'Come on,' she murmured under her breath. Duncan looked up the road, saw no sign of a taxi approaching and, digging his hands in his pockets, turned towards the tube. 'Bugger!' Jan said aloud. There was no way she could get away with following him on foot. But just then a cab drew up alongside him, he spoke to the driver and climbed in. Jan knocked on the connecting window inside her own cab. 'That's it,' she said. 'The one that's just pulled up over there.' She pointed. 'OK?'

The driver gave her the thumbs-up and pulled out into the traffic. Sitting back, Jan let out a breath and kept her eyes firmly on the cab ahead.

As Duncan's taxi headed out of the city and up towards

King's Cross, Jan became wary. If he got out and decided to walk to his meeting, then she wasn't sure she felt safe enough in that area to follow him. But she needn't have worried because moments later his taxi pulled up alongside the kerb and Duncan climbed out. Her own cab stopped twenty yards behind and he turned, glancing in her direction as it did so.

'I think you need to get out, love,' the driver called over his shoulder, 'and look as if you're paying me.' Jan nodded. Duncan was staring now as he waited for his change, and it would look odd if no one climbed out of the cab behind him.

'Go into the bank,' the driver suggested. 'Wait for five minutes, then I'll collect you outside.'

Opening the door, Jan got out and leaned into the front of the cab with her purse in her hand. She could see Duncan out of the corner of her eye. He looked at her once, up and down; then, completely unaware of who she was, he ignored her. She smiled at the driver. 'You're pretty good at this,' she told him.

'Do it all the time, love,' he answered and, smiling back, he pulled out and drove off. Jan glanced up to see that Duncan had gone. Making a mental note of the name on the door of the office he was visiting, she walked into the bank and sat down feeling both shaken and ridiculous at the same time. She took off the hat, found a pen in her bag and wrote down: 'Rickman Levy Solicitors', placing a large question mark alongside. Then she let out a long breath, waited for the allocated time and left to find the taxi outside.

But what Jan missed was almost as important as what she saw. As her taxi drove off, another cab pulled up in front of the solicitors' and two people climbed out of it: a woman, chic and stylish but very impatient; and a man, his suit crumpled, his face worried and his manner subservient and ingratiating to absolutely no effect.

It was lunch-time in the still-room, but no one had eaten. It was hot, the atmosphere was thick with tension and everything was ready to go. The botanicals had been steeped in the grain spirit overnight, the still had been boiling the mixture all day, condensing the re-distilled spirit, and now they were ready for the first run. Kate stood next to the Reverend Gallagher in the still-room and watched Rory attach a hose to the still and line up a bucket to take the foreshot. This done, he then rolled a 21-kilo drum into place, ready to take the run. The whole process was complete in a matter of minutes and she could hardly believe they had come this far in so short a space of time.

'Ready?' he called across. They both gave him the thumbs-up.

'This foreshot, the stuff that comes off first. You really can't drink that?'

'No, Kate, it's pretty rough,' said Michael Gallagher. 'It's a really strong concentration of the botanicals; it's wasted, I'm afraid. Same as the last bit – the feint or tail, when the botanicals start to run out – the gin loses its flavour and that's wasted too.'

'But the bit in the middle's OK?'

He raised an eyebrow. 'I hope so, Kate,' he said. 'I certainly hope so.'

Rory came across to them and took a towel from Kate. He wiped his face and neck with it and said, 'Once the foreshot's come off, we're ready to go. Is the water all ready?'

Kate nodded. They were using spring water from a natural well on the estate, but they'd had to deionise it first and that had been the biggest expense; the chemical pack had cost hundreds. She crossed her fingers and held them up. 'We're all set,' she said.

'Right,' Rory answered. 'Let's go!'

He and Kate moved across to the still, he bent to the valve, glanced up at her, then opened it and the foreshot ran down the pipe and into the bucket. In the notes, it had said that the normal foreshot run was about ten minutes; so as soon as the valve was open and the gin was down the pipe, Rory switched on the stop-watch. 'We're off,' he said, and they both just stood and stared at the liquid which flowed into the bucket.

'God, it's hot,' Kate commented. Even the smallest movement made her sweat.

'Hardly surprising,' Rory replied. The fire to boil the still had been going for about seven hours; both Rory and Kate had kept it stoked, taking it in turns, and even though it had died down now the heat in there was still fierce. Up close to the still, Kate was sweating heavily now and had been on and off all day. She was beginning to feel a bit faint, but the adrenaline and excitement buoyed her up. She glanced at the watch. 'Three more minutes,' she said and Rory smiled. They waited, the stop-watch bleeped and then he said, 'You transfer the hose, Kate, it's your gin.' She flashed him a smile, and did exactly as he said. The hose fitted into the drum and the first run of Tonsbry gin began.

*   *   *

As Jan's taxi left King's Cross, she decided that she'd had enough for one day and would go straight home. She left the wig on until she was inside her own front door; then she took it off, along with the beige mac and black boots, and went up to the bedroom to re-style her hair. As she sat in front of the mirror, she thought: Rickman Levy Solicitors – who the hell are they, and what was Duncan doing there? It was doubtful it was a social call; Duncan had few friends and he never wasted time on them during a working day. So what business would take him, on several occasions, to a small solicitors' office in the back end of King's Cross? Particularly – and this was a major point – when all his career he had been so insistent on using top advisers for Ingram Lawd: a respected partnership of lawyers in Chancery Lane, a well-known bank and the biggest firm of chartered accountants in the City. And why was it never written in to his diary? Jan put down the hairdryer and ran a comb through her hair. There was only one thing for it; she had to find out.

Going down to the bureau, she telephoned directory enquiries, asking for Rickman Levy and noting down the number. That done, she dialled the number and got straight through.

'Hello,' she said. 'I'm looking for a solicitor in the King's Cross area, and I wondered if you could tell me what sort of business you specialise in?'

'Yes, madam,' a pleasant voice on the other end replied. 'It's primarily conveyancing, contracts on properties, leases, and repossessions. The property market in general, really. Can I take your name and perhaps get one of the partners to call you back?'

'Thank you but no; I was looking for matrimonial. Can you recommend someone?'

The voice asked her to hold, then told Jan that she was sorry but she didn't know of anyone in the area. Jan thanked her and hung up. The next thing she had to do was find out if Duncan did business with them, but that wouldn't be quite so easy. She picked up the phone again and rang her office.

'Hello, Molly? Can you do something for me, confidentially? Good. If I give you a number, could you make a call from my office in private, saying that you're Mr Lawd's new secretary and that you're updating his files and which partner is it who looks after Mr Lawd there? Good, OK, and ring me straight back if you get an answer. Thanks, Molly. Bye.' Jan hung up. She sat where she was and made small patterns on a blotter pad as she waited for the reply. The phone rang and she picked it up.

'Hello? OK, yes – I've got that, Molly, thanks.' She wrote down the name Rickman, circled it, then said, 'Oh, really? Say that again, will you? "Mr Rickman deals with all Mr Lawd's business" – and that's exactly what she said was it? "All Mr Lawd's business"? I see. Yes, yes, I will. Thanks, Molly, bye.'

Jan hung up a second time and stared down at her pad thoughtfully. So Duncan has a series of appointments, all through the year, that he wishes to keep strictly private, she thought. These appointments are with a firm of solicitors who deal exclusively with the property market, and Mr Lawd is a regular client. Oh dear, where on earth is all this leading me? Wherever it is, she concluded, I don't think it's going to be nice. And taking up her coat and bag, then slipping on her shoes, she grabbed the front-door keys and left the house. She was going to talk to Stefan for no specific reason other than that she couldn't think of anyone else to share this with.

Rory, Kate and Michael Gallagher sat at the table in the kitchen at Tonsbry in stony silence. Kate had Flora on her lap, and she gently stroked the little girl's hair as they sat there. In front of them the table was littered with glasses, jugs, bottles and pages of notes. The air was heavy with disappointment.

'I just don't understand it,' said Rory. 'We followed the instructions to the letter, put in all the right botanicals, used high-quality grain spirit, re-distilled the spirit for the length of time required, timed the run, diluted the alcohol . . .' He shook his head. 'What more could we have done? Where did we go wrong?'

Kate glanced up. 'Rory, for God's sake! We've been through all this. I don't know where we went wrong, nor does your father! All we know is that we have a hundred and fifty litres of gin that tastes nothing like the original. Please, stop going on. It doesn't solve anything.'

'But, Kate, we've got a hundred and fifty litres of gin that's practically undrinkable!'

'Not undrinkable, Rory,' Michael put in. 'Not saleable no, but I think most would drink it as a home-made gin.'

'But that's not the point, Dad!' Rory was exhausted and the disappointment had frayed his temper. 'If we want to market this stuff, we've got to get it up to a commercial level.'

His father gently touched his arm. He was getting too wound up; there would be a solution, Michael Gallagher was sure of it, there always was. 'You will get it right, Rory,' he said. 'This was just a first attempt.'

'But we haven't got time to mess about with umpteen attempts, or the money for that matter. This whole run is wasted! It's money down the drain, plus we have to pay duty to Customs and Excise on all gin produced, regardless of whether we sell it or not. I just can't think what's happened, I—'

'Rory?'

He stopped and looked at Kate. 'Rory, it's late and Flora's tired. Let's think about all this in the morning. I think she should go home for some supper.'

'Kate take me, Daddy.'

Rory stood. 'No, sweetheart, I'll take you,' he said, his patience wearing thin. 'Kate's tired, it's been a long day.'

Flora sat up. 'No, Daddy! Kate take me!'

Kate shrugged and looked away, embarrassed. 'I'm quite happy to take her, Rory, I—'

'You've done enough for today!' Rory said sharply. Kate's jaw tensed, but she said nothing. 'Come on, Flora,' he went on, 'Daddy will take you and no fuss. OK?'

Flora sat where she was, rigid in Kate's lap. 'Jump down, Flora, and let me stand up.' But Flora huddled in closer to Kate and tightened her grip.

'Flora!' Rory snapped.

Flora looked up, her bottom lip trembling, and Michael Gallagher said, 'Rory?'

Rory ran his hands through his hair and sighed. 'OK, Flora, if Kate doesn't mind then she can take you home.'

'No, I don't mind at all.' She was glad to get out of there; the tense, gloomy atmosphere was depressing. 'Right, then,' she said gently. 'Jump down, then I can stand up and you can have a carry home, OK?'

Thumb stuck firmly in mouth now, Flora nodded dumbly and did as she was asked. Kate stood up, lifted Flora up on to her hip and turned to Michael Gallagher. 'Do you think we should try another run?'

He nodded. 'Yes, Kate, I do.'

'Can you set it up, Rory, so that it's ready to re-distil tomorrow?'

Rory didn't answer.

'Rory?'

'If that's what you want, Kate, yes, but—'

'Look, let's give it one more try. We'd have been pretty lucky to get it right first time, wouldn't we?'

He shrugged.

'Well, wouldn't we?'

'Yes! But that doesn't mean we should just go ahead and do the same thing all over again.'

'Have you got any other ideas?'

'No, but . . .'

'But that settles it then!' Kate turned away from Rory. 'Come on, Flora,' she said, her voice immediately softening. 'Kiss Daddy and Grandpa goodbye.' Still clinging on to Kate's neck, Flora planted a kiss on Rory's and Michael Gallagher's cheeks, then they turned towards the door.

'I'll put her in the bath after tea, shall I?' she called over her shoulder.

Rory was already clearing up the mess on the table. 'If you want to!' he said sourly, but Kate didn't bother to answer. Without another word, she closed the door behind her and left Rory alone with his father.

'Right, we'd better get the botanicals out,' he said. 'We'll need to order in another delivery of grain spirit in the morning. I wonder if it has anything to do with that? It might be a completely different quality now from what it was forty years ago . . .' Rory glanced up and saw his father staring.

'What?'

Michael Gallagher didn't answer. How sad, he was thinking, that so much happiness once between two people could have come to this. And, not for the first time in his spiritual career, he wanted to shout out loud at God for such a terrible waste.

'You all right, Dad?' Rory asked.

His father shook his head to clear it, then shrugged. 'Yes, fine,' he answered. 'I was just thinking . . .' He broke off, unable to put his thoughts into words. 'I was just thinking how close Kate and Flora seem,' he said finally.

Rory said nothing. He simply turned away and went on with clearing up the mess.

Chapter Fifteen

Stefan was in the shower when the doorbell rang. He only just heard it during the pause between the first and second movements of the Elgar Cello Concerto which he was listening to at full blast on the CD player in the bedroom. He turned off the water, ran his fingers through his hair and stepped out, grabbing a towel and wrapping it round his waist. He padded along to the front door, buzzed the intercom and heard Jan's voice.

'Jan! This is great. Come on up, I'll just release the door for you.' He hurried back into his bedroom, found a towelling robe and pulled it on. As the front door sounded, he glanced at the suit lying ready on the bed, his shirt pressed, his tie draped over the back of the chair, and he cursed. He was due out at seven-thirty; it was now six-fifteen, and the last thing he wanted to do was rush Jan. He wondered whether to cancel his appointment, but it was a long-standing client and, besides, there simply wasn't time. The knock came again and he hurried back to the front door. When he opened it, he was surprised just how pleased he was to see her.

'Hello,' he said, not in the least embarrassed about being in his bath-robe. 'Come in.'

Jan stepped inside the flat. Stefan smelled of cologne, citrus and slightly floral, strong and sharp. She was acutely conscious of the fact that he wasn't dressed and found herself focusing on the visible patch of dark, smooth skin on his chest.

Stefan motioned behind him. 'Come on, come inside. Did you get my message, then?'

'No. What message?'

'Messages actually, plural. I rang your secretary several times and asked you to call back.'

'I wasn't in today, and when I spoke to Molly it was only briefly. Sorry.' Jan immediately felt better. If she'd had her doubts earlier in the day about never seeing him again, they were now dispelled.

Stefan shrugged. 'Would you like a drink?'

'Yes, please, I'd love one.' Jan followed him down a corridor lined with black and white framed photographic prints to his sitting-room. 'I'm sorry – I mean, to just call in like this and for Friday night of course. I was working and I know it sounds silly, but I completely forgot.'

'It doesn't sound silly at all and you're forgiven, think nothing more of it.' He found her an ashtray and placed it on the sofa table by her side. 'Is there a reason for this visit or is it purely social?'

Jan reached for her cigarettes. 'There is a reason,' she said. 'And I'm sure this is going to sound silly as well, but I wanted to talk to you about something and I couldn't think of anyone else to discuss it with. I think – although it's simply a hunch, I've not got any evidence at all – I think that it's connected with your friend Kate Dowie, so I thought you might be interested.' She stopped. 'Does that make sense?'

Stefan nodded. 'Perfect sense. I'll get us a drink,' he said, 'then you can explain what's going on. White wine OK?'

'Yes, lovely, thanks.'

He disappeared into the kitchen and came back a few minutes later with two glasses. 'Here.'

'Thanks.' Jan sipped, then sat on the edge of the sofa and slipped off her coat. As she looked up she saw Stefan glancing at his watch and said, 'Oh God, I'm sorry, were you going out?'

'Sort of – well, yes I was, actually, but I'll ring and say I'm going to be late. I'll just pop into the bedroom and make the call, OK?'

'Yes, fine!' Jan was sitting right by the phone and wondered why he had to go into the bedroom. She sipped her wine and waited for him to return. He came back five minutes later and said, 'That's fixed, we're meeting a bit later now.' He picked up his wine. 'Sorry, go on.'

'Well.' Jan glanced down at her hands. 'I'm not really sure if I've got anything to go on or if this isn't all a bit far-fetched, but the thing is that I'm not convinced in the slightest that the loan on the Tonsbry Estate should be foreclosed – that's what I was doing on Friday, by the way – and yet Duncan is desperate to do it. That rang alarm bells for me and well, to be frank, I had a snoop around his office on Friday night and I came across something really odd in his diary.' She lit a cigarette. 'I won't bore you with the details, but it led me to the bizarre act of following him this morning and he ended up at a rather seedy-looking solicitors' office in King's Cross, a firm I've never heard of – and all very odd considering Duncan always insists on using the best advisers for Ingram Lawd.'

'Maybe it was personal?'

'I don't think so. I rang them; apparently they handle mainly property deals and one of their partners, Mr Rickman, deals with all Mr Lawd's business.'

'Sorry, you've lost me.'

'OK, sorry. Look, Ingram Lawd are a loan company and in the past five years of recession we've had to repossess a great number of properties, owing to mortgages and loans people can't meet – properties which we then sell on. This has made us quite a considerable amount of money, and I'd say that a large proportion of our business has been this type of property. So, one: Duncan wants to foreclose on the Tonsbry Estate with no buyer or developer in sight; and two: I then discover that he has regular meetings with a firm of solicitors who have him down as a client and who handle mainly property deals.'

'So?'

'Exactly,' Jan said, reaching for her wine. 'I think it sounds dodgy, but I've got no idea why.' She smiled. 'Am I being completely paranoid? And if not, what do I do next?'

'Blimey!' said Stefan, sitting down opposite her. 'You're asking me, Stefan Vladimar, ace detective?' He shook his head. 'I'm afraid I haven't got a clue.' He sipped his wine, there was a silence, then he asked, 'So you think Duncan is pulling a fast one on the property side?'

'I don't know, is that what it sounds like to you?'

'I think so. Have you been through the records of sales over the past year or so?'

'No, do you think I should?'

Stefan smiled. 'Jan, you'd have far more idea about that than I would! But, in my humble opinion, I'd have thought it was a good place to start.'

'Yes,' she murmured. She thought for a moment, then said, 'I think you're right.' She took a large gulp of wine, stubbed out her cigarette and got up. 'Thanks, Stefan, I really appreciate this.'

He shrugged. 'I haven't done anything.'

'Yes, you have, you've . . .' She broke off, suddenly embarrassed, sure that she was gushing. Then she smiled. 'You've given me a nice glass of wine,' she said, and Stefan smiled back.

'Any time,' he remarked. 'How about tomorrow night?'

Harry Drummond turned off the main A road towards Tonsbry and glanced at his watch. It was way past his supper and he was hungry, but with any luck he knew his way there now and he might just convince Kate to rustle up something to eat when he arrived. He slowed as he approached a junction, looked at the signs and turned right. Just as he did so, his new mobile phone – a gift from Sasha – rang.

'Oh, blast!' It was in his overnight bag on the floor of the passenger side, so Harry slowed again, pulled on to a grass verge and stopped. Leaning across, he fumbled frantically for the phone and ended up pulling out all his neatly folded clothes before remembering he'd put it in the side pocket for easy access. He hurriedly unzipped that and finally found it, but it took him several seconds more to remember how to turn it on.

'Hello?' He was not in a good humour when he eventually answered it.

'Harry? Hi, it's me.'

There was a silence while he tried to think who 'me' was.

'It's Sasha, Harry!'

'Oh God, yes!' It had to be Sasha, she was the only one who knew the number as yet. 'Sasha! Sorry, I'm on my mobile, it's a bad reception.'

'Yes, I know.'

'You know?'

'That you're on your mobile.'

'Oh. Yes, of course.' His stomach rumbled and he glanced at his watch. 'So?'

'So, how are you?'

'How am I?'

'Yes? I rang to ask you how you were!'

Harry sighed. 'But, Sasha, I only left you a few hours ago.'

'Gosh, was it only a few hours ago? It feels like ages.' She put a special little kittenish purr into her voice as she said that, and almost felt Harry's reaction down the line.

'It does, doesn't it?' he murmured wistfully.

'When will you be back, Harry darling?'

He sighed again, this time differently. 'I don't know – soon, I hope. Shall I ring you?'

'Hmmm, please. I'd like that.' She giggled. 'I like everything you do – you know that, don't you, Harry?'

Harry felt a rush of blood to his groin and smiled. 'Do I?'

'Yes, and you'd better go, you naughty boy!'

'Oooh,' Harry teased. 'Do I have to?'

Sasha giggled again. 'Yes,' she whispered. 'Think of me.' And without another word, she cut him off.

'Bugger!' Harry said. 'I was enjoying that!' And throwing the phone across on to the passenger seat, he switched the engine back on and shifted the car into first. He was annoyed and Sasha was delighted. Little did he know that she had just completed phase one of her new plan and there was lots, lots more to come.

The atmosphere in the still-room was taut with anxiety. There were about fifteen minutes to go before the second gin run was ready. Kate sat back from the still by an open window, her face flushed from the heat but drawn from exhaustion, while Rory paced the floor. They were alone, they had hardly spoken for the past hour and they both watched the clock.

'Ten to go,' Rory said a short while later. Kate nodded and he continued to pace. They had the bucket and a second drum in place to take the run; the hose was attached. The silence lengthened and Kate felt sick. 'Five more minutes,' Rory said. He came and sat down next to her. 'You OK, Kate?'

'Yes!' she snapped; but she didn't sound it.

He glanced at his watch for the umpteenth time that hour and stood up again; he couldn't keep still. Finally he said, 'Come on, Kate, it's ready. Let's do it.' Kate got to her feet, her limbs stiff from the intense motion of shovelling coal. She joined him at the still and watched as he opened the valve.

'Watch set?' She nodded and at that moment the gin began to pour. 'It looks the same,' she ventured, but Rory ignored her; there was no point in being negative at this juncture.

'Wait and see,' he told her. As they both stared at the colourless liquid that flowed down the hose into the bucket, the vapour of alcohol made Kate's eyes smart. 'I think that's about all the foreshot,' Rory said.

Kate glanced at the stop-watch. 'No, another minute to go,' she answered.

'Are you sure?' asked Rory. But Kate didn't reply. She had heard her name, swung round and saw Harry at the entrance to the still-room.

'Harry! What on earth . . .' She hurried across to him. 'Harry, what are you doing here?'

He handed her the flowers he'd brought. 'I wanted to see you, Kate. I hope you don't mind.'

She shrugged.

'Can we talk?'

'Look, Harry, I don't know, I—' The stop-watch started bleeping. 'Harry, hold on a minute, will you?'

She started to move off, but he caught her arm. 'Kate, don't go, please, say you'll just talk to me.'

'Harry! I've got to—' She broke free and turned to look at him. 'You'll have to wait, I've got to—'

'Kate!' Rory hollered across at her. 'Is it time yet?'

'Oh, yes! It's . . .' She glanced down at the watch; she was a minute over, and a lot of liquid drained in that time. 'Sorry, quick! Change the hose over!'

Rory scowled at her, but did it with speed and efficiency.

'What's going on?' Harry asked.

'I'll tell you later,' Kate answered, crossing to Rory. 'OK?' she asked him. He nodded, but kept his head down. 'Rory, I'm going up to the house with Harry.'

'What does he want?' Rory asked, not daring to look at her.

'I don't know,' she said. 'Probably his records back.'

Rory glanced up and she smiled at him. It was the first sign of friendship in a very long time.

'I'll bring this up to the house when it's ready, shall I?'

Kate nodded and went to turn away but glanced back.

'Thanks,' she said. Then she turned on her heel and left. Rory watched her go. She was holding the flowers Harry had brought and she was saying something that Harry seemed to find hugely amusing. Oh God, he thought, not him, not after the first tiny glimmer of hope in years – please, not now!

Kate led Harry into the kitchen, filled the sink, dunked the flowers and turned to face him. 'Harry,' she said coldly, 'what do you want?'

Harry eased his feet apart to distribute his weight evenly and clasped his hands behind his back. It was a nervous habit which Kate was used to. 'Kate,' he said, 'I owe you an apology.'

She raised a cynical eyebrow. The fact that he looked as if he were standing at ease on parade didn't help his credibility. 'Really?'

'Yes, really. Will you hear me out?'

Kate looked across at him, stiff, a bit dull but, despite last week, for the most part kind, loving and committed. She sighed. 'Shall we sit down?'

'I'd prefer to stand if that's all right,' he answered stiffly.

She shrugged and pulled out a chair. 'Fine,' she said. 'Apologise.'

Harry winced. 'You're not making this very easy for me, Kate,' he said.

'Did you expect me to?'

'No, of course not, I . . .' He broke off, coughed, then said, 'Look, I was unfair last week—'

'Yes, you were.'

'I was? Oh, yes, I was, I'm sorry. I shouldn't have walked out on you, that was the last thing you needed, but I had to have some time to think. You do understand that, don't you?'

Kate said nothing. Somehow she had never imagined that Harry had it in him to come and apologise, to open himself up like this; it had never been part of the equation. Harry was just Harry and, if she was honest with herself, Kate had never given him that much thought. She supposed she loved him, if she was still capable of love, but it wasn't the sort of love to shape or change her life. She was comfortable with him, but then she was equally as comfortable without him. Where did that leave her, she wondered, where did it leave both of them?

'Kate? Did you hear what I said?'

She looked up. 'Sorry, Harry – no, I didn't. I was thinking about . . .' She stopped, then shrugged. 'Never mind. Go on.'

'I said that I needed time to think, and I've had it. I was confused—'

'*You* were confused?'

'I didn't know what to do, I've never been in a situation like that before—'

'Oh, and I have?'

'No, Kate, I didn't mean that, I . . .' Harry moved across to her, knelt down to her level and said, 'Look, Kate, I'm sorry.'

Embarrassed, Kate nodded. 'OK,' she said quickly. 'Fine.' She didn't actually know what to say, but saw no point in Harry on his knees.

'D'you want a cup of tea?'

He blinked. 'But, Kate—'

'I'm having one. I'll put the kettle on, shall I?'

Harry stood up. He moved aside to let her get up and watched her fill the kettle, then put it on to boil.

'Kate?' She glanced over her shoulder. 'The thing is that I've had an idea – well, a scheme, actually – for Tonsbry.'

'Really?' Not particularly interested, she went back to making the tea.

'Yes! Listen, Kate, have you ever thought . . .' Harry stopped, walked across to Kate and took the tea-pot out of her hands. He placed it on the side and said, 'Have you ever thought of starting a restaurant?'

'Starting a restaurant? What? Here, at Tonsbry?'

'No! No, in London.'

'Yes, I've thought about it, I've put money away for it in the hope of being able to do it one day, but that's as far as I've got, a small nest-egg. Why?'

'Well, because I've been thinking that perhaps you should go ahead and do it. I've been wondering about this house and the debt and us and—'

'Whoa, hold on a minute, Harry! This is fantasy land we're entering now. Whatever you've been thinking, I certainly haven't got enough money to open a restaurant and keep it afloat for the first year before it starts to make a living.'

'No, no of course not, I wasn't meaning that, I was . . .' Harry stopped and took her hands in his. They were cracked and stained with juniper juice and they smelled of the WD40 she had been using to oil the capping machine. 'Kate, what I was thinking is that I've got some money, quite a bit actually, that I inherited from an aunt several years ago and, well, I thought I could use it to set you up in a small restaurant in London. Nothing fancy, maybe

Battersea Park, Fulham . . .' He stopped as Kate pulled her hands away and held them up to silence him. 'What's the matter?'

'Harry, how much money are you talking about here?'

'I don't know, I . . .' Shit, he hadn't discussed an actual sum with Adriana! He faltered for a moment, then plucked a figure from the air. 'Fifty thousand?'

'Double it!' Kate said and turned away to take the tea-caddy from the shelf. She opened the drawer and found a spoon. When she turned back she saw his face, aghast with shock. 'Oh, Harry,' she said, feeling immediately guilty for brushing aside such kindness. 'Harry, it really is so sweet of you to think of me in that way but I'm afraid it's impossible, completely impossible. Besides,' she went on, 'there are other things to consider now, and—' She was interrupted by the kitchen door bursting open.

'Kate, Kate! Daddy says come on, the gin's ready!'

Harry and Kate turned to see Flora Gallagher, pink and out of breath. 'Who's that?' Harry demanded.

'Flora,' Kate said. 'Right then, Flora, we'll come back to the still-room with you.'

'Flora?' Harry asked. 'Still-room?'

'Flora Gallagher,' Kate explained. 'And we're making gin.'

'Making gin?' As Harry stared down at the little girl, a snippet of his drunken conversation with Adriana came back to him. Kate made her way across to the door with Flora hanging on to her arm.

'Kate! Hang on, wait a minute!' he called and she stopped. 'Kate, think about my idea, will you?'

She was about to refuse point-blank, but there was something about his imploring face and the fact that she couldn't bear to reject him. She hesitated, then nodded.

'Oh . . . and Kate?'

She turned a second time.

'We are still engaged, are we?'

'Oh, Harry, I . . .' No, they weren't still engaged, he had broken it off and she hadn't really given it much thought since. 'Harry, I don't know, I don't think so.'

He hung his head and all the old feelings about rejection swamped her. 'Please, Kate, don't say no.'

She bit her lip, agonised for a minute or so, then finally shrugged.

'Great!' Harry said. He made his way over to her. 'I'll come with you to have a look at this gin. What possessed you to have a bash at distilling gin? Not an easy job, I shouldn't think; you have to know when to strike the still and tons of stuff like that . . .' He took Kate's other arm. 'Oh, and by the way,' he said, as they headed out of the house, 'the Colonel's having a drinks party in the next couple of weeks; I don't suppose you fancy coming, do you . . . ?'

Rory sat alone in the still room waiting for Kate. He had diluted the gin and it stood in front of him in a measuring jug, not unpleasant, not as bad as the last batch but definitely not saleable. It was nothing like the Tonsbry gin they had found cases of, even taking into account the change in the gin over the years it had been stored.

Kate came in, saw him and her heart plummeted.

'It's no good, is it?'

Rory shook his head. 'It's better,' he said.

'But it's still not right?'

'No.'

Harry looked confused.

'I've rung Dad, he's coming over.'

'With all due respect, Rory, I don't see what your father can do.'

'Pray?'

'That's not funny!'

'It wasn't meant to be!'

'Will someone tell me what's going on?' Both Kate and Rory turned to look at Harry.

'Sorry,' Kate said. 'It's a long story, Harry, but we decided to try making Tonsbry gin; it used to be distilled on the estate about fifty years ago and it was pretty good. Rory and I thought we might be able to revive it.'

'And sell it,' Rory said. 'There's a niche market for drinks like this and Kate has all her catering contacts, so we, I . . .'

'Making gin!' Harry exclaimed. The use of 'we' upset him. What was going on? Was there some kind of arrangement between these two? The last thing Harry knew, Rory had jilted Kate virtually at the altar and gone off with another woman, and she never mentioned his name. Now it was 'we' this, and 'we' that. Harry was more than upset; he felt excluded. He'd been gone five minutes and already that bastard had muscled in. 'Are you mad, Kate?' he demanded. 'And you thought my idea was a money drain!' He turned to Rory. 'What the hell do you know about making gin, Gallagher? It's hardly the same as putting the kettle on for a nice cuppa!' He was into his stride. 'This is totally irresponsible, to involve Kate in something like this. Wasting her money! Making gin! It hasn't worked, has it? How many independent gin distillers do you know of, eh?

No, none, exactly my point! If it was that easy, don't you think there'd be one on every street cor—'

'Boller's!'

Harry stopped, unsure whether he'd heard right. He swung round and the Reverend Gallagher, in dog collar and cassock, said again, 'Boller's, Kate!'

Harry's mouth dropped open. 'Boller's?'

'Gin!' He came into the room, pulling the cassock over his head and throwing it over the back of the chair. 'Boller's gin! Of course you won't have heard of it, either of you, it was before your time, but there was a local company in Winchester and your grandfather, Kate, worked quite closely with one of their men; it was the two of them who developed Tonsbry Original, back in the late thirties when Edward Alder was a young man.'

'Dad! How do you know all this?' Rory was genuinely taken aback and Michael Gallagher smiled. 'It's a bit of a specialist subject for me, local history and gin.'

'So what does all this mean?' Kate asked, sure that it must have some relevance even if she couldn't see it.

Michael Gallagher turned. 'Well, Boller's were swallowed up back in the seventies by a huge drinks company, but old Boller is still around. I saw something on the family in the local paper months back, and as soon as Rory rang me tonight I thought of them. In fact, I don't know why it didn't occur to me before but we should contact him, or the family at least, and see if there are any records. Old Boller is very elderly and, you never know, he might even remember.' Michael crossed to the table and picked up the measuring jug of sample gin, smelled it and went on, 'I can't help thinking that perhaps there's something we don't know, that we're missing in this process, something records or even Boller himself might be able to tell us.'

'So how do we go about contacting him?' Rory asked. He was sceptical, didn't see it happening at all. 'It could take weeks. Presumably we'd have to find his address and write?'

Suddenly Michael Gallagher grinned. For a man of the cloth he had a rather manic and wicked grin. 'The phone book!' he announced and, unable to contain his delight, the grin widened to a broad smile. 'I rang directory enquiries a short while ago and found the number, or what I'm pretty sure is the number. It was listed under Boller, H.J.!'

'Dad, that's brilliant!'

'Of course!' He dug in his pocket and brought out a piece of paper. 'Divine inspiration!' He handed it to a doubtful-looking Kate. 'You should ring,' he said. 'I've written a list of questions to ask, but the main thing is are there any records and is there anyone alive now who might be able to help us?' He looked at Kate. 'OK?'

She hesitated. 'Are you really sure about this? I can't help thinking that it's a bit obscure.'

Michael shrugged. 'No, Kate,' he replied. 'I'm not at all sure, but it's a start. If it doesn't work – and chances are it might not – then we sit down and think again. OK?'

Again she hesitated, then finally nodded.

'D'you want me to come with you, Kate?'

She glanced up. 'No. Thanks, Rory, but I'm a big girl now.'

Michael Gallagher sighed. Was this constant sniping ever going to end? She heard the sigh and immediately felt embarrassed.

'Sorry,' she mumbled. 'If you want to come, then do.' It was a grudging apology, but the best she could offer.

'I will, thanks.' Rory took a handkerchief out of his pocket and wiped his face and hands, then he headed towards the door.

'I say, shouldn't I . . . ?' Harry began, but the Reverend Gallagher put a hand on his arm. 'Have you seen this capping machine?' he asked. 'Splendid bit of old machinery, let me show you.' And by the time Harry looked round, Kate and Rory had gone.

Henry Jacob Boller sat in the conservatory in his wheel-chair, a wheel-chair he found almost impossible to manoeuvre himself, and sprayed the long, shiny leaf of a Yucca plant with leaf cleaner, then wiped it carefully and lovingly with a soft cloth. Satisfied with its glossy surface, he moved on to the next leaf and did the same. He was completely absorbed in what he was doing, yet every now and then his hand crept down to the rug over his knees and the small hard object concealed there. It was the second week he'd had it, a secret gift from his grand-daughter, and already it had opened up a whole new world for him. Henry Boller was the proud new owner of a cordless telephone, a cordless telephone which his son and daughter-in-law knew nothing about – its extension plugged into a hidden socket in the conservatory – and a piece of modern technology that at long last had put an end to his isolation in old age. For the first time in years he was free to make and receive calls, something he had previously been denied owing to what his son called 'an irresponsible running up of phone bills'. It wasn't so much the opportunity to make calls that he wanted – most of his friends were dead – it was more the link with the outside world. He loved to answer the phone virtually on the first ring and way before anyone else in the house had any idea there had been a call. Of course he could only do it for a couple of hours in the evening, the hours he spent in the conservatory after dinner, and there were rarely more than one or two calls, but those two hours were the best of the day.

Moving slowly and with great effort from the Yucca to his beloved orchid collection, Henry Boller changed the leaf spray for a water spray and laid a fine mist on the leaves and flowers of the first orchid. He leaned forward to inspect what he had done and, just as he did so, the phone rang. Deftly, considering his age, he pulled the phone from under the blanket and switched the button to speak. When the bleeping stopped, he put it to his ear and said, 'Good evening, Henry Boller speaking.'

On the other end of the phone, Kate was taken aback to get straight through. 'Good evening,' she said quickly. 'Is that the Henry Boller of Boller's gin?'

'It is? And to whom am I speaking?'

Kate took a breath. The voice was frail but determined, the manner rather old-fashioned. 'You don't know me,' she began. 'My name is Kate Dowie and I'm the grand-daughter of Edward Alder, from Tonsbry House.'

'Good Lord! Edward Alder? Haven't heard from him in a long time. How is he?'

Kate coughed. 'Well, he's . . . he died several years ago, I'm afraid.' Twenty, to be precise.

'Oh dear, I am sorry to hear that. Not many left now, you know, most of 'em dead. Gets a bit lonely at times.'

'I'm sure it must do.' Kate motioned frantically for Rory

to pick up the other phone and listen in. 'Mr Boller, I wonder if you can help me . . .'

'I'll do my best, my dear.'

'Well, I don't know if you remember, but my grandfather used to make gin on the estate, Tonsbry Original, and I—'

'Tonsbry Original! Haven't heard of that for years! Used to be made by a chap called Edward Alder, over on the Tonsbry Estate.'

Kate glanced worriedly across at Rory who was mouthing the words: KEEP HIM GOING! 'That's right,' she said, 'it's . . .'

'Now who was it that worked with him? Goddammit, I can't remember the chap's name. He was one of the best master distillers we had, and Alder went and pinched the blighter! Left us high and dry for a while! Can't say I blame him, it was—'

'Master distillers?' Kate interrupted gently. 'What's a master distiller?'

'Master distiller?! Why, he's the fellow who makes the gin! Knows exactly when to strike the still, how to handle the drink – all that sort of stuff. Essential, a good master distiller! Can't make the stuff without him. Now what was that chappie's name, local man, came from a long line of gin workers, good fellow too . . .'

'I wonder if there might be any records of all this, would you know—'

'Tommy Vince! That was it, old Tommy Vince! From Westhampnet. Good Lord, I wonder what he's doing now, haven't seen him since 'thirty-five – not that I wanted to, mind you, not after all that business. I . . .' Henry Boller broke off and Kate heard a scuffle, then muffled voices, one angry. She held on and moments later another voice came on the line. 'Good evening, William Boller speaking. Can I help you?'

Kate breathed a sigh of relief. 'Yes, yes I hope so. I was just talking to Mr Henry Boller about Tonsbry Original gin. I wonder if—'

'Who is this?'

'I'm sorry, my name is Kate Dowie, I'm Edward Alder's grand-daughter. He was a friend of Mr Henry Boller, and I wondered if I might be able to ask you a few questions about Tonsbry Original.'

'Tonsbry Original?'

'Yes, it used to be made by my family and I'm trying to revive it. I gather there was some connection between the two families and I wondered what that was, or if there were any records of it—'

'I'm sorry,' William Boller cut in, 'but it is very late and I really can't discuss this now. If you have an enquiry I suggest that you put it in writing and send it to our parent company, Worldwide Drinks. Thank you and good night.'

Instantly the line went dead. Kate looked at it, then at Rory and replaced the receiver. 'That's that, then,' she said.

Rory nodded. 'Yes,' he answered. 'I'm afraid I think it is.' And too frustrated to say anything more, he turned and walked out of the room.

Chapter Sixteen

The following morning, Kate woke alone in her white four-poster bed and lay for a while staring at the empty space beside her. She had slept badly; she felt that her whole life was unresolved – Harry, her business in London, Tonsbry – and that she really had no direction at all. The one thing she was clear about was a deep-seated determination not to give up on any of it.

Climbing out of bed, she pulled on her dressing-gown and crossed to the basin to brush her teeth. She had a mouth full of toothpaste when she heard a knock and Harry popped his head round the door.

'Morning. Coffee?'

'Hmmmmmmm!'

'Sorry?'

Kate spat out a big globule of toothpaste and saliva into the basin and said, 'Thanks, lovely.'

Harry, fully dressed and smelling strongly of aftershave, came in and placed the cup on the chest of drawers, then retreated towards the door. 'So what are you doing today?' he asked. 'Now that the gin thing has fallen through?'

'It hasn't fallen through exactly, Harry, it's . . .'

'It's what?'

Kate sighed irritably. 'Oh, I don't know, but I'm not sure it's over yet.'

'Well, over or not, why don't we take a drive in the MG? It's a nice morning, we could dress up warm and put the roof down.'

'I don't think so, Harry,' she said abruptly. 'I've got things to do.'

'I see.' Harry's face was the epitome of boyish disappointment; it was a look he had been practising, and it worked.

Kate was immediately moved and said, 'I'm sorry, it's not that I don't want to, it's just that there's so much to do here and, well . . .' She looked at him. 'You don't mind, do you?'

'No, I don't mind.' He shrugged and dug his hands in his pockets. 'See you at breakfast, then?'

She nodded and went back to brushing her teeth. 'I'll be down in a minute,' she said, with the brush stuck in her mouth. But it came out too garbled for Harry to understand.

Down in the kitchen half an hour later, Kate found Harry cooking himself eggs and bacon and Mrs Able, sour-tempered, with a malevolent look on her face.

'Good morning,' Kate said, realising instantly that it wasn't. No one, with the very rare exception of Kate – and then only on occasions – was allowed the free run of Mrs Able's kitchen.

'Why don't you let Mrs Able do that for you, Harry?' she asked hurriedly.

'Good Lord, no!' Harry shot back. 'Bacon and eggs are a supremely male art, and one with a long tradition in the armed forces.'

Kate winced, Mrs Able huffed. 'But you haven't read the paper,' she tried.

'Plenty of time for that.'

Mrs Able clucked disapprovingly; it went right over Harry's head.

'Good morning!' said Rory, coming into the kitchen still in his coat. He paused, sensed the atmosphere and turned to Kate.

'Kate, would you like to go for a drive?'

'Not you as well!' she remarked.

'Sorry?'

'Never mind. And no, no thanks.'

Rory bristled at her rudeness. 'OK, I'll put it like this, shall I? Kate, come out in the car with me, please, because there's somewhere I'd like to take you. Purely business, of course.'

Kate looked at him; he wasn't smiling. 'Will we be long?'

'I don't know,' he answered honestly. 'Are you coming?'

Glancing sidelong at Harry and Mrs Able, locked in silent battle, she shrugged and reached for her coat. 'See you later, Harry,' she said and, before he could reply, she darted out of the kitchen after Rory.

It was nine-thirty in the morning and Jan was already at her desk with the door to her office firmly closed. Molly, at her work station out front, had been given strict instructions not to interrupt her, and Duncan was out of the office. That gave her a clear run of about four hours and, as she looked at the box of files on her desk, she reckoned she was going to need it.

*　　*　　*

Rory swung the Land-Rover hard right off the main A road, down a narrow country lane that cut across swaths of prime arable farming land and towards the village of Westhampnet. Kate glanced at the sign as they passed it and said, 'So that's what this is all about.' It was the first time she had spoken since she got in the car.

'I don't know if it'll lead us anywhere, but it's worth a try,' Rory answered. 'At least *I* think so.' They drove on, over a small one-vehicle bridge and down a gentle incline into Westhampnet village.

'Post office, village stores, church. Where first?' Rory pulled up by a bus-stop.

'Let's try the churchyard and see if this Tommy Vince is buried here. You never know, he might still be alive.'

'Highly doubtful and, if he is, knowing our luck he's probably a hundred and two and gaga.'

Kate arched an eyebrow. 'I do admire your confidence.'

'I'm here, aren't I?' Rory fired back and, quite unexpectedly, Kate smiled.

'Yes, you are,' she said. 'Thank you.'

They drove off towards the church.

In the churchyard, they walked together and looked at the headstones. They were silent but, for the first time since they had met again, the silence was not underpinned by animosity.

'He's not here, then?' Kate said.

'No.'

'Which means that either he's still alive, or that he moved away and died some place we have no hope of finding.'

'Or,' Rory added, 'that he's still alive and has moved away to some place we have no hope of finding.'

'Great.' They both turned away and walked back to the Land-Rover. 'Where now? The post office?'

'Yes, you do that and I'll do the village stores, OK?'

Kate nodded. They drove the short distance and parked, then Kate climbed out and disappeared into the post office.

'Good morning, may I help you?' Kate glanced up at the woman who addressed her. She crossed to the counter and looked through the glass shield.

'I'm not sure really,' she said. 'I'm trying to locate someone by the name of Vince.'

'Vince what?'

'I'm sorry?'

'Vince, you said? What's his last name?'

'No, sorry, that is his last name, it's Tommy Vince. I'm afraid I've got nothing to go on, no address or anything, and all I know is that he lived here back in the thirties. He worked for Boller's gin apparently.'

'No, sorry, my dear, I can't help you.' The woman smiled sympathetically. 'My husband and I bought the post office three years ago and, although we know the locals, we don't know much village history. Have you tried the doctor's surgery? It's in the next village: Easthampnet.'

'No, but thanks, I'll give it a go.'

As Kate opened the door the woman called out, 'Try the pub too, dear. The landlord's been here years.'

Kate held up her hand in thanks and joined Rory outside on the pavement. 'Any luck?' He shook his head.

'Pub and doctor's surgery,' Kate said, and strode towards the Land-Rover. 'Come on,' she said over her shoulder. 'We haven't got any time to waste.'

*   *   *

271

Halfway through the morning Jan stood up, thought about getting herself a cup of coffee, paced the office for a few minutes, then changed her mind and went back to work. She lifted three more files from the box, put them in front of her and opened the first. Another Letchworth Housing Association purchase, so she settled down in her seat, lit one more cigarette and got to work. The property sales policy of Ingram Lawd was beginning to develop a pattern and, if she'd been a gambling woman, she would have bet her last penny on the fact that the pattern wasn't coincidence. She didn't know why, but another thing she would have bet on was that she was going to find out.

Rory and Kate stood in the reception area of the West- and Easthampnet doctor's surgery and waited for the secretary to finish on the phone. A few yards away from them, a middle-aged woman strapped her baby into its pushchair with an exhausting struggle and Rory found himself staring at her, remembering the same scene himself little over a year ago. She looked down-at-heel and drained, and her patience was stretched. It might have been him, and so strong were the feelings she aroused that he crossed to her and asked, 'D'you need a hand?'

She looked up, startled. 'No, no thanks.' The baby was secure but screaming and she pushed a greasy, limp strand of hair off her face.

'Can I open the door for you?'

'I'm going to sit here for a moment and catch my breath, but thanks anyway.' Suddenly she smiled. 'There's not many who'd offer.' Rory shrugged and smiled back. As he heard Kate ask the receptionist if she knew how they could locate the Vince family or Tommy Vince, the smile on the woman's face abruptly died.

''Scuse me,' she said, pushing past him. 'I've got to go.' He looked at her, but she'd averted her face and her whole manner was suddenly anxious. Kicking the door hard with her foot, she shoved the pushchair through it and let it slam behind her.

On a hunch, Rory hurried out after her and caught up with her in a couple of strides. 'Hey! Wait!' He gently stopped her. 'You wouldn't know Tommy Vince, would you?'

The woman flushed and kept her face averted. 'No, why should I?'

'I don't know, I just thought . . .' He broke off. 'We're looking for him, if he's still alive, or anyone who can tell us about him because we might have some work for him.'

The hostility swiftly changed to curiosity. 'What sort of work?'

'I don't know. I need to find out if he's the right Tommy Vince first. The man we're looking for used to work for Boller's gin, he'd be about—'

'Eighty-six,' the woman interrupted, tonelessly, 'and he's dead; he died ten years ago, stroke.' She went to move off.

'Wait! Are you related to him?'

She stopped and turned to look Rory in the face. She was pale, her lips were chapped with the cold, her hair was unwashed, her clothes shabby and her nails chewed. 'No,' she said sharply. 'Is that all?'

Rory nodded as Kate came up behind him. 'We're not from the Social Services or anything,' he said. 'We're not wanting to catch anyone out; we just need some help, that's all.'

The woman turned to go, hesitated, then glanced back. 'What's in it for me?'

Rory looked at her. 'D'you want cash?' She shrugged, but her eyes were desperate. So he took out his wallet, pulled all the cash he had from it – £20 – and handed it to her.

She took it and avoiding his gaze, said, 'I'm Tommy Vince's daughter-in-law. But I don't know how I can help you 'cause he's been dead ten years, like I told you.'

'Did he ever talk about the gin industry? Can you remember anything—'

'Talk about it?' she suddenly cried. 'It were his bloody life! And my Tommy's too! Got his son into the same line, didn't he? Only there's no work now, what with this recession and it being so specialised. My Tommy wanted to be a chippie, work with his hands but no, his dad insisted; good living he said, unique. Unique! Look where it's got us! Unemployed for five years now, five kids and scrubbing around to make a living, that's where it's got us. At least as a carpenter he would have always found work. Bloody unique! Bloody useless, if you ask me!'

She thrust the money down into the pocket of her coat and her baby started crying. 'Now, look!' she said, bouncing the pushchair violently up and down and making the baby cry harder. 'I gotta go,' she snapped. 'Baby needs feeding.'

Rory gently moved forward and took hold of the pushchair. 'Here, let me.' She stood back and relinquished it, almost with relief. Calmly and smoothly, he wheeled the pushchair backwards and forwards with a very slight rocking motion. The baby quietened.

'Look, can we help you home with this? Maybe talk to Tommy? Did he work for Boller's as well?'

She nodded and looked away, trying to make up her mind. All the time Kate stood silent beside them, not daring to speak. The woman finally turned back. 'It's this way,' she said, 'it's a bit of a walk.' And she lumbered on ahead, leaving Rory and Kate to follow with her baby and pushchair.

Jan sat at her desk for several minutes, thinking hard about what she might or might not have found, then she picked up the phone and spoke to Molly. 'Can you get me the number of Companies House, please, Molly,' she said. 'And I'd love a coffee if you've got a minute. Thanks.' She replaced the receiver, stood up and rubbed her hands wearily over her face. When the phone rang, she noted down the number that Molly gave her and dialled.

'Good morning, I wonder if you can help me? I wanted to find a list of directors. Sorry? Oh, right, a directors' screen print, that's a list of company directors, is it? Right – yes, that's what I want. Oh, can I? Great, I'll do that then. How long would a fax take to come through? OK, fine. Visa card please, yes, hang on a minute.' Jan reached for her purse, took out her personal credit card and gave the number, followed by her fax number. 'Yes,' she said, 'it is a limited company, the name is: the Letchworth Housing Association Limited . . .'

Just as she hung up, Molly came into the office with her coffee. 'Molly, there's a confidential fax coming through to me in about an hour from Companies House, Cardiff,' she said. 'I'm going to go out and grab a sandwich; can you collect it for me?'

'Of course. Do you want it on your desk?'

'No.' Jan didn't want anyone to know what she was

looking into. 'Keep it for me, will you?' She took a sip of her coffee and lit another cigarette. 'When I say confidential, Molly, I mean *strictly* P and C.'

Kate sat in the Land-Rover and waited for Rory to climb in. He was saying goodbye, shaking hands, exchanging a few more words and she stared at him from inside the car, across the small, scruffy front garden of the terraced cottage, as if she'd never seen him before. Perhaps she hadn't, perhaps she had only seen the Rory she wanted to see – the one she despised and distrusted, the one who had let her down. And if she'd done that, had she misjudged everything else? Certainly this wasn't the man she had assumed him to be over the past ten days; this was a man who had just been sensitive, caring, persuasive and dynamic. This was a man who had just been totally honest. She turned as he climbed into the car.

'So that's that, then,' he said, smiling. 'To quote someone we know and love!'

Kate took the jibe and smiled back.

'Tommy starts work at Tonsbry tomorrow morning, I will pick him up myself at seven-thirty.' He looked at Kate. 'You know, for the first time, Kate, I've got a good feeling about all this.'

Kate's smile dissolved into laughter. 'So have I!' she said. And without thinking, she leaned across and planted a kiss firmly on Rory's mouth.

It was late afternoon by the time Jan made it across London to Egerton Square. As she climbed out of the taxi she thought, I must stop just turning up like this, and experienced a moment of doubt. But she needed to talk to Stefan; he had become her sounding board and, after her discoveries today, she had an awful lot to try on him.

Ringing at the main door, she waited, heard the intercom and said, 'Hi, it's Jan.' Stefan sounded surprised and a bit distant, but he told her to come up and she did so, wondering again if this was the right thing to do. She rang the bell, waited a few minutes and heard what sounded like a scuffle in the flat before Stefan appeared at the door in tracksuit bottoms and a torn sweat-shirt. He looked as if he'd just got up. 'Sorry, Jan, come on in.'

Jan followed him along the corridor to the sitting-room and saw the remains of what appeared to be an intimate scene. As she walked in behind him, the head of a young woman popped up from the sofa and she felt her heart plummet.

'Hi, I'm Rebecca, but most people call me Becca.'

'Hello.'

'Sorry about the mess, but we've been frantic trying to arrange schedules and menus and things for Kate.'

'Menus?'

Stefan bent to tidy a pile of papers on the floor. 'I'm running Kate's catering business in her absence; well, managing it really. Becca does most of the cooking, I do the bookings, orders, all the boring stuff.'

'Oh, I see.'

'Yes, well . . .'

'I'd better go,' Becca said, getting to her feet. 'We can finish these tomorrow morning.'

'No, don't go, not on my account,' said Jan. 'I just wanted to have a quick word with Stefan and then I'll disappear. Do you mind, Stefan?'

'No, of course not. Becca, I'll get you a coffee and we'll have a quick break. Jan, we can talk in the kitchen. OK?'

'Fine.'

Becca sat down again and Jan followed Stefan into the kitchen.

'Sorry,' she said as soon as he'd closed the door behind them. 'I thought I was interrupting something intimate.'

Stefan smiled. 'You were, stuffed quails' eggs or slivers of warm smoked salmon with raspberry vinegar. Very intimate!'

Jan laughed. 'Is this what you do, then? Food and catering?'

Stefan turned away and filled the kettle. 'Not all the time,' he replied.

'Oh?'

This was an ideal opportunity to tell Jan what he did for a living, to get it all out in the open, establish the honesty she deserved, but somehow he just couldn't do it.

'But mostly,' he lied. 'I'm helping Kate out at the moment.' He turned back. 'So, what was it that you wanted to talk to me about?'

Jan's curiosity was forgotten, she had other, far more important things on her mind. 'Well, I think I've come across something odd. Can I run it past you and see what you think?'

'Sure. Let me give Becca a coffee first. Would you like one?'

'No, thanks. May I smoke?'

'No problem. I'll be back in a tick.' Stefan left the kitchen, and Jan lit up, conscious of the fact that during the past few days she had been smoking far too much. He was back just as she reached for the ashtray.

'Right, fire away.'

'OK. After our conversation last night, I decided to look through the company's property sales this morning and I went through all the files going back the past two years.'

'And?'

'And I've found that certain discrepancies have arisen, all concerning a housing association called the Letchworth Housing Association Limited.'

'What sort of discrepancies?'

Jan smiled. 'Hang on, I'll get there all in my own time!'

'Sorry, go on.'

'Well, firstly, housing associations usually buy the same sort of properties, cheap housing basically, but this one has bought anything; there's no pattern to their purchasing, and it seems that they buy it as long as the price is right. And, secondly, the price is always right. In fact, there are times when I'd have said that they got one hell of a bargain – ten, fifteen, sometimes twenty thousand pounds under the market price. So, I decided to check them out with Companies House, just to see who they are, and it turns out that one of their directors is a P. Rickman. Next thing, I rang them, checked and lo and behold, he's the same P. Rickman of Rickman Levy Solicitors.' She stubbed out her cigarette, reached for another and Stefan leaned across to open a window. 'Now does that sound odd to you?'

'I'm not sure, though I think so. But where does Duncan fit into all this? And what about Kate and Tonsbry? Is there any connection to them, do you think?'

Jan shook her head. 'That's the problem; I really don't know and I have no idea how to find out either. The only thing I can guess is that when Tonsbry comes to be bought, the chances are it'll be bought by the Letchworth—'

'Housing Association. Yes, I get that feeling too. So why would Duncan knowingly undersell properties? What would be in it for him?'

'Cash under the table?'

'Hold on! Are we talking embezzlement here, Jan?'

Jan sighed wearily. 'I don't know, Stefan, I really don't.' She stubbed out her cigarette and dropped her head in her hands.

Stefan crossed to her, gently pulled them away from her face and tilted up her chin. 'So we've got to find out, then, haven't we?'

'We? You don't have to get involved, Stefan, it might not even be connected to your friend Kate, it might just be . . .'

He silenced her with a kiss on her forehead. 'All that matters is we get it straight,' he said. 'We find out what Duncan is up to with the Housing Association and why he's in such a hurry to foreclose on Tonsbry. OK?'

Jan glanced away. He made it sound so simple, banal almost, and she wanted to shout: No, it's not OK, this is serious stuff, painful, gut-wrenching stuff! But she didn't voice any of that, she simply nodded and extracted herself from his embrace. 'OK,' she answered. 'Fine.' But of course, she didn't mean it in the least.

Alice sat on a teak deck-lounger on the beechwood terrace of an apartment in Neutral Bay, Sydney. She wore a white bath-robe, and there was a cup of Earl Grey tea by her side. It was early morning and she lay with her head back against the blue-and-white striped calico cushion, her eyes closed. Reading an old copy of *The Times* – something she had picked up in the lobby of a restaurant last night – she had found an announcement of Leo Alder's death and it had thoroughly upset her.

'Alice?' She opened her eyes and put her hand up to shield them from the sun. Tom Sullivan stood in the doorway. 'You all right?'

She nodded and shifted, placing her feet on the floor. 'Would you like some more tea?' he asked.

'No, thanks.'

He walked across to the edge of the terrace and stood looking out at the ocean for a few minutes, then he turned and said, 'It's not like you to be maudlin.'

'No. Alice the original good-time girl,' she said. 'Sorry.'

'What on earth for?'

She shrugged and finished her tea, then picked up the paper from the floor. 'It's this,' she said. 'Someone I knew died last week, there's an announcement in here.'

'I'm sorry. Were you close?'

No, he wasn't close – in fact she had never met Leo Alder – but she knew all about him from Rory. 'No,' she said, 'not really. It just makes me feel very homesick, that's all.'

'It's understandable.'

'Is it? The "someone" was Kate Dowie's uncle.'

'I see.'

'Do you? Because I don't. I couldn't even say her name for years, and now I see a mention of Leo Alder's death and I want to go home. It doesn't make any sense to me.'

'Perhaps you're ready to go home now, Alice, to face up to things.'

'But I did face up to things, Tom! I told Rory the truth and left him to get on with his life. Wasn't that facing up to things?'

Tom said nothing.

'You don't think it was?'

He didn't answer. There was a long silence and Alice sat very still, just staring out at the blue sky and blue sea. Then she said, 'I ran away, didn't I?'

'Yes, I think you did.'

Alice stood up and walked across to stand next to Tom, facing the ocean. He watched her, waiting. When she finally turned to him she was crying. She wiped the tears away with the back of her hand. 'I should be paying you for this.'

'I'm not your analyst any more, Alice.'

'Perhaps you should recommend a colleague?' She tried to laugh, but it died in her throat. 'Am I getting ill again, Tom? I've thought about nothing but all this since I saw the paper last night. I can't get it out of my head.'

Tom took both her hands in his. 'No, Alice,' he answered, 'you are not getting ill again, you are healing yourself.' He looked at her face and wondered if it was the right time to tell her that he loved her. 'You must go home and deal with whatever it is that haunts you, Alice.'

She pulled her hands away. 'Will that make this guilt go away?'

'It might do.'

'But what if I don't want to come back?'

He shrugged. No, it wasn't the right time. 'If you do, then I'll be here,' he said. Then he smiled and held out his arms. Alice stepped into his embrace and felt safer than she had ever felt in her life before. 'And if you don't,' he whispered, 'well, I'll still be here.'

Chapter Seventeen

Tommy Vince sat in the kitchen at Tonsbry with the tools of his trade in front of him: a bottle of Tonsbry gin, a bottle of the last run that failed, the water, the botanicals, the pages of the old Tonsbry records and pages of his own notes, various measuring jugs, the grain spirit and several tasting glasses. As he worked – sniffing, tasting, diluting, re-tasting and crushing the spices between his fingers to release their aroma – Kate and Rory sat watching him. They were both nervous, Kate most of all, and they were all slightly in awe of this small, compact man who did everything in total silence and with intense concentration. They had been there for over an hour when he finally spoke.

'Right,' he said. 'First off, your botanicals are wrong.'

'But—'

Tommy held up his hands to silence Kate 'Yes,' he said, 'I know what it says here, and you were right to follow it, but this juniper isn't as sound as it should be; it's a bit past it, and we need to up it a bit to get it right. Look . . .' He took some juniper berries and crushed them in his palm. 'See the oil here? There's not enough of it – that should be much darker, smell much stronger. It's a bit dried out, been there too long, I should say.' He dropped the berries on the table and Kate picked them up to smell them. She nodded. 'Then there's these cornflowers,' he went on. 'They give it the colour and a distinctive flavour, but here's the opposite – they're too strong, much stronger I'd gauge than they were forty years ago, too concentrated, giving too many high notes. Nope . . .' He picked up the cornflowers and rubbed them between his fingers. 'Nope, I'm right,' he said. 'Here, smell.' He held out his hand and they each took a quick sniff. 'Pungent! Too strong.' Again he dropped the crushed flowers on the table. 'Then there's the run. Spirit's good, top quality, water's lovely, very nice – is it local?'

'Yes, we've got a spring on the estate.'

'Good. But the run was too quick, the foreshot hadn't quite come off in both cases and it ruined the run.'

'How do you know when the foreshot has gone then?' Kate asked.

Tommy tapped the side of his nose and raised an eyebrow. 'It's all in here,' he said, 'in the nose. I can smell it.'

'So what next?' Rory asked. 'Where do we go from here?'

'Well . . .' Tommy Vince scraped back his chair and stretched his legs. 'If you're happy with what I've said, and happy for me to do it, then I reckon I could produce your Tonsbry gin for you next run.'

'Really?' Kate was excited. 'You really think we can get there that quickly?'

'You done most of the work yourselves, you just need me to finish off for you.'

'And what sort of fee are we talking about?' As cautious as ever, Rory was concerned that this was going to cost and it was an expense they hadn't bargained for.

Tommy clasped his hands together and looked at them both squarely.

'No fee,' he said.

'No fee? What, you mean you want some sort of salary?'

'No, not that either.' Tommy wasn't sure he had the nerve for this, but for Mary's sake he had to give it a try, at least. 'I'd like a share of the business,' he said. 'A small partnership and a share of the profits, in return for my services for as long as they're needed.' He'd said it, it had been easier than he'd thought it would be, just like Mary said it would. 'They need you, Tommy,' she'd said, 'and this time they're not going to just use you and dump you when they're ready. You ask them, Tommy, you have to ask to get!' 'The thing is . . .' he went on, 'well, we're on the Social, me and Mary, and we've got a lot to lose if you start giving me money – I mean, it's fraud, isn't it?'

Kate nodded silently. 'So well, we, I mean me and Mary, we thought that if I got this up and running for you, and I was still getting my payments, then when you think it's making enough, as much as my Social, then I would give up the dole and start taking a share of the profits. If it doesn't work, then I've not lost anything, have I?'

'But you'd have worked for free,' said Rory.

Tommy shrugged. 'That's my risk, isn't it?' Then suddenly he grinned. 'Only I don't think it's going to come to that.'

Kate looked at Rory and they were silent for a few moments, then she said, 'Would you excuse us, Tommy? I think we need to talk about this.'

'Of course. I'll take a walk down to the still-room and

look things over.' He stood and picked up his notepad. 'Might need to note something down,' he remarked.

Kate nodded, but said nothing. She and Rory were silent until he had gone. 'Oh dear,' she said, as the door closed behind him, 'I wasn't expecting that.'

'No, nor was I.' He looked at the paraphernalia on the table. 'He knows what he's doing, Kate, and without him we're struggling. If he can get this thing up and running in the next week, then he's very probably worth a small share of the business.'

'But why? Why does he want to get involved? He hardly knows us.'

'Perhaps he thinks the gin is worth it, that we're on to something big.' Rory shrugged. 'Perhaps he just wants to be part of the management, rather than an employee, and he's right about the Social Security – if we pay him it's fraud.' He held up his hands. 'Look, I don't know, your guess is as good as mine.'

She bit her lip. 'What sort of partnership could we give him? This isn't really a proper business yet – and if he gets a share then to be honest, Rory, so should you.'

Rory stared at her, astounded by her comment. This was his Kate talking – a Kate he thought had died several years ago – and it was so typical of the woman he remembered, honest and fair.

'Thanks,' he said, 'but I don't want a share, Kate, I just want you to succeed.' He stood and crossed to the sink, filled the kettle and put it on to boil. 'Kate, you have to face up to the fact that without this man you won't have a business, not within the time frame we need. You have to either take him into the business or forget it.' He took a couple of mugs from the draining-board and spooned coffee into them. 'Why don't you ring David Lowther and ask him to draw up some kind of legal arrangement? If that's what Tommy Vince wants, then give it to him and let's get on with it!'

Kate picked up the bottle of Tonsbry Original that was on the table and looked at it. The last couple of weeks had been an emotional roller-coaster; she had been up and down so many times that she didn't know where she was. She was hopeful, excited and yet still nagged by doubt. 'Do you really think this can work, Rory?' she asked finally.

Rory waited for the kettle to boil, filled the mugs and brought them across to the table. He handed Kate hers. 'Yes,' he said, 'I do. Now,' he passed her a carton of milk and the sugar-bowl, 'stop fretting, drink your coffee, call David Lowther, get him to draw up a contract and, while you're at it, get him to draft some sort of legal appeal against the foreclosure now that we know what we're doing. OK?'

Kate shrugged. 'OK, if you really think so.' She dolloped two heaped spoonsful of sugar into her coffee, stirred and took a sip. 'Right, then.' She stood up, mug in hand, and gave a half-smile. 'Come on, Rory,' she said, 'let's make gin!'

David Lowther put down the telephone after speaking to Kate and stood up from his desk to walk over to the window. He looked out across the Chartwell market square and thought about Adriana. For years now – virtually most of his adult life – he had thought about Adriana, longingly and with an almost desperate love. She consumed his every spare waking moment and as he had aged – unmarried and lonely, carrying on a family legal firm that did nothing more challenging than a tricky will in probate – his work for her had become an obsession. And now, with the prospect of calling her so close, he could feel his excitement rise, a youthful, vigorous excitement which no one and nothing on earth except her could make him feel.

He turned away, went back to the desk and picked up the phone. He knew that what he was doing wasn't right, it was unethical and very probably illegal, but he was unable to stop himself. The thought of pleasing her, of basking even briefly in the glow of her admiration, blotted out any doubts and negated any risks. He dialled the number of her London hotel and felt a dart of exhilaration pass through him as he asked the switchboard to connect him.

Rory walked into Tonsbry House mid-afternoon and saw Mrs Able standing uneasily in the hall. She held a duster, but it hung limply in her hand and she had one ear turned towards the door to Leo's study.

'Hello?' Rory called. The housekeeper started, then coloured slightly.

'Oh, Rory dear, it's you.' She turned towards him and pointed at the study. 'He's been in there on the phone for over an hour now.'

'He?'

'That Harry chap of Kate's!' she hissed. 'He's up to something, must be, to be on the phone that long.'

Rory shrugged and said, 'I'm sure it's all perfectly harmless.' But he didn't mean it; he was as irritated as she was.

'Harmless or not,' said Mrs Able, 'he shouldn't be making calls on Kate's bill. It makes my blood boil to think of—'

Rory placed a hand on her arm to interrupt. 'Look, I'll have a word with him, shall I?'

'Would you mind?'

Yes, he would mind — any exchange with Harry he wanted to keep to a minimum — but Rory had discovered a new-found self-confidence in the past twenty-four hours and it gave him a good deal of tolerance. 'I don't mind,' he said. 'I'll go in now.' And leaving Mrs Able, he crossed to the study, went in and closed the door behind him.

'I don't know if I can arrange that, she seems pretty fired up about this gin,' Harry was saying. 'But I have made the calls you asked and—'

'Calls?'

Harry jerked round. 'Oh God! Rory, I . . .' He had been sitting in Leo's wing chair talking on the phone to Adriana and now he jumped up, dropping the phone as he did so. 'Rory, hang on a minute, I'll . . .' He went back on the line. 'I'll call you back,' he said, 'later.' And immediately he cut the line.

'Calls?' Rory repeated.

'Oh, um, yes, I . . .' Harry shifted his weight uncomfortably from foot to foot. He had to think fast and struggled to do it. 'Calls, yes, I was . . . er . . . calling the regiment.'

'The regiment?'

'Yes, about this gin.'

'What? You mean selling it? To the regiment?'

Harry looked momentarily stunned. That wasn't what he'd meant at all, but he saw Rory's face change and kept quiet.

'That's not a bad idea, Harry, not bad at all. What was their reaction?'

'Well . . . er, reasonable.'

'What does reasonable mean? Yes or no?'

'Er . . . maybe.'

Rory came across to the desk. 'Well, maybe's a start,

I suppose. Listen, I wonder if it's worth trying all the regiments? What do you think?'

Harry nodded numbly. Shit, this wasn't what he'd planned at all. Adriana had expressly asked him to get Kate away from all this, not to involve her more. He began to sweat.

'Who would I speak to, Harry, if I rang round?'

'I don't know, the . . . er . . .'

Rory looked across at him.

'The Mess Sergeant,' Harry finished.

'Brilliant! What I'll do is get a list of all the regiments in the south, south-east and south-west, maybe even include some TAs in that and start ringing round. I am right in thinking that I'd ring the MOD for a list, am I?'

Harry nodded.

'Great.' Rory cuffed him on the back. 'Great idea, Harry, thanks.' And, picking up the phone, he was too busy to see Harry slink silently and miserably out of the study.

It was about eight-thirty in the evening and Jan was sitting at home watching television when the phone rang. She had come to a dead end in her search to find out what Duncan was up to, and at dinner last night Stefan had questioned her motives. Perhaps he was right in doing so; perhaps this whole thing was a vendetta more than anything else, her chance to vilify her husband. Perhaps she was just chasing around in circles, getting all vexed about nothing.

She picked up the receiver.

'Hello?'

'Hi, Jan, it's Stefan.'

Snuggling back into the sofa, Jan settled herself for a comfortable chat but Stefan had other ideas.

'Jan, I've been thinking about the Letchworth Housing Association, and it seems to me that the next step is to have a look at their books.'

'Their books?'

'Yes, to see if anything is awry there.'

'I agree, but there's no way we can do that without arousing suspicion. They'd have to agree first and—'

'No, not my way they wouldn't.'

'What do you mean, your way?'

'Jan, you don't have to agree to this because I've decided to do it anyway, but I'm going along to the company offices at the end of the week and posing as a VAT inspector . . .'

'A VAT inspector! Stefan, are you mad? You can't possibly—'

'Wait, let me finish! I've thought it through, honestly. I've got a fake ID, I've photocopied something from Kate's files with a Customs and Excise heading on it and I'm certain I can get away with it. I'll go in and ask to look at their books, and by law they have to let me. They'll know that – and the chances of it having happened recently are pretty remote. I'll stay a couple of hours, in private, and get what we need. They won't be suspicious, why should they be? I'm not handling any money; all I'm doing is looking at information . . .'

'But, Stefan—'

'No buts, Jan, I've made up my mind and—'

'Stefan, listen, you can't do it! I won't let you.'

'Jan, I'm not going to argue with you about this . . .'

'All right, then, let me come with you. VAT inspectors nearly always work in pairs, and I know what I'm looking for in the books.'

He was silent.

'Stefan? Did you hear me?'

'Jan, I don't want you involved in anything that could ruin your business.'

'Stefan, I *am* involved. Come on, we—'

'No, no, I really don't want you to come, Jan. I'm sorry, but that's my last word.'

'But how will you know what to look for?'

He had been told specifically, that's how, by one of his oldest and best clients, a senior partner in a firm of accountants. 'I'm not an idiot, Jan,' he replied. 'I'll work it out.'

Jan sighed. He was determined and she was wasting her breath. 'OK,' she said, 'if you're absolutely sure?'

'Absolutely.'

'Right. I'll wait to hear from you then, shall I?'

'I'll ring as soon as I've done it.'

'When? I mean, is it definitely Friday?'

'I think so? Why?'

'Because if it is I won't worry until then.' Jan heard Stefan laugh and went to hang up, but she wanted to ask one more thing. 'Stefan, how did you think of all this? I mean, knowing about VAT inspectors and everything?'

Stefan was silent. He knew about it because he'd discussed it, hypothetically of course, with his client. 'I'm not sure,' he replied, conscious of the lie. 'It just came to me.' And wishing he had never had to do it, he said goodbye to Jan and hung up.

It was late in the still-room, well after midnight, and Tommy Vince had a measure of spirits in his hand. He took it over to the table and poured it into a jug, tested the gravity, added the water and tested the gravity again. Then he held it up to the light, sniffed it, and poured the gin into a glass. He put it to his lips, took a sip, swilled it around his mouth and spat it out.

Kate was exhausted; the wait had seemed interminable and, as she watched him repeat the process, she began to shiver.

Finally, Tommy looked up and, without even a flicker of a smile, he said, 'That's your gin, Kate!' He handed the glass to her and waited for her to taste it. As she did so, relief swamped her; she bit back the tears. Then Tommy turned towards Rory. 'OK, Rory, mate,' he called. And suddenly his face broke into a grin. 'Strike the still!'

Chapter Eighteen

Kate was awake. It was five a.m. and she thought she must have slept the past few hours, on and off; but if she had, it had been fretful sleep with no rest. She felt peculiar, not tired, quite the contrary, wide-eyed and alert, her whole body receptive to every minute movement and sound in the house. It was still dark, not even the faintest hint of daybreak in the sky, and as she crept from her bed and dressed, she had only the eerie light from the fading moon outside to guide her. Slipping on some clothes, she pulled a coat around her shoulders and padded barefoot down the stairs, through the house and along the passage to the back door. There she found some boots, stuffed her feet into them and quietly let herself out into the cold dawn air. She ran, not knowing why and powerless to stop herself, down past the side lawns, across the courtyard and towards the outbuildings. At the still-room she stopped, put her face near the door to feel the rush of warm air that escaped and then silently turned the handle and went in. This was hers – the pungent smell of the botanicals, the acrid, over-powering smell of alcohol, the heat, the whiff of damp glue, empty blue glass bottles, labels, caps and lastly Tonsbry Original gin. She picked up a bottle and looked at it.

'It's fantastic, isn't it?'

Startled, she jumped and almost dropped the bottle, then spun round.

'My God, Rory, you gave me a fright!'

He came out from behind the still, wearing yesterday's clothes, and smiled at her. 'Sorry, I couldn't sleep.' He came across and picked up a filled bottle of gin himself. 'I didn't bother to try, actually.'

Kate touched his shirt-sleeve, dirty and rolled up to the elbow. 'So I see. As your daughter would say: yeuch!' They both laughed quietly.

'You know I haven't really thanked you,' Kate said, 'for finding Tommy and getting the orders from the regiments.'

Rory ran his hand over the bottle. 'Not bad for a first try. Fifty bottles, and we haven't even started selling!'

Kate poked him gently in the ribs. 'All right, no need to show off your modesty to me. I know you, remember?'

Rory laughed. 'Ooh, Kate, how could I forget? You're one of the few living witnesses of the purple velvet jeans and hand-tooled cowboy boots; one of the handful of survivors to see me as Olivia in *Twelfth Night*. Remember the dress?'

She started laughing. 'The padding down the front was a bit iffy, but the rest was very pretty!'

'Thank you.' He raised an eyebrow. 'Anyway, I hardly recall you being the picture of sartorial elegance – what was it? Turquoise, zip-up, satin bomber-jacket and pink eye-shadow?'

'Hey!' Kate poked him again, this time a little harder. 'You're not supposed to mention a lady's gaffes, it's impolite.'

'Sorry!' Rory poked her back and she yelped, jumping away.

'Don't you dare!' she cried, laughing and darting forward to get him right under the arm. He shouted and laughed too, made another lunge for her and got her just under her ribs. She burst out laughing. 'God, you fiend! Take that!' She jabbed him, quickly and sharply in the side, 'And that!'

But this time, as she lunged for him he grabbed her hand and held it tight. 'Got you!' She tried to wrestle it free but couldn't because they were both laughing so much.

'Rory! Stop it!' He held her fast. 'No, I mean it. Stop—'

With one sudden movement, Rory pulled Kate against him and kissed her. It was completely unexpected and their laughter instantly died. For a second she stared fleetingly at Rory's face, but moments later she surrendered to the bliss of his kiss and shut her eyes tightly. The kiss was long and deep, Rory's body was hard and warm and the blood pounded in Kate's chest. She felt a rush of heat down in the pit of her stomach which spread between her thighs and eased her legs apart so that she could feel him harder and tighter against her pelvis. He moved his mouth and it crept down her neck, biting, kissing, his lips hot on her skin. She shivered. Moments later she felt herself being lifted up, her shoulder-blade hit the light-switch on the wall behind her and the still-room was swamped by darkness which took them over and destroyed any last vestige of judgement or reason.

Kate clung to Rory, her thighs wrapped around his hips, her mouth open to his. The dawning light outside made some sense of the shapes in the room and he turned, still holding her, kissing her as they fell against the edge of the table. Kate's hands went back to support herself and Rory struggled with her clothes. She didn't think, she couldn't; it was as if nothing else in the world mattered at that moment. Rory tore the shirt up over her body, his mouth caressing her exposed stomach, her breasts, his tongue darting over her nipples. She gasped as a wave of something she was totally unused to swept through her and moved her legs up higher round his hips. She felt in the darkness for Rory, unzipping him, feeling him jolt as she wrapped her hands around him. Then she arched her back, he pulled her jeans down over her long slim thighs, kissed the smooth, scented skin between them, and then, wrapping his hands in her hair, he let her guide him into her. Their bodies locked tight and, knowing she had no control over what she was doing, Kate cried out.

For a few seconds afterwards, Kate was totally still. She felt as if her mind and body had exploded; great waves of heat and pleasure coursed through her and she shuddered, releasing them. Rory's breath was hot on her shoulder, his heart pounded and the damp skin on the back of his neck slithered under her fingers. She opened her eyes and then, as he moved, easing himself gently back from her, she saw his face, she saw them both, saw what they had become . . . two separate, lonely people . . . and, swamped with guilt, she started to cry.

Turning away from him, she made an attempt to hide her face. It crumpled under the pressure of the sobs which came, harsh and uncontrollable, tears streaming down her cheeks. He released her, she hugged her arms around her naked body and curled into herself. Rory said nothing. He stood back, pulled up his jeans and fumbled behind him for his jacket. When he found it he carefully placed it around her naked shoulders, then he gently stroked her hair. He looked at her face, swollen and blotchy, and wished he was sufficiently organised to have a clean handkerchief somewhere about his person. 'D'you want some tissues?' was all he could offer, having spotted some on a nearby shelf. Kate nodded and he gave her some.

'I'm sorry,' Kate said. 'It wasn't you. I mean . . . well, it sort of was . . .' She flushed, only Rory couldn't see it in the dark. 'It was everything, really.'

Rory touched her cheek. 'It doesn't matter.' He was embarrassed, not in the least by her tears but by the fact that she felt she had to explain herself. He wanted to wrap her up in his coat, carry her up to bed in the house and tell her that he didn't care if she howled the place down, it was so fantastic making love to her. But he didn't dare. Instead he thought of nothing except how soft her skin was and how the smell of her now was making him hard again. 'It really doesn't matter,' he murmured again.

Oh, but it does, Kate wanted to cry out, it matters terribly! I have just done to Harry what you did to me. Shame welled up inside her and made her shudder with guilt. Uncurling herself and reaching for her clothes, she dressed silently – trembling, suddenly icy cold, despite the warmth in there.

'Kate,' Rory murmured, 'I have to go.' It was the last thing he wanted but he remembered Flora; she would be up soon and needing him. Kate nodded. She felt nothing but relief. 'God, I'm really sorry, I wish I didn't have to, I wish—'

'But you do,' she said. 'There's no point in wishing.'

'No.' He picked up his jacket. 'Can I walk you back to the house?' She nodded again and a silence descended on them. How could such intimacy evaporate? He didn't know and had no idea how to salvage the situation, but he reached for Kate's hand and held it in his own. The silence deepened and seemed to envelop them.

Opening the door, he followed her out. She turned to him and said gently, 'Don't bother to come up to the house. You get home, you look exhausted.'

He kept hold of her hand and she tried to smile. His Kate. He kissed the tip of her nose. 'I'll see you later, then?'

'Yes.' Kate was suddenly tired too. She felt that she had come to some kind of awful turning point, but didn't know what it was. They stood together for a few moments longer, then she freed her hand and dug it in her pocket. 'Goodbye, Rory,' she said.

He looked at her. 'Don't say goodbye. I'll see you later.'

Kate shrugged, miserable and ashamed. Then, without saying anything else, she walked away and back up to the house alone.

At Heathrow Airport, Alice lugged all three of her bags off the luggage carousel and on to her trolley in quick succession; then she stood straight and rubbed her back. It happened like that, in her experience – something to do with sod's law. Bags either came so quickly that you missed one or did your back in trying to get them all in a rush; or you got one case at the beginning and one, an hour later, at the end. Why weren't they ever evenly spaced, she thought, so that you could collect them calmly one at a time and stack them neatly? She released the brake on her trolley and wheeled it towards customs, steadying a precarious bag on top with one hand as she went.

Out in the main airport, Alice walked the length of the

roped-off area, scanning the small crowd. Of course no one would be there, she'd told no one she was coming, but she couldn't help looking, nor could she help the disappointment. She should have told someone, her brother maybe; she should have had someone there to meet her. It was depressing to be so alone.

Crossing to the public telephones, Alice took her address book out of her bag and looked up 'Gallagher'. It was ridiculous; she had lived in that flat with Rory and Flora for nearly two years, yet now she had no idea of the phone number. All she could think was that the whole situation had been so ghastly that she had blanked it from her mind.

Having found the number, the only change in her purse was Australian and so, shifting booths, Alice found her credit card and swiped it to pay for the call. She glanced at her watch to check London time, six-thirty a.m., then dialled the London number and waited. The line came up as unobtainable.

'Oh, blast!' She wondered momentarily what to do. Perhaps they had moved? Then she glanced at her address book a second time and saw Rory's parents' number directly after his and Flora's. She dialled again. The phone rang several times, and finally it was answered.

'Hello? Mrs Gallagher?'

Faye Gallagher hesitated. She recognised the voice, it was familiar and yet unnerving. 'Yes?' she said. Her hand instinctively tightened round the telephone wire.

'Hello, Faye, it's Alice here.'

'Alice!' Faye Gallagher was shocked, and Alice heard that shock in her voice. She flinched.

'Faye, I'm in London,' she went on. 'I've just arrived, and I'm trying to get hold of Rory.'

There was a silence. Alice watched the units of money flash up on the small electronic screen and her heart sank.

'Oh,' Faye said, then, 'I see.' And that was the only comment she made.

Chapter Nineteen

In just a few days, the dining-room at Tonsbry had changed beyond all recognition and become the centre of the business. The furniture was stacked neatly on one side of the room, the long fake Chippendale table – the real one had been sold years ago by Leo – hidden under a protective cloth and covered with the equipment for labelling bottles, the machine itself, glue, labels and a neat row of bottles done and bottles to do.

Tommy Vince, when he wasn't working in the still-room, was often in here with John and Mrs Able, sticking labels and packing bottles, keeping the records up to date. He had rapidly become part of the team, a new experience for him after working for Boller's, where an employee knew his or her place and stayed in it if they wanted to keep their job. He liked Kate and he liked Rory; he enjoyed the work, it was exciting and he felt part of it. He'd told Mary the truth when he said he was happier here than he could remember ever being and that the money, if they made any, didn't really matter all that much now. He thrived on activity, on hard graft; he liked the atmosphere here, and he was beginning to really believe that he had a stake in what he was doing. And as he sat with Mrs Able, sticking on labels, he thought about his hobby and about an idea that had been going round and round his head all night.

'Morning, Tommy.' Kate strode into the room in her habitual faded jeans, Doc Martens and black skinny-ribbed sweater, her hair a neat bob of dark brown. She was eating an apple – not really eating it, more devouring it with huge bites and virtually chewing the core as well. Finishing it, she crossed to the table, dropped the remains on the rubbish pile and said, 'Crikey! You've done masses, well done!'

It was then that Tommy decided to mention it. 'Kate,' he said, 'I've had a bit of an idea.'

'Have you? Great!' She turned to him and gave him her full attention. It was something he truly admired about Kate, her ability to listen, not superficially but properly, with total concentration, to what anyone had to say. She pulled out a chair and sat down.

'It concerns a hobby of mine,' Tommy said, 'making cocktails.' He paused to allow room for her to make some sort of joke, most people did, but she said nothing. She simply waited for him to go on.

'I've been experimenting with Tonsbry Original, trying to find something long and cool and a bit exotic but not naff. A sort of alternative to gin and tonic really – and I came up with this.' Tommy delved in his pocket, shifted on his seat to dig further and finally pulled out a scrap of paper. 'I'm pretty pleased with it, and Mary likes it too. We've been drinking it most evenings now.' He handed the paper across to Kate. She read the ingredients and said, 'Hmmm, sounds delicious.'

'You want to try it?'

Kate looked up quizzically. 'I'd love to but—'

'Oh!' Tommy smiled. 'Sorry, I didn't quite explain myself, did I? Well, it's just that when I was at Boller's I had the idea of putting a cocktail recipe on the back of their special reserve gin, and the marketing people loved it; only the thing was, we couldn't find the right cocktail – and then I was booted out and it all sort of faded away . . .' He broke off, shrugged, then went on. 'Anyway,' he said, 'if you like the cocktail, then maybe we could put the recipe on a separate label on the back, an extra selling point that is—'

'Tommy, that's a wonderful idea!' Kate burst out. 'Can we make the cocktail now and try it? If it works and we're all agreed, I could ring the printer and get a stack of labels done for the first few cases. What d'you think?' She turned as the door opened. There was a change in her manner, a slight tensing, a wariness, but it was so subtle that it went unnoticed to everyone except Rory. 'Hello, Rory,' she said. 'Just in time! Tommy's had a brilliant idea about a cocktail recipe for the back of the bottle. He . . .' She stopped. 'Rory? Is something wrong?'

Rory didn't come into the room, he hovered by the door. He was going to tell her about Alice right away – his mother having finally plucked up the courage to tell him – but he wasn't sure he could. The unfairness of it, of her timing was almost too much to bear. He knew things hadn't been exactly healed between him and Kate and that Kate was confused, but perhaps if they were together enough, perhaps if he could prove himself to her and do everything in his power to make Tonsbry Original work . . . perhaps if he just had a chance . . . Rory stopped himself; he saw Kate looking at him and said, 'Sorry, no . . . nothing.'

Kate wasn't sure. 'Is Flora OK?'

'Yes, she's fine. She's coming up later, she's with my mother at the moment.'

'Right.' Kate turned back to Tommy, but she had lost some of the glow, some of the excitement – even Tommy could see it.

Rory came into the room and pulled out a chair. 'What's all this about a cocktail?' he asked.

'It's a hobby of mine,' Tommy explained, 'making cocktails. I've come up with rather a good 'un made with Tonsbry gin. You want to try it?'

'Love to.' Rory did his best to show enthusiasm. 'D'you have all the ingredients, Tommy?'

Tommy scraped back his chair and stood up. 'Yes,' he answered. 'I took the liberty of bringing in some things this morning, in the hope that you might be interested. I'll get them, they're in the Land-Rover.'

Mrs Able got up as well. 'D'you want a hand, Tommy? You could use the kitchen.'

'Yeah, thanks.'

'Right then,' the housekeeper said. 'We'll be back in a few minutes.' And, leaving Kate with a knowing glance, she followed Tommy out of the room.

Kate wasn't sure what the look had meant. She supposed it had something to do with her and Rory, and Rory's obvious unease, but before she had gathered the nerve to broach the subject the door opened again and, true to her word, Mrs Able and Tommy returned just five minutes or so after they'd gone.

Tommy carried a tray loaded with glasses, a bowl of ice and a jug of his cocktail, while Mrs Able ceremoniously held the door open for him. 'Here we are,' she said, clearing the table with a great deal of fuss. 'The cocktails!'

Tommy set down the tray, threw some ice into each glass, poured the cocktail, added a wedge of lime and finally a thin blade of lemon grass to each drink. He handed them round. 'Cheers!' he said. 'A Tonsbry Original Cooler.'

Kate took a sip. She let the cocktail sit in her mouth for a few moments, savouring the taste, then swallowed, immediately feeling the kick in the back of her throat. She took another sip, exchanged glances with Rory, sipped again and finally said, 'Wow! That is some drink, Tommy!' Tommy's face broke into a broad grin.

'Rory? What do you think?'

'I think it's terrific!' Rory agreed.

'You want to put it on the bottle, Kate?'

She hesitated. 'I think so, Tommy, but what about copyright or patent?'

Tommy waved his hand in the air dismissively. 'There's no need for all that,' he said. 'I'm a partner now; this is all part and parcel of the business, isn't it?'

Kate smiled. She had drunk half a glass already and had no head for drinking. It slipped down very easily, probably a bit too easily. She sneaked a glance at Rory, he caught her eye and they stared at each other for a few moments, then a deep blush crept over her cheeks and Kate looked away. She couldn't stand the guilt, the terrible shame of having deceived Harry, yet she couldn't think of Rory without her stomach churning. What the hell did it all mean?

'Kate?'

She looked up. Rory was still staring at her and, unable to put it off any longer, he said, 'Can we have a word?'

He glanced briefly at Tommy and Mrs Able. 'In private.'

Kate frowned, scraped back her chair and got to her feet.

'Of course.' She glanced at Tommy. 'I'll ring the printers while I'm up,' she said. 'Get them to do some label designs for this drink on their computer and fax them over. What did you call it, Tommy?'

'The Tonsbry Original Cooler.' Tommy held out his list of ingredients. 'Here, you'll need this.' Kate took it, tucked it into her pocket, and following Rory she left the room.

As they walked into the hall, she stopped, dug her hands in her pockets and said, 'So, what did you want to say?' Somehow being alone with him made her all the more confused.

Rory faced her. He didn't *want* to say anything, but he had to.

'Alice is coming,' he said and all of a sudden Kate felt as if the world had stopped, completely stopped, dead still. She drew in her breath as the memory that name evoked crushed her chest, like a heart attack. She wrapped her arms around her body.

'Alice?' She could hardly say it. '*Alice?* What do you mean, Alice is coming?'

'Alice rang my mother. She's in England, at her brother's, she's coming—'

'What do you mean, coming?' The panic stabbed at her and her voice rose. 'Coming here, coming for dinner, coming to live with you and Flora, coming to take Flora away?' She threw her hands up in the air and her eyes blurred. 'What do you *mean*? I don't understand?'

'Kate,' Rory said. 'Kate, look at me.'

But she couldn't look at him. There was a big, hard lump in her throat that she kept trying to swallow and her eyes stung. 'Alice?' she cried. 'What's Alice—?'

Suddenly Rory took hold of her arms. 'Kate, look at me. Please!'

She stood still and blinked. The tears slid out from under her eyelids and she had no idea why she was crying. There was no more confusion, no more churning, just a sudden sense of loss. That's it then, she thought, but she didn't know what *it* was.

'Alice is *not* coming to live with me and Flora, and she is *not* coming to take Flora away. She wants to see me, I don't know why – I've been racking my brains to try and think why, but I can't – so I just have to go with it. Kate, please don't worry.' He fumbled in his pocket and brought out a crumpled handkerchief which he handed to her. She blew her nose, then smoothed it to give it back.

'Rory?' she said. He looked at her and she glanced down at her hand. 'You've given me a pair of Flora's knickers!'

And suddenly they both started to laugh.

'I always keep a spare pair,' he said a moment later, 'in case of accidents.' He took them back. 'Kate,' he began, 'Alice isn't a threat.'

Kate frowned. 'A threat?' she asked. 'To what? There's nothing that she can threaten. Is there?'

Rory took a breath. 'Kate, I . . .' But the phone rang and he didn't say any more.

They both turned towards Leo's study and Kate said, 'I should get that.'

He nodded. 'Of course.' He had been about to say, a threat to us, to all this, to what we've built up over the past few weeks, the last two days. But of course he didn't say it. He simply shrugged and, without a word, let her go.

Jan was in the office when Stefan rang. It was Friday, mid-morning, and although she had made an effort to work her concentration wasn't good. She had thought of nothing but Stefan, of what he was doing for her, and was anxious for it all to be over with. The nature of the task had become almost irrelevant; it was the fact that he was doing it and taking a risk for her that mattered. Earlier on she had asked Molly to hold all calls but his, so when she picked up the receiver she knew it was him and immediately asked, 'Are you all right?' It was really all that was important.

'I'm fine. It all went according to plan,' Stefan replied. 'We need to talk, though. Can you come to the flat?'

Jan didn't hesitate. 'Of course. When?'

Stefan wanted to see her, he too had realised something through the course of action he'd taken. 'As soon as you can?'

She smiled. 'I'll leave now,' she said. 'Is that all right?'

'That's perfect.'

Jan stood, picked up her coat and bag and left the office without telling Molly where she was going or when to expect her back.

Stefan opened the door of his flat and for a few moments he and Jan just stood and looked at each other. Then, as she stepped inside, he moved forward to her and eased her gently back against the wall.

'Thank you, I mean for . . .'

He put his finger to her lips. 'I'd do anything for you,' he whispered. Slipping her coat off her shoulders, he slowly

unbuttoned her shirt to the waist and ran his finger and
thumb over her nipple through the thin lace of her bra.
He bent his head and sucked for a few moments. Jan
caught her breath and pulled him away. 'Don't! I . . .'
But he silenced her with his mouth and freed her breasts,
holding the weight of them in his hands before he kissed
them and darted his tongue across the tips of her nipples.
She shivered, but had no more power to resist. Parting
her thighs, she pressed herself back and felt his hands
under her buttocks, lifting her. As she closed her eyes,
he straightened and, without a word, carried her to bed.

Some time later, when Jan was asleep, Stefan got out of
bed and went through to the kitchen to make tea. He had
some serious thinking to do; he had uncovered something
in the accounts that even an idiot wouldn't miss, and he
had a strong idea what it meant. However, he had no
clear evidence. According to the accounts of the Letchworth Housing Association for 1991–92 and 1992–93,
they had purchased twenty-three properties from Ingram
Lawd and each time had paid a sum of £5,000–£10,000
– an unbelievable figure – in legal fees. The solicitors they
had paid it to were Rickman Levy of King's Cross.

Stefan filled the kettle and found himself a tea-pot. Now
no one, he thought, spooning leaf tea into the pot, pays
that sort of sum in legal fees unless it's a scam. It isn't
illegal of course, but the chances were – and this is where
he entered the realms of speculation – that those fees were
a payment for a cheap property and were going straight into
the pocket of the vendor: one Mr Duncan Lawd. The kettle
boiled and Stefan made tea. Which meant, he concluded,
that Duncan has been embezzling the company out of up

to a quarter of a million pounds. And that was one hell of a charge.

Stefan poured himself a cup, added a slice of lemon, carried it over to the small bistro table in the corner and sat down. So what did he do next, he wondered miserably? Did he tell Jan, knowing that he had no proof? Or did he try to find out a bit more first? Of course, it really wasn't his business and there was no reason to get even more involved, but then the way he felt about Jan meant that he wanted everything that concerned her to concern him as well. Wrapping his hands around his cup, he lifted it, let the steam drift up into his face and closed his eyes. He had thought loving someone would make life easier, not complicate it.

The door-bell rang.

Standing, Stefan walked into the hall and spoke into the intercom. 'Loïs?' He felt a sharp jolt of panic; it was Loïs Makinny. 'What on earth are you doing here?' This was so unlike her – she had never turned up at his flat before, never. He could hear that she was upset, her voice was thick with tears. 'Loïs, look, I can't talk. I was . . . I was in bed . . .'

He heard a short, bitter laugh, then Loïs's voice was so loud that she seemed to be in the room with him. 'In bed?' It was then that he knew she was drunk. He began to sweat. 'Tell me, Stefan?' she went on, slurring her words. 'Is that business or pleasure?'

Jan heard voices, Stefan's mainly, and sat up. As she reached across to switch on the lamp on the bedside table, she knocked off Stefan's diary. Climbing out of bed, she pulled on a dressing-gown, then bent and retrieved it.

She glanced at the page where it had fallen open before closing it and noticed a couple of entries; they were both appointments with women.

Strange, Jan thought, and her curiosity got the better of her as she read the entries for the rest of that week: all women. Her pulse rate quickened and she felt a rush of blood to her cheeks. Flicking back, she read the previous week's entries, then the week before that. All women! Stefan was seeing two women a day, on average, three days a week. For some of the dinners he had scribbled a line going through one day to the next. What did that mean? That the date lasted all night? Jan felt sick. She hurriedly glanced through the rest of the diary, much the same, and made for the door. What the hell was going on? This deserved some sort of explanation. She pulled open the door to the bedroom and was about to storm out when she heard Stefan. She stopped dead in her tracks, listened for several minutes, then went back to the bedroom to dress.

'Loïs, why don't you just go on home? Please, I can't see you now and you can't stand out there for ever. Please, Loïs!' Stefan's voice was a desperate raised whisper.

'I don't want to go home,' she whined above the crackle of the intercom. 'I want to see you. I'm one of your best clients, Stefan. Let me in, please, I demand that you let me in . . . !'

Stefan turned and he caught the breath in the back of his throat as behind him Jan appeared, fully dressed, with her coat and bag in her hand.

'Oh God, Jan! This isn't what it seems, it—'

'Stefan?' Loïs called. 'I'm cold, I need to see you, please.'

He moved across to Jan and took her arm. 'Jan?'

'Don't touch me!' she suddenly snapped, yanking her arm free. She walked past him to the front door and opened it. 'I didn't pay for extras,' she said coldly. And moments later, she was gone.

'Stefan? I'm freezing out here, I . . .' But Stefan ignored Loïs Makinny outside and went back into the bedroom. He saw the lamp on, the disarray of bed-covers, his clothes thrown on the floor. Then he saw his diary. It was on his pillow and his heart sank. As he was picking it up, something fell out; he took the piece of paper up off the bed and saw that it was a cheque in Jan's handwriting, from her personal account, and made out for £200. In his diary – on the page she had marked by the cheque, and on the space for that day – Jan had written her own name. So she knows, he thought. And closing the little black book, he climbed into bed, switched off the light and lay in the dark feeling totally desolate and alone.

Duncan's new secretary, a pretty graduate who was temping before a world trip, knocked on his door and popped her head round.

'Duncan?'

Few employees called him that, but he liked this girl; she had potential. 'Yes?' He glanced up briefly, then went back to his work.

'There's a Comtesse de Grand Blès on the phone. She said it's urgent.'

Duncan sighed, screwed the lid on his pen and placed it carefully on top of the pile of letters he was signing. 'OK, put her through.'

Coughing lightly, he picked up the phone and said, 'Adriana, how are you?'

'Fine,' she snapped. 'No thanks to you! What the hell are you playing at, Duncan?' She was in a vitriolic mood.

'I'm sorry?' This was Duncan's first taste of her temper; he was taken aback.

'When we had our meeting the other day, you assured me that you had everything under control! And now, *now* I find that my daughter has telephoned her solicitor to file an appeal against your foreclosure and that you are no further on with the legal work!'

'That's not quite fair, I—'

'He also told me that apparently you have lost the file!' she continued. 'Title deeds to the house and land, all the loan agreements, signatures, everything! Is this right?'

'No! Absolutely not.' He felt himself pinned down. 'I can assure you—'

'You can assure me of nothing! I bloody well hope that the file isn't lost, Duncan. I have already given you a large cash payment which only we two know about in order to secure your full attention to my business, and I am not happy to learn that you are making mistakes.'

'Adriana, I—'

'Don't Adriana me! Just get a move on. I want this business done and dealt with immediately. Is that understood?'

'Yes, yes, of course.' Duncan buzzed his secretary. 'I can only apologise for . . .' But he stopped mid-way through the sentence and replaced the receiver. Adriana had hung up on him.

'Suzie?'

The bright young thing appeared in the doorway. 'Er . . . it's Suzanne, actually,' she said.

Suddenly Duncan lost it. 'I don't give a flying fuck what it is!' he roared. 'Get me my wife on the line and do it now!'

Chapter Twenty

Stefan sat on the floor in the hall of his flat with the telephone in front of him and pressed the re-dial button. Jan's number was rung, the line connected and he listened to the ringing tone, unanswered, for as long as he could bear it before hanging up. He knew she was there; he had rung Molly at the office and he had to keep on trying.

Laying his head back against the wall, he waited for several minutes and then repeated the same procedure. As it began to ring, Stefan found himself gripping the receiver. 'Please pick up the phone, Jan,' he murmured, making a conscious effort to relax. 'Please pick up the phone!'

Jan lay in bed and listened to the phone ringing in the sitting-room, too depressed to go downstairs and unplug it, too depressed even to get out of bed to make a cup of tea. She felt ill – indeed she was ill, she was sick to her heart, sick and tired of being used and being made a fool of. She knew it was Stefan ringing; who else would it be every five minutes? Ringing to make sure she wasn't going to change her mind about the Tonsbry file, no doubt; ringing to tell her more lies. Jan slid down the bed and pulled the covers up over her face. She was so ashamed that she wanted to disappear, to stay hidden and cocooned for ever. She wasn't ashamed of her feelings – who wouldn't have found him attractive in all his youthful glory? – but she was ashamed of falling for the same old line. She had honestly believed that he liked her, honestly believed that it was more than just a fling.

The phone stopped and Jan exhaled slowly. She found herself holding her breath all the time it rang, digging her nails into the soft flesh of her palms. There was a silence and she began to relax. She rolled over, curled herself up into the foetal position and closed her eyes. Perhaps he'd leave her alone for a while now, perhaps there would be a little peace? But just as she thought this, the phone started to ring again.

Silently and desperately, Jan began to cry.

It was lunch-time and Flora was hungry. She had been helping with the labels, if sticking labels on everyone and everything could be described as helping, and she had come to the end of her attention span. She was fed up and growing mischievous. Kate decided that enough was enough.

'I think,' she said to Mrs Able, 'that someone needs to go home for some lunch.'

'Who's someone?' piped Flora.

'You,' Kate said, smiling. 'Come on, I'll take you back to the cottage, and we'll stop and let Daddy know on the way.'

'No!' Flora whined. 'I don't *want* to go!'

'OK,' Kate said, 'no problem. I'll go home with Daddy, then, and eat the fairy-cakes Mrs Able baked for you all by myself. I might give Daddy one, but if I do then there's still two for—' But Flora was up like a shot and over by Kate, holding on to her hand before she finished her sentence. 'Ready, then?' Kate asked.

Flora handed Kate her coat, Kate helped her on with it and smiled across at the housekeeper. 'We'll see you later, Mrs Able. Say goodbye nicely, Flora.'

'Goodbye nicely, Flora!' Flora called. Mrs Able blew a kiss and clucked as the two went out of the door.

'They've grown very close, those two, haven't they?' Tommy commented, picking up on the disapproving cluck.

Mrs Able clucked a second time, to emphasise the first one. 'A bit too close I wouldn't warrant,' she said. 'I don't want that girl hurt again.' And without explaining herself, she left Tommy to his own conclusions and went on with the labelling in silence.

Kate and Flora stopped off at the still-room and called out to Rory. He came across immediately and picked Flora up for a cuddle. 'Where're you off to, pudding?'

'I'm not a pudding!' Flora protested.

'What are you, then?'

'Flora Gallagher!' Flora said solemnly.

'Are you sure?' Rory asked, grinning.

She nodded and he looked at Kate.

'I'm taking her back for lunch,' she explained. 'She's had enough of labelling.'

'You don't have to do that,' Rory said. 'I'll ring Mum and ask her to come up, I—'

'No, it's OK. I'd like to.'

'Well . . . thanks.' Rory dropped Flora on to her feet. 'Now you be a good girl for Kate, no messing about.'

'I am a good girl!' Flora said.

Kate tapped the plastic box she was holding. 'I've got a secret weapon,' she said, 'just in case!'

'Secret weapon?'

'Mrs Able's fairy-cakes.'

Rory smiled. There was a brief moment when neither of them knew what to say or do, then Flora tugged at Kate's hand and said, 'Come on, I'm hungry.' And Kate moved off. 'See you later, Daddy!' Flora called out.

'Yes,' he said. 'See you later.'

Alice climbed out of the taxi at the entrance to Tonsbry House, paid the driver and took her small piece of luggage off the back seat. As the cab drove off, Alice straightened, put on her glasses and took a good look at her surroundings. She had only been to Tonsbry once before, on the day of Rory's wedding, and she hardly remembered it. Looking at it now, she realised it was quite some place. She dug in her pocket for the instructions that Rory's mother had given her, under duress, and saw that Gully Cottage was to the right of the entrance. 'Damn,' she muttered, realising that she should have taken the small lane before the entrance to the house. Now she would have to go across the fields. Alice glanced down at her shoes and experienced the first sense of doubt since she had embarked on this mission. Perhaps this was a sign that she shouldn't have come? She pinched herself and picked up her case. Nonsense, she told herself, don't be so wet. And following her sense of direction, she walked off across the fields towards Gully Cottage.

Flora sat on Kate's lap and listened intently to the story. It was one of her favourites, a real scarer, with the full gamut of monsters, ghosts, creepy-crawlies and things that went bump in the night. She didn't suck her thumb or cuddle a teddy, but she had a peculiar attachment to one of Rory's old ties which she held close to her face, rubbing the silk against her cheek.

Kate told the story with great gusto. In truth, she probably enjoyed it more than Flora, doing all the voices and all the noises. She was just getting into her stride when she thought she heard someone outside in the courtyard; she stopped, listened for a minute or so to check and Flora said, 'Go on, Kate – read it, please.' Kate took a breath to continue, glanced up and saw Alice standing in the open doorway.

'My God!' Kate started so violently that she almost toppled Flora off her lap. She stared at Alice and Alice stared back at her – they said nothing.

Flora glanced behind her at Kate, saw her look and followed it to the woman at the door. 'Who's that?' Flora asked, a slightly puzzled frown on her face, and Alice felt her whole body sag with sadness.

'That's Alice,' Kate said quietly. 'Alice is . . .' She stopped and gazed for a moment at Flora, at her trusting, alert little face, and she didn't know what to say.

'Alice is a friend of Daddy's,' Alice finished for her. She was shaking so hard that she had to hold on to the door-frame for support. 'I've come to visit you both.'

'Does Daddy know?'

'Yes,' Alice said, 'I rang him to tell him.'

'Oh.' Flora returned to the book. 'Come on, Kate,' she said.

Alice turned away. Of course she doesn't remember me, she told herself, how could she? She hardly knew you, you disappeared two years ago. But Alice couldn't stop the heartache. She didn't know what she had expected, but she knew that she had lost her daughter . . . no, not lost her, given her up. 'Can you let Rory know I'm here?' she asked Kate.

Kate nodded. She had never thought she might feel sorry for Alice, but for that one moment she did. 'I'll ring him now,' she said.

'Good.' Alice attempted to smile but failed. 'I'll wait for him outside.'

Jan had kept the marital home. It wasn't particularly big or smart, a medium-sized maisonette on two floors in Putney, but she had decorated and furnished it lovingly herself and felt that Duncan and Carol-Anne would get it only over her dead body. It was hers; she watered the window-boxes, got on with the neighbours and parked her car in the same space each night. It might have been suburban, but Jan loved it.

Stefan wasn't surprised, when his taxi pulled up outside the red-brick Edwardian building late that night, that this was what Jan had dug her heels in for. It suited her, a neat, careful property with no pretensions. He had badgered the address out of Molly at the office, and had struggled with the idea of coming all afternoon. In the end, his sense had given in to his emotions. He knew Jan wouldn't be happy to see him, but he had to talk to her; he couldn't go on any longer in this state of desperate misery. He didn't know what it was about Jan, but he had never felt so wretched. His whole body hurt just thinking about her – and if that wasn't love, then bugger it, he didn't know what was.

Stefan rang on the door-bell of No. 3 Ashmore House, stood back to see if any lights were on, saw that there were and rang again. He waited, glanced at his watch and put his face against the glass panel in the door. He could make out the shape of the hall and the sitting-room beyond, and saw Jan's figure move across the doorway to switch off a light. 'Damn,' he muttered. He bent, pushed open the letter-box and shouted, 'Jan, I know you're in there, there's no point in turning off lights and pretending that you're not! I want to speak to you, Jan, we've got to talk. Jan? Answer me!'

Peering through the slot, he saw the bottom half of her figure in the sitting-room. 'Jan!' he called again, 'Please, we've got—'

'Go away!' she cried. 'Go away and leave me alone!'

Stefan stood up and banged on the door. 'No,' he shouted, 'I won't go away. I want to talk to you, Jan, I can't leave it like this, I can't let you—'

'Excuse me!' A voice called down from a second-floor window. 'Will you keep the noise down, please! Some of us are trying to watch television.'

Stefan banged louder on the door. 'Jan!' he shouted. 'You're disturbing the neighbours. Let me in, for God's sake, or I'll stand out here and say what I have to say!' As he bent and peered through the letter-box again, another light went off. 'Jan! Jan, please!' He stood and moved back, wondering for one brief, insane moment whether to break the glass and let himself in. Christ, Stefan, he thought, get a grip. He moved close to the door again and laid his face against the glass. 'Jan,' he said quietly, 'please listen to me, that's all I—'

Suddenly Jan opened the door; Stefan fell forward, lost his balance and stumbled inside. She closed the door behind him and, as he righted himself, she said, 'You've got five minutes, then I want you out of here and out of my life. The only reason I've let you in is because I want to keep on good terms with my neighbours. Now say what you have to and then go. Is that clear?'

Stefan turned and looked at her.

'Is that clear?' she repeated.

He nodded. She looked terrible, almost as bad as he did. He wanted to touch her. 'Jan, I'm sorry,' he said.

'Sorry!' she snorted derisively. She hadn't planned to say anything, but couldn't help herself. 'You're *sorry*?'

Stefan looked down at his hands. 'Jan, I'm sorry that I didn't tell you what I do for a living.'

'And what exactly *do* you do, Stefan?'

'I'm a male escort. I take people like Loïs Makinny to dinners and parties; I escort women who don't want to be seen in public alone.'

Jan shook her head. 'For God's sake, Stefan, be honest! You're a prostitute! You sleep with women for money.' She couldn't keep the revulsion out of her voice and he winced. 'You sell sex!'

'No, Jan, I don't sell sex!'

'Isn't it part of the service?'

Stefan hesitated. He wanted her so much that he was tempted to lie, to tell her anything to convince her. He bit his nail, the hesitation lengthening into a painful silence.

'There are certain clients, women I particularly like, that I sleep with.' He'd said it, the truth; there wasn't any going back now. 'I get paid for the whole evening, not for sex. I never meet anyone just for sex; if it happens, then it usually comes at the end of the evening, as it might if I had taken them out anyway.'

'Oh, and that makes it all right, does it? I don't believe you, Stefan. You really can't see what's wrong, can you?'

'I can see that it's not everyone's idea of a good career, but there's nothing truly terrible in what I do. I like sex, I like women, the relationships I have with my clients are honest, I make a difference.'

'Well, if you believe that, then more fool you!'

Stefan put out his hand and touched her arm. 'Jan?'

She shrugged him off. 'You lied to me,' she said quietly, 'and you used me. Even if I could accept what you do, I can't take any more lies. You may be honest with your clients, but you didn't have the decency to be honest with me.'

'I didn't lie to you, Jan, and I didn't use you. When you asked me what I did, I just didn't say, but I never told lies to protect myself.' He stopped and put his head in his hands. 'Jan, after last night, after what's happened between us, what does it really matter?'

Jan's whole body ached. She wanted to believe him, she wanted to think that all this drama was because he cared, but she couldn't. This time her morale had sunk too low. 'It matters,' she said. 'It matters to me. You used me to get things done for your friend. I don't know – maybe I was just another client?'

'No, Jan, never that.'

'But you don't deny that you wanted to help Kate Dowie?'

Stefan looked at her. The truth was a peculiar thing; once embarked upon, it was impossible to rescind. 'No, I can't deny that, but . . .'

Jan turned away. 'Don't say any more,' she murmured. 'Please.'

Stefan stood apart from her and wondered how just a few feet could seem so distant. A gulf lay between them, and he hadn't said any of what he'd wanted to say. 'What if I did something else, Jan? What if I had another job?'

She glanced back at him. 'Like what? I presume you're not a fully qualified lawyer?'

'No.'

'Exactly, no.' Jan shrugged. 'Forget it, Stefan.'

'Forget what? Us?'

She nodded and moved towards the door. 'There is no us, there never was.' Opening the door, she held it wide for him. 'And just for the record, what I did on the Tonsbry Estate file I did for myself, not for you. I may have made a fool of myself in taking you seriously, but I didn't let it affect my business decisions.'

Stefan swallowed hard, took one last look at her face and walked out. He went to turn to say goodbye, to say anything to prolong his leaving, but Jan had already closed the door. He stared at it for a few moments, then pulled up the collar of his coat and made his way to the main road to hail a taxi. Only when he was halfway back to Pimlico did he realise that he hadn't told her anything about the Letchworth Housing Association or Duncan's idea of a cash bonus.

Alice stood at the sink with a tea-towel in her hand and dried the dishes that Rory passed to her. Never having been one for domesticity, the part she found herself playing now was very alien to her. Flora was upstairs in bed; supper had been eaten at the small kitchen table, the three of them together, and Alice had helped with bath-time, despite Flora's reluctance for her to do so. She stacked the last three plates on the table, folded the cloth and hung it over the back of the chair. Leaning against the sideboard facing Rory, she said, 'Kate and Flora seem close.'

Rory tensed. 'Do they?'

'Quite a cosy little scene, really.' Alice folded her arms across her chest and looked down at the floor. 'It's a shame that I had to come and break it all up, but then Flora is mine by rights—'

The crash came out of nowhere. Loud and sharp, it stopped Alice in her tracks. She leaped back as fragments of broken china splayed across the floor towards her and stared at Rory. 'Don't,' he snarled, 'ever say that again! *Ever*!' There was no question of the plate having fallen accidentally and Alice backed away from him. 'Flora is not yours by right and if you do anything to hurt her, or Kate for that matter, then so help me God, Alice, I'll kill you!'

Alice stayed perfectly still. For some time she simply stood and stared down at the mess. In all the time she had known Rory – through her illness, through his obvious pain at losing Kate, in the midst of their desperation – he had never threatened her, never lost his temper, not really, not properly. The shock took several minutes to recede, then Alice knelt and silently began to pick up the broken china. When she had finished, she swept the remains into a pile with the tea-towel and stood up. 'I'm sorry,' she said 'It isn't true, of course. I shouldn't have said it.'

'No, you shouldn't.'

Alice pulled out a chair and sat down, feeling suddenly very tired and very sad. 'Flora's a lovely child,' she said, 'all credit to you . . .' She closed her eyes in an attempt to stop the tears, but couldn't. Fumbling in her pocket, she pulled out a dog-eared tissue. 'I'm sorry,' she mumbled, blowing her nose. 'I didn't want it to be like this, I imagined it all so different—'

'Didn't we all!'

Alice looked up. As she stared at Rory, it was as if she saw him for the first time, really saw him, as an individual and not just an appendage to her own life, and she was suddenly horrified by what she had done. 'Oh God, Rory, I'm so sorry.'

'So you said.'

She swallowed. 'I really made a mess of things, didn't I?'

Rory shook his head. 'You fucked up my life, Alice, and Kate's and Flora's to a certain extent.'

'You're still bitter.'

'No, not any more. I've got Flora, you see.'

Alice flinched. He was right, but it wasn't easy to accept.

'Is that why you came back? For Flora?' he asked her.

She was silent. In a way, yes, it had been why she'd come back – to claim her daughter, to salve the guilt, to set things right. Only now she was here she knew that Flora wasn't for claiming, she wasn't a possession and she didn't belong to Alice any more than she belonged to Rory. As for salving the guilt, she wasn't sure if she would ever be able to do that, and putting things right . . . well, perhaps that had just been a fantasy.

'I came home to see Flora,' she said finally. 'Maybe, if you wouldn't mind, we could keep in touch?'

Rory looked away. For so long now he had been angry at Alice, had felt betrayed and used. Now, seeing her small, sad figure across the room, he just felt sorry for her. 'Of course.' He came and sat down. 'Do you want a drink?'

Alice shrugged. 'I should get going.'

'Stay,' Rory said. 'I've got some pictures of Flora if you'd like to see them?'

She smiled. 'Yes, I'd love to see them.'

He stood up and went over to the dresser.

'Rory?' He turned. 'Thanks,' Alice said, 'for everything.'

It was much later than she had expected when Alice looked at her watch. There had been a cry from upstairs and Rory had gone to see if Flora was all right. Alice finished her glass of Tonsbry Original and stood up. She had booked a room in the village, but she didn't think she'd take it now. If she hurried, she might just get back to the station for the last train up to London.

Picking up a photo of Flora from the pile she and Rory had been looking through, Alice tucked it into her pocket and pulled on her coat. She could hear Rory's voice upstairs, low and reassuring; taking a pencil from the dresser, she scribbled him a quick note, wished him luck with the gin enterprise and thanked him again. She placed it under the gin bottle, found her case and, holding Flora's scarf close to her face for a few moments, breathing in the smell of child that lingered on it, she opened the door and silently left the cottage.

By the time Rory had settled Flora back to sleep and come downstairs, Alice was long gone.

It was late when the telephone rang, and Kate was in the bath. She had had an extension line put in her bedroom, but still cursed as it meant climbing out of the warm water into the damp, chilly air and cutting short her one luxury of the day. It might be Harry, she thought, leaving it to ring and then immediately feeling guilty because she'd not thought of him or called him since he'd left Tonsbry two days previously. She stood, shivered and reached for a towel as the phone rang on. 'Whoever it is, they're pretty determined,' she muttered, drying herself vigorously and pulling on her dressing-gown. As she padded back to her room, one singular thought struck her: it had to be her mother.

'Hello?' Kate wished she'd taken the trouble to light a fire in her room. It was icy cold, and she grabbed a rug to wrap round her.

'Kate, darling, it's Mummy!'

'Hello, Mummy. I thought it might be you.'

'Did you, darling? How awfully clever of you!'

Kate smiled. This was the second time her mother had broken a lifelong pledge never to ring Tonsbry and her bright, charming tone was rather unnerving. Was she up to something?

'Kate, darling, I've been thinking. I know that you didn't want to come up last week what with all that was going on, but I really do think you could do with a little break, even if it's just for lunch and . . . well, Pierre is in London now and I've asked him to send the car down for you tomorrow, mid-morning, and bring you up for lunch.' Adriana paused only to draw breath. 'I thought we could go somewhere quiet, the RAC Club, and then potter round St James's? I've seen a lovely coat in—'

'Mummy—'

'Harvey Nicks,' Adriana went on, ignoring the interruption. 'We could take a cab up to Knightsbridge and—'

'Mummy, I can't! It's terribly kind of you, but really I can't.'

'Nonsense! Of course you can.' The charm slipped. 'What on earth is there to stop you, Kate?'

'I can't leave the business at this point. I—'

'Business? For goodness' sake, Kate, you're not still going on about all that, are you?' Adriana made a concerted effort to rein in her temper. 'Oh, do say yes, Kate darling, it'll be lovely, just the two of us . . .' She glanced up as Pierre came into the room and mouthed: 'It's Kate.'

'I'd love to, really,' Kate said, 'but I'm sorry, I can't.'

'Well really, Kate!' Adriana suddenly snapped. 'I don't know what's got into you, I really don't, I . . .' She stopped and looked at Pierre; he was watching her with mild irritation and she flushed. 'Kate, we will talk about this another time,' she said, a little more calmly. 'I have to go now, Pierre has just come in.'

Kate shivered and wrapped the rug in tighter. 'OK,' she said wearily. 'Whatever you want, Mummy.' They exchanged goodbyes and Kate hung up, but she sat staring at the phone for quite some time before getting up. She found a pair of thick pyjamas in the drawer, pulled them on and climbed into bed. I wonder why it is, she thought, that whenever my mother tries to be kind I can't help feeling suspicious? She pulled the covers up to her chin and snuggled down. It really isn't fair of me; after all, this is the second time she's rung and she's only got my best welfare at heart. Closing her eyes and forgetting to switch off the lamp, Kate began to drift swiftly towards sleep. I really must do more for Mummy and Harry, the people who love me, she pledged. And those were her last conscious thoughts of the day.

Chapter Twenty-One

Just over a week after the first successful run of Tonsbry gin, the centre of the business operation, formerly the dining-room, was a hub of activity. Two telephone lines had been newly connected; separate tables had been set up for labelling, packing and orders; and once the bottles had been filled and capped down in the still-room, they were finished off here, counted and packed, ready for delivery.

It was a Friday morning. Rory had just brought up another crate of bottles and Kate had just finished on the phone. She made a few notes on her pad, then glanced up and smiled at him.

'Another case sold,' she said, 'to the Queensbury Hotel in Kensington. They had one at the beginning of the week and apparently it's gone like a bullet.'

'Well done.' Rory placed the crate of bottles on the labelling table and Mrs Able made a note of it. Everything had to be counted and recounted for Customs and Excise; every drop of gin produced accounted for.

The phone rang again. 'Your line, Rory,' Kate called. He slid into his chair and picked it up. 'Good morning, Tonsbry Original.'

Kate watched him as he handled the call, chatted and

sold half a case of gin. He made it look so easy that it surprised her. She had never considered Rory a natural salesman and she had a sneaking suspicion that he'd had to work very hard at it indeed. He put down the phone, scribbled his order note and placed it in the filing tray. 'Are you back up to London tomorrow, Kate?' he asked.

'Yes, I'm doing the brokers tomorrow. I've got that tasting at Kennings – thanks to one of their directors I did quite a bit of catering for – and then I'll probably do the rounds. Stefan's kept the sandwich and salad drop going, so I'll go along with Rebecca and see if I can shift a few bottles there—'

The phone went again on Rory's desk. 'Sorry.' He picked it up and Kate turned away as he went into his spiel. She watched Mrs Able and wondered about Alice. She had done an awful lot of wondering about Alice in the last week, but had got no further in her conclusions. Rory said nothing and she wasn't going to ask him. Only, was Alice coming back? Why had she just arrived one day and gone the next? And if she was coming back, then what did Rory think about it? As Kate sighed, Mrs Able looked up, caught her staring and huffed. She turned back to her order forms just as Rory put down his phone and suddenly threw his pencil up in the air. 'Yes!' He caught it and put it between his teeth, grinning. 'Four cases to the Blues and Royals, two cases to the Infantry at Coalport, two cases to the Scots Guards and a case to our own Hampshire Blues.'

'Rory, that's marvellous!'

He took the pencil out of his mouth. 'Yes, it is rather, isn't it!'

'That's ten cases in all, and that's just this morning. John? Did you hear that?' John Able had just come into the room.

Each member of the household had a specific job, and John had taken on the day-to-day accounting. 'It's great, isn't it? We must be getting somewhere with all these sales.'

John shrugged, glancing at Rory, and Kate said, 'Well, aren't we?'

'I'll have a look,' he said. He took a file from the table and opened it, pulling out several sheets of paper. 'We've done three runs at forty-four cases per run, so that's a hundred and thirty-two cases and we've sold so far . . .' He paused, reached for the calculator and added up some figures. 'Forty-eight cases.'

Kate's face fell. 'Forty-eight cases?'

He nodded.

'That doesn't sound like a great deal.' She looked at Rory.

'No,' he said, 'I'm afraid it's not.'

Kate put her head in her hands for a moment.

'Well, more correctly, it is and it isn't,' Rory said quickly. She looked up. 'You see, if we had lots of time to build the business, or even a normal amount of time, then the speed we're going at now would be pretty damn good. But as it is, this business has had to hit the ground running, so to speak, and we need to be able to prove in a very short space of time that we can make it work, get good profit margins – shift a hell of a lot of booze, in other words.' He stopped talking and looked at a silent and depressed audience. 'We *must* have some hefty ammunition to be able to appeal against foreclosure.'

There was another silence, then Kate said, 'Great! So we're all working our butts off and it's still not enough?'

Rory honestly didn't know what to say. This was the sort of information the company accountant kept to himself until absolutely necessary.

'I just don't see what else we can do!' she exclaimed.

He avoided her eye and stared down at his hands. 'No,' he said, quietly, 'nor do I.'

Duncan ordered two coffees, one Danish and one croissant with butter and jam, both of which were for him. Carol-Anne had him on a strict diet and he was starving half the time, depressed for the rest of it. Any opportunity he got, he would stuff his face with goodies he would never have been allowed in her company. There was something rather pathetic about it, but he wasn't about to admit that.

The coffees arrived and he handed Jan hers – black, no sugar – adding cream and two packets of sweetener to his own.

'Is it really worth it?' Jan asked.

'What?'

'The sweetener? You're just about to eat two days' worth of calories, so why bother with a sweetener?'

Duncan ignored her. He stirred, took a sip of his coffee and sat back.

'So?' Jan said.

'So what?'

'Why the meeting? And why here?' The food arrived and Duncan motioned for the waitress to put it in front of him. 'Unless of course Carol-Anne has put you on a diet, and this is the only way you can satisfy your sugar addiction.'

'Don't be ridiculous!'

Jan smirked. 'How much weight have you lost?'

'Nine pounds,' Duncan said automatically and she started to laugh. 'Very clever,' he remarked. He bit into the pastry, chewed and licked the sugar off his lips. 'Tell me, Jan,' he said, 'how is your own relationship going?'

Jan narrowed her eyes. She could just about detect a sneer behind the smile and had a pretty shrewd idea that Duncan already knew.

'It isn't,' she answered. 'There is no relationship.'

'I'm sorry.'

'Bullshit!'

Duncan held up his hands. 'No need to be aggressive, Jan.' He finished the pastry. 'The reason for this meeting is the Tonsbry Estate file.' Moving one plate aside, he exchanged it for the next and broke the croissant into small pieces. 'I think we both know what's happened to it and I want it back, Jan.' He buttered a piece of croissant and spread a thick dollop of jam on top. 'It's company property, you've got it and, if you don't give it back to the company or me, I shall be forced to consult a solicitor.'

'You're joking!'

'I'm not smiling, Jan.' Duncan ate his piece of croissant, went to butter another but changed his mind and pushed the plate away. 'That file is an important piece of business, and removal of it amounts to theft.'

Jan stared at him, not quite able to believe what she was hearing. 'If you're going to play it like that,' she said, 'then I'm afraid that I don't know what you're talking about, Duncan.' She stood and reached for her cigarettes.

Duncan caught hold of her wrist. 'Cut it out, Jan!' he hissed. 'This isn't a game. I want that file and I'm going to get it. Now why don't you save us all a great deal of trouble and just tell me where it is?'

'Duncan, let go of my arm or I will scream, very loudly!'

He looked up at her, his lip curled in disdain and he twisted his grip, making her wince. The next moment he let go.

'You bastard!'

Duncan smiled and suddenly, unable to help herself, Jan lashed out and kicked him hard in the shin.

'Ouch! Shit! Christ, you—' Several people turned and looked at him. He shut up, rubbed his shin and glared at Jan.

'Oh, Duncan?' she said, turning to leave. 'I forgot to ask, how's the bad leg?' And throwing her bag on to her shoulder, she stalked off and left him to pay the bill.

Stefan was in the large Shaker-style kitchen of a huge white Nash house in Regents Park. Rebecca was arranging Thai canapés on several long oval dishes while he made up another jug of Tonsbry Original cooler. It was lunchtime, and this was his second job of the day. Champagne breakfast for twenty had been the first, and he still had drinks in the City to cater for at six and a dinner that another of Kate's girls was cooking in Chelsea at eight. No wonder Kate was so bloody thin, he thought; food, food everywhere and not a speck to eat.

'You nearly finished, Becca?'

Rebecca was just adding roses carved out of carrot to the dishes, on a bed of watercress. She glanced up. 'What time's kick-off?'

'In about ten minutes. I'll get out there now with the drinks, you come out as soon as you're done. Once it starts filling up, we'll get the nibbles out.'

He turned and dried his hands on a tea-towel. Just as he'd finished, the hostess came into the kitchen in a cloud of Jo Malone scent. 'Stefan? A word, if you don't mind.'

Stefan exchanged glances with Becca, who then placed the last of the garnish on the dish and straightened. 'I'll take the first tray out,' she said; she disappeared with the cocktails and Stefan faced his client. As she perched on the edge of the table, the skirt of her suit rose to show a decent expanse of thigh and she said, 'Stefan, I've heard that you don't just do catering.'

Stefan remained impassive.

'The thing is . . .' She paused, letting her eyes travel from his face down over his body, in fitted white shirt and black jeans. 'I was wondering if you might like to take me out for dinner, somewhere quiet. I'd pay, of course . . .' Her voice trailed off and she smiled, a little embarrassed. 'For everything.'

Stefan tensed. He looked down at the floor, briefly considered his options and decided that Mrs Dolby could be a very good potential client – for catering.

'Mrs Dolby,' he said, 'I'm afraid that there's been a slight misunderstanding. I only do catering now.' He looked at her for a moment, saw her blush, then picked up a jug of cocktail. 'Have you tried this drink?' He reached over, took a glass from the table behind her and poured out a Tonsbry Original cooler. He gave it to her and briefly touched her hand. 'Thanks,' he said, very quietly, 'and I'm sorry, really.' Then he left the kitchen and went out to see how Becca was getting on.

The party was in full swing, Stefan was on his fifth round of cocktails and Becca was piling canapés on to plates as fast as she could. 'They're going like hot cakes,' she said over her shoulder. 'Must be the amount people are drinking.' She glanced back at him. 'It was a good idea, Stef, we'll have to try it again. That cocktail's a whammy!'

Stefan finished cutting limes and began squeezing. 'No

time to chat, Becca,' he said. 'People out there are dying of thirst!' She laughed, picked up a tray and disappeared out of the kitchen.

The next time Stefan looked up, a small, scruffy man in jeans, trainers and a grey marl T-shirt under an Armani jacket was standing in the doorway watching him. How long he'd been there, Stefan had no idea. He stopped what he was doing, faced the man and said, 'Forget it. I don't do men, never have.' He went back to his task.

'I beg your pardon!'

Stefan turned. Perhaps he'd been mistaken? 'Sorry,' he said. 'Misunderstanding, I think. What can I do for you?'

The man came into the room. 'This the first time you've done a party like this?'

He was American, which explained a great deal. 'Yes. You mean the lime cocktails and Thai food?'

'Yup.'

'Yes, yes, it is. D'you like it?'

'Who, me? Nah, can't stand cocktails.' He took one of the canapés off the tray which was waiting to go out. 'My daughter Dolores loves 'em, though.' Pulling the satay off its skewer with his teeth in one bite, he barely chewed it before swallowing it down. 'It's her birthday next week. We got a party for her, a few friends in a tent in the garden. I got the food all lined up, all that stuff, but I was wanting something a bit different – you know, to set the scene. What about these cocktails?'

'What about them?'

'You think you could do them for me, and these nibbly things? It's short notice, but I'll pay extra for the inconvenience.'

Stefan's pulse was beating so hard that he was convinced

the vein in his neck was throbbing. He took a breath. Act cool, he told himself, this could be big, so act cool. 'How many people exactly?'

'I dunno, about five hundred.'

Five hundred? *Five hundred*! Who the hell was this Dolores, American royalty?

'Look,' he said, 'can you give me ten minutes or so to see if I can get it organised?' He'd have to phone Rory, see if he could get the gin – God, they were talking twenty, twenty-five cases, almost an entire run, had to be.

'Tell you what, call me on this number tonight.' The man pulled a card out of his pocket and handed it to Stefan. 'Justin North', it said, 'Executive Producer, ACE Films'. Stefan clutched the card in a hand which had started to sweat.

'Any time before ten; we turn the phone off at ten.'

'Thanks, Mr North,' said Stefan. 'And I'm sure I can help you.' As North left the kitchen, Stefan threw the card up in the air and shouted so loudly that Rebecca, coming back with an empty tray, wondered what on earth had happened.

Duncan had been closeted in his office for the entire afternoon, snarling at anyone who had the nerve to interrupt him. He had been on the phone to the bank, the company solicitors, Jan's personal legal people . . . Christ, he'd even called her mother! No one had any idea of a file she might have deposited with them, or if they did they bloody well weren't saying. He reckoned he'd now tried every route and come up with nothing. Bugger-all! Jan might have been easy to manipulate in the past, but she was getting her own back now. She was one bright woman, and Duncan was beginning to wonder if he hadn't been a bit rash in pitching himself against her.

Sitting back, he stretched and rubbed his eyes. Hours in bright office lighting affected his vision, and his sight was beginning to blur. He heard a knock on his door, shouted, 'Go away! I'm busy!' and reached for the computer manual. He was flicking through it for ideas when the door opened, despite his request, and someone came into the room.

'I said I'm busy,' he snapped, not even looking up from the book. 'And no, I don't want coffee, tea or any bloody thing to drink. Thank you.'

'I wasn't offering refreshment,' said Carol-Anne.

Duncan jerked round. 'Oh, hello, sweetheart. Sorry, I thought it was someone else.'

She crossed the room and came to stand behind him. 'What, one of your little floozies!' Gently, she massaged his shoulders with the tips of her fingers and felt him relax at her touch. 'They'll have to go, Duncan.'

Duncan closed his eyes and let out a deep sigh. 'Who will, sweetie?'

'The receptionist and your secretary, for starters.' Carol-Anne moved her fingers up from his shoulders to the sensitive part of his neck.

'Don't be ridiculous,' Duncan murmured.

'I'm not.' As Carol-Anne bent her head and kissed around his ear, Duncan shivered. Her tongue darted in and out of his ear and her breath was hot on his skin. Moments later, she spun the chair round to face her and Duncan opened his eyes.

'My God—' Carol-Anne had slipped her coat off her shoulders and was wearing nothing underneath but a black net body, a pair of black stockings and spiky, shiny black stilettos. It was outrageous, but Duncan loved it. Silencing him with her mouth, she unfastened his trousers with long, deft fingers and straddled him.

'Carol-Anne, I . . .' The chair rocked back with their weight. 'Christ, what if someone comes—' But he got no further. As Carol-Anne moved astride him, he forgot what he was going to say and drew in a breath. The chair bounced, creaking on its hinges, and Duncan gave himself up to the pleasures of a dominant woman. But just as he did so, he raised his eyes heavenward and caught sight of a company team photograph on the wall opposite. Jan, in navy suit and sensible shoes, was watching him and he was sure, despite the fact that it was a serious photo, that she was smiling at him.

It was dusk and, as Alice walked the beach in Norfolk with her brother Philip, the dying sun laid a sheen on the blue-black water. Alice picked up a stone and threw it; it skimmed the surface for several yards, then disappeared.

'You were always good at that, Al, far better than me.'

She turned. 'It's so long since I was good at anything that I can't remember what it feels like,' she said.

Philip put an arm around her shoulders. 'Come on, don't be gloomy.' He squeezed and she smiled. 'That's better.'

They walked on in silence for a while.

'Alice, you know Cath and I didn't expect you back so soon, we thought you might stay down in London for a while.'

'There was no point.' Alice looked at him. 'You don't mind me staying, do you?'

He smiled. 'Oh, heavens, of course not, it's just that we wondered . . .' He stopped and faced her. 'Look, tell me if

I'm interfering, Alice, but we thought you'd want to spend more time with Flora – get to know her, maybe?'

Alice shrugged and turned to stare out at the sea. 'I messed up again,' she said. 'It didn't work out as I'd expected and I said things I shouldn't have and, well . . .' She turned back. 'I thought it best to leave.' Philip frowned. 'Yes, I know,' Alice said. 'Same old story; stupid Alice, when will I ever grow up, when will I stop making a hash of my life?'

'No, that's not what I was thinking.'

'What were you thinking then, Philip? Tell me, be honest.'

'I was thinking that it must be very hard to be you, that it's not an easy situation to have to face up to but . . .'

'But what?'

'But, oh I don't know, perhaps you shouldn't have left, Alice. I can't help thinking that at some point you're going to have to put things right, and the sooner you do it the easier it will be. If you leave it until Flora's grown up, then maybe it'll be too late.'

Alice picked up another stone but she didn't throw this one, she held it in her hand. It was smooth and round and it felt good, heavy and solid. 'How do I put things right, Philip? God knows I've thought about it, but being there was such a disaster. Kate blanked me, Rory was still angry and bitter. What could I possibly do to change all that? In the space of a few hours I got nowhere, I just upset everything.' She tucked the stone into her pocket.

Philip asked, 'Didn't you say something about gin a few days ago? Isn't Rory involved in some sort of business venture with Kate, making gin?'

'Yes, but I don't see what that's got to do with—' Alice

broke off, narrowed her eyes and looked at her brother. 'How long have you been harbouring this idea, Philip?'

'Cath and I talked about it last night.'

'Hence the long walk?'

He smiled. 'Alice,' he said, 'you used to work for a big drinks company, you were in marketing, you put the drinks they made into people's shopping baskets. What more do I have to say? It's staring you in the face, the chance to put things right! Ring Rory and offer to help. You've got years of experience, experience they could use.'

'Oh, Philip, I don't know. How would they react to having me, the arch enemy, working alongside them? And I've been out of the business since before Flora was born, I haven't worked since I was made redundant. Even if they did want me to help, I don't know if I'm still up to it, I—'

'You're making excuses, that's what you're doing! Rory will agree. He's an accountant and a businessman, he'll know a good offer when he sees one. It'll give you a chance to be close to Flora, without any pressure on either of you, and the opportunity to do something positive for once. I think Rory deserves that much, don't you?'

Alice was silent, remembering their conversation. She hadn't just made a mess of things, she had fucked up his life. Yes, Rory deserved something positive from Alice, he more than deserved it, he was owed it. 'Oh, I don't know, Philip, I'm not sure . . .'

Philip took both her hands in his. 'We can never be sure,' he said, 'of anything in this life, Alice. Go, go and put things to rest. For Rory's sake, for Flora's and' – he looked at her – 'most of all for your own.'

*　　*　　*

Pierre Glibert, Comte de Grand Blès, sat in the back of the chauffeur-driven Mercedes with his wife, Adriana, in complete silence. It was he who had insisted they come, telephoning Kate from the car to tell her they were on their way for dinner, and it was he who was determined to find out exactly what Adriana was up to. He had had enough. Urgent, unexplained departures, irrational anger with Kate, secret meetings with lawyers and endless telephone calls which ended immediately he entered the room. He was a patient man and he loved his wife very much, but now he was bored with her deviousness – it failed to intrigue him, it simply irritated him.

As they turned off the main road into the network of country lanes, he leaned across and took her hand.

'Where shall we have dinner, my darling?' he asked. 'I wonder if Kate will know anywhere?'

But Adriana didn't answer. She sat and stared out of the window at the unfolding familiarity of the countryside and silently ground her teeth. At the signpost to Tonsbry village she visibly tensed, and Pierre held her hand a little tighter. They followed a route he recognised and, as they slowed at the gates to Tonsbry House and the driver indicated he was about to turn, Adriana suddenly snatched her hand away. 'Stop!' she cried. 'Stop the car, Pierre, I want to go home.' As Pierre leaned forward and touched the driver on the shoulder, the car ground to a halt.

'Adriana,' Pierre said, 'are you going to tell me what this is all about?'

She sat, stony-faced and silent.

'I will not go in,' she said. 'I did it once for that disastrous wedding and that was the one and only time, ever! I will not go in there, Pierre. You'll have to phone Kate and tell her to meet us in the village.'

Pierre was silent for a short while, then he said, 'Adriana, I have tolerated your secrecy for many years now regarding Tonsbry, but recently it has become excessive. What is David Lowther doing for you, and what connection do you have with the company that has mortgaged the house and estate?'

'How did you—?'

He held up his hand to silence her; the question didn't even need answering. Pierre knew everything his wife did, and she was well aware of that fact. It was the sort of man he was. 'I am giving you the chance to tell me yourself, Adriana. Shall I go on?'

She turned and stared out of the window.

'You are doing everything in your power to influence Kate against this lovely house, lying to her, entertaining her boyfriend, a young man I do not think you even like—'

'All right!' she snapped. 'All right! Yes, I am trying to get Kate away from here, but it's for her own good. She hasn't got a clue about what she's taken on, she's making a fool of herself and she can't see it. She's—'

'She's doing what you always dreamed you would do,' Pierre cut in. 'She is trying to salvage this house and estate, as you would have done had it been yours. Am I right?'

'No! I never wanted this place, it's a mausoleum, dead, worthless—'

'Adriana.' He looked at her. 'Adriana, if it's worthless, then why have you been buying parcels of its land for the past ten years? Every time your brother needed cash David Lowther came up with a buyer and, unknown to Leo, it

was always you.' He waited for her to speak. 'Was it not?'
There was a silence.

'Was it not, Adriana?' he insisted.

'Yes, it was me!' she said. 'Oh, for God's sake, Pierre,
do we have go through all this now?' She reached for her
handbag and opened it, taking out a small compact mirror
and her lipstick. She started to apply it, but Pierre gently
stopped her. 'Why, Adriana? I want to know why!'

Adriana shrugged, slipping the top on her lipstick and
ignoring the question as she snapped the compact shut
with a sharp click.

'I asked you a question, Adriana, and you will answer
it. We will sit here at the entrance to Tonsbry House until
you do.'

Again she shrugged.

'*Adriana!*' he suddenly shouted.

'All right!' she snapped back. 'All right, Pierre, I'll tell
you why.' She turned and looked out of the window at
the stone pillars and rusting iron gates to Tonsbry House –
her house, her inheritance and hers by right. 'It should have
been mine,' she said, her face averted. 'I was the first-born,
I loved it, I was the one who worked with my father, kept
the books for him and learned about the estate. I loved
it, Pierre. I loved every brick and tree and blade of grass.'
She turned to him. 'And then he told me, he told me on
my eighteenth birthday that he was giving me a small flat
in town, Chelsea to be precise, because Leo would inherit
the house and it was only fair that I should have a bit of
property too.' She snorted. 'A bit of property, that was my
present, a little three-roomed flat while he, the sniveller –
a snotty, pathetic little brat who couldn't tell a sheep from
a goat – got all of it, the house and the entire estate, and all

because he was male, the male heir!' She nodded through the window to the view outside. 'And look what he did to it! He hadn't a clue. Pathetic doesn't even sum it up, it was bloody disastrous! He riddled it with debt. He sold anything that was of any value and mortgaged the place down to the rubber plugs in the bath. He was an idiot! He should never have been given possession of a property like that. *Never*, he—'

'He was your brother, Adriana,' Pierre interrupted, 'and he did his best.'

'His best? His *best*! And what would you know about that?'

'More than you would give me credit for.' Pierre shook his head. 'Leo told me once that running Tonsbry was draining, Adriana; he said that it bled him dry, literally, with its constant repairs and maintenance, low crop prices, low rentals, the odd disaster like dry rot in the roof and the second-floor bathroom flooding. It haemorrhaged money and he would need to have been a very wealthy man to be able to keep up with it.'

'He *was* a very wealthy man! He—'

Pierre shook his head again. 'He was not a wealthy man, and you know that as well as I do.'

She sniffed. 'Wealthy or not, Pierre, that doesn't alter the fact that if I had inherited that place it would still be up and running and probably doing very nicely indeed, thank you. I would have—'

'You would have done everything that Kate is doing!' Pierre said sharply. 'Which is why I do not understand your desire to thwart her.'

'I am not trying to thwart her. I am simply trying to stop her from making a fool of herself. If she makes a mess of things, then she'll be lumbered with debt for the rest of her life. You don't see that, do you, Pierre? You think that I am the villain. You don't see that I am only trying to do what's best for Kate . . .' She broke off tearfully and reached for a handkerchief from her bag.

Pierre watched her, unmoved. 'Adriana, if you take this away from Kate, she will never forgive you. She is trying to prove herself, take possession of her own life, and you want to take that from her.'

'I do not, Pierre! I am trying to stop her getting hurt, with the house and with Rory and—'

'What will you do with it, Adriana?'

She stopped, taken aback by the question. 'What do you mean?'

'With Tonsbry? If you are able to get Ingram Lawd to repossess the property, that is. Presumably they will sell it directly to you?'

Adriana sat silent. The extent of Pierre's knowledge stunned her for a moment, then she recovered herself and said, 'It's none of your business.'

Pierre took her hand and he held it tightly in his own; very tightly. 'Oh, but I think it is, Adriana. You must never forget who pays the bills.' He squeezed.

Adriana turned away from Pierre's gaze; she did not want him to see that he was hurting her. 'I shall leave it to rot,' she said coldly. 'And when it is decayed and ruined, I shall sell it to developers who want to knock it down and build over it. All of it!'

Pierre released her hand and she took it back, gently massaging her fingers to get the circulation going again.

He sighed. 'Oh, Adriana,' he said wearily 'Poor, poor Kate.' He leaned forward and asked the driver to turn round and head back to London, then he sat back and looked out of the window. 'And poor you,' he added sadly. 'Poor, poor you.'

It was nine-thirty when the phone rang at Gully Cottage. Rory was sitting alone in the small front room, looking through a pile of back copies of *Drinks International*, the trade magazine for the industry. He had been making notes on launch campaigns in an attempt to find any other routes they could go down to sell Tonsbry gin, but hadn't got very far. He couldn't concentrate. For the first time since its conception, he had serious doubts that they were going to succeed with this business. It was all there, it had all the potential, but they just didn't have the time. It would take little short of a miracle to propel them forward to where they needed to be and, never having been a believer, he simply couldn't see that happening. He had just finished another magazine when the phone rang.

'Hello? Rory Gallagher.'

'Rory – hi, it's Stefan. Sorry to ring so late, I've been up to my eyes in catering all day and this is the first time I've got to the phone. Even now I'm ringing from my car on the way home.'

'Good for you. How's it going?' Stefan had rung Kate last week and offered to take over the catering business completely until she was ready to return to it. She had jumped at the chance.

'Actually I've surprised myself. It's going pretty damn well! I've got a good set of cooks and this cocktail thing – well, that's why I'm ringing. Rebecca and I tried something new today, at lunch and then this evening at drinks in the

City. We did the Tonsbry Original cooler with Thai food, and it's gone down a storm!'

'You're kidding?'

'No! We were staggered. I've got three more bookings for drinks and, wait for it, a bloody great party a week on Friday. Can you supply the gin?'

Rory was already reaching for his file. 'How many bottles do you need?'

'Cases! For the party, I'd like twenty cases on sale or return, and for the drinks another ten cases. Can you do it?'

Rory smiled. 'Of course we can bloody do it! We'd love to.' He made a note on his pad. 'You want them delivered?'

'Yes, by the middle of next week if you can.'

'We can.' Rory was pacing the floor now. 'I'll get someone to drive them up.'

'Thanks,' Stefan said. 'I'll be in touch.'

'No, thank *you*,' Rory finished. 'Thank you very much indeed.' He hung up and was just about to pick up the phone to call Kate when it rang again. 'Hello? Rory Gallagher.'

'Hello, Rory. It's Alice.'

His mood died almost instantly. 'Alice,' he said. 'What can I do for you?'

Alice heard the edge in his voice and had to steel herself to say the next sentence. 'Rory, you know this gin business? Well, I wondered if I might be able to help.'

'Help? Is this some kind of a joke?'

She swallowed hard. 'No, no joke. I used to market Virtual Vodka. You probably don't remember, but I worked for Worldwide Distillers before we . . . before I had Flora.'

'I don't remember.'

'Well, the thing is . . .' Alice stopped. The silence on the other end of the phone overpowered her for a moment, then she braced herself and went on. 'Look, Rory, I've got years of experience in the drinks industry and you could use it. There are no strings. I'd come, market the gin for you for as long as you like and then go when it's done. It's as simple as that.'

'Is it?' Rory tightened the telephone wire round his fingers. 'Alice, nothing has ever been simple with you.'

'No, well maybe now's the time to change all that.'

There was another long, tense silence, which Alice made no attempt to fill. Then Rory said, 'What sort of marketing are you talking about?'

Alice let out the breath she had been holding. 'How about basic publicity to start with? That way you wouldn't have to spend much, it'd be a case of a few free samples and lots of me chatting up the media. If that works, then maybe we can think of more of a marketing spend, but only when we've seen the response to the publicity. We'd have to get a customer profile in order to target the right people, and that would dictate the POS material and the advertising. Then we could—'

'OK, OK!' Rory sat down on the edge of the bed. It wasn't exactly a miracle but something, somewhere, had been stage-managed. 'Can you really put all this together, Alice?' he asked.

'Yes, of course I can.'

'What time frame are we talking about?'

'Whatever time frame you have.'

'How about a couple of weeks?' Rory asked miserably.

'If that's all you've got, then yes, a couple of weeks.'

'Really?'

It was the first time she had heard any warmth in his voice at all and Alice smiled. 'Yes, really,' she said. 'If you want it, then you've got it.' And it felt good, really good in fact, to do something positive for a change.

Chapter Twenty-Two

One Month Later

Alice was on the phone.

'Yes, of course we can send you a couple of bottles,' she said. 'No problem, and I'll get Kate Dowie to call you when she comes in; she can give you all the details. Can I make a note of your number? OK, got it. Yes, thanks . . .'

Kate walked into the study and Alice put a finger to her lips and went on talking. 'And the show is going out when? This Monday – OK, great! Yup, we'll call you in a while. Thanks again. Bye.'

Kate waited impatiently by the door. 'Can I speak now?' she snapped.

'Sorry.' Alice stood up. 'That was the producer of *Food and Drink*, they're doing a feature on Christmas spirits and want to talk to you about Tonsbry. I think I might just have persuaded them to do a couple of minutes on it, apparently one of the researchers had it at Harry's Bar last week and loved it. I thought we should just go over what to say . . .' She broke off; Kate had turned away and was staring out of the window. 'Kate?'

Kate glanced back. 'What, you mean you don't trust me to speak to them on my own?'

'No, I didn't mean that, I just think it's always better if you know what I've said and I know what you've said. I don't want them to know, for example, that we've got it on to the *Good Morning* feature. They might change their minds if they think it's been done.' Alice gathered up her notes. She had never expected any warmth from Kate, she had anticipated that she would be ignored for the most part, but the extent of the hostility had taken her aback. It was almost impossible to work with – a cold war situation. Every thing she did was received with distinct indifference, often open dislike. 'I think I'm about finished for today. Do you want to ring the Beeb now?'

Kate shrugged and Alice had to hold down a flash of temper. 'Kate,' she said, as calmly as she could. 'This publicity is free, but it's worth a hell of a lot of money in marketing terms. I've had to really badger to get Tonsbry on and—'

'It's OK, I'll ring now.'

This was one of the things that Kate did; she never let Alice have her full say, always cut her off short, and it was driving Alice insane. She counted to ten, found herself grinding her teeth as she did so and had to open her mouth to relax her jaw. 'The number's here,' she said. 'If you could emphasise the debt side of the story, and the fact that you discovered the distillery by accident and it all fell into place . . .'

'That isn't strictly true.'

'No, but it makes for better press and that's really all I'm interested in.' Alice dropped her notes into a file and made her way across to the door. As she turned, she saw Kate glaring at her.

'Kate, is there . . .' She stopped and took a deep breath. She was going to ask if there was really any point in her being there and working so hard when Kate was so uncooperative. It was her business Alice was working for, after all. But she didn't say it; Alice was learning.

'Is there what?' Kate asked.

'Is there dinner tonight?' Alice enquired.

'Of course,' Kate said. 'It's Friday!' It had become tradition; a Friday-night dinner for everyone involved in the business, to talk over the week and to relax. Kate always cooked.

'Right,' said Alice. 'Fine. I'll see you later, then.' And without bothering to say anything else or attempt any sort of smile, she left the room and went off to find Rory.

Duncan pulled into Redview Road and felt the warmth of familiarity as he drove up towards Ashmore House. He parked his car on the main road and sat in it for a while, thinking about Jan and about all the years spent getting to that address. It was his home, it had had his name on the door the day they viewed it with the estate agent, and he missed it. He missed Jan too, if he was honest with himself, in the strangest and most mundane ways.

Duncan climbed out of the car. Oh well, he was here for a purpose; it had taken a good deal of hard work and careful manoeuvring on his part to get this far, and he wasn't about to ruin it all now with sentimentality. Straightening his tie, he walked up the small gravelled drive to the house and rang on the door of No. 3. It felt odd, ringing on what legally was still his front door.

Jan answered it, dressed in a white towelling robe. They looked at each other for a moment, Duncan thinking how much she had changed in the past year; Jan thinking that despite all that had happened, recently Duncan had been far more like the man she married. Then she opened the door wide and said, 'Come in. I'm not ready yet, I'm afraid.'

Duncan walked into the hall.

'Why don't you get yourself a drink? I'll be down in about five minutes.'

He nodded and waited for her to show him through to the sitting-room. He knew the way, of course, he could have done it blindfolded, but it was Jan's house now and if he wanted her on his side then he would have to humour her.

Jan disappeared upstairs while Duncan poured himself a whisky and went into the kitchen to add some ice.

Up in the bedroom, Jan sat down on the bed and took a couple of deep breaths. She looked at the two outfits she had laid on the bed, stood up and tried one up against herself in the mirror, then decided on the other. She fiddled a while with her hair, then combed it back into the style she had started with. She put on the suit, changed the shirt, tried an alternative pair of shoes, then took the whole thing off and pulled a black wool shift dress with matching jacket out of her wardrobe. She put this on, then found some black suede shoes, a pair of black stockings and a silver necklace Duncan had bought her three years ago. Ready, she stood and stared at herself in the mirror. Oh God, she thought suddenly, what on earth am I doing? She sat down on the bed again and dropped her head in her hands.

Duncan had been working on her, that's what he'd been

doing, charming her, carefully manipulating her, and she knew it; she was perfectly aware of it, yet somehow she didn't really care. He was back to his old affable self, calling into her office several times a day, chatting, talking things over with her, having the odd lunch, lingering after meetings – the whole Duncan thing; effortless and likeable. And it was all so easy to slip into it again, to go with the flow. Jan knew she didn't love him any more, not in the same way, but she was forty-five and alone, with one brief disastrous fling behind her, and if Duncan wanted to resume something then why fight it? Perhaps twenty-odd years of marriage with just one ugly hiccup wasn't so bad?

Jan stood up, smoothed the skirt of her dress down over her hips and went to the mirror. Applying a thin coat of lipstick, she ran the comb through her hair one last time, took her handbag off the bed and, reasonably content, made her way downstairs.

'Hello, d'you want a drink?'

Jan shook her head. Duncan was drinking whisky; she never touched it and the bottle on the sideboard was exactly as he'd left it six months previously. She took a packet of cigarettes from the sofa table and lit up while she waited for him to finish his drink.

'The patio looks nice,' Duncan said. 'I like the pots. You don't usually do them in winter, do you?'

'I needed cheering up,' Jan said, then regretted it.

Duncan ignored this and smiled. 'You've always had green fingers, Jan,' he said. 'You even manage to make flowers last that little bit longer.' Which is more than Carol-Anne does, he almost added. Twenty quid a week on flowers, she spends, and they're dead by bloody Wednesday. He reached for Jan's cigarettes. 'D'you mind?'

'Of course not, help yourself.' She passed him the lighter and an ashtray. The ashtray was glass, heavy-bottomed, and it gleamed.

That was another thing he didn't like; Carol-Anne might be hot in the bedroom, but she was lukewarm everywhere else. Nothing ever gleamed in the flat, nothing ever looked clean even, including his shirts. Duncan lit up and finished his whisky.

'Do you want another?' Jan moved across to the sideboard and Duncan noticed that her dress showed exactly how much weight she'd lost.

'Is it new? The dress?'

Jan shrugged. Carol-Anne would never shrug in answer to a question like that; she loved to shop and she loved to regale Duncan with every intimate detail of each purchase.

'We'd better go,' he said. 'No more whisky, thanks, Jan.' He left his glass on the sideboard. 'The invitation said six; it's half-past five.'

'Right, I'll get my coat.' Jan went into the hall and took her overcoat out of the cupboard. Duncan followed her and saw the neat empty space – one overcoat, one jacket, one fleece – and longed for it. Clean and fresh and tidy; those words didn't exist in his life any more. Jan opened the front door and waited for Duncan to go out ahead of her.

'Shall I do the alarm?' he asked.

'Don't worry, I changed the number,' she answered. That was the reality; it wasn't his home any longer. He walked out into the cold night air. In a matter of half an hour it had got dark and Duncan stood under a street light waiting for Jan. She joined him on the pavement and he said, 'Just like old times, eh? Drinks party in the City, Christmas around the corner, you and me.'

Jan looked at him for a moment and tried hard to convince herself. She failed. 'Not really,' she replied. And they walked on to the car in silence.

Jan stood next to Duncan, holding a glass of some sort of gin cocktail which had gone straight to her head, and laughed at the punch-line of his joke. She had heard it before, twice actually, but it was still funny. He had a talent for entertaining people, when he was in the right frame of mind.

As the chap they had been talking to moved off, Duncan turned to her and said, 'Carol-Anne's gone out tonight with some friends. I don't suppose you fancy dinner, do you?'

Jan's hand tightened round her glass. Yes, she fancied dinner, she hated eating alone, but she didn't want to be available when Carol-Anne wasn't, she didn't want to get into that sort of set-up. 'Thanks, Duncan,' she replied, 'but I've got other plans.'

'Other plans?' He stopped. 'Sorry, none of my business.'

She smiled, adamant that she wasn't going to admit the truth. 'You're right, it isn't. Excuse me.' She placed her empty glass on a passing tray and made her way out of the room towards the ladies'.

The drinks party was in the entertaining suite of one of the broking houses, downstairs, all big expanses of grey carpet with white walls and signed, framed prints by big-name contemporary artists. It wasn't Jan's scene but she did like the pictures and, walking along, she took her time to look at them all individually, admiring them. She stopped by one in particular and was just looking at

the colour and form when she heard a familiar voice. She
turned and a few yards away, dressed in a crisp white shirt
and black jeans and talking to a woman much older than
himself, was Stefan. Her mouth dropped open, from the
surprise and from the instant physical attraction she still
felt. Then she saw him give the woman a card and realised
she was witnessing a business transaction in progress. It
outraged her. She was about to walk off when Stefan
saw her.

'Jan!' He came straight across, impervious to her glare,
and stopped her from going anywhere. 'Hello! Are you at
the Kennings party?'

'Yes.' Her voice was icy. 'And you?'

'Yes, I'm—'

But before he could finish, Jan exploded; she couldn't
help herself. 'I know exactly what you're doing, Stefan,
and it still appals me!' She turned to leave but glanced
back at him. 'No,' she said, 'more than that, it disgusts
me!' And shoving past him, she headed for the ladies'
and disappeared inside. Stefan went after her, on the way
knocking into Rebecca who said, 'We're running short
of gin, Stef, can you bring up another three or four
bottles from the car? Pete's cocktail-shaking for England
in there.'

He stopped, looked towards the cloakroom, then at
Rebecca, and let out a groan.

'You OK, Stefan?'

He shrugged, dug in his pockets for his car keys and said,
'Fine – just fine, thanks, Becca. I'll get that gin.' Heading
off towards the entrance, he stopped and looked back. 'I
just took another booking,' he called, 'provisionally for the
twenty-third.'

'Great,' Rebecca replied. She smiled. 'Well done!'

'Yeah,' he muttered under his breath. 'Bloody well done, Stefan.'

Jan found Duncan in exactly the same spot where she had left him. She walked across the room towards him and he turned as she approached. 'Jan?' Hurrying forward, he took her arm. 'What's up? You look awful.'

She made a joke. 'Thanks. You do know how to charm a girl!' But her voice was leaden and her face had drained of all colour.

'Come on,' Duncan said. 'We're going.'

'No, Duncan, I'm fine, really, don't spoil the party just for . . .' But he kept hold of her arm and started towards the door.

'Plans or no plans, I am going to take you somewhere really nice for dinner.'

Jan let herself be led. She hated scenes and seeing Stefan just now had thrown her. God, she thought, I really am pathetic, but the worst had passed and Duncan had taken charge.

'So,' he said as they left the building. 'Noisy, fashionable and expensive or quiet, intimate and expensive? What's it to be?'

Jan shrugged. 'I don't care, as long as it's really expensive.'

Duncan put his arm round her and she found she really didn't mind. 'That's my girl,' he said. And they made their way along to where he had left the car.

Kate came down the stairs dressed for dinner. She spent the best part of the week in jeans and DMs, but on Friday night she made an effort to change out of her work clothes, once the food was prepared, and put on something different. Tonight she wore a long wool dress in dark red, fitted down to the hips and flaring out from mid-thigh, a pair of black lace-up ankle boots with a square heel and a black scarf in her hair. All in all she looked quite startling and as Tommy glanced up from the phone in the study and saw her coming towards him, he wondered where she got the spirit and verve to look like that after such an exhausting week.

'Kate,' he said, putting his hand over the mouthpiece. 'You look lovely.'

Kate smiled. 'Is it Mary?'

'Yes.'

'Is she coming?'

He shook his head. 'Can't get a baby-sitter,' he said and went back on the line. He finished his call, hung up and asked, 'Is Harry coming tonight?'

Kate shrugged. 'No idea,' she said. She didn't mean to sound dismissive, but Harry had that effect on her. During the past month he had been acting really strangely. He had become obsessed with the idea of opening a restaurant and whenever he turned up — which wasn't often — he was no help at all, just went on and on about it, and he always had his mobile phone in his pocket which rang at the oddest moments, making him all secretive and embarrassed. Kate was trying hard to love Harry, but he didn't make it very easy.

'You miss him, I suppose,' Tommy said, 'when he's not here.'

'Sorry?' Kate had gone over to the desk and was flicking through Alice's notes.

Tommy realised once he'd said it that it was a wasted comment. Much as he liked Kate, he couldn't work out what the hell was going on with her and Harry and her and Rory, or what Alice had to do with it all. 'I'd better change,' he said, 'get this filthy kit off.'

Kate glanced up. 'Great. See you in time for a Tonsbry Original cooler, Tommy.' And she waved as he disappeared into the hall.

Some time later, Kate was still sitting at Leo's old desk reading through the file on publicity when she heard Alice's voice out in the hall. She tensed and sat still, waiting to see if Alice was heading that way. Then she heard Rory's voice as well; she couldn't hear what he'd said exactly, but it must have been a joke as Alice began to laugh. Kate's stomach churned. Despite the business taking off – largely due to Alice's marketing skills – and despite the bubble of confidence that enveloped them all, she couldn't help wondering if it hadn't been better when it was just her and Rory, when she'd needed him and he had wanted to be there for her.

She looked up as they came into the room, still laughing, and Rory said, 'Oh, Kate, what're you doing here on your own?'

She shrugged and tried to smile, but it didn't happen and her face sort of froze in a grimace. 'A bit of work,' she mumbled. 'Some sales figures.'

Alice moved round Rory and walked across to the big square vase of freesias which Kate always kept fresh on the mantelpiece for Leo. She reached up and smelled the sharp, sweet fragrance, rearranging a stem. As she glanced up, she caught sight of Kate's face in the mirror behind her and for an instant the shock of what she saw took her breath away. Then she closed her eyes and wondered why she hadn't seen it before. And immediately she thought that, a spirit of the old Alice emerged: the manipulative Alice, the Alice who lied. She opened her eyes and turned as Rory asked, 'Is Harry coming tonight?'

Kate shrugged her shoulders. 'No, not that I know of. But,' she looked away, 'you know Harry!'

Of course Alice hadn't seen it before; it was so heavily snowed under the weight of Harry, so wrapped in his disguise, that nobody had picked it up, not even Kate. Moving to Rory, Alice laid her hand very gently on his arm. He looked puzzled for a moment, but Alice wasn't concerned with him. Out of the corner of her eye she saw Kate flinch, and she knew she was right. And if she was right, then this was the final part of the equation, her last chance. Alice removed her arm and smiled up at Rory. 'Come on,' she said. 'Let's leave Kate to work, I'm dying for a drink.' And taking his hand, she led him out of the study and along to the kitchen, leaving the echo of her voice and the scent of her perfume behind in the study for Kate.

It was very late when Duncan finally looked at his watch. He was lounging on the sofa, just across from Jan, he had his jacket and tie off, his feet were up on the coffee table and he nursed a large, vintage Armagnac. He was content; comfortable, relaxed and content – indeed, the most content he had been for quite some time.

Jan too held a large brandy balloon, but it contained a healthy measure of iced orange liqueur. She sipped, but she didn't really want it; she had gone past it and, although not drunk, she wasn't thinking at all clearly. She had kicked off her shoes and pulled her legs up under her, revealing the tops of her stockings and making Duncan wonder just what the hell she had been up to while he'd been away. Jan had never been one for sexy underwear but, judging from what he could see now, that had all changed. He let his eyes rest on the sight of her thighs, much slimmer than they had been, and felt the warm hardness of an erection. As his gaze travelled up, he saw that Jan had been watching him.

'I can see your stockings,' he said.

'So? There's nothing there that you haven't seen before.'

Duncan took a gulp of brandy. 'Oh, I don't know, Jan.' He let out a long, heavy sigh. 'You're different now, not the same woman I once knew.'

'Oh, I'm the same, Duncan,' she said. 'I've got very few surprises up my sleeve.' She laid her head back and uncurled her legs, putting her feet up to rest on the coffee table. As she did so, her toes touched Duncan's.

'God, I've missed you, Jan!' he burst out. 'I've really missed you.'

Jan lifted her head. Her vision was blurred and she suddenly felt exhausted. 'Duncan, I'm going to bed,' she said. She pulled herself up and stood a little unsteadily. Wrapping her arms round her body, she looked at him.

'Can I stay?' he murmured.

Jan said nothing. He held out his hand and she placed hers in it. He squeezed. 'Shall I finish up here?'

She nodded and, dropping his hand, turned towards the stairs. It was strange, she thought briefly, how easy it was to slip back into a lifetime's habits. She always went to bed first, Duncan always switched off the lights and followed her later.

'I'll see you in bed,' she murmured. Duncan smiled and, sipping his brandy, watched her go.

Alone a few moments later, he looked round the room at Jan's things, at the familiar order and neatness, then he stood up. Out of curiosity he thought, I'll have a look. I bet I know her far better than she thinks; I bet I understand her, I always have. He went to the antique bureau, turned the key, opened it and pulled out the small secret drawer. There, in a plain brown folder, was the Tonsbry Estate file.

Duncan lifted it out, closed the drawer, then the bureau and locked it. Crossing to the sofa, he picked up his jacket, found his car keys and slipped his feet into his shoes. She'll have forgotten all about it by now, he thought, she'll never notice it's gone. She was proving a point, and now she's proved it she no longer needs the file. This was how he justified to himself what he did next as, aware that Jan had neglected to set the alarm, he went out to his car, unlocked it, placed the file in the glove compartment and locked the car again.

Back indoors, he switched off the lamp in the sitting-room, took his brandy through to the kitchen, finished it and left the glass alongside Jan's by the sink. He remembered Carol-Anne, thought he should give her a quick ring, so went back into the sitting-room to dial the flat and leave a message on the answerphone. He said that he was staying in a hotel because the business dinner had gone on too late. Then he unplugged the phone.

Climbing the stairs, Duncan felt a mild excitement overlain with tiredness. Bed with Carol-Anne meant sexual athletics and very little sleep. The prospect of a good nine hours was powerfully welcome. In the bedroom, he undressed. It was dark, there was no parading around naked showing off his erection, no holding his stomach in, just comfort and ease. Duncan climbed into bed without brushing his teeth and moved towards Jan.

Jan was half-asleep. She opened her eyes only for a moment and put out her arms to fold Duncan into her embrace. Then she relaxed against him and let the pleasure of familiarity and warmth overwhelm her. It was over in minutes and, rolling apart, they both took up their separate sides of the bed, nestling into the dips and bumps of the worn old mattress as they relaxed into contented and drunken sleep.

Chapter Twenty-Three

Jan woke up with a thumping head.

The ache started at the base of her skull and moved up the back of her head, across to her temples. She opened her eyes, felt it worsen and closed them again. Then she remembered Duncan. Rolling over on to her side, she reached out an arm to touch him and was almost surprised he was still there. She stroked the warm, heavy flesh of his thigh, heard him moan in his sleep, and rolling over again, dropped her legs out of the bed and stood up. Immediately she put her hands to her head. 'Ouch!' She staggered into the bathroom and slumped down on the side of the bath. Reaching for a flannel, she ran the cold tap and soaked it, putting it up to her forehead. She sat there for some time until the coldness eased the pain and she could open her eyes. What she needed was a swim and a sauna to sweat out all the alcohol, she thought, standing up. She took a grey track suit from the heated towel rail and pulled it on, cleaned her teeth and went back into the bedroom.

Duncan was awake. 'Where're you off to?' he muttered.

Jan bent down and picked his underpants up off the floor. She folded them and put them on the chair. 'I'm going to the health club.'

Duncan sat up, punching the pillows to make them more comfortable. 'You joined a health club?'

'Yes, a couple of months ago. It's in Chiswick.'

He watched her bend and retrieve his socks from under the counterpane. 'You off now?'

'Yes.' She was irritated by the mess. Tidy by nature, she liked her bedroom neat and orderly. Crossing to the window, she raised the blinds and opened it, letting in a cold gust of air.

'Blimey, Jan, it's freezing!' Duncan pulled the duvet up to his chin. 'If you want me to go, then just say so.'

Jan stopped and turned. She was getting set in her ways, that's what, in only six months. 'Of course I don't want you to go,' she said. 'Sorry, I'll close the window.' She did so and took her trainers out of the wardrobe. Sitting on the edge of the bed to pull them on, she asked, 'You don't mind me going, do you?'

'No, course not.' Duncan reached forward and planted a kiss on her cheek. 'You couldn't make me a cup of tea before you go, could you?'

Outside it was cold, below freezing, but Jan didn't mind. There was something about icy air when you had a hangover. She'd heard once that you never got a hangover on a skiing holiday and wondered now if that were true. Perhaps, if things worked out, when they'd sold Ingram Lawd she and Duncan might go on a skiing holiday. Perhaps.

She pulled her jacket in tight around her and jangled the car keys in her pocket. As she walked out on to the drive towards her little car, she realised that another car had parked right across the entrance and blocked her in. She swore under her breath and walked towards it. It was iced-up but there was someone in it, probably trying to start it though Jan couldn't see that clearly.

She knocked politely on the side window and called, 'Hello? Good morning, I wonder if you could move your car, I . . .'

The person inside wound down the window and looked out.

'Stefan?'

'Jan!'

Stefan was bleary-eyed and icy-cold. He had a couple of rugs over him and a sheepskin coat, but they hadn't kept him warm. 'God, Jan, I'm so glad it's you! I came here after work, I tried to ring you but there was no answer. I must have fallen asleep.'

Jan looked into the car. It was full of boxes of glasses, plates and empty bottles. She took a pace back, not sure what to do, and saw a small printed sign in the side window which said: *KATE DOWIE – HIGH-QUALITY CATERING SERVICES.*

'Work?' she asked.

'We did the party last night, the Kennings party? That woman you saw me with, I was taking another booking, I . . .'

Jan caught her breath, the realisation of her mistake hit her with a thud and she felt the overwhelming urge to cry. 'Oh God,' she muttered. 'You changed jobs . . .'

'Jan?' Stefan grabbed the door-handle as she turned and fled. He pulled open the door and tried to leap out of the car, but his legs had seized up with the cold and sleeping in one position and they failed him. Stumbling on to the pavement, he called out after her: 'Jan! Jan, come back, please! Jan?'

But Jan had disappeared up the road, abandoning her car and flagging down a taxi round the corner. By the time Stefan managed to get some feeling back into his limbs and jog up the road after her, she had long gone.

'Jan!' he shouted desperately at the empty street. Then; 'Oh, bugger it!' And he turned and stomped back to his car.

Harry jumped down out of the Jeep and reached into the back for his bags. His men all delivered safely to the NAAFI, he had taken a lift up to the Mess and, tired, damp and cold, was well and truly pleased to be shot of that particular exercise. Brecon Beacons might have been a holiday destination for some, but they were the byword for discomfort, cold and exhaustion for his regiment. Carrying his kit into the entrance of the Mess, Harry picked up his post and messages, then made his way along to his room. He wanted a bloody long, hot shower, a huge plate of eggs and bacon and a kip. He was a simple man at heart and that was all he needed. Sadly, on opening the door of his room, it wasn't all he got.

'Sasha!'

'Hello, Harry.'

He came in and dropped his stuff just by the door. 'You're beginning to make a habit of this.'

Sasha rose from the armchair she had been sitting in. 'Hardly. I didn't have anything on last time, remember?'

Harry smiled. 'How could I forget?' He began taking off his combat fatigues and dumping them in a pile on the floor. Sasha moved towards him. 'I shouldn't come over here if I were you,' he said. 'I stink! This gear stinks as well.'

Sasha frowned. 'It's been ages, Harry. Haven't you missed me?'

Harry looked up at her. She was blond and fair-skinned, with pink cheeks and soft rounded features. She always smelled deliciously of vanilla and he carried that smell with him, remembering it at the strangest moments. She smiled and Harry smiled back. Sasha was so intensely female that she made him feel the opposite, strong and masculine, always in command.

'Of course I missed you, Sasha,' he said, and was surprised how much he meant it. 'Look, let me have a shower and get some fresh kit on, ring Kate to see if she's made any decisions and then we can go and get breakfast in the Mess. How does that sound?'

It sounded fine, apart from the bit about ringing Kate, but Sasha wasn't going to mention that. She was on to the final stage of her plan.

'How is Kate?' she asked. 'Did you set a date?'

Harry was down to a pair of particularly gruesome Y-fronts and was kneeling, ferreting in his bag for his mobile. 'A date?'

'For the wedding?' Sasha held her breath.

'Good Lord, no! It's been far too busy for anything like that. In fact,' he glanced up, 'the Colonel asked me the same thing the other day on exercise. I explained to him that there hadn't been time for any of that, what with the exercise and that wretched bloody house.' Harry found the phone and reached for a towel. 'Sasha, I'm off to the bathroom, I'll call Kate from there.'

As he peeled off his underpants and dropped them on

the pile of dirty clothes, she noticed a burgeoning interest down there and smiled. 'Shall I come and scrub your back?' she asked.

Harry laughed. That was another thing about Sasha, he thought, she always made him laugh. He thought briefly of Kate, of the dismal, gloomy attempts at bed recently, and was sorely tempted to take Sasha up on her offer. A man needed to be needed, but his conscience got the better of him. 'Thanks, Sasha, but I don't think we should be going in for all that now.'

She raised an eyebrow. 'Really?'

He tucked his towel round his waist and picked up his wash-bag. 'Don't tempt me,' he said, really hoping despite his conscience that she would. And opening the door, he went along the corridor to the bathroom.

Harry decided on a bath rather than a shower. He was tired and wanted a good, long soak. Besides, he could phone Kate lying in the luxury of hot, soapy water and have a nice long chat. He ran the taps and took off his towel, hanging it on a hook. With Sasha in mind, he left the door unlocked and climbed into the bath. Settling into the warm water, he let it caress the semi-erection he'd had since seeing Sasha and reached for his phone. When he dialled Kate, it rang twice and was answered by Mrs Able.

'Hello, Mrs Able, it's Harry.' He sighed. That woman had never liked him, he was sure she did it on purpose. 'Harry Drummond,' he said. 'Kate's fiancé, remember? Is Kate there, please?'

Asked to wait, he closed his eyes as he hung on the line. He didn't notice the door quietly open, or hear Sasha creep into the room. As Kate came on the line, he was just about to say hello when a warm, soft mouth closed over him and the semi-erection burst to life.

'Oh God, ahh . . . !'

'Harry?'

He opened his eyes to Sasha's head bent over the bath.

'Yes, Kate,' he managed.

'Harry, what's going on?' Kate was peeved. 'Are you still on exercise?'

'Yes . . .' Harry hissed through clenched teeth. Kate sighed irritably.

'Look, Harry, it's a bad line, I'm going to hang up.' She was in the kitchen and could see Rory and Alice walking up towards the house together. For some reason that made her even more cross. 'Call me another time, all right?' She heard a muffled answer but couldn't make it out. 'Look, I'm going now. Bye, Harry.' She hung up.

Harry sank down into the bath. Sasha, naked, knelt over his groin and the smell of vanilla wafted over the steam. He closed his eyes, Kate vanished from his mind and a huge wave of pure pleasure engulfed him.

Duncan helped himself to orange juice from Jan's fridge, made a couple of slices of toast and some fresh coffee and took his time over his breakfast. She had a Saturday paper delivered, so he read the business section and took the magazine to look at later. Jan never read the colour supplements. Then he showered, dressed and left his wet towel on the unmade bed. Scribbling her a note to say that he'd had to go but would see her on Monday, he gave Carol-Anne a quick ring and left the flat.

He walked briskly to his car, climbed inside and switched

on the engine, turning the heating up to full. Then he made a call on his mobile.

'Paul Rickman, please. Hello, Paul, it's Duncan Lawd. Fine, thanks – you? Good. Look, I've got hold of the Tonsbry Estate file and we need to move ahead with it now. I'm just about to drive up to the office, so can you meet me there in an hour?' He listened to the reply, then said coldly, 'Yes, I'm well aware of the fact that it's Saturday, but presumably you'll bill me for double time or whatever it is you charge for working out of hours and I want this business sorted, Paul. I want it sorted now, today. I can't afford to wait any longer!'

Duncan turned the hot air down while his solicitor spoke. 'Good,' he said a few minutes later. 'I'll see you at eleven, then.' And without even a backward glance at Ashmore House, he shifted the car into gear and drove off.

Kate was surprised how few people it took to make a television programme. She had always imagined a crowd: make-up people, sound engineers, scriptwriters, directors, producers, her fictitious list went on. In reality, the *Food and Drink* team arrived at lunch-time on Saturday in a small van, just three of them, with one camera, a couple of lights and some sound equipment. She was amazed, and she was also very nervous.

'Is this all you've got?' she asked, leading the way through the house to the dining-room so that they could see the business in operation.

'It's only a three-minute feature, dearie,' a rather sour-looking producer said. 'Not *Ben Hur*.' Kate winced.

There were cases of bottles everywhere, the finished

product piled up in the hall ready to go and empties just delivered back, empties ready to fill, full bottles ready to label. 'Sorry about the muddle,' Kate called over her shoulder. 'I suppose it's all part of running a family business.'

'What is?'

'The muddle.' She opened the door of the dining-room, her confidence failing fast. 'This is where we—' She stopped. 'Oh, Alice, I didn't know you were in here.'

Alice came forward. 'Hello – Mike Sawyer, isn't it?' The producer nodded. 'We met some time ago, you won't remember me: Alice White. I used to work for Virtual Vodka and you did a feature on it.' She smiled. 'It was a really good piece, you filmed our vodka in bars in three different parts of the country to see who drank it.'

The sour producer turned almost instantly and smiled back. 'It was a good piece,' he said. 'Very funny, as I remember. I don't remember you, but I remember Virtual Vodka.'

Alice crossed the room. 'Good, at least I did my job then.' She picked up a bottle of Tonsbry. 'Have you tried this? It's fabulous.'

He shrugged. 'Not much of a drinker.'

'Here.' She handed him one and uncorked the other, pouring them all a shot. 'You can drink it neat.' She sniffed and Kate watched as the film crew all did the same. She was staggered; Alice had them in the palm of her hand. She sipped and so did they. 'Good, isn't it?' She drank down her measure in one, then reached behind her for a couple more bottles to give to the cameraman and sound engineer. 'Perk of the job,' she said, handing them out. 'It's a bit more glamorous than country crafts.'

They all laughed and Alice poured another shot of gin. The door opened as she did so and she turned. 'Ah, Rory!' she cried. 'Rory Gallagher, one of the most important players in this whole operation.' She glanced towards Kate. 'Along with Kate Dowie, of course,' she added as an afterthought. Rory looked at Kate's face, then at Alice. Oh Christ, he thought, what the hell's going on here?

Alice smiled and crossed to him, laying her hand affectionately on his arm. 'Rory not only manages the estate, but he's been an integral part of the whole business. Hasn't he, Kate?' She glanced back over her shoulder and Kate nodded blankly, glared, then looked away.

Kate had a sudden sick, sinking feeling in the pit of her stomach. 'Look,' she said, turning to the film crew. 'Do you want to see round the distillery? See what there is to film?' She had to get out of there, get some air.

'What a good idea,' said Alice. 'Why don't we leave you to it, Kate?'

'Yes, well . . .'

'I think I ought to go with Kate,' Rory piped up.

'I'm sure she can manage, Rory,' Alice cut in. 'It's always easier with just one, isn't it, Mike?'

The producer, tucking into his third gin, smiled at her and said, 'Whatever you think, Alice.'

Kate wanted to scream. 'Right,' she said, 'I'll get going, then.' She headed towards the door, glancing over at the producer as she did so. 'D'you want to take that with you?' she asked tersely, nodding at the bottle of gin. Embarrassed, he put down the bottle and made his way over to her.

'We'll see you later,' Kate said.

'Yes, I . . .' But Rory didn't finish. Kate had opened the

door and stepped out into the hall without even hearing him. The film crew followed immediately after her and he turned to Alice with a thunderous look on his face.

'What the bloody hell are you playing at, Alice? That was open flirting and I don't like it. I don't like it one bit!'

Alice let out a sigh and moved across to the table. She sat on the edge of it and looked at Rory. 'Tell me something,' she said. 'Do you still love Kate?'

'Love Kate? She's engaged to be married to that dunderhead Drummond.'

'You didn't answer my question.'

'What question?'

'Do you still love Kate?'

Rory stared at the floor. He folded his hands together, then dropped them apart. He picked at a fingernail.

'Rory?'

He looked up, and his face was so wretched that for a moment Alice wished she hadn't asked him. Then he said, 'Yes, I still love Kate. I never stopped loving Kate, and I don't suppose I ever will.'

'Well, then,' Alice said.

'Well then, what?'

'You'll have to trust me.'

'Trust you?' Rory suddenly exploded. 'The last time I trusted you, Alice, you lied to me and ruined my life. Why the hell should I trust you?'

'Good question.' Alice stared down at the floor but said nothing more.

Rory came threateningly close. 'What the hell is this all about, Alice?' he spat.

Alice gritted her teeth but remained silent.

'Are you going to tell me or do I have to throttle it out of you?'

She glanced up at him, not sure if he meant it, then stood and faced him. 'I do not want to spend the rest of my life regretting things. That's all I'm going to say. OK?'

Rory's face was menacingly close. 'No, it isn't bloody well OK! I warned you once before, Alice, and that warning still stands. Do you understand me?'

Alice shrank back.

'Do you?' He didn't touch her, but his breath burned where it touched her skin. Finally she nodded.

'Good,' he said. And turning, he walked out of the room.

Chapter Twenty-Four

It was Monday, the *Food and Drink* feature had gone out the previous night and in the dining-room at Tonsbry the phone lines were jammed.

It had all happened so fast that there had been no time to get organised with order sheets or a layout on the computer, and as fast as the calls came in, Kate and Rory were scribbling out the orders and throwing them into a box. Alice was writing them up, along with handling the sudden renewed interest in the whole thing from the media and fielding calls on that front in the study, while Mrs Able was sorting orders into areas and Tommy Vince and John Able were labelling new bottles as fast as the old-fashioned labelling machine would go. It was chaotic, but what else could they do? Tonsbry Original gin had shot to stardom, literally overnight, and they were as much bemused and overwhelmed by the whole thing as surprised.

'Kate, I've got three magazines on hold,' Alice called out, striding into the room and seeing a brief moment in between calls. '*Country Life* want to do you in a feature on country houses and cottage industries, BBC *Good Food* mag want to do something on making the gin and the *Telegraph*

Saturday mag are doing a piece on "Jobs for the Girls" and want to interview you for it.'

The phone rang and Kate picked it up. 'Sorry,' she mouthed across the room.

Alice groaned. 'When the bloody hell is the cavalry arriving?' she cried, but everyone was far too busy to hear her.

Rory finished his call and took the phone off the hook. 'I've got to pee,' he said. 'Did I hear you calling for the reserves?'

'You're not kidding! I've got media queuing up for Kate and she's too bloody busy to speak to anyone. People would kill for this kind of coverage, and Kate's chained to that telephone.'

Rory stopped by the door. 'There's not much else we can do,' he said, a little sharply. 'Do you want to man the phones in here for a while?'

'No. Point taken.' Alice wasn't anywhere near Kate's and Rory's league. 'It's just so frustrating!'

'I know. Look, chances are Harry'll be here some time this morning. I couldn't get out of Kate exactly when, but she said he was back off exercise on Sunday and had a few days off so was coming down to help. I don't know how good he is, but—'

'Great! The cavalry, but no one knows when.'

'Alice!' Rory warned and she shrugged.

'I'll go back to writing up the orders then,' she said, taking the full box of paper slips and leaving an empty one in its place. 'Let me know when, or even if, Harry arrives, won't you? The sooner Kate speaks—'

'Yes, all right!' Rory pulled a face. 'Look, sorry, have to go.' And he disappeared out of the room. Alice, knowing that she was better off out of it, followed immediately after him.

Jan buzzed Molly from her office. 'Is Duncan in yet?'

'No.' The intercom went dead and Molly stood up. That was the third time Jan had asked and it was barely ten o'clock. She knocked on Jan's door.

'Yes?'

Molly poked her head round. 'Can I have a word?'

'Yes, sure, come on in.'

Molly did so but stood just inside the office with her back to the door and her palms pressed against it. 'Jan . . .' She wasn't sure how to begin, she didn't know what had been going on but something had, of that she was certain.

Jan looked up. There was something in Molly's voice that put her on edge. 'What is it, Molly? You're not going to resign, are you?'

'Oh, no! Nothing like that.'

'Good!'

'Jan, Duncan's not in this morning, he's not in until later on this afternoon – or so that temp said, the graduate one.'

'Suzanne?'

'Yes, that's her. Apparently he's been in the office all weekend working on something very important, and he's finishing it off today with the lawyers.'

Jan bit her lip. 'And Suzanne told you all this?'

Molly nodded. 'She was in herself on Saturday afternoon, typing up some documents.'

'What documents?'

'I don't know, she wouldn't say.'

Jan felt a sudden stab of panic. She turned to her

computer. 'Whatever it was she was typing will be in the system, Molly. Let's have a quick look at it, shall we?'

'I've tried already.'

Jan glanced up. 'And?'

'Nothing. No documents were saved. The system was up all weekend according to the time and date information, but there's nothing stored.'

'Shit!' Jan drummed her fingers on the desk. 'What the hell is he up to?'

Molly shrugged. 'Whatever it is,' she said, 'he doesn't want anyone knowing about it. Suzanne's not saying a word, and you know what a blabbermouth she is.'

'I certainly do.'

Jan reached for her cigarettes. Her decision that morning to try cutting down with a view to giving up had lasted all of three hours. Lighting up, she asked, 'What do you think, Molly?' Molly was a first-class secretary and she had her finger on the pulse of the whole office.

'I think it might be something to do with the Tonsbry Estate file,' she said. 'I think—' The phone rang.

'Sorry, Molly, I'll just get this.' She picked it up. 'Hello, Jan Ingram.' It was Stefan and Jan felt a peculiar shifting of the ground under her. 'What do you want?' she asked coldly.

'Jan, I'm down in reception on the ground floor. We need to meet. We have to talk.'

'No, sorry, not now.'

'Yes, *now*! It's about Duncan. Please, Jan!'

'Duncan?'

'Yes. Sorry, but it's important. Can I come up?'

Jan stubbed out her cigarette. 'No, stay there, I'll come

down and we can go for a coffee. What's it all about, Stefan?'

'I'll tell you when you get here.' And with that he hung up.

Jan stood. 'Molly, things are beginning to look a bit odd,' she said. 'I've got to go out. I'll be back in' – she glanced at her watch – 'half an hour.'

'Right.' Molly moved towards the door.

'If Duncan calls,' Jan said, 'ask him to ring back about eleven, can you?'

Molly nodded. *If* Duncan calls, she thought; I wouldn't place a bet on it. But she held her tongue as Jan walked past her and out of the office.

Stefan was waiting by the lifts.

'Hi, thanks for coming to meet me.'

Jan shrugged. 'We can get some coffee at the Cumberland, is that OK?'

'Fine.'

Together they made their way out of the building and along the main road up to the hotel on the corner. Jan led the way inside and they were shown to a table in the morning-room.

'Coffee?'

'Actually, no, thanks.' Jan glanced at her watch.

'Look, Jan, I was going to tell you this ages ago when I found out, but I never got the chance and then I seriously wondered if I should. What I am about to say is one hell of an accusation and it may well be completely untrue, but you must make up your own mind about that.' He waited for her to light the cigarette she held between her lips. 'When I looked at the books for the Letchworth

Housing Association I basically found that every purchase made from Ingram Lawd was first, under market price, and second, included a large sum of money to Rickman Levy in the name of legal fees. The conclusion I drew from this was that someone, maybe the vendor, was taking cash payments for offering below market-price properties for sale. But it was only my personal view. There was no direct evidence and—'

'How much?' Jan broke in.

Stefan hesitated, then said, 'I worked out that if the vendor was Duncan Lawd, then he stood to have made nearly a quarter of a million pounds over the past two years, under the table.'

Jan put her hand up to her mouth; the sudden shock made her feel sick. She said nothing, unable to get any words out.

'Jan?' Stefan reached across to touch her but she pulled her hand away. 'Jan, it might not even be true,' he argued. 'There's no evidence.'

Standing, she held on tightly to the edge of the table, her vision blurring for a moment. Then she dropped her cigarette into the ashtray and stumbled towards the door.

'Jan?' Stefan jumped up and went after her. 'Jan, stop! Let me help you, please. You've had a shock, you look . . .'

'No, really, don't! I'm fine.' She gulped down lungsful of air heavy with carbon monoxide.

'Jan, please.'

She turned to look at him. 'No, really. I'm OK, there's something I have to do. Can you er . . . call me a cab?'

Stefan glanced quickly round, saw an orange light on a passing black taxi and leaped out into the road to flag it down, narrowly missing two oncoming cars. 'Where to?' he asked, pulling open the door.

'Home,' Jan told him.

'Ashmore House, Redview Road, Putney,' he told the cabbie. He went to climb in.

'Alone,' Jan said. Stefan looked at her and wondered what to do, then he slammed the door shut and stood back. Watching her as the car pulled out into the traffic and drove off, he thought how slight and broken she looked, staring out of the window with a blank, unseeing gaze.

At Ashmore House, Jan paid the driver and went into her maisonette. She walked across to the bureau, her stomach churning, opened it and pulled out the small secret drawer. It was empty; the file had gone. She picked up the phone, dialled Stefan's number and willed him to answer it. The line rang, on and on, but she waited.

Duncan Lawd walked into the offices of Rickman Levy and saw Adriana in reception with her solicitor. For the first time since they had met, she greeted him with one of her rare, disarming smiles. She was an exceptional-looking woman, and Duncan felt the power of that smile.

'Are you ready, Comtesse?'

She took the arm he offered her. 'Perfectly,' she answered.

'Let's go and close that deal, then, shall we?'

She smelled divine and her laughter cut through the air like rays of sunlight. 'Yes, let's,' she said and they left a sour and miserable David Lowther to follow in the wake of their glory.

Harry had arrived at Tonsbry House as promised, and

immediately he stepped inside he was roped into filling out order forms, much against his will, whilst Rory and Kate took calls. At last they had some kind of system going, and the chaos was a proportion organised. They were inundated, the orders flowed in and the tally of cases to go out kept rising and rising. This is it, Rory thought, with a subdued sense of exhilaration, we are going to make it! He made a note of one more case of Tonsbry Original ordered, then took another call. Despite everything, he thought, we are finally going to make it!

Stefan jumped out of his stationary taxi, thrust a tenner at the driver and told him to keep the change. He ran along the line of traffic they had been stuck in and up towards Rickman Levy Solicitors. He got there just as a black cab pulled off and, flinging open the door, he dashed in and asked, 'Is Duncan Lawd here?'

The receptionist shook her head. 'Mr Lawd has just left,' she said. 'Sorry.'

Stefan sagged. 'Just left?'

'Yes, he went outside to find a taxi just a few minutes ago.'

Stefan darted back out on to the main road. 'Shit!' said aloud as he noted the same black cab moving off into the distance. Inside he could just make out the figures of a stunning, immaculately turned-out woman and a middle-aged man.

It was nearing the end of the day and Alice had been busy. She'd finally got Kate on the line to her various journalists, she had written up hundreds of orders, made teas, coffees and sandwiches, taken calls, made calls – yet all that time she had been trying to puzzle out the situation here and wondering what the hell she was going to do about it.

Sitting in the dining-room as the calls were winding down and listening to Kate recording the answerphone message, she dropped her head in her hands, too weary to puzzle through it again. She heard a bleep, glanced at the phones, saw they were all occupied and asked, 'Is there a mobile in here?'

No one looked up. 'Is there a mobile in here?' Alice shouted.

Harry broke off from counting his order forms out loud, a habit that was driving everyone insane, and said, 'God, sorry, yes! It's mine. You couldn't get it for me, could you?' He nodded at his pile of forms. 'I'll lose my place otherwise.'

Alice shrugged, thinking, God forbid if he starts counting from the beginning again, and stood up. 'Where is it?'

'In my bag, I think, or my coat pocket.'

She tried the coat first but couldn't find it, so unzipped the bag, delved in and pulled out the phone, still ringing. 'Hello? Harry Drummond's phone.'

'Hello? Who's that?'

'Alice, I'm taking the call for Harry, he's tied up at the moment. Who's speaking, please?'

'Alice who?' The voice sounded immediately wary, upset even.

'Alice White. Who's that?'

'Oh, never mind!' said the voice. 'If he's busy. Can you just tell him Sasha called?'

'Yes, sure.'

'Are you . . . er . . . are you a friend of his?'

Alice thought for a moment. In the broadest sense, she supposed she was. 'Yes,' she said. 'Why?'

'Oh.' Again the hint of distress. 'Could you tell him . . .' There was a pause. 'Er, just that I called – here's my number.'

Alice frowned. 'Of course.' She scribbled Sasha's name and number on a piece of paper. 'Are you sure you won't hold, he's . . .' She shrugged and switched off the phone. Sasha had hung up.

Dropping the phone back in Harry's bag, Alice walked over and put down the piece of paper by his order forms. He glanced at it, flushed a deep red and hissed, 'Alice, come here!' Alice went back. 'Sasha . . . did she leave a message?'

Alice looked at him. She narrowed her eyes, took in his stance, the blush, the nervousness, an excitement she had never seen before, and suddenly it all fell into place.

'No,' she replied. 'No message, just that she called.'

Harry nodded. 'I see.'

Alice watched him. He smiled, not at her though but to himself, and folded the piece of paper neatly in two, tucking it into the breast pocket of his shirt. 'Right, then,' Alice said.

'Oh, yes, right.' Harry seemed to connect with the real world again and went back to his forms. 'One-oh-six,' he continued, 'one-oh-seven, one-oh-eight . . .'

Alice walked away, but she carried with her Sasha's voice in her head and the memory of her telephone number imprinted on her brain.

Duncan was sending the papers to Tonsbry House by courier, and he was doing it from his solicitors' office. He was giving a notice period of twelve hours because he did not want any last-minute surprises. He waited until five o'clock that evening, then he ordered the bike which arrived within half an hour. Witnessed by Paul Rickman, his solicitor, he signed the repossession notice on Tonsbry House and Estate and sent it on its way. Jan knew nothing about it, but then he had gone beyond caring whether she did or not. At that point he had gone beyond caring about very much at all except getting this deal done. It had become a turning point for Duncan, a very large sum of money carefully, successfully and deviously procured and the final proof that he was as clever as he had always thought he was.

'So that's it, then,' said Kate, switching on the answerphone and turning down the volume so that no more calls could be heard. 'I suggest we have a drink!' She smiled, tired eyes in a pale face, and uncorked a bottle of Tonsbry Original. She poured out a glass for each person and handed them round. 'Tommy, John, Mrs Able.' The room was suddenly quiet. 'Alice, Harry and . . .' She turned and looked for Rory. 'Ah, Rory! Here.' She held out a glass for him as he stood in the doorway. 'We're going to drink a toast, to success and—' She broke off. 'Rory?'

Rory hadn't moved from the doorway. 'Kate, there's a courier here for you, says he's got some documents and has to hand them over to you in person.'

'A courier?' She put down her glass. 'Wait, everyone, we'll have that toast when I get back.' Moving towards Rory, she said, 'Where is he?'

'He's in the hall,' Rory told her. 'He's come down from London.' Kate glanced at him as she walked past and he shrugged.

'Miss Kate Dowie?'

In the hall, the courier lifted his visor and held out a thick brown A4 envelope.

'Yes?'

'Could you sign here, please?' He handed her a clip-board and the envelope.

Kate looked at the envelope, then at the paper attached to the clip-board. 'It's from Ingram Lawd,' she said, as Rory moved to her side. Signing, she turned to the courier, handed back the clip-board and asked, 'Do you want a drink or something before you go back to London?'

'No, thanks.' He flipped down his visor. 'Thanks a lot.' He was anxious to be off. With the clump of boots on stone and the heavy rustle of leathers, he turned and left the house.

Kate opened the envelope, pulled out the first legal document and looked down at it. She read for a few moments, then closed her eyes. 'Oh, God,' she said. 'It's a repossession notice for Tonsbry.' Then she glanced across at Rory, her face stricken. 'They're going to take the house away.'

Chapter Twenty-Five

Jan lay on the bed still wearing her suit, crumpled and unwashed, and opened her eyes for a moment as the phone rang. It pierced the blackness and she struggled to sit up. Somehow she managed it and dropped her legs over the side of the bed, but as she stood they gave way and she slumped down on to the floor. Crawling across to the phone, she reached for it just as it stopped. She collapsed where she was and closed her eyes again as the blackness rose up and swamped her.

The atmosphere at Tonsbry House was one of stunned silence. The full glasses of gin were placed on the table untouched as Kate sat and Rory stood beside her, reading the papers over her shoulder. When she had finished, she looked up at him first, then at the people around her. 'It says here that as of nine a.m. tomorrow morning, the property detailed above, Tonsbry House and grounds, will be repossessed by Ingram Lawd Ltd.' She shook her head. 'I don't believe it! They can't do this to us, can they, Rory? Surely our appeal must be in motion, surely . . .'

Rory took up a pencil and scribbled a list on a scrap of paper. 'Right, first you've got to ring David Lowther, then Stefan and see if he can get hold of this Ingram woman.' He glanced at his watch. 'Shit! That's pretty bloody devious, to bike the documents round after the close of day so that we wouldn't be able to get hold of anyone.'

Kate stood up. 'I'll call David Lowther at home and see if he's in. If not, then what?'

Rory touched her arm. 'We'll face it when we come to it, Kate,' he said. 'Go on, get Lowther's number and I'll ring Stefan.' He looked at Mrs Able. 'Would you be kind enough to make some coffee, Mrs Able?'

She nodded. 'Why don't we all go into the kitchen and leave Kate and Rory to get on?' she suggested. There was a general consensus and move towards the door as Kate came back with her address book.

She sat down to make her call and Rory said, 'Don't worry, Kate, I'm sure we can sort something out.'

'Are you?' she asked. 'Are you really?' But all he could do was shrug. He had never been less sure of anything.

Stefan replaced the receiver, having called Jan once again, and started to pace the floor. When the phone rang he answered it, spoke briefly to Rory and made up his mind. Grabbing his jacket off the chair, he pulled it on and left the flat. Minutes later he was in his car and on his way across London to Putney.

'Stefan's going over to speak to the Ingram woman, Kate. I'm sure she'll be able to help us,' Rory said. 'I'm positive she will.'

'Well, that's more than can be said for David Lowther! Where the hell has he disappeared to? Leo used to say that he only went out one night a year and that was to midnight mass.'

Rory felt the knot of tension in the pit of his stomach tighten. 'He'll turn up, Kate,' he said. 'He's bound to.'

At Ashmore House, the curtains were drawn downstairs and up. Stefan rang the bell, got no reply and looked in through the letter-box. The house was dark and empty, but Jan's car was outside, she had milk on the doorstep and her morning newspaper was on the floor in the hall. He was certain she was in there.

Climbing the fence, he jumped down into the back garden and saw that the curtains were drawn at the rear windows of the maisonette as well. This unnerved him; it didn't feel right. He glanced up at the house, spotted a window open in the bathroom and decided to chance it. He clambered up the drainpipe, managing a grip on the wall with his trainers, and got on to the flat roof of the dining-room. Then he reached up to the small top window of the bathroom, dropping his hand down inside as far as he could to try and release the catch of the bigger window. He couldn't do it. Climbing up on to the sill, he peered in through the gap, his sense of unease rapidly turning to panic. He could just see the bedroom in darkness – the bed, the telephone on the bedside table . . . then he saw Jan's legs.

'Jan?' There was no reply, the legs were motionless. 'Jan? Oh, shit!' He jumped down and looked frantically around for something to throw. Nothing. Then he saw that a part of the guttering was loose and bent to grab hold of it; he struggled for several minutes and freed it with a sharp snap. Scrambling to his feet, he held the guttering up high, then looked away and cracked it against the bathroom window with all his might. There was an almighty crash, glass flew everywhere and Stefan dropped the pipe. He climbed in through the broken window and ran towards Jan.

The lady in the flat above dialled 999.

'Jan!' He knelt down beside her, turned her over and checked her pulse. It was there, weak but still there. 'Thank God,' he murmured. Lifting her head, he placed a pillow under it and her eyelids fluttered open. She was conscious.

'Jan, what happened? Jan?' They closed again. Stefan looked up and saw an empty pill bottle on the floor beside the bed. He reached for it, read the label and jumped up. Not thinking properly, he didn't register the phone by the bed but ran downstairs, sick with panic, and searched the sitting-room for the telephone. Finally locating it, he picked up the receiver and dialled 999. 'Ambulance!' he said. 'Quickly!' He heard a resounding crack in the hall. 'What the hell . . . ? Oh God, yes, sorry, yes, a suspected overdose. It's 3 Ashmore House, Redview Road, SW15. No, oh God, I don't know the number here, I . . .' He jumped with fright as a hand suddenly grabbed him by the shoulder and he jerked round.

'Got you!' a voice said. 'Stay where you are! You're nicked!'

It was three a.m. when Rory arrived back at Tonsbry House. As a last resort, he had taken a drive in to Chartwell to David Lowther's office, then to his home address, but there was no sign of the man. Parking the Land-Rover in front of the house, he climbed out and walked in through the open front door to see John Able still up, waiting for him in the hall.

'Mrs Able's found beds for them all,' he said. 'No one wants to go home.'

'Of course not.'

'Any luck?'

Rory shook his head. 'I'll go and find Kate,' he said. 'See if Stefan's called.' John nodded. 'Thanks, John,' said Rory, and he made his way along to the dining-room.

Standing in the doorway for a few moments, Rory looked across at Kate – her head on her arms, her coat wrapped round her and her soft even breathing the only sound in the silent house. He crossed and laid a hand gently on the top of her head, as he did with Flora, then he turned to go. Just as he did so, the phone rang and Kate woke with a start.

Jan sat up in a bed in a side ward off Casualty and Stefan arrived back from making his call to Kate just as a nurse took her temperature and pulse.

'I still don't think it's a very good idea, Mrs Ingram. You should rest. The bed's free, you know – I really think it might be a good idea to stay in overnight. I'm sure your son thinks so too – don't you, Mr Ingram?' She looked at Stefan and Jan winced.

'I'm not her son,' he said. 'I'm her boyfriend. And yes, I do think so.'

Jan ignored him. As soon as the nurse had released her arm, she pushed back the covers and dropped her legs over the side of the bed. Stefan moved forward to help her. 'I can manage, thank you,' she said and he backed off.

'You've signed the discharge sheets then, have you?' The

nurse watched as Jan collected her wash-bag and the towel that Stefan had brought in.

'I have,' Jan replied. 'Could you show me where the bathroom is, please?'

The nurse tutted. 'It's this way,' she said. 'Come on – and hold the gown together at the back, it's very revealing.'

Ten minutes later Jan was ready. She looked a mess – ashen, with deep blue smudges under her eyes, and her face was swollen – but she didn't care. She felt a mess too, she felt as if someone had punched her about the head and kicked her in the stomach. Her legs were weak and she had to accept Stefan's help down to the car. As he opened the door, she climbed in and slumped down into the seat. Stefan got into the driver's side and glanced across at her. 'I really don't see what on earth you can do now, Jan. I'm not at all sure that this is a good idea.'

She turned to face him, unashamed of her appearance. 'No,' she said. 'Nor am I, to be frank, but I feel responsible, Stefan, and I want to be there. You never know, there might just be the faintest possibility of some mistake with the papers, some procedure not gone through in the rush . . .' She put her hands up to her face and wearily rubbed her eyes. 'I don't know, but I have to go, that's all.'

Stefan nodded and started the engine, then he glanced at his watch. 'We've got five hours before the repossession order takes effect.' He shifted into gear. 'Ready?'

'Yes.' Jan placed a hand on his arm. 'Thanks, Stefan.'

He shrugged. 'Right, then,' he said. 'Let's go.'

Chapter Twenty-Six

It was five a.m. by the time Jan and Stefan arrived at Tonsbry House. Kate met them in the hall and Jan's stomach lurched at the sight of her shining hope. 'I don't know if I can do anything,' she said immediately she stepped inside. 'I really don't expect I can, but well, I just thought . . .'

'Of course,' Kate said quickly and the hope died. 'Where are the papers?'

'In the study. Come on, I'll show you the way.' Jan followed her across the stone floor, her heels clicking sharply.

'Here.' Kate opened the door and Jan walked in. 'Do you want some coffee?'

'Please. Are those the papers there?' The envelope lay on the desk, a notepad beside it with various numbers and names scribbled down.

'Yes. Shall I leave you to it?'

'OK.' Kate turned to leave.

'Kate?' She glanced back. 'Kate, I'm sorry,' Jan said. 'I really am.'

'Yes,' Kate answered. 'So am I.' And she closed the door and left Jan to get on with what she was sure would be a fruitless task.

*   *   *

In the hall, Rory and Stefan stood together.

'You OK?' Rory asked as Kate approached them. She shrugged.

'Look, I think I'll join Jan,' said Stefan, and started towards the study.

'Stefan?' Kate called after him; he turned. 'What happened?' she asked.

'I don't know,' he answered honestly. 'Whatever it was, Jan had no part in it; she didn't want it to come to this, I know she didn't.' Kate nodded and he went on into the study.

'Not that it made any difference,' she said. 'It's over, whether Jan wanted it to be or not.'

'Is it?'

'I think so.' Kate hung her head and Rory placed an arm around her shoulder. She did nothing to resist and he found himself gently stroking her hair.

'Kate,' he said quietly, 'I know you probably don't want to hear this, but I have to say it, as a last resort. Had you thought of phoning your mother?'

Kate eased gently away from him.

'What are you smiling at?' he asked.

But she wasn't really smiling, it was an expression of amused sadness. 'I've done it already,' she said. 'After you left for Chartwell, I swallowed my pride and decided to beg for help. I woke Pierre and he said that he would speak to Adriana. He said she would phone me back, but of course she hasn't.'

'She might still do.'

Kate shook her head. 'No, that's not my mother's style. If she had wanted in, she'd have phoned immediately.' She sighed. 'I don't blame her, she's only doing what she thinks is the best for me.'

'You could try again?'

'No.' Kate wrapped her arms around her body and shivered. 'No, that's it,' she said. 'It all really rests on Jan now . . .' She stopped and glanced up as the study door opened. Taking one long look at Jan's face, she was silent for a few moments, then she turned to Rory and said, 'Could you organise everyone in the kitchen, please? I have to tell them what's going on.'

Half an hour later, holding herself up with yet another cup of endless coffee, she faced the small group of people who had worked so hard and tried to say what she felt.

'I'm afraid I have some bad news,' she began. 'The repossession notice that was served last night will be enforced this morning as of nine a.m.' She clasped her hands together in front of her and, when she released them for a moment, Rory saw that they were trembling. 'Last night,' she said, 'we thought, Rory and I, that there might be some small hope of appeal, but we have been unable to get hold of David Lowther, our solicitor, and as the night wore on we realised it was hopeless.' She stopped and swallowed hard. 'This means that we will all have to vacate the property, very probably today, and certainly that production of Tonsbry Original will cease.'

The silence in the room was thick and tense and as Kate looked at the faces around her she felt tears well up. She coughed and stared hard at a blank spot on the wall. 'I really am so very sorry, not only to be losing my home but all of you as well . . .' She stopped as the front door-bell sounded. 'Sorry, Mrs Able, could you answer the door?'

The housekeeper hurried out of the kitchen. No one said

a word; the silence deepened. Footsteps were heard across the hall, then along the passage. Mrs Able came in first, then everyone turned round as Sasha walked in after her.

'Sasha!' Harry jumped up.

'Sasha?' Kate frowned. 'Who's Sasha?'

'A friend,' Harry butted in.

'More than a friend, Harry! I've been thinking about you all night. I had been planning to come and then when Alice rang . . .' She broke off and stared hard at Kate. This was the final part of Sasha's plan: confrontation. She had planned it and planned it, but had lost her nerve at the last moment. It was only the phone call from Alice that had convinced her.

Kate frowned again, not really conscious of the scene unfolding in front of her and trying to pick up her lost train of thought. 'Anyway, I'm so sorry that you have all worked so hard for nothing and that—' She suddenly broke off and turned to Sasha. 'Sorry, but who the hell are you?'

'Sasha Tully.' Sasha swallowed hard and braced herself. 'I've been seeing Harry for a couple of years now and—'

'Seeing Harry?' Kate shook her head. None of this was making sense. She put her hand up to her brow and thought for a moment, then said, 'Look, I don't understand, what exactly are you saying?'

'Harry Drummond and I have been sleeping together for a couple of years now.'

'Sasha!'

'But Harry, it's true! I'm sick of all this deceit! It's true and you have to face up to it.'

The room swam and Kate closed her eyes.

'Oh, Christ!' muttered Tommy Vince.

'It was Alice who decided me to finally come,' Sasha went on. 'We have to get this straight, we have to—'

'Alice?' Kate stammered. The past had risen up and swallowed her whole. She held on to the table for support.

'Where the hell is Alice anyway?' Rory demanded.

'Oh, God!' Harry murmured. Alice had disappeared. All of a sudden Kate started to cry; her face collapsed and she put up her hands to cover it.

'Kate?' Rory called, hurrying across to her. But Kate couldn't answer; she dropped her hands away and ran, shoving past him and out into the passage, her footsteps echoing in the stunned silence that she left.

Rory turned. 'Is this true, Harry? Have you been seeing this girl Sasha?'

Harry nodded.

'You don't love Kate, do you?'

Harry opened his mouth to protest, but glanced at Sasha. She stood looking at him, pale-faced, her lip trembling, and all at once he saw how stupid he had been. 'No,' he said. 'I'm sorry, I don't.' He moved towards the woman he did love and took her hand.

Rory didn't wait another second. He ran out after Kate and shouted back at Harry, at anyone who could hear him, 'Well, I do! I bloody well do!'

The room remained silent for several minutes, then Mrs Able tutted loudly and said, 'About bloody time too.' And she filled the kettle for tea.

Rory finally found Kate sitting alone on the wall of the old York stone terrace that ran along the back of the house. He had been looking for over an hour, the terrace being a last thought. She had no coat on, and when he got to her she was chilled to the marrow and shivering in the icy dawn air. Gently he laid a thickly lined waxed jacket around her shoulders and silently he sat down next to her. He took her hand and rubbed it between both of his to warm her fingers.

'It's all over,' she said quietly.

'Not all of it,' Rory answered, tucking her hand down into his pocket. 'There's something else, two things actually, that have to be dealt with.'

She continued to look away.

'First, Flora is not my daughter.'

Kate caught her breath and swung round. 'What do you mean? I thought—'

'I know, so did I.' He looked at her. 'Kate, I'm sorry. I wanted to tell you, I really did, but I never had the chance, I never felt it was right.'

'And it is now?'

'Probably not, but I haven't exactly got much of a choice, have I?'

'No.' She looked away again. 'I suppose not.' Without facing him, her heart thundering in her chest, she said, 'Does that mean that you never slept with Alice?'

'No, I never slept with Alice. I got drunk, woke up in her bed, but she put me there, I was too out of it to even undress myself.'

'I see.'

'Do you, Kate? Do you really?'

She turned to him, looked at him for several moments, then shrugged. 'I don't know,' she answered honestly.

There was a silence, then Rory said, 'Look, Kate, there's something else.'

Suddenly Kate jumped up. 'Rory, how much more do

you expect me to take?' she cried, throwing her arms up in the air. 'I am at saturation point – the house, Harry, this!' She backed away from him. 'This is all too much. I can't take it. I don't want to hear it, you can keep it to yourself, you—'

'I can't!' Rory shouted. 'I love you, and I can no longer go on pretending that I don't!' He too jumped up and grabbed hold of her hands. 'Kate, listen to me, please, because I have to say it. It's not all over, not for me it isn't! There's still us; I think that you love me too and now that that pompous . . .' He stopped himself and took a deep breath. 'Now that Harry is out of the way then there's nothing to stop us, nothing at all . . . I mean, providing that I'm right and that you do love me.' He pulled her in towards him. 'Kate, I will stick by you whatever happens – repossession, debt, bankruptcy. I'm here, you're here and even if we've lost everything – the house, the gin business, your catering – we've got each other and Flora and that's all that matters! All you need to do is say you love me and—'

'Rory!'

He stopped.

'Rory! Kate!'

They both glanced behind them. The dining-room window had been flung open and Stefan hung out shouting to them. There seemed to be a crowd behind him. 'Kate! Rory! Come in here, now!'

'Bugger it!' Rory said.

'What the—?'

'*Kate! Rory!*'

'Come on,' said Kate. 'We might as well see what's going on!'

They turned, headed round to the kitchen entrance at

the back of the house. She held the door for him and Rory went in ahead. The first thing he heard was some sort of commotion in the hallway. Fearing the worst, he broke into a run.

'Rory!'

'Dad? What's happened?' Rory's stomach lurched. 'It's not Flora, is it?'

'No, no, calm down, it's fine. Ah, Kate!'

Kate's face suddenly drained of all colour. 'Mr Gallagher! What's happened? Is Flora—?'

'No, no, she's fine – really, Kate dear, fine. This is nothing to do with Flora. Come with me, I think I've got some very, very good news for you.' He went to her and took her hand.

'What's going on?' Rory looked at his father, then Mrs Able and John. 'Who're these people?'

Michael Gallagher stopped. 'Lord, sorry! Kate, let me introduce you. This is a solicitor that one of my parishioners uses, Henry Pascoe, and this is Kirk Bradshaw – I think you've met Kirk before, he runs the local antiques shop.'

Kate nodded, completely baffled. Rory glanced at his watch. 'Dad, it's eight forty-five! What on earth—?'

His father held up his hand. 'This way, come on!' He led Kate and Rory along to the dining-room, where Jan and Stefan stood facing the wall by the fireplace, carefully chipping away the panelling.

'What on earth are you doing?' Kate cried.

Stefan spun round. 'Kate!' He grinned. 'Kate, come over here.' She walked towards him. 'Do you know what this is?' he asked, stepping aside to show her a gaping hole in the panelling and the glow of black and gold behind it.

'No.'

'No, nor did I, but Jan did!' He looked at Jan and the grin softened to a gentle smile. 'We were sitting in here talking and she went across to the mantelpiece to fetch some matches for her cigarette. As she stood here smoking, she noticed a small hole in the panelling, chipped it away and there it was!'

'There what was?' Kate shook her head, bafflement turning to confusion.

'Black and gold marble!'

'Black and gold marble?'

'I ran to fetch Mrs Able; she rang Reverend Gallagher, then Jan suggested we call a solicitor to lodge an appeal and get an antiques dealer to authenticate it all and—'

'Hang on a minute! What? Authenticate what?'

'Black and gold marble,' said Kirk Bradshaw, 'is extremely rare and very valuable. My guess is that the entire dining-room is panelled with it, and that it's worth between a quarter and half a million pounds!'

Kate's mouth dropped open. 'You're kidding!'

'Absolutely not!' Stefan said. 'Jan has briefed Mr Pascoe here on how to appeal against the repossession notice; he has typed up a document and now all we are doing is waiting for Ingram Lawd's representative to arrive in order to lodge the appeal.'

Feeling suddenly faint, Kate leaned back against the wall and closed her eyes for a moment. 'I don't believe it,' she murmured. There was a silence which went on for several moments and Rory found himself holding his breath. Then suddenly Kate smiled.

'That's it, then!' she said, the smile breaking into laughter. 'We've done it! You've done it!' she cried. 'I can repay the loan, carry on with the business, keep Tonsbry. That's it, all of it, nothing left outstanding.'

Rory dropped his head; except me, he thought. Everyone had started talking at once, there was a celebratory air in the room and, as he edged towards the door, he hated himself for not being magnanimous enough to join in. He eased out into the passage-way and let out the breath he had been holding.

'Except you,' Kate said.

He looked round. 'Sorry?'

'Nothing left outstanding except you.'

He stared at her.

'You said that all I had to do was say that I love you.'

'Yes.'

'But I don't think that's enough.'

He didn't answer; she moved closer to him. 'I think it's important to say that I love you and . . .' She was right in front of him now, her body only a fraction of an inch away. 'That if you ever leave me again, Rory Gallagher, I'll smash your ruddy face in!' And erupting into laughter, she leaned forward to kiss him.

Epilogue

Adriana, the Comtesse de Grand Blès, was in triumphant mood. She sat at breakfast with a very surly Pierre and buttered her croissant with lashings of creamy Irish butter and French blueberry conserve. Pouring coffee for them both, she said, 'Oh, do cheer up, Pierre!'

Her husband didn't answer; he merely lifted the *Financial Times* a fraction higher so as to block out all view of her.

'It would have been no good me ringing Kate at that hour,' she went on. 'It was all done and dusted anyway!' She bit, chewed and let out a tiny sigh of pleasure. 'I'm sorry you don't approve, but it was all done in her best interests and—'

'Adriana!' Pierre lowered the paper. 'Please, do not insult me by lying to me. The only person whose interests you have ever considered is yourself.'

Unperturbed, Adriana took another bite of her croissant. The phone rang and she rose swiftly from the table. 'Saved by the bell,' she said gaily, and crossed the suite to answer it.

'Ah, Kate, darling!'

Pierre glanced up.

'I'm sorry?' There was a brief, tense silence. 'Marble?

Don't be so bloody ridiculous, Kate! There can't possibly be! I'd have known about it if there was.' Another brief silence followed. Pierre raised an eyebrow. 'Sorry?' Adriana snapped, 'You did what?'

Pierre put down the paper now and watched with open curiosity.

'But you can't possibly do that!' Adriana suddenly cried. 'You can't! It's . . .' She stopped, wound the telephone wire tightly around her finger and, changing key, said, 'David Lowther? No, I've no idea where he could have gone. Unethical? Not lodging an appeal? Really? Can you sue a solicitor?' Her voice softened and she took a deep breath. 'Well, Kate dear,' she said, not kindly but tolerantly, 'if you really think that business will work and if you really want to keep the house, then of course Pierre and I have to congratulate you.' She felt a hard lump in her throat and had to cough to clear it. 'Yes, Kate; I hope it does work out for you.' The wire was so tight now that all the blood had drained from Adriana's finger. 'Yes, I will give your love to Pierre.' Pierre smiled. 'Thank you, Kate. Yes, goodbye, dear.'

Replacing the receiver, Adriana held her head up high and came back to the breakfast table. Pierre went to speak.

'Don't . . .' Adriana managed, 'say a word!' And sitting straight-backed and rigid in her chair, she continued to eat her croissant while the tears streamed down her face.